SHOCK

In the mess blocking ⟨...⟩ ⟨...⟩ something small suddenly slithered and jumped away, making Tabitha shout in fright. Only a lizard, she told herself. But there were bigger things out there, roaming the jungle. She had heard about them. The crash would have scared them away. They would be back.

Meanwhile there was an immense, omnipresent, utterly hostile monster facing them, surrounding them, not about to go away for anything: the planet.

―――――

"A grandly realized broad-brush painting that sweeps the reader along with its sheer panache . . . A book to be enjoyed, a rich collection of inventive situations . . . Another milestone in the promising career of Colin Greenland."

Vector

"A throughly good read with depth to it . . . The people are marvelous and real . . . And good aliens. I love and admire good aliens."

Diana Wynne Jones,
author of *ARCHER'S GOON*

Other Avon Books by
Colin Greenland

HARM'S WAY

TAKE BACK PLENTY

COLIN GREENLAND

AVON BOOKS • NEW YORK

AVON BOOKS
A division of
The Hearst Corporation
1350 Avenue of the Americas
New York, New York 10019

First AvoNova Printing: January 1992

AVON TRADEMARK REG. U.S. PAT. OFF. AND IN OTHER COUNTRIES, MARCA REGISTRADA, HECHO EN CANADA

Printed in Canada

UNV 10 9 8 7 6 5 4 3 2

To the women behind the wheel

CONTENTS

—

ONE

Encounters at the Moebius Strip

1

"Nabe?" said the port inspector.

"Jute," she told him.

"Giv'd nabe?"

"Tabitha."

"Status?"

"Owner operator."

"Shib?"

"The *Alice Liddell*," said Tabitha.

He lifted his close-shaven muzzle and looked at her hard over the monitor of his reader. "Tybe and *registratiod* ob shib," he said.

"Oh, right," said Tabitha. "Bergen Kobold. BGK zero—"

She shot her cuff and checked her wrist monitor. She could never remember the *Alice*'s registration number without looking it up, though she saw it twenty times a day. "Zero-nine-zero-five-nine."

"Burbose ob bisit?"

"I've got to see a man about a job," she said. "Look, could you hurry it up, do you think?"

But he was an Eladeldi, he was entering everything with his paw stylus and checking her record. His tongue was hanging out. Tabitha sighed in annoyance and drummed her fingers on the desktop.

She looked around the hall. All the other queues were moving right along. Locals simply had to slot a tag and step through the gate. Just her luck to get an Eladeldi.

She knew what he was going to say next as soon as he opened his little purple mouth.

"Records show registratiod ob debectib axis lock crystal,'' he said. "Two budths ago."

"Yes," said Tabitha.

"Not yet reblaced," he observed.

"No," she said. "That's why I've got to see a man about a job."

But he still had to print out yet another copy of the Capellan regulations about acceptable levels of degradation on axis lock crystals before he let her through the gate.

She stuffed the printout into her bag, where—some-where—three other copies were already lurking, and looked at the time.

"Shit," she said.

The commercial terminal was closed for some kind of police operation. Tabitha found herself being diverted down a long underground tunnel to the civil concourse. It was swarming with people. Spacers in livery jostled with porters, human and drone. Eager evangelists pressed prophecies of the imminent Total Merge into the paws, fans and hands of glazed-looking tourists. Holos for local businesses, net stations and archaeological attractions competed for attention, whooping and gyrating on their daises. The hubbub was even more deafening than usual.

Of course: it was carnival.

Tabitha's headset suddenly locked into an ambient channel and began to tinkle with tinny salsa. Irritated, she snatched out the earpiece and let the set dangle round her neck. She had to get a move on if she was going to make it to the city before noon. Hoisting her bag, she sidestepped a cargo float, waded through a crowd of squabbling Perks and elbowed between two Alteceans and a city guide they were trying to haggle. Stepping high in the light gravity and brandishing the bag before her, she ploughed her way out into the open air.

Outside, it was dusty and cold. Grit whirled in the biting desert winds. Half-naked children with slit eyes and matchstick limbs worked the emerging crowd with grim efficiency. Tabitha Jute pulled up the collar of her old foil jacket and strode off past the concession stalls, looking for transport.

The queues for air taxis would be impossible. She took the slidewalk to the canal. The queues there were just as bad. Fortunately most of the tourists were after a robot hover, which she couldn't afford anyway. Then—a stroke of luck—she cut in front of a white family still cooing over the color of the water, and managed to sling her bag into an arriving boat.

"The Moebius Strip," she called.

The cries of the annoyed sightseers dying away behind them, they left the wharf and slid off downstream. Tabitha sat in the stern and watched the olive groves and sponge gardens on either bank swiftly give way to ship-yards, silica refineries and air plants. In the distance for a moment the complicated towers of Schiaparelli rose. Then coral pink walls of rock closed about them as they took the deep cut into Wells.

"Here for carnival?" the driver asked Tabitha, in tones of boredom and resentment which didn't lessen when Tabitha said no. She was a Vespan, brooding with hostile humility, like all of them. The atmosphere had mottled her long cheeks with brown blotches. She complained about the cold.

"It was better before they knock the dome down," she said. "Was you ever here when we had the dome?"

"Before my time," said Tabitha.

"We had good warm then," said the driver. "Then they knock the dome down. They say they gone put up solar." Her mobile features squeezed themselves around sulkily. "They never. They still argue, argue, who gone pay."

She lifted her elbows. She looked like a bundle of spoiled green peppers in a brown felt overcoat. Her glossy lobes were withered and shrunken, the soft pouches of her face sagging in permanent despair. Tabitha wondered how long the woman had been scratching a living on the waterways, complaining to uncaring passengers, never quite summoning up the cash or the strength to take the long haul home.

They swept along the crimson canal into the purlieus of the new city. There the cries of the watersellers and the buzz of taxis came wafting on the wind, strident and echoing across the dirty water. A team of Palernian prostitutes, their wool in frizzy perms, sat smoking and dangling their legs in the sunlight on the steps below the Malibu Arcade. They hooted and waved at the boats as they whizzed by. Tabitha's driver started to complain about them. Tabitha shifted forward along the cracked red bench.

"I've got some calls to make," she said.

She ducked into the phone hood, unreeled the plug from her headset and plugged in. The scratched little screen played her a little tune and showed a phone company logo. Then there were ads, more than ever for the sake of the season. In a window in the bottom left hand corner of the screen Tabitha watched her credit flickering merrily away.

She tried the Moebius Strip, but all she got was an answering routine. She tried another number. She waited.

They passed a sulphur felucca with a crew of children. They were towing a desert manta on a long black line. It dipped and fluttered in the chilly air, its wings drab and flaky.

At last Tabitha got through. On the phone an oily face cracked a smile as she identified herself. "In for the carnival?"

"No, business," she said. "Carlos, how much is an axis lock crystal these days?"

"What you got?"

"A Kobold."

"Still driving that old thing? She's gonna fall apart on you one of these days."

"That's what she keeps telling me," said Tabitha. "Come on, Carlos, I'm in a hurry, how much?"

He told her. She swore.

He shrugged.

"That's what you get for flying antiques," he said unsympathetically. "Can't get the parts." He scratched his ear. "I could do you a great deal on a Navajo Scorpion."

"Piss off, Carlos."

She thought of the Alteceans, back at the port, snuffling over their bags and parcels. "Look, have you seen Captain Frank lately?"

"A crystal for a Kobold, yeah, that's about ol' Frank's speed," he grinned. "Try the flea market."

"Thanks very much, Carlos."

"Cheer up, Tabitha," he bade her. "It's carnival!"

Carnival in Schiaparelli. The canals are thronged with tour buses, the bridges festooned with banners. Balloons escape and fireworks fly. The city seethes in the smoky red light. Though officers of the Eladeldi can be seen patrolling everywhere, pleasure is the only master. Shall we go to the Ruby Pool? To watch the glider duels over the al-Kazara? Or to the old city, where the cavernous ancient silos throb with the latest raga, and the wine of Astarte quickens the veins of the young and beautiful? A thousand smells, of sausages and sweat, phosphorus and patchouli, mingle promiscuously in the arcades. Glasses clash and cutlery clatters in the all-night cantinas where drunken revellers confuse the robot waiters and flee along the colonnades, their bills unpaid, their breath steaming in the thin and wintry air.

Reflected off the oily water, a thousand colored lights flicker and glow on the scoured faces of the buildings. A thousand noises batter the attendant ear, calliopes and stridulators, cannonades and sirens, all mingling with the babble and slur of happy voices. Even the screeching rasp of a police hover forcing its slow way upstream can scarcely cut the din. The cop, a human, leans on his screamer, twice, and stalls. In the shiny black carapace of his servo-armor he looks stiff and offended, like a gigantic beetle beset by ants.

They pulled in at Mustique Boulevard, below the skate bowl. Grubby urchins stood on the wall, sucking steaming mossballs and shouting abuse at each other.

"This isn't the Moebius Strip," said Tabitha.

The morose boatwoman jerked an elbow. "Close as I can, sister. Grand's closed for the procession."

Annoyed, Tabitha paid her and leapt easily to the landing stage. Her jacket flashed and sparkled with sodium light, her boots crunched on the sandy boards.

Picture her, Tabitha Jute: not as the net media show her, heroine of hyperspace, capable, canny and cosmetically enhanced, smiling confidently as she reaches with one hand for the spangled mist of the Milky Way; but a small, weary young woman in a cracked foil jacket and oil-stained trousers, determinedly elbowing herself through an exuberant Schiaparelli crowd. She stands 162 in her socks, broad in the shoulder and the hip, and weighs about 60k at 1 g, which she very rarely is. Her hair is darkest ginger, cut in a conservative spacer's square crop. Her skin is an ordinary milky coffee, and freckles easily, which she hates. Here she was, in after a stiff haul back from Chateaubriand, spacelagged and frazzled, needing a shower. There were dark olive bags under her hazel eyes. You wouldn't have given her a second glance that evening, amid the florid, the fancy and the flash.

Not that there was much of that around here. This was definitely the scrag end of the festivities. She ducked beneath the concrete walkway and strode along an avenue of makeshift stalls lashed together from pipes and planking, weaving a path between the strolling browsers. Overhead, lines of bioflourescents snaked from pole to pole, tied on with string. Tabitha had come to the flea market after all.

Some of the stallholders had made an effort for the carnival. There were masks and bunting decorating their displays of scuffed cassettes and second-hand knitting. Here were bright clothes: everything from aluminium shoes to cheap and garish movie shirts of winking kittens and prancing unicorns and swivelling strippers. Collectors rummaged in boxes of sunglasses, discussed the merits of filched scraps of cruiseliner trim. Two scrawny women in tiny dresses sat behind a table of china animals, painting each other's faces by the warmth of a dilapidated reactor stove. One of them whistled at Tabitha as she squeezed by.

A decommissioned shop robot leaned from under its canopy and fired a burst of sublim at her, filling her head with sun-dappled pools, the smell of honeysuckle, desire. A yellow child tried to interest her in a jar of dead flies. Round the corner were the Alteceans in their cardigans, their conical caps of brown felt, presiding over accumulations of human refuse. On high stools they squatted, hunched in their habitual dolour, their snouts inflamed and dripping in the irritant air. They snuffled and sighed to each other, beckoning Tabitha, knowing a haulier when they saw one.

"Axis lock crystal?" she shouted. "For a Bergen Kobold?"

The Alteceans wheezed moistly at her, waving their paws at their mounds of surplus respirators and dismantled heat-exchangers as if these treasures were all one could possibly require in life. Tabitha spent a valuable minute dragging out from under a heap something that looked promising but proved to be a caustic diffraction coil. She threw it back. She was wasting time.

Dodging a band of spacers in Shenandoah colors braying drunkenly out of a bar and shoving one another about, Tabitha pushed ahead into the crowd that lined the banks of the Grand Canal. She circumvented fat tourists in fancy dress, civic marshals in baggy overalls, then a personal camera drone, its head swivelling back and forth as it scanned the canal for its owner at home. A sailing ship was passing, its mylar sails flapping in the gusty wind. Behind it crawled a hoverbus of MivvyCorp employees having a party. Through the rigging of the schooner a five of Palernians could be seen, making a nuisance of themselves on a flimsy raft. They were hoot-

ing and flapping their great woolly arms as they tried to
climb on to a private jetty. A tall woman leaned from a
balcony and emptied a bucket of water over them. Hanging over parapets and out of windows, clustering in the
streets and on the rooftops, the crowd whistled and ap-
plauded.

As Tabitha was trying to get past a couple of coked-
up Thrants in expensive shakos and boiled leather, one
of the Palernians turned a clumsy somersault, and one
of the others pushed her into the canal. They yoicked
and whooped. A spark-boat sputtered by, filling the air
with the smell of ozone. In it a couple in electric suits
were arcing and fizzing to the hefty thump of a jumpbox.
The Palernians bounded up and down in excitement,
flooding the raft and endangering their coolers. As a cop
arrived, his cyclops helmet protruding above the heads
of the crowd, the woman was lowering her bucket at the
end of a rope, shouting to a gaggle of little painted boys
for a refill.

Tabitha leaned out over the railing. She could see the
Moebius Strip. It was only another hundred meters: there,
just beyond the float full of oversized Capellans, dum-
mies, their huge bald heads bobbing with grave benevolence as if conferring blessings on the excited crowd.

Carnival in Schiaparelli. Cold, dusty city, full of hol-
idaymakers and noise and smells and dirt. Wherever you
go, now, you will meet people who will tell you that
Schiaparelli was a fateful city for Tabitha Jute. It was in
Schiaparelli that she met Tricarico, who brought her
aboard the *Resplendent Trogon*, which led her into the
presence of Balthazar Plum—and if it hadn't been for
all that, she would never have acquired the *Alice* in the
first place. Likewise, here she was now, years later, in
Schiaparelli, heading for a fateful encounter which would
completely and utterly change her life, my life, all our
lives. She was at the top of the steps leading down to
the front door of the Moebius Strip. She could see the
lights inside, the drinkers and gamblers.

And then the Perks came, scurrying up the steps on
all fours like rats out of a cellar.

3

Tabitha made a mistake. She made the mistake of trying to go forward, down the steps, through the upcoming Perks.

"Hey, woman! Woman watch it!"

An oily-pelted male with piercing green eyes reared up under her feet, knocking her sprawling on her bottom.

At once they were all around her, perching up on their hindlegs like scrawny otters in black leather and chrome earbands.

Not about to argue, Tabitha started to get her feet under her.

They grabbed her. Twenty thorny little paws caught hold of her jacket, her trousers, her arms. They scrabbled at her bag.

"Hey! Get *off!*"

They pulled her down on her back again. She wallowed in the flimsy gravity. As she scraped her heels against the steps, trying for purchase, the alpha male jumped up on to her hip, then down between her legs. He stood there in her crotch, weaving sinuously from side to side, hunching his shoulders, his flat little head squealing down into her face.

"Cheeeeeeee!"

Tabitha sat up fast, jerking her hips back from the snarling Perk. Several of his cousins and brothers went flying. She hauled her arm from the grip of two more and jabbed a finger at the little alien.

"Get out of my way!"

"In our way, woman."

"Cheee!" they all went. "Cheeeeee!"

11

The feathers were all bristling up the backs of their heads, on the tiny muscular shins that protruded from the legs of their breeches. They flexed their claws on their medallions, up and down the zips of their jerkins. The ones she had just knocked down were on their feet again, hopping on the steps around her. Some of them were clutching tubes of beer, bottles of chianti. The men had exaggerated their black eye-sockets with kohl and mascara. They sneered at her, baring their tiny incisors. Their breath smelled of stale fish.

"Whass'n hurry, woman?" said the Perk between her legs, taunting her. "Missa parade!"

Tabitha realized he was drunk stupid. She cooled a degree or two. She hadn't time for a fight. Clutching her bag, she tried to get up again, but they were hanging on her shoulders.

"Get *off* me!"

"Whassa fire, woman? Whassa party, woman?"

He made a lunge at her. She threw up an arm, fending him off. Another one, older, the barbs of his feathers going soft and ashy, burrowed under her raised arm.

"You tread on us! You'n knock us down!"

"Okay, I'm sorry! All right? I'm sorry! Now just let go of me, all right?"

She tried again to stand up. When the wiry little creatures obstructed her again, she hauled them off their feet. They all squealed, "Cheee! Cheee!"

A couple came out of the Moebius Strip, a yellow woman in video shades and a black one in a tubecoat, basilisk teeth plaited into her hair. They glanced at Tabitha encumbered with perks, forcing their claws from their arms, standing on one foot trying to shake one that was hanging on to her leg. The women glanced at the fracas and stepped delicately aside on the steps as they passed by. The yellow one muttered a remark to her companion, who laughed and sucked on a cigarette.

A tall man in a cloth cap came after, hurrying to catch them up. Tabitha heard his bootheels tap up the steps behind her. She winced as long black claws met in the flesh above her elbow. It was like being wrapped in barbed wire by a gang of fox terriers.

She heard something rip.

The Perks come from the third planet of a G class system in the region of Betelgeuse, where they live in warrens, underground, which is perhaps why they took so readily to the tunnels of Plenty. There may be something endemic to the more ferocious subterranean dweller about suspicion, aggression, an unquestioning pack instinct backed up by heedless hostility to all outsiders. Leaving the deep hearth for whatever reason, hunger, duty, sexual imperatives, you trot along the lightless, complicated corridors of the buried labyrinth, their ambient odor a composite of you and all your kin. Suddenly you hear the scrabble of claws coming in the opposite direction. Friend, foe, relative, rival? Behind you lie your siblings, perhaps your own offspring, curled and mewing, tender in the warm dark. What option have you in that moment of social uncertainty but to bare your teeth, to ready your claws?

At any rate, it seems to be so for the Perks. There is nothing Perks like so much as a good fight. When the time came for civilization on the planet of the Perks, they built war-trains, undermining engines, mole bombs. It is unclear what motivated Capella to bestow the space drive on the little rodents. In all possibility the Perks merely infested their own elusive craft, following their urge to burrow into whatever comes along.

Tabitha lost all patience with them. She could see her goal ahead of her, so close she was practically inside. She had struggled halfway across Schiaparelli to get there. She was not about to stop and engage in a scrap on the very doorstep of the bar. Nor was she about to lose her jacket to a gaggle of overdressed hooligans. With a yell she thrust herself at their leader.

The neck of the Perk is very long. It accounts for the curious, rather comical way they have of standing perfectly upright and perfectly still while surveying their surroundings with a quick 240° swivel, like a furry periscope. Tabitha seized her chief aggressor by the neck with both hands. She swept him off his feet as the forward momentum of her lunge carried her upright, shedding Perks left and right with a shake of her shoulders.

All might still have gone well. Or ill, depending on your view of all that happened in consequence. But Tabitha's blood was up. She flung the choking, clawing creature from her. She flung him into the Grand Canal.

"*Cheeeeeeee*—!"

Instinctively drawing in his limbs and curling his long back, the Perk sailed out of her grasp and over the edge of the steps like a furry stone in a leather jerkin. Horrorstruck for the instant, his cronies stood and squawled with outrage. Spectators and bystanders on the canal bank turned and stared, not knowing what it was that had flashed past them, hurtling towards the water. The filthy, carmine, oily water. The water he never actually hit.

For at the moment, directly below the steps that led down to the Moebius Strip, the float of dummy Capellans was purring serenely by.

Tabitha watched in diminishing triumph and mounting dismay as the Perk fell through the smoky air and struck one of the huge statues directly on the head. With a crack audible above the gasp of the crowd, the impact smashed a large hole in the fabric of the great white dome. Knocked from its invisible supporting cradle of needle-thin tractor beams, the effigy swayed. It bowed its ruined head to its chest as if to inspect the squealing assailant now hanging from its buckled shoulder with frantic claws. It swayed, and continued to sway. Its arm fell off, clattering to the deck with the Perk still clinging to it. Its benevolently smiling head fell off and bounced with a sickening crunch from the beam projector into another of the statues, knocking it off the deck of the float and into the canal. Meanwhile, breaking apart like a toppling chimneystack, its body collapsed and felled another, which threw up an arm as it went down, as if thinking to save itself by grabbing hold of one of its remaining upright companions.

There was no hope it could save itself; nor any for Tabitha either. Standing staring appalled at the devastation she had caused, she became aware that the Perks had not instantly attacked her in retaliation for their leader's ignominious defeat. Indeed, they had melted away into the crowd. The hand that fell upon her arm was a paw; but not a tiny black-clawed paw, a hefty one with silky blue fur protruding from the sleeve of a night-black uniform.

It was the cops.

BGK009059 LOG

TXJ.STD

PRINT

Øf§§ü§TXXXJ!åinterintelin%ter&& &

MODE? VOX

SD? 31.31.31

READY

I can't stand it in there, Alice.

WHAT HAVE YOU DONE, CAPTAIN?

I don't want to talk about it.

Why do I do these things, Alice? Why do I get myself into things like this?

INSUFFICIENT DATA

Is that an answer?

NO, CAPTAIN, I SIMPLY MEANT THAT IF YOU DON'T TELL ME WHAT YOU'VE DONE I CAN'T MANUAL OVERRIDE

Sorry, Alice.

HELLO, CAPTAIN. WHY ARE YOU APOLOGIZING TO ME?

Oh, nothing, Alice. Don't worry about me. I'm just in a foul mood. I just wanted some company.

THAT SEEMS TO BE ABUNDANT INSIDE AT PRESENT, CAPTAIN.

That's why I'm out here.

DO YOU WANT TO TELL ME ABOUT IT?

No.

TELL ME A STORY, THEN.

A story? I don't know any stories. I'm from the Moon.

WE'VE NEVER BEEN TO THE MOON, HAVE WE?

It's boring. Nothing happens there. Nothing happened to me until I got off the Moon.

BUT YOU WERE BORN ON THE MOON.

Yes, I was born on the Moon.

WHAT WAS THAT LIKE, BEING BORN?

I don't know! I don't remember.

THAT'S A PITY.

There's nothing to remember. It's a pit, the Moon. A dead end. A black hole.

THIS IS LUNA WE'RE SPEAKING OF, ISN'T IT.

Yes.

THOSE ARE METAPHORS, THEN.

Of course they're bloody metaphors.

YOU ARE IN A FOUL MOOD.

Well, when you tell people you come from the Moon they always say, Really? And I say, Somebody has to be. And they say, Well, yes, I suppose so.

The next thing is, especially if they're Terrans, they say, I've been to the Moon. And I say, Everybody's been there, but they don't have to live there. And they say, well, yes, and they sort of smile. They think, She's got a chip on her shoulder. You can see them thinking it. I haven't got a chip on my shoulder. It's them, always saying the same thing.

The other thing they say, if they're Terrans, or actually, especially if they're not, is, Well, you must have spent a good deal of time on Good Old Mother Earth. And we didn't. We went down twice, to see grandma and grandpa. We hated it, Angie and me. We didn't like grandma and grandpa, and we didn't like their gravity either. I fell out of a tree. We reckoned Earth was horrible and backward. They didn't even have network, where grandma and grandpa lived.

DID YOU NETWORK WITH ANGIE?

Oh, yes, we all did, a lot, though nobody ever talked about it. Everybody had a secret identity, so you could say what you liked and nobody knew who you really were. Networking was encouraged. It was supposed to be educational. It was, as long as you skipped all the educational stuff. What was good was the gossip and the lies. Angie was a Capellan princess in exile.

ARE THERE PRINCESSES ON CAPELLA? I DIDN'T KNOW THAT.

I don't know, Alice. I don't suppose anyone does. But that's what you need on the Moon. To be a Capellan princess in exile, I mean. Otherwise it's all just civics classes, vacuum drill, t'ai chi, monthly medicals, cleaning and maintenance rosters and not being able to go outside. Not that there's anywhere to go.

I had one place I used to go sometimes, when Angie was off with her friends. I'd take a bike and head out from Posidon across the Lake of Dreams. If you went all the way across the Lake of Dreams you'd end up in the Lake of Death. I always thought that was about right. Five minutes out of Posidon there was no sign of humans, no sign anyone had been there ever. Just boring brown rock and shadows black as the sky. You didn't go in the shadows. It was too cold.

I'd put a tape on and turn the radio off. You weren't supposed to turn the radio off, but I used to so they couldn't hear me singing along with the tape.

YOU DON'T SING MUCH THESE DAYS, DO YOU, CAPTAIN?

Be grateful. I talk to myself instead.

YOU TALK TO ME.

Same thing.

YOU CAN BE TERRIBLY RUDE SOMETIMES. I DON'T WONDER ANGIE DIDN'T WANT TO PLAY WITH YOU.

I didn't hang around with her much anyway. The only thing we ever did together was network. And sometimes Dad used to take us down to Serenity, to see the ships.

It was at Serenity we lost Angie, a few years later. We liked it there, when we were kids, though I suppose it wasn't that brilliant, looking back. The Rush Years were well over. Nobody put in there unless they had to. The starships passed us by. It was all just small stuff, tenders and shuttles. No offense, Alice.

On the Moon, everyone's into austerity and teamwork. Or like my mum and dad, who were as keen as anyone to get off Earth, but hadn't the gumption or the connections to get a work permit on an orbital. We used to watch them arrive, looking dazed and disappointed. Nervous tourists who couldn't afford or probably couldn't bear to go out any further, or bottom-rate passengers on a stopover. Fat couples in vacation plaids, bouncing about like toddlers in the low g and cooing over the moondirt souvenir jewelry. Bureaucrats with grey skin and grey denims. They were always arguing schedules with the clerks and crowding the phone stations. My dad would say, Stay well away from them, he was always afraid they were after him for all the taxes he hadn't paid. Engineers with goggles on their headsets and drones hovering at their heels. Netball teams from the Church of the Star Shepherd, all perfect bodies and gleaming white teeth. Then you'd get a bunch of compulsory emigrants, once in a while, Indians or Chinese, all wearing identical pyjamas and shuffling along in a crowd.

There weren't even any interesting aliens. There were only Alteceans dragging black plastic bags everywhere, and Perks, and Eladeldi, looking like big dogs dressed up in uniforms.

I wanted a dog, when I was a little girl.

DID YOU, CAPTAIN? THEY'RE MESSY CREATURES, AREN'T THEY, DOGS?

You'd go down very well on the Moon, Alice. The only dog I ever saw there was very clean, and very small, only about ten centimeters high. It was a holo. There was one with a

monkey in too, crammed in this little shell with the side cut
away so you could see in. There was only room for the
monkey. Its mouth was open, I didn't like that, I thought it
was screaming. The dog didn't look very happy either. It
was white, with black spots.

I'M NOT SURE I FOLLOW THIS PART, CAPTAIN.

It was at the museum. The Museum of the Big Step. My
mum used to take me when I was really little. I always went
straight to the dog and the monkey. They were with all the
boring stuff at the beginning, the primitive stuff all the other
kids used to run past to get to the Frasque fighter. It was a
display, a what do you call it, diorama, showing the cruelties
of Pre-Capellan flight. Then they had the first "aided" flights—
that was what they called them then; the first skips; some
of the disasters, the ships that disappeared. There was the
fighter, a crashed one they'd rebuilt, and some stirring stuff
about how "we" helped Capella beat the Frasque. And in
the middle there was an area open to space, just a circle
of bare surface with a window all the way round it, and a
sign on the window that said it was the site of the Capellan
arrival in the solar system.

There was another diorama there, in front of the window.
It had a man with a big bald head, wearing a sheet and
shiny sandals, saying hello to a couple of stupid-looking
"astronauts," they called them, in clumsy old Gore-Tex suits.
The Capellan was floating above the ground, standing on
nothing, smiling. There was something funny about it, as if
it had a deliberate mistake you were supposed to spot or
something.

CAPELLANS DON'T MAKE MISTAKES, CAPTAIN.

That's what dad used to say. Dad said, Keep away from
Eladeldi, because everything they see goes straight back to
the Capellans. He said stay away from Perks too. I should
have listened to him.

WHY DOES YOUR FATHER DISLIKE THEM?

Oh, dad isn't fond of any kind of aliens, really. Dad didn't even like the Capellan at the museum, the one in the diorama, and he had a smile like a great big teddy bear. He looked as if he was going to pat the astronauts on the head. They just looked startled.

Dad was happy enough on the Moon, really. It was the rest of us that were so bored.

WHAT HAPPENED TO YOUR SISTER?

One day she was at Serenity and she met a boy from the Holy Sepulchre of the Expanded Neurosphere, and he told her she didn't have to be an imaginary princess any more. She could be a little bit of God instead.

I didn't know about God, but that was when I knew it was serious, when she told him her secret identity. Mum and dad argued, but it was no good. Angie was into it all the way. The Great Network in the Sky. Sockets, wetware, the lot. She was only on the Moon in transit after all, like everybody else.

So that was Angie's way out. It was a few more years before I found mine.

Tabitha flung herself at the hard bunk with an angry sigh. She looked around the cell. Four porous dirty pink walls, concrete. Matt steel door, flush-fitted, shielded lock, no handle. No windows. A grille in the door and another above, the glint of a camera lens behind it. Dirty pink concrete ceiling, biofluorescent ring, not working. Dirty pink concrete floor. The bunk was a solid platform against one wall. Some kind of chemical toilet, scuffed white, was already stinking in the corner. There was no room for anything else.

The Eladeldi had dragged her from the steps into an alley, shoved her against a wall and searched her. Then, deciding she was no political, just another stroppy trucker, they'd handed her over to the locals, which was a big relief. They could sometimes turn very nasty where the Capellans were concerned. In the Mirabeau Precinct she'd only get pushed around and ignored. In Eladeldi custody, people tended to disappear.

The cop who'd collected her had been a crowd control unit, the full cyborg. His grey visor flickered with read-outs, obscuring the implants.

"Jute, Tabitha, Captain," he intoned, as his cyclops lens scanned and recorded her. He was very tall and shiny. His augmented hand whirred out to take her arm.

She tried to get him to let her check in the bar first. "I've got to tell my employer! He's in there. I was going to report to him when those bloody vermin tripped me up."

It was no use, of course.

The Eladeldi watched as the cop marched her to the end of the alley, where his double was waiting in the hover. They sat her between them.

The traffic was plentiful and sluggish. All the way downtown the cops' disfigured faces glittered with electronic traceries of red and blue data, analysis, file reports, yellow nets, video idents, updates on other cases. When they cut the engine, Tabitha could hear tiny voices whispering to them. They didn't speak to each other, or to her.

At the precinct a stolid desk sergeant ran all Tabitha's ID through a reader and took it away. Her arresting officer stood behind her like a statue, his brain off-line. He made a macabre figure standing there with wires up his nose and the whites of his uprolled eyes showing through his empty faceplate. Electronic man attending to the high singing voices from another star that compliment him, sooth him, accept his duty.

The sergeant tipped out the contents of Tabitha's bag

on the counter between them. She stirred it all around and poked it about.

"Been in trouble before, have we, Tabitha?" she murmured, ritually.

Tabitha didn't answer. Damn and blast them. They were all the same, when it came down to it. Cops and Perks and Eladeldi and the bloody Capellans out on Charon for all she knew. Life was hard enough without all that. Rules and regulations and protocol. Tribal stuff. These days it was hard enough trying to hold everything together without all that.

Antagonism got you nowhere.

That never seemed to stop her trying.

She leaned both arms on the counter, watching the sergeant with sarcastic fascination.

"I bet you love your job," said Tabitha.

The sergeant focused her mild eyes on her.

"Were you thinking of applying?" she asked. "I'd like to see you try. All of you. I'd like to see you try. Do you a power of good."

There was loathing in her voice, loathing restrained by laziness and boredom. Tabitha was just another cowboy at the carnival. They knew she'd been drinking on the way in. They only had to look at the floor of her cockpit to prove that.

"I'd rather shovel shit," said Tabitha.

The sergeant nodded. "We'll arrange it."

"I bet you see the whole rich pageant of sapient life," said Tabitha, "going through people's bags."

The sergeant held up a dogeared copy of a disreputable magazine.

She raised an eyebrow.

Tabitha ignored her. "I'm just going to make a phone call, all right?"

"No you're not."

"I've just got to make a *phone* call."

"No you haven't."

"Look," said Tabitha. "You're going to fine me, right? And I haven't got any money, have I? You've read my data."

"You haven't been charged yet," said the woman. She had a huge square jaw and a look of iron self-satisfaction that kept the boredom and loathing intact and extended them to as many other people as possible.

"It was self-defense," said Tabitha. "I told him." She swung around and tapped the arresting officer on the breastplate.

"They don't like aliens picking fights," the sergeant said. She meant the Eladeldi.

"It was a bloody Perk," Tabitha said. "Come on." She knew she was lost now, when she started to plead. "Haven't you ever wanted to chuck one of them in the canal? I bet you have. I bet you've done a lot worse than chuck a Perk in a canal."

She leaned across the desk. "Well, mine was self-defense!" she said.

"I bet you think you're a right hero, don't you," said the sergeant. "Throwing little Perks about."

She shoved Tabitha's belongings back into her arms, buzzed a restraint drone and sent her downstairs.

Now Tabitha sat on the bunk, trying to stuff everything back into the bag. There were sheaves of yellowed print-out and mislaid documentation; tubes of Shigenaga beer empty and full; an assortment of abused rayons and grey underwear; a grimy pair of zero-g's; a squashed box with two organic tampons in it; a circuit tester; an inertial screwdriver; a bag of aging fruitdrops; and a broken-backed paperback book, its pages creased, its cover fused and inert.

"Why do I carry all this junk everywhere?"

The Eladeldi had been so quick arriving she hadn't even seen what had happened to the Capellan float. She thought about the one with the smashed head crumpling up. She had a little laugh about that.

She wondered how the Perk was feeling.

It wasn't the end of the world. How much might they fine her? It wouldn't be that much. Maybe she could trade some haulage klicks for the crystal and take along a couple of pods on the open market, legit, for the fine. She was pissed off at missing Triste at the bar, but there would be other jobs.

There would have to be.

Tabitha was soon bored. There was nothing to do. She thought about playing her harmonica, but that seemed to be the one thing that wasn't in her bag. She remembered detention on Integrity 2. At least the cells there had muzak. Though they also put stuff in the air that made you passive. In-cell slot video, that would be a good idea, she didn't know why someone hadn't come up with it already. The captive audience.

Tabitha yawned. She curled up facing the wall and shut her eyes.

Time passed. She was dead tired, but she couldn't fall asleep. Once in a while she heard footsteps and obscured voices, the hum of drones. Once there was a yell, and a violent clattering of metal. Another noise, a continuous whistle, very faint and high, she couldn't decide was in the walls or in her ears. She found herself tracing with her finger a pale, silvery track where graffiti had been erased from the wall. She didn't know how long she'd been lying there. Time stopped here, as it did in space. The concrete walls shut it out like walls of stars.

Suddenly the door opened.

She leaned up on her elbow.

It was a cop. She couldn't tell whether it was the first cop or a different one.

"Jute, Tabitha, Captain," he said.

Data scrolled across his faceplate, reconfigured, froze.

"Get up," he said.

Not in any great hurry to accompany the cop, she did.

The desk sergeant was listening to her headset. She'd become very formal all of a sudden. Obviously someone was now listening to her. "Jute, Tabitha, Captain. Current address a ship docked at Schiaparelli Port, Bergen Kobold registration BGK009059."

"Yes," Tabitha said, although it wasn't a question.

"Aggravated assault, breach of the peace, causing a public nuisance, degrading interspecies harmony, ditto civic ditto, grievous damage, treasonous damage, reckless behavior. Two hundred and fifty scutari," said the desk sergeant, with a broad smile.

"*How* much?" It was three times what she'd been expecting.

"You have twenty-four hours to return here with the money or phone it in."

"Yeah, yeah."

"Or forfeit your ship."

The Moebius Strip stands on the southern bank of the Grand Canal about a kilometer along from the Baratha Arcade, between the Church of the Directed Panspermia and a crustacean restaurant. Now past its notorious hey-day, it has become a favorite attraction for Schiaparelli's less sophisticated visitors, who fondly imagine they have located a corner of the city that retains the historic charm of frontier days. In fact, the fiberglass decor was artificially aged by being exposed in the desert for a week before fitting, by the first owners, emigrants from Europe who had reason to foresee the nostalgia boom.

That evening, when Tabitha Jute finally set her hand on the battered aluminium doorknob, it was still a cheerfully disreputable establishment, catering to the social needs of those who felt more comfortable doing business in an environment with a degree of sleaze to it. Whores of all sexes, augmented and non—, came here at the start and end of their shift to meet pimps, pushers, and "privileged" clients. Superannuated net scribes maintained a bleary outpost at one end of the bar, from which to garner the increasingly hermetic gossip which was all they had left to peddle. At the other end was a low stage, where failing acts established the poise with which they were about to endure their professional decline. When you fell off the bottom of the bill at the Nash Pavilion, you came straight to the stage of the Moebius Strip. There was a man there now, a short tubby man, quite good-looking, Tabitha thought, checking him automatically as she entered. He had a parrot on his shoulder. It looked like a real one. He was playing music of some kind, it was hard to hear for the din.

She went up to the bar. Heidi was on. "I'm looking for a man called Triste," Tabitha said.

"He left," said Heidi.

Tabitha grunted. She had expected no less. "Where can I get hold of him, Heidi, do you know?"

"Callisto," said Heidi, wiping the bar.

"Shit," said Tabitha, with a degree of warmth. "He had a job ad on the net, do you know anything about that?"

Heidi shook her head. Her eyes flickered to the cabaret. The man had his arms stretched out to either side. The parrot was scuttling along from arm to arm across his shoulders.

"Not bad, is he?" said Heidi.

"I can't hear," Tabitha said.

"I wasn't talking about the music," Heidi said.

Tabitha gave her a wintry smile. But she checked him out anyway. He was playing a glove, she could see that now, through the smoke and hi-tech gloom. He was singing, or somebody was. She couldn't see him moving his lips. They were nice lips, beautifully curved, and his eyes were brown and very round. All the while she eyed him, somewhere in the back of her mind Tabitha was thinking, Twenty-four hours. Bastards.

She said, "Know anyone else who needs a barge?" They'd never done that to her before, never threatened to take her ship away. She didn't like to think of the *Alice*, falling into cop hands.

"Anyone that's not a Perk," she added.

Taking her eyes from the man onstage, she gave the punters a swift once-over. In the front window, some sort of complicated tile game was going on, thick wads of soft old cash changing hands at a brisk clip. A poison courier was sharing a jar with a waterman. Two coltish three-year-old Thrants in cream leather were posing by the antiquated music generator, wearing sunglasses and toying with licorice liqueurs.

"Nobody's working now," Heidi said. "It's carnival. Can I get you a drink?"

Tabitha sighed. "Beer," she said.

Heidi listed seven varieties in one breath.

"Whatever's nearest," said Tabitha.

Carlos would know someone. She went to the phone, which was on the basement stairs, below the stage. As she passed by, she realized it was the bird that was singing. It looked like a parrot, but it didn't sound like one. It could sing. It sang in a sweet trembling voice about a yellow bird up high in a banana tree.

Carlos was out. She left a message, said she'd call him later, but she thought she probably wouldn't. She might as well cut her losses and take off for Phobos or Longevity, see if there was anything there, see if there was anyone that hadn't flown down for carnival.

She drank up, watching the gloveman. She could quite fancy him. He was tanned and sleek, with glossy black hair. He was wearing a natty scarlet and white pinstripe blouse, pseude trousers and espadrilles. He seemed to have talent too, though the neural induction gauntlet was a bit old-fashioned now, even in Schiaparelli where things hang on forever. The sound was deep, electronically slick and fluid, but feathered with a tremolo so fine you could only just distinguish the individual notes. The melody swooped and split into two, harmonizing with itself. People clapped. The man smiled. The bird perched on his shoulder, nestling against his cheek with his eyes closed, and sang along now in an eerie, wordless croon.

Heidi wiped the bar by Tabitha's elbow.

"Another drink?" she said.

"Okay," said Tabitha, draining her glass. One more drink, try Carlos again, and then take off. "I'll be back, Heidi," she said, and went back to the phone.

Carlos was still out. His smiling photo asked her to leave her name and number. She hit the wall.

"You're at a party somewhere, aren't you, Carlos? I hope you're having fun, 'cause I'm certainly not."

"Wrong number?" asked a voice above her.

She looked up. It was the gloveman and his bird, descending the stairs. They'd finished their show and were coming back down to the damp and squalid cellar the management refused to redecorate because of its "classic atmosphere."

"Right number, wrong planet," she said.

He came down to the half-landing and stood behind her, peering over her shoulder at Carlos's face on the little phone. She could smell his bird. It smelled like a parrot too.

"This guy stand you up?" asked the musician. "He didn't take you to the party? That's what you just said, wasn't it? I mean, pardon me, it's not my habit, you understand, to pick up on other people's phone conversations, I was just coming down the stairs here, I couldn't—"

The bird stretched its neck and made a sudden loud trilling noise like a fire alarm. Tabitha winced. She pulled her plug from the phone.

"Shut up Tal! Tal, shut up! Will you shut up? Hey, Tal?" the musician shouted, swatting at the bird with his glove. It fell silent as suddenly as it had begun.

"This is Tal," said the gloveman. "I have to apologize. Artistic temperament. Very very sensitive. How do you do, I'm Marco, Marco Metz. What?" he said, though she hadn't spoken, "What? You've heard of me?"

"No," said Tabitha. Close up his eyes were even more luscious than they'd looked on stage.

"You're pretty good," she said.

"I am," he said. "I'm really very good. I mean, as it happens. Yes, I am, very good. In fact. But why should you know that? You're a busy woman, I'm a busy man, it's a big system . . ."

All the while he was burbling inanities, his eyes were

roving up and down her body.

She hadn't got time for this.

But still.

"Tal?" she said, gesturing to the parrot.

"That's right, yes."

"Can I stroke him?" she suggested.

He shrugged lightly. "They're your fingers," he said. "No, no, I'm only kidding. Sure. Like this. See?"

He took her hand lightly in his own. His touch was warm and dry. He lifted her fingers to the head of his parrot and stroked them down along its back. Tal wriggled.

"Where's it from?" she asked.

"This? A long way away. You couldn't even pronounce it. Look at him, he can't even pronounce it. Hey," he said, bringing his face close to the bird's, "she wants to know where you're from, see, even he can't pronounce it."

"Shoe polish!" fluted the bird suddenly. "Intrigue in the corps de ballet! Intrigue in shoes!"

Surprised, they both laughed.

"He's a little excited," said Marco.

Tabitha stroked the bird's head again. "Does he drink?"

"Tal? No."

"Do you?"

"Sure."

"I'll be at the bar," she said.

"So," he said, when he joined her three minutes later without the bird, "you in town for carnival?"

"No, I'm looking for work. I just got in from Chateaubriand."

"In the Belt?" He looked at her with new respect, the way they always did when she said something like that. "What sort of work was that?" he wanted to know.

"Just a delivery run for a drug house. Carboys of vacuum barnacle serum, mostly. Nothing interesting."

"You're a driver, then?"

"I'm a driver."

"You always work for this drug house?"

"I'll work for anyone," she said, "if the money's right."

"What, you have your own ship?"

"I have my own ship," said Tabitha. He was impressed, you could see. After all these years she still couldn't resist a feeling of pride when she said that to a total stranger. She knew she would feel a good deal less proud when she told *Alice* about the penalty clause. She hoped she wouldn't have to.

She looked at Marco. She wished she could take him back with her.

She wanted to take him to her cabin and tear all his smart clothes off. "I'd ask you aboard," she said, "but I'm not staying around."

"That's too bad," he said. "That would be fascinating. What have you got?"

Tabitha stared at him. She suddenly realized he really was interested in the ship. She felt vaguely insulted.

"Just an old crate," she said.

"Scouter?"

"No, a barge."

He looked thoroughly animated, as if he was bursting with a gleeful secret.

"And it's yours? There's nobody else?"

"No," she said, nettled.

"You want to take me to Plenty?"

"You're going to Plenty?"

"Yes."

"Tonight?"

"No, no. First thing tomorrow."

Tabitha gaped at him. "Well, yes!" she said. Then she remembered the axis lock crystal. "Well, no," she said, "I mean, I'd love to, but I need more than that."

He chuckled. "Oh, there's more," he said. "Plenty more! What do you need?"

She sucked her teeth. "Two hundred and fifty," she said. "Up front. And then, hell, I don't know, I have to get a repair."

"No problem," he said.

"I don't believe this," said Tabitha. "You're serious."

"Sometimes I am."

He ran his hand lightly down her arm. He had a gentle touch, a musician's touch.

He said, "Do you want to go to a party?"

They went out together into the cold and dusty night.

Though the parade had long gone by, the water was still crowded.

There were kids tussling on rafts of planks and plastic drums; couples in rowing boats; powerboats limping, out of charge. On the landing-stage below the Moebius Strip a dozen people were standing, sitting, lounging, arguing, drinking. There was a small speedboat moored to a red and white pole. The green bird flew straight down to it, its shadow confused and doubled by the moons.

The moons shone down, on desert and steppe; on the polar settlements and the canyonlands where the somnolent canals flow deep and wide. They painted the deserts, swept the pampas, glinted on the glass farms, glistened on the algae lakes of the intertwining towns. They floodlit the arena at Barsoom and silvered the lawns of suburban Bradbury. Without discrimination they illuminated the somber, monolithic blocks of the old city and the arrogant, hectic jumble of the new, observing without comment how it sprawled and spilled beyond the circumference of the dismantled dome.

Tabitha sat back in the boat, amazed and astonished by her own luck, as they nosed out across the filthy water, under the acid glare of a video wall. Mars, she herself would later remark, had all been parcelled up; the smartmoney had moved on. It was only a few years since Schiaparelli had been a living pan-cultural matrix, a cosmopolitan crossroads of the solar system, where all the client races of Capella could co-exist in noisy harmony, or pass through, haggling, to the caravanserais of the south. These days, the tourist buses were shouldering the caiques and drays off the al-Kazara; imported souvenirs filling the shelves of the pawnshops where hungover spacers had once come shuffling in clutching their tapers and accordions.

Tabitha liked it well enough as it was, though she remembered better days, not so many years ago, when the jazz bands in the bodegas had been almost loud enough to drown the furious rattle of the old spice prospectors playing mah-jongg. You could sleep anywhere that was warm enough and even the cops wouldn't move you on. When you woke, at first light, you'd find an untended llama nosing in your pocket and a party of Thrant flake traders setting up their market all around your bed.

Pulling on your boots, you blinked and stumbled across the souk, stealing a chapati from the old women, and wove your way along the arcade, following the smell of roasting coffee. People leaned from upstairs windows to chat with their neighbors passing on the canal. Across the hundred and ninety-nine little backwaters, their colorful washing hung rigid in the bitter morning air. As you crossed the Copper Bridge, the sun brimmed over the rooftops, bright as butter in a cinnamon sky. Robot tenders puttered briskly through the water, humming to themselves. Beyond, in the Hamishawari Gardens, the fountains came on.

To those humans who, given mastery of space, preferred to vault across it than to linger in orbit and build there, Mars and its hurtling moons had been the first great benefit of the gift. Capellan hands directed the operations, Capellan machinery accomplished the construction, but it was by and for the humans of Earth, her nearest neighbor, that the great work of habilitating Mars was undertaken. One can understand their zeal. Suddenly, a whole new planet was accessible; and not only accessible but available, unoccupied, deserted. Abandoned.

It is difficult to imagine, now that the Red Planet is knee-deep in silicite replicas and sentimental re-creations of the "Ancients" owing more to fancy than to archaeology, but at the time of the Big Step the only vestiges of that once proud race of architects and engineers were the great canals.

For all their impressive size, they were in a sorry state: their courses choked with silt, their beds cracked and their banks decayed by centuries of long, hard Martian winters. Where they disappeared amid the crazed valleys and jumbled boulders of the dusty scablands, the first explorers drew back in defeat, unable to decipher the wild terrain. Only the expert eye of their Capellan advisor could tell where, in all that wilderness of basalt and shale, might lie hidden a clue to the world that had been lost. Following her pointing finger, they went out into the raw desert, and dug in the sand. Then and only then it was that the vast seamless blocks and slabs of the buried city came back to light.

They built a dome over it to keep the duststorms out and the new air in. They called it Schiaparelli, in honor of a hero of the art of astronomy. Elsewhere, they were scaling the volcanoes of Tharsis, draining the Argyre Basin, and hacking down whole forests of the Red Weed. Here was a gravity you could argue with; here was a horizon close enough to reach out and grasp hold of. With the primitive microclimate generators just beginning to emerge from the orbital factories of Domino Valparaiso, they woke the slumbering ecology and shook it rudely. Stunted saguaro sprouted from the rusty dunes. Prospectors trailed back into town babbling of grassy oases, trailed out again into the desert, discovered Martian frostbite.

The years were long, the company was colorful, and if the air was raw, well, didn't that lend a zest of danger to the enterprise? The presence of Capellan directors and

Eladeldi police did not seem so oppressively dispiriting when you stood a good chance of killing yourself, if you pushed it. That so much of the Rio Maas was opened out by sandschooner instead of by plane and caterpillar truck was probably exactly for that reason: because it was a distinctly more perilous way of going about it. Sailors who chanced on a sudden sand blizzard or capsized in the Neck of Mithridates were rarely rescued. The directors advised against it. "They knew the risks," they said, sorrowfully shaking their huge heads. A popular contemporary poster for recruiting emigrants shows a grinning human infant wearing an enormous pair of grown-up boots caked with red sand. Sentimental it may be, but the image clearly captured that exhilarating feeling humanity had of striding into something too big to manage—yet.

But the Martians, that vanished race of titans, what can we say of them? Little more, even today, than the architecture of old Schiaparelli so eloquently declares. Titans they were, to judge by their buildings, which take full advantage of the undemanding gravity. They were large, and strong, and had grand and far-reaching plans. They worked in stone and iron and brick. Though natural light was obviously not an amenity they thought much of, there are traces of glazing in a few of those infrequent and shapeless holes that howl in the wind; elsewhere, of a primitive and not altogether unsuccessful stab at ferrocrete.

What those buildings actually were is still doubtful. Certainly they are not very domestic. Scoured as they have been by the turbulent and freezing sands that eroded every trace of fittings and furnishings whatsoever, their walls and ceilings do bear signs: remnants of incised and sometimes inlaid strings of rectangular shapes that numerous experts have confidently identified as writing, though no truly plausible translation has ever been constructed.

The Martians were, if we may venture a fanciful interpretation of their character from the gantries, the dry vats, oubliettes and occluded vaults, the forthright aspect

of their stairways, gutters and conduits, as of the famous
canals themselves, a serious and resolute people, thorough in their undertakings, not given to digression or
frivolity. Further than this it would be frivolous of us to
speculate. The sixty-seven ruins on the Plain of Barsoom
commonly called "temples" may have been just that; or
equally well may have been army barracks, isolated quarters for the mentally disturbed or victims of plague, or
holiday camps for Martian urbanites. There is not a shred
of evidence that fearsome beasts were ritually slaughtered
in the arena or lissome slave-girls routinely sacrificed on
the altars of scowling deities.

What happened to the Martians? Where did they go?
If the Capellan directors had any idea, they never said.
Resentful souls on Earth, tethered there by obligation or
obstinacy, muttered that Capella knew from the first what
would be found on Mars and why. Some, perhaps not
without malice, averred that Capella was what did for
Mars in the first place, god knows how many aeons ago.

Still as a great dumb necropolis at the heart of the
teeming city, the ancient empty bunkers and barren silos
shuffle their enormous overlapping shadows across the
stone streets and the slick canals. Tenebrous, sepulchral,
their interiors speak mutely of their absent architects.
The archaeologists camped uncomfortably inside them
for a while, then moved out into the townships that had
mushroomed around the site. The old city was abandoned
a second time, given over to romantics, theorists, tran-
sients and dogs. Teenagers began to go there and drive
their buggies round the docklands, round and round and
round. When they grew up, it became fashionable to
return to the warehouses and hold huge parties there.

Tabitha looked up at the colossal walls of seamless
pink stone rising hundreds of meters overhead, disappearing up into the dark. Between them girders and gantries of black iron ran like gigantic roadways spanning
gulfs of empty air. She could have set the *Alice Liddell*
down comfortably on any of them, with room to spare.

The speedboat moved steadily past the empty wharves
of the giant, gaunt buildings. Lights shone out here and

there. Music and voices came gusting from moored pleasure boats across the plum-red water. The coarse whine
of the engine took on a dead, flat echo.

They tied up in a backwater under a sky black as old
blood, and walked along a pontoon to the apron of an
enormous dock. In the gloom, the basin looked like a
dim pool of deep red wine with Deimos like a giant pearl
sunk in it. People were gathered on the dock, spilling
from a warehouse full of food and drink and fresh air,
and thunderous with moth raga.

BGK009059 LOG

TXJ.STD

PRINT

¢// Basprr§ TXJ!å222/ in%ter&& &

MODE? VOX

SD? 07.31.33

READY

Hello, Alice.

HELLO, CAPTAIN. HAVE YOU COME TO TALK TO ME
AGAIN?

It's like a madhouse in there.

SO I SEE. I HOPE THEY WON'T DAMAGE ANYTHING.

They're damaging me.

SURELY NOT, CAPTAIN.

It's like having a permanent party in your own home.

YOU LIKE PARTIES.

I like going to parties. Other people's parties. I don't like throwing them. And I definitely don't like having them thrown at me.

Actually I did have a good party once. On Ucopia Plat. When I got you. I had a big party to celebrate. It was a real success, that party. Everybody came: Sam, May Lee, Muni Vega. Fritz Juventi from the *Valenzuela Perseverance*, looking not a day older in his tricorn and spats. Some of the girls from HiBrazil were teasing him, but Fritz always pretends to be charmed. Butter wouldn't melt in his mouth.

Some of them had come quite a way, from Phobos, even, people I knew when I was still hustling for my white card. I saw Dodger Gillespie, flashing her sockets and cadging a smoke off an awestruck spaceline stewardess.

"Dodger!" I said, hugging her. "I thought you were in the Belt."

"I was," she growled. "Passed up a couple of total certs to come to your bloody bun-flight," she complained, though she was looking at the poor child all the time, with her eyes half-closed and tossing her head so the sockets would catch the light. The stewardess was dutifully holding out a packet of cigarettes. Dodger deigned to take one off her. "Thank you, darling," she said and punched me vigorously on the arm to tell me to get lost, though it was half a joke, it's always half a joke with Dodger.

So I decided to stay there, just to get up her nose.

I asked her victim, "Are you having a good time?"

"Oh yes," she said. She looked at Dodger inquiringly and back at me, but Dodger was just staring at me with her head on one side and drop dead in her eyes. She wasn't doing introductions.

"I'm Tabitha," I said, smiling ingratiatingly. "Tabitha Jute."

"Oh, then this is your party!" squeaked Dodger's stewardess.

"That's right," I said.

Dodger sighed and blew smoke all over us.

"So you're going solo now," said the victim, fumbling for her smokes again. I let her get them out and offer me one before I shook my head.

It's being around Dodger. She has a bad effect on me.

"Sorry," the stewardess gulped. "I'm Moira. How do you do."

"Delighted," rumbled Dodger.

Moira looked at her, confused. But it was me she wanted to talk to now.

"I wish I had a boat," she sighed. "I'd love to fly."

"Well, you fly," I pointed out.

She flashed me a glance that made it clear there was some backbone in there, it was just the training that made her act like a dipstick. "I help old ladies in and out of webs, you mean," she said, caustically. "I serve cocktails and smile."

"Well, I used to do that," I admitted.

After that, there was no stopping her. To think you could go from herding tourists to owning your own boat!

I couldn't tell her mine wasn't a route she'd stand much chance of following. She'd have thought I was just being snotty. I ended up leaving her looking disappointed and Dodger sardonically grateful.

"Enjoy yourselves," I told them.

I went off to circulate. I had no idea I'd invited so many people. There was even a freedrone or two, I don't know how they got in, and everyone from the hiring hall, it looked like. I was showing off because I didn't have to go there any more. No more contract flying, being treated like dirt by all the owner-drivers. No more wanted boards, no more hiring hall!

WHAT DOES THAT MEAN, CAPTAIN?

Well, when you first come to a station you don't know anybody, so you're stuck with the official net, the boards for incoming business, the hall for the locals. You don't do that long before you realize it's a waste of time. The Eladeldi supervise everything, and anyway the jobs worth having all go on word of mouth. But by the time you've found that out, you've met a few people, and you don't need to hang around the hall any more. What you do is stake out a corner of one of the canteens, the zero-gyms. Somewhere news flows through. Some of the old hands have got themselves in at the cop stations and traffic control rooms. But if you've got your own boat and you're not allergic to work, you can pick and choose.

WE DON'T ALWAYS FIND IT THAT EASY, THOUGH, DO WE?

No. We don't. We make stupid mistakes and end up with rotten little capers like this one.

I'M SORRY, CAPTAIN, I DIDN'T MEAN TO FIND FAULT. GO ON ABOUT YOUR PARTY. YOUR REAL SUCCESS.

It was a success too. There wasn't a dull bit or a wrong note in the whole evening. The only time things went a bit quiet was when a couple of Eladeldi came in and sniffed around, on patrol, because all gatherings on the plat are at their sufferance, public or private. I offered them drinks and they just bared their teeth, being civil.

I spotted an Altecean burrowing under the tablecloth. I wondered if he was trying to hide from the Eladeldi, but he was just nosing for something somebody else had dropped. I was thinking of Captain Frank, you see. I wish I hadn't lost touch with him. I lose touch with so many people, Alice.

PEOPLE COME AND GO.

I'll tell you who I did see that night I wished I hadn't. One of the HiBrazil lot, Vera Shawe, with her head shaved, toga, sandals, the lot. "Hello, Tabitha," she said. "I hear congratulations are in order."

She made it sound as if I was having a baby.

"I should get her registered as soon as possible if I were you," she said. "Make sure the log's all in order."

"She hasn't worked for seven years," I said. "She was with Sanczau. She's clean."

Vera put her hand on my arm. "Even so, Tabitha," she said. "You'll want to let the Eladeldi give her the once over."

"No." I said. What a wanker, honestly. "They'd shed all over the plumbing," I said.

She gave me a prissy look. "You are naughty, Tabitha," she said. "You know you're supposed to let them check her."

I stared at her. "I forgot," I said blankly.

She would have been rude back, but she was drinking my booze. I patted her silken shoulder.

"Have a good time, Vera," I said. I was trying to get away, but she started telling me everything she knew about Kobolds, everything that had happened when she'd flown one, everything that had happened when somebody she knew had flown one, everything that had happened whenever anyone had flown one, whether she knew them or not.

I WISH I COULD HAVE HEARD THAT. I'D LIKE TO MEET VERA SHAWE, SHE SOUNDS FASCINATING.

She isn't. She's a nerd. I hate people like Vera. All right, so we owe everything to Capella. That doesn't mean we have to go around in a great lather of gratitude all the time. I wouldn't even want that, if I were a Capellan.

WHAT DO YOU SUPPOSE YOU WOULD WANT, IF YOU WERE?

If I were a Capellan, I'd have everything I want, wouldn't I?

SURELY THEY EXPECT SOMETHING.

Maybe not. Maybe it was a mistake.

CAPELLANS DON'T MAKE MISTAKES.

You said that before. It was a mistake them giving the drive
to the Frasque, wasn't it?

THE FRASQUE HAD THEIR OWN DRIVE, CAPTAIN.

Did they?

THEY DID.

How do you know that?

I SUPPOSE I PICKED IT UP SOMEWHERE.

Well, it didn't do them much good. May Lee came and
rescued me. In fact she seized me by the arm. "Well?" she
said.
    "Well what?" I said.
    "Hello, Vera," she said, flashing a steely smile over my
shoulder, and then, before Vera could reply, she went on:
"When are you going to take us to see the ship? Everybody's
just dying to see her."
    "Is it true she's a Sanczau Kobold?" Molly asked. "One
of *the* Sanczau Kobolds?"
    I was going to ask her what she meant, but May inter-
rupted. She was rounding up a party to come and inspect
the property, and everybody wanted my attention.
    May Lee and Molly Jane. I wonder what happened to
those two. May Lee is probably still there. Probably running
a repair shop by now. Or somebody's fleet. Do you remember
May Lee, Alice? She insisted on checking you over there
and then.

I REMEMBER MAY LEE. SHE HAD WONDERFUL HANDS.

You're not going to tell me you could feel her hands.

OF COURSE NOT. BUT I DID NOTICE THEM. SHE WAS
VERY DEFT. SHE MADE ME FEEL LIKE A MUSICAL IN-
STRUMENT.

All right.

PERFECTLY TUNED.

All right!

SORRY, CAPTAIN, I WAS REMINISCING. YOU KNOW I
WOULDN'T DREAM OF COMPLAINING ABOUT YOUR
OWN STYLE OF MAINTENANCE. I'M QUITE USED TO IT
BY NOW.

Will you shut up?

SORRY.

Alice. I promise you, the minute we're out of this, whatever
it is—the minute I get paid, I promise you a proper overhaul,
rebore, decontam, the works.

THE MOST IMPORTANT THING IS THE AXIS LOCK.

Everything! You can have everything. As soon as I get paid.

I HOPE IT'S QUITE SOON, CAPTAIN. I'D HATE TO LET YOU
DOWN.

9

White fire blossomed suddenly in the sky, chrysanthemums on velvet, turning the crimson black. Blue magnesium flares went spiralling up into the chilly night. Staccato tracers splashed scarlet light across a scene of jollity and confusion. Tiny figures with wands of fire were milling about the canalside, hopping from boat to boat, their shadows leaping up the faces of the buildings on the other bank as the fleeting light caught them and threw them about. Through the glass the sound of horns and drunken cheering came faintly up from below.

Tabitha Jute stood, swaying slightly, at the window of Marco Metz's penthouse flat, looking down at the determined remnants of the Schiaparelli carnival. Would they never go home to bed?

She prodded the force field that kept the cold out. It bit her finger with dull teeth. The window was floor-to-ceiling, the field generators invisible and silent. There was music playing. She tried to lean on the field.

"Don't do that," said Marco. "You only just got here."

He came up behind her, put one hand over her shoulder and one around her waist. He nuzzled her neck.

Tabitha turned, into his arms. She kissed his muscular lips, pressed herself against his compact little body.

He kissed her cheek, murmured in her ear. "Maybe you should take your coat off."

"Maybe," she said. She was perfectly smashed. Everything seemed to be moving in fast forward, yet she was darting lightly between the moments like a Rigelian sylph. Everything was glossy, filmed with silver. She scattered stardust from her feet. She reached for her gorgeous man, but he was being practical, taking her bag, her bag!

"I'll just put it here," he said, taking it to a table which was just a long low slab of something transparent. "What have you got in here anyway, you lift weights?"

"I pick things up," she said. "On my travels. I pick up some strange things," she said, looking at him. He was very close up, hard to focus on. She started to undo the buttons of his blouse. He had a thermal undershirt on, she got impatient, rucked it up with her hands, bent her head to kiss his broad brown chest.

"I don't believe you," she said.

She felt him tense. "What's that?" he said. "What do you mean?"

"I drive a barge," said Tabitha. "I meet a lot of men. I meet a lot of women. But you, you, you're an interplanetary artiste—" She said this very carefully, it was getting hard to speak properly, her tongue kept getting in the way. "You," she said, running her fingers through the rug of hair on his chest, "you, this place—and you're going to hire me!"

He relaxed.

"You," he said, kissing her lightly, "are very smashed."

"Perfectly smashed," she said. "It's perfect. Did you get any of that?"

"Any of what?"

"Whatever it was," she said. "At the party."

He chuckled. "Whatever it was," he repeated. "Whatever it was, I think I got some of it."

"It was crystal," she said. "Good stuff." She blinked at him. "Really." Perhaps he didn't believe her.

She reached for him. Her arm went through the mercury suspension like the *Alice* going into warp, sleek and cool and shimmering all along its length. He had his undershirt off now. She took hold of his belt. The buckle was modern and complicated, but it melted in her hands.

Beyond him, she caught sight of something standing in the corner. It was tall and slender and silvery. Tabitha thought it was some kind of antenna; then she realized it was an empty perch.

"Where's your little friend?" she said.

"Tal? He's around. I think he thought we should be alone together."

For some reason this struck her as extraordinarily funny. A tactful parrot! She laughed and laughed. When she laughed, the laugh came out of her mouth like mirror bubbles of liquid oxygen and spattered the iridescent walls, the scintillating ceiling, the miraculous man, his wonderful glossy chestnut eyes. She was showering him in pleasure, did he understand?

She thought it was important to tell him. "When I saw you," she said, "I was so pissed *off*. Do you know what they said?"

"What did they say?"

"They called it degrading interspish—" Her tongue was in the way again. "—interspecies harmony," she said. Talking was not as easy as laughing.

It seemed important to tell him this too.

"Talking," she said, squatting gracefully as she slipped down his trousers, real pseude trousers, "is not as easy as laughing." She thought about it as she said it. "Only sometimes," she added, "it's easier."

She started puzzling over his shoes.

He came down to join her on the floor.

She smiled. She was blissful. She caressed his luminous face. "But now everything's all right," she said. The music soared and swayed.

"Everything's fucking wonderful," he said. He growled it like a bear, and grinned like a shark. He was a miracle, truly, truly a miracle!

He took off her jacket, her grimy shirt. He kissed her nipples through the fabric of her T-shirt, opened her shoes, took them off. She sat on the floor and watched him take away her shoes and his shoes. He scuttled across the rich thick carpet like a toddler, making her laugh. He was naked. He was going to give her a job. Her jaw hurt with smiling. He came back and hugged her for a while. He was warm and supple, flesh like golden leather amidst the rippling silver air. They coped with her jeans.

There was a jump. She was standing up in just her T-shirt, pants and socks. He was sitting cross-legged at her feet. She felt distressed, she didn't know why.

Tabitha, Tabitha, she thought, sternly. And she remembered.

"I've got to get my device," she said.

He held out a hand, stroked her shin. "We can—"

"No," she said. "I must. I must be sensible. Sensible!"

She lurched lightly over to her bag, opened the zip, delved inside. She pulled something out. It was a matt black plastic box. A cassette.

She didn't remember it. All the rest of the stuff in there looked pretty much familiar, but not this.

"What's this?"

"Looks like a tape," he said, equably.

She looked at him, the tape in her hand. "I don't remember it."

The man was grinning again. "You're not in much of a state to remember anything right now, are you, sweetie?"

"But I don't remember it *at all*," she said solemnly.

While she spoke he got to his feet, turned away from her, and strolled briskly across the room to straighten a shelf of magazines. "Probably it's one of the strange things you pick up," he said, quoting her. "Why don't you go and fit your scrambler before you forget what that is?"

He was right. He was right. He was miraculous. She put the tape on the table. "Bathroom," she said.

"Second on the left."

Tabitha pranced slowly along the hallway. The music followed her into the bathroom. There were mirrors all over the place.

She sat and addressed her reflection silently and strictly. You're breaking the rules, aren't you, Tabitha? she said. Yes, she admitted. She didn't really care, though. He was so beautiful. She had a beautiful place to sleep tonight, and a beautiful man to sleep with, and in the morning he was going to pay her fine. And buy the *Alice* a new crystal.

These were the rules. She never went off with anyone, especially a man, except on her own terms. She never went to anyone else's place without checking it first. And she never entrusted herself to anyone else, *especially* a man, when she was out of her head.

All these rules she had already broken tonight.

But tonight was not a normal night. Marco was not a normal man, not her usual standard. For one thing, the men she went with didn't usually have bathrooms with bidets, or loo seats in real Earth wood. How could he afford a place like this if he was playing dives like the Moebius Strip? He must be on the way down. As long as the money held out for her, that was enough.

She had lost him for a while, at the party, but she'd already been too drunk to worry. She'd danced with a five of Palernians, all of them at once. They gave her some astonishing Ophir crystal that made her feel three meters tall and very sharp. That was when the world had turned to silver. There was a generator blowing bubble holos all around the room, snatches of old movies, adverts, random faces, alien landscapes. It was like rummaging through someone else's dreams. She laughed and jumped about with the Palernians, trying to burst the bubbles. Then Marco came back. She kissed him.

There was no pushbutton by the loo. Tabitha looked around in vain for a few minutes. When she stepped back from it, it hummed and emptied itself. She shrugged, went over to the bidet, washed herself and inserted her tiny scrambler. She could hear a tiny voice somewhere, talking and pausing, as if somebody's radio was interfering with the music, but by the time she left the room it had stopped. The light turned itself out.

"Tabitha," called the voice of her beautiful man.

The walls of the hallway dipped and rippled. She was starting to come down.

"Where are you?" she said.

"In here."

Disoriented, she tried to locate his voice. The music wandered around her as she searched. At last she found him. He was standing in the dark, in front of a picture window, fireworks exploding silently behind him. She went in and kissed him all over. There was a bed. It was a bedroom.

On a table by the bed was a flask of something, gin, tequila, wine, she hardly knew the difference any more. They drank from the flask. He drank from her mouth.

Then they took off her T-shirt. It was a very involved and complicated process.

The light of the fireworks strobed around the room. Metallic circles spread like ripples across the walls.

Tabitha said, "You are going to fix everything, in the morning?"

The lovely man was kissing her navel, running his lips along the top edge of her panties. He started kissing her crotch, very gently, his lips barely touching the fabric. He said, "Of course I'm going to fix everything. How could I pass up a chance of hiring the most beautiful bargee in the solar system?"

He took off her panties with his teeth. Apparently he was something of an acrobat as well.

She caressed his perineum with her tongue. The fireworks seemed to pulse with the music, her skin seemed to melt and reform from moment to moment. She was no longer sure where he ended and she began.

10

When Tabitha Jute woke up, she immediately wished she hadn't. She discovered she'd been sleeping on her back. Her head felt as if it had been hit with a bag of cement, or replaced with one. Her sinuses were all gummed together in a lump between her eyes.

"Kgn," she said faintly.

She was in a strange bed, in a strange room. It was something approaching day. Limp orange light was leaking in around the edges of a grey blind. In the corner by the window was a stringy plant straggling desperately out of a blurry brown pot, as if in search of water. Tabitha knew how it felt.

She blinked and tried to focus. On the wall behind the plant she could just make out irregular painted spirals of pale gold. Next to it stood an empty tubular blue clothes rack, a tubular blue chair, a tubular blue AV rig.

She shut her eyes again.

The bed was warm, and extraordinarily comfortable.

Tabitha turned over on her side, and saw the man. He was fast asleep with his back to her, snoring very quietly. He was wrapped in so much of the duvet all she could see was the top of his head.

She remembered everything at once then, in one big bright colorful blurt of sound and light and music and immensely accelerated action.

"Ngk," she said.

It was a sound of guilt and astonishment and relief, all at once.

She moved her mouth about a bit to see if she could

find her tongue. It seemed to have become stuck somewhere back there during the night.

She urgently needed a piss.

Tentatively, she sat up.

Marco didn't stir.

After a moment, when her head had settled, muddily,
Tabitha slowly turned back the duvet. She noticed she
still had her socks on. And she smelled just terrible.

Marco Metz snored on.

Tabitha swung her feet to the floor. Her eyesight was
vague and muzzy, her mouth felt like the bottom of a
sandpit. She wondered, not for the first time, how it was
that her body could be desperate for liquid at one end
while bursting to get rid of it at the other.

In the bathroom she confronted her reflection again.
Even with the blinds down, she could see the dark shadows under her eyes.

Slut, she told herself. It was a word her father had
used frequently. Slut, she thought again, comfortably.

Tabitha took a pee and a shower, with real water.
Soaped and rinsed, the world looked rather better. She
went to the window and, carefully, raised the blind.

It was still very early. The sun was a tangerine blob
in a swirling blackcurrant sky. Below, dim curds of refuse lay clotted about the glass pillars of the Maserati
Mall. Across the rooftops, a lone cop prowler was the
only thing moving on the cold expanse of the Grand
Canal.

Wrapped in a big green towel, Tabitha left the bathroom. She looked in the bedroom. The hump in the duvet
had not moved.

She padded around until she located the kitchen. It
was large and very, very white. Tabitha wondered if there
was any fruit juice in the fridge. Grapefruit, she thought.
She willed there to be grapefruit juice in the fridge.

But it was empty. Or as good as. There was a transparent sachet of something brown and thick, chocolate
paste or miso; one dried-up anchovy in an open tin, its
coat of salt dried to a hard crust; and a smear of something

on a saucer that might once have been pesto sauce. Or
parrot vomit, she thought, grumpily.

Tal was in the living room, on his futuristic perch.

"Good evening," he said.

"Morning, Tal," murmured Tabitha.

"Good evening," he said. He sounded like a perky
little old man.

There were clothes strewn around on the floor. Some
of them were hers. She picked out the ones that were
and put them on. Solemnly, the parrot watched her dress.
"Stop looking at me, Tal." But he didn't. She found it
slightly uncomfortable, being scrutinized by a bird.

Next she looked for her bag, and found it on a long
low table. She thought her toothbrush was in there somewhere, and rummaged for it. She didn't find it, but buried
right down at the bottom she did find a tape cassette in
a box.

She pulled it out and looked at it. She vaguely remembered taking it out of the bag last night. She didn't
remember putting it back in. Whatever it was, she still
had no recollection of it at all. It was plain black: no
label, not even a brand name. She wondered where she'd
picked it up, and who was missing it.

There was a reader in the dusty rig next to the tape-
shelves. Tabitha went over and turned it on.

"Grievous tale in all forlorn!" whooped Tal suddenly.

Tabitha nearly jumped out of her skin. "Christ, bird,
don't do that," she muttered. He was beginning to get
on her nerves.

She slotted the anonymous tape.

But she was none the wiser for what came out of the
speakers: a soft sea of hiss, a hint of ultrasonics, and a
persistent, repetitive creaking noise. It was so nearly
nothing she wondered if she hadn't loaded it properly.
She crouched down to make sure it was turning, and
check the settings on the amps.

Marco reached over her shoulder and pressed stop,
twice.

The tape ejected.

He put his hands under her arms and raised her up, turning her about, away from the AV.

He was unshaven and wearing a shabby toweling bathrobe with threads hanging off it. His big brown eyes were dull, unexpressive. He smelled of warmth and sleep.

She stepped into his arms and kissed him. "There's nothing on it," she said.

Reaching past her again, he took the tape out of the reader and slipped it back into its case. "You want music, I'll find you some music," he said rapidly, looking away from her. He plucked a tape from the shelf and put it on.

It started in the middle of something, something hollow and highly polished that fed into itself in ever-increasing rounds. It was quiet and quite pleasant.

"Is this you?" asked Tabitha.

"This?" said Marco, glancing at the tape he'd just slotted. "Yeah," he said.

He threw the mystery tape on the table beside her bag.

"Good morning, Tal," he said. He went and fondled the bird, which chirped and squeaked and nibbled his finger.

"I feel terrible," Tabitha said. "Don't you?"

"Sure," he said, non-commitally. "You want some coffee? I'll get it."

He did. He also shaved and dressed, in a blockneck and yesterday's trousers.

"I need to go to Plenty," he said, "pick up the rest of the band and all our gear." He was sitting on the couch facing her, his arm stretched out along the back. "We play there tonight. Then you can take us on to our next engagement."

"Where's your next engagement?" she asked.

"Titan," he said. He drank his coffee.

"How many of you are there?"

"Me. Tal. A couple of others. Say five altogether. Say four, maybe, Tal doesn't count."

The parrot, hearing his name, gave a loud hoot.

"It's funny," Tabitha said, "he looks just like a parrot."

"Well, he is a parrot, a kind of parrot. He's from Altecea, a planet there somewhere. I won him in a poker game, taught him to sing. Do tricks. He doesn't like space, do you, guy?"

"Banana tree!" chirped Tal. "Sriti naogar demestica! In Mongu Town, where I was born, there lived a merry maid, up high in banana tree!"

"Shut up, Tal!" Marco shouted loudly.

The bird subsided, twittering.

"He hates being on the road," said Marco. "He has a box he has to ride in. It's around here somewhere."

He looked around, negligently.

"So," he said. "Are you up for all this?"

Tabitha nodded. "But we need a new axis lock crystal," she told him.

"We? Who's this we, I thought there was just you?"

"I mean Alice does."

"Who's Alice?"

"The ship. She has to have a new crystal."

"We'll pick one up. On Plenty."

Tabitha considered it. She didn't like the idea of it. Plenty was bad news. And Titan was way off her patch, there wasn't much chance of a return load. But Titan was a long way off. And Marco was here. And he had the money.

She cleared her throat. "Well, we'll have to take our chance on Plenty. But I need the two-fifty in advance." She looked at the clock. "To pay the fine."

Marco became very still. "What fine?" he said.

"Didn't I tell you about that?"

She told him. He laughed. He laughed and laughed.

"It's not that funny."

"Sure it is! That little feller sailing through the air . . ."

Tabitha drank some more coffee. "Expensive joke," she said.

"Well, let's see. Two-fifty."

"Three with the port tax and stuff. Three-seventy-five with fuel."

"Hell, we can cover that. We can do that for you."

Tabitha was relieved. She hated bargaining. She never seemed to be in a very good position to bargain from, somehow.

"So how much is this crystal?"

Tabitha told Marco what Carlos had told her.

He didn't even blink. She wondered if she was wrong about what you got playing the Moebius Strip.

Marco said, "Let's say we pay the fine and the crystal and you take us to Titan."

"Have you got that much?"

"Sure. Sure we have. Well, Hannah has."

"Who's Hannah?" Tabitha asked, hearing an edge on her voice and not liking it.

"Our manager," he said. "This is her apartment."

"Does she live here?" She couldn't believe it. For all the furniture and appliances, the tapes on the shelves, the place had a desolate air. Everything seemed like stuff abandoned, or in transit. There was no resident personality holding it together.

"No. No, I'll take you to meet her. You'll like Hannah."

"Does she live on Titan?"

"On Titan? No."

"Oh, she lives on Plenty."

"She doesn't exactly live there, no," he said. "She kind of—operates from there."

He could be bloody evasive sometimes. She supposed it was the effect of being famous—or having been famous—being wary of your privacy. Well, she wasn't famous at all, and she was wary of her privacy. She didn't mind taking him to Plenty, that was no distance. It could even be fun. She wasn't at all sure she could cope with him and a band of strangers, all the way to Titan, through the depths of hyperspace where there's no escape from your companions.

She gave it up. Maybe she could renegotiate when they got to Plenty and she had her crystal.

She got to her feet and went and picked up the phone.

"Who are you calling?" he asked.

"The cops," she said. "So we can pay the two-fifty and get on the road."

"Oh," he said. He sounded unenthusiastic.

Tabitha paused, the phone in her hand. "Is that okay?"

"Sure," he said, "Sure. Sure."

BGK009059 LOG

TXJ.STD

PRINT

/¡β*[ÑXO]$!'ˆrT:/9/Ç%222m

MODE? VOX

SD? 07.07.52

READY

Have I ever told you about Rella, Alice?

NO, CAPTAIN. NOT THAT I REMEMBER.

She was quite important, in her way.

She was in her fifties, I suppose. She was about my height, but chunky. Hefty. She had awful teeth, with black fillings, and long ratty hair that always seemed to be just coming out of a perm. She had lots of rings, on both hands, and she always wore overalls. She said they didn't notice you if you wore overalls.

Rella lived in a store room under Posidon transport station. Sometimes, I mean. That was her base. That's where I see her when I think of her, though she didn't take me there at first. The first time I met her was up on the platform. I was twelve or thirteen. I was coming back from the labs at Menelaus, after some work detail or other. Rella was going through the bins.

She stopped as soon as she saw me. She said, "What are you staring at?" She hated anyone to watch her when she was going through the bins. It was something she'd never admit doing, though she was always doing it.

That's not fair. Rella could hold down jobs, when she wanted to. She was a cleaner, more than once, and she worked in the hydroponics, and in kitchens. But she could never keep her mind on the job. Sooner or later she'd end up drifting innocently around the bins.

"What are you staring at?" she said. She had a pathetic, ruined, smoky kind of voice that used to go right through me. I don't know why she spoke to me, what was special about me, why she didn't ignore me the way she ignored everyone else. There was a whole transport of people in the station coming home from early shift. I suppose I was the only one dawdling to look at her instead of going by as if she didn't exist.

I went on by, that first time. I was embarrassed.

She called after me, "Cat got your tongue?"

I hadn't the first idea what she meant.

THERE WEREN'T CATS ON THE MOON, SURELY, ANY MORE THAN THERE WERE DOGS?

I never saw one. But after that I was always seeing her, all over the place. She kept moving around; she kept them guessing. They all had to. If they'd caught her, they'd have stuck her in Imbrium or somewhere, some institution. She'd been in places like that before. That was like death to her. There must have been a lot of them caught like that, at the end.

Whenever I saw her, she always smiled at me. It was as if she'd got me confused with someone else, someone important. Once I had half an hour to wait for a transport. She came waddling up to me. She was drunk.

"I've got papers," she assured me. "I'll show you."

I really didn't want to know.

"I don't carry them around," she said. "You never know who's looking. Bastards."

The thing was, she really did have papers, a resident's card, a work category check, that sort of thing. Half of them didn't, they were up illegally in the first place, working the underside of the system, the jobs nobody wants. But Rella was a Lunar citizen. She did show me her papers, later on. She had them hidden in a box, in the store room. She made me promise to destroy them, "if anything ever happens to me," she said. Other times she made me promise to keep them forever, to remember her by, and say a prayer. She was a bit vague who it was I was to pray to. She had a lot of time for religion, prophecy, looking for her star. She took everything to heart. I don't know if she understood any of it.

"I'm misplaced," was a thing she'd often say. She didn't just mean like a misplaced person, floating loose in society.

LIKE DATA MISPLACED IN A FILE.

She was certainly that. But she meant on a larger scale. A cosmic scale. We were all lost; but one day we'd be saved. One day we'd all rise up together into the sun.

"Everyone will be there," she told me. "You will. You're one of us. You don't know it, but you are." But other times she'd say: "You wouldn't understand." And she'd give me that look, like at first, half wary, half defiant, as if she had a secret to defend from me.

God knows she'd told me her secret enough times.

"This isn't my home," she'd say. "Not here, not Earth either. One day I go home. The ship will come for me."

I can see her now, sitting on her shelf in the store room, surrounded by bottles of detergent, pointing at her box.

"That's not me," she said. " The woman in those papers." It was confusing, sometimes, when she'd go on about her papers. Sometimes she meant the ones that proved she was a citizen, sometimes the others, the ones that proved she wasn't. So she believed.

She had these maps. One of them was drawn on an old envelope, a paper one. I don't know how she came by it. Maybe she drew it herself, when she was young, and forgot. Maybe it was something she found in one of her bins. It was just six dots, anyway, and some lines joining them up. Five of the dots had names. Sometimes she said they were stars, sometimes they were the names of cities. They certainly weren't anywhere on the Moon, or anywhere else I've ever heard of, before or since. Rella would point to the sixth dot and say solemnly: "This is here," and she'd point at the floor, to make sure I understood. "The prison planet," she said. "Babylon. Maya."

But she was always changing her mind about that too. Sometimes the sixth dot was her star, the one she was going home to, when the ship came for her.

And one day she had this other map, and I don't know where she got that either, or what happened to it. She only showed it me the once, and after that whenever I mentioned it she didn't know what I was talking about. It was made of something absolutely rigid but incredibly thin. Edge on, you couldn't see it at all. I mean it. I've never seen anything like it anywhere.

So it was transparent, with these little black circles in it that seemed to jump backwards and forwards at you. If you concentrated you could make them all line up, in 3-D; and then it would all just collapse and be jiggling spots again. And it had lots of tiny writing at the top in some alien alphabet. Rella said it was a map. It might have been some sort of optician's test thing, for all I could say, or a kids' puzzle.

"Don't put it down," Rella warned me. "You won't be able to pick it up again." She laughed. She was in a good mood that day.

She told me I was the only person she could trust, though I often saw her around with other people, misplaced people, I suppose. Most often with a woman, a real whitey, in dark glasses. She was about twice my age, about half Rella's. Rella pretended she didn't know me when they were together. She looked straight through me.

Rella used to tell me stories, about places she'd been, only sometimes I thought she meant herself and it turned out it was her mother she was talking about. Sometimes it was her grandmother.

WHAT DID THEY DO?

Oh, roamed about all over Earth, as far as I could make out, traveled on foot across huge mountain ranges and vast great deserts where nothing lived. I can't remember any of it now, but I used to sit on a crate and listen to her, and think about freedom, stupid things you think when you're a kid, you know.

NOT REALLY, NO.

Well, you do. We do. I thought she was marvelous. Sometimes I'd bring her food and things. Steal little bits of money so she could buy drink. I thought I was doing something important, helping Rella along. One day I had to go to the clinic and I lied about the time of the appointment so I could skip a suit inspection, so I had an hour to waste. I didn't want anyone to see me, so I went to see Rella, but she wasn't there.

I wandered back up to the station concourse. I went over to the screens to see if there was a movie on anywhere. There were these two men there, talking, and one was saying there was trouble at Serenity, some problem about a ship trying to come down without an Eladeldi registration.

"A kit job," he said. "Bits and pieces from I don't know where. All held together with string and faith, by the look of it."

I was only listening because I was bored. I was thinking about something else. I'd found a movie to go to, at an off-center commons. When the transport pulled in, I got on.

Then, just as the doors were closing, I dived back out to the platform. Everyone stared at me, but I didn't care. I ran to the stairs, and down to the basement, to the empty store room. I went straight to Rella's box. It was empty. I never saw her again. I never saw the other woman either. And when I got to the clinic everyone was in a mess because half the domestic staff had disappeared, walked out without a word.

12

Tabitha Jute and Marco Metz took the lift to street level. They went out into the bloodshot Schiaparelli day.

No one was about. A Scarab Minor dawdled along, dusting and watering the gutter. Tabitha's boots crunched on the sandy pavement. The chill in the air began to clear her head. She'd let herself go, last night—but she was none the worse for it, was she? No. Which was the spirit of carnival, wasn't it? Loosen up, she told herself. Stop worrying.

She took them by a short cut to the Weinbaum Canal. Brown barges puttered slowly through the turbid water. At waterside tables mustachioed wharfingers sucked soup ponderously from steaming bowls. Altecean street cleaners were piling the litter with their long rakes. Everyone looked hung over. The sky had turned streaky, the atmosphere raw, too much sulphur in it.

They caught a flier out to the port, out of Schiaparelli on the Graben Road, past the Devil's Fingers, those soaring pinnacles of rock, vermilion and cerise. In some lights they seem to glisten, as if they were red hot, molten. Under Deimos at full they look like gigantic pink fungi, or worse. This morning, looming through a yellow haze, they might have been the eroded spires of a lost city of cathedrals, buried beneath the omnipresent sand. At least, so Marco said, and expatiated freely on the idea of a performance he had always thought of mounting there, a mood piece, a son et lumiére.

"Tell me about your band," she said.

"Oh, you'll meet them," he said.

She pressed him. "Who are they?"

He shifted in his seat, rubbing the window with the knuckle of his index finger. "You'll get along," he promised her.

He would say no more.

Tabitha didn't like being told no, told nothing. She bit back on her irritation. He was obviously used to having his own way. Well, she could put up with that until they got on board. Then things would be different. He did take things for granted, though. She had not been pleased when it turned out the credit chip he needed to pay her fine was with the rest of his stuff on Plenty. "See, I like to travel light," he said. "It's no problem. We'll phone it through when we get there," he said. "First thing. Promise."

He had kissed her and fondled her breasts. Then he pulled on a well-worn jacket of aerated leather and strolled out of the flat, with Tal in a box on one shoulder and a duffel over the other.

She hoped this wasn't going to turn out to be a mistake.

Especially having people on her ship.

Not that there was anything delicate or vulnerable about the *Alice Liddell*. She was a working ship, like all the ships of her line. She had quirks, of course: her drive was a Capellan one, like everyone else's, and nobody understood them. Only the ship's personae, through some elusive twist of code deep in the programming, were enabled to master the Capellan drive.

This was quite as true when Tabitha Jute met Marco Metz in Schiaparelli as it had been in the days of the Big Step, years before she was born. Nobody had really made any significant progress in discovering how they worked, these engines Capella handed out so liberally. The Capellans didn't prohibit research, not in so many words; they simply assured humankind that for them, with their small brains, the mechanics of hyperspatial foreshortening would be incomprehensible. Those who persisted discovered the drives' disconcerting tendency to implode or deliquesce at the merest touch of a screwdriver. If you did manage to open one, it would turn out to be full of dead leaves.

Humans are inquisitive creatures by nature. Not everyone was content to remain an unenlightened beneficiary of a superior technology. But even those who tried to think their way in were obliged to retreat, baffled. Ace hackers on clandestine projects for ruthless outfits like Frewin Maisang Tobermory were taken away at midnight in unmarked ambulances after collapsing with mysterious new conceptual diseases and cognitive dysfunctions. Some ingrates and irresponsible rumor-mongers tried to implicate the Eladeldi in these abrupt disappearances, which made no sense at all. The Eladeldi were never known to involve themselves in medical matters.

In the absence of understanding, superstitions proliferated. Oh, how they proliferated. How many times had Tabitha heard, in casual conversation in some dorm, some station bar, from pilots who had found their craft taking a route they had never intended, never charted? A route which nonetheless delivered them to their destinations safely and on time, and proved, on later inquiry, to have avoided an entirely unforeseeble hazard or delay? How many ships suddenly developed strange ghost personae; mechanical poltergeists in the engine room; voices where they had none before? And how many times, on re-entering occupied space, did the phenomena depart as suddenly as they came? "It's as true as I'm sitting here telling you," insisted Dodger Gillespie, never one to be subject to fancies or unsought hallucinations. "Electric blue caterpillar long as my arm, coiled up around the reactor! Then, when I come back with the welding torch, no sign of the bastard. Only a trail of blue sticky stuff all on the gratings. True as I'm sitting here," she said, draining her pint. "True as the fact it's your round, gel."

The seeds of this new mythology of space had been sown, back in the days of the Big Step, by so many alien races appearing suddenly in the system, in vessels as various in shape and size as their owners. Nowadays we are used to these things—the spinning jeweled diadems of Rigel; the quasi-organic models of the Frasque, that echo the shapes of the hives and cocoons built by insects; the Palernian Brisk, which looks nothing like its name, more like a bundle of sausages. But think how they marveled then, the first time they glimpsed the grandiose space architecture of the Eladeldi, or the shining needle, a kilometer long, of the Vespa Omicron.

There were theories about all of these, some of them frankly theological. The Witnesses of the Total Merge catalogued all those ships believed to belong to other client species of the Capellans. Allocating them to niches of higher or lower favor on a cabbalistic tree, they claimed to detect some principle of metamorphosis. Human craft too, they prophesied, would pass through all these forms on their way to the ultimate, transcendental spaceship. On the day of its perfection, aeons hence, the arcana of the Capellan engine would finally be comprehended, and the invisible barrier around the orbit of Pluto would silently dissolve. On that day, argued one heresy, humans too would complete their evolution, and become Capellans. The prophecy of the Total Merge would be fulfilled, and aliens be aliens no more.

How much truth there was in all these myths you now know as well as I. Certainly the Witnesses hit early on the fact that, rippling in and out of hyperspace, even ships as basic as the Bergen Kobold change slightly every time. The abused particles that constitute them never reintegrate quite exactly. That would be rather too much to ask of the laws of conservation. Sometimes their pilots notice these aberrations, and sometimes they don't; because, after all, their particles have been transubstantiated too.

About the evolution of the human being I know nothing that is not obvious just by looking at me. But I did know the *Alice Liddell*—who better?—and I remember her well. I remember her intimately from the beginning, from the third year of the Big Step, when she was built and christened. For she was old when Tabitha Jute first set eyes upon her, when she dragged the tarpaulins from her in the long grass of that neglected vineyard. Her bronze was bruised and discolored from the raw cold burn of space. Her pile was spent, her hydraulics dry and full of spiders' webs. She had done sterling service already, and was as inert as a ship can be—which is actually, as we have already speculated, not quite inert after all. People used to believe (permit me this, one last one) that once you activated the Capellan drive it could never be entirely deactivated again, not until it suffered ruin or physical destruction. And I, where was I, during those years when chipmunks scampered through the undercarriage of the battered little Kobold? I was asleep.

The ship that bore the name of Liddell was, frankly, primitive. She was low and she was lumpy. I remember her as cramped. Her cockpit seated two, a pilot and a co-pilot, each in a standard zero-g web. Aft she had two small single cabins with modest personal storage, a minute galley and ablute. She measured a shade under twenty-one meters from nose to tail, and a shade over half that across, from wingtip to stubby wingtip. Her number BGK009059 said that she was one of the first of the Bergen K line, the Kobolds that plied the spaceways of the solar system, taking this here and that there, for nearly fifty years.

She was built to labor, and built to last. Her middle could hold loose goods to 250 cubic meters or be replaced with any one of seventeen styles of container. Her four loading extensors and four cargo drones stowed themselves, during flight, in the double wall of the hull. She bore sixteen directional plasma jets, four for each axis, and three huge fixed "roundmouths." She had scanners all over her, more than the Bergen yards supplied as standard. Her solar had also been much improved, as if her commissioner had expected more of her than her designers. Any trouble she gave her last pilot was more to do with adverse conditions and those middle years of neglect than any flaw in her constitution. Also, Tabitha never quite got around to doing as much maintenance as she meant to.

Call it whimsy if you will, but I have always thought,

privately, there was something very similar about the two of them, the *Alice Liddell* and her captain Tabitha Jute. Both were small, stocky and strong. Neither came of anything but the most commonplace, workaday material; yet each hid an adventurous spirit and surprising resources beneath her utilitarian exterior.

Or perhaps this is just the wisdom of hindsight, a rosy blur of sentiment cast by nostalgia over the scene. Picture them, Tabitha Jute and Marco Metz, as they walk out across the spaceport tarmac this chilly Schiaparelli evening, to climb aboard the not-quite-redeemed *Alice* and take off into the Martian sky, bound on a journey that will take them to Plenty—and far, far beyond.

TWO

Lost in the Caverns
of Plenty

13

"You can have this cabin," she said, sliding the door open. "I'll clear all this stuff out."

Anyone would think he'd never seen a Kobold before. "This is terrific! Absolutely terrific! What a ship!" Now he hugged her from behind. "I want to ride up the front with you."

"No," said Tabitha. "I never have anyone in the cockpit." She looked into his big brown eyes. "I'm sorry!"

"What's this," he said, "safety regulations now?"

"Well, yes," she said.

"I don't believe this," he said, holding her tight and leaning back to look at her. "You're telling me a woman like you actually obeys that stuff?"

Tabitha turned and shoved at the passenger cabin door, which was stuck halfway. "I don't like having anyone else in the cockpit while I'm driving," she said, "that's all."

He seemed to be mollified. "Well, okay," he said. His hands roved around her body. He nuzzled her ear. "I'm going to miss you," he said. "All the way to Plenty . . . what's that, three, four hours subjective?"

"Five," she said, extricating herself. "I'm not skipping. Not with that crystal. Not with a passenger."

"Five hours!" he said. "What am I supposed to do all that time without you?"

She was irritated, amused. "I don't know! Practice your glove. Talk to Tal," she said.

"He's out," he said. Tal lay behind him in the passageway, in his white porcelite traveling case. In customs, the Eladeldi had drawn back their lips at the sedated parrot, but all the processing was in order, and Marco had hustled them through. "He'll sleep a while now. He hates flying."

Marco's hands found their way back to Tabitha's hips. He looked over her shoulder. "That's a lot of stuff in there," he commented.

Tabitha leaned on the door. It wouldn't budge. "It's just kipple," she said. "I'll clear it up," she repeated, but her intention was waning. There was so much of it. Spare overalls, loose packaging, an inflatable life raft, most of the parts of a second-hand galley robot she'd picked up cheap and never quite got round to reassembling . . . She let it float around in there, mostly unsecured. "I haven't had anyone in here for a while," she said, semi-apologetically. "It just builds up."

"You never know half the things you've got until you have to do something about them," he said amiably.

She shoved at the door again. There was a loud clatter of something falling down inside.

"Come on," said Marco quietly.

"Don't hustle me," she said. But she was weakening.

What he'd just said reminded her of that business last night with the tape. Probably it was simply one of those things that happen, or that you think happen, when you're smashed and half-asleep. But she kept thinking about it.

She turned away from the door, stood irresolute outside the door of her own cabin. Logically, she could put him in there. Tired and hungover as she was, she wasn't going to be sleeping in the next five hours; not until they docked at Plenty.

"Tabitha. Relax," he said, drawing her back toward him in the cramped confines of the passage. "Look at you, you're so tense. How can you possibly drive when you're all wound up that way?'' He massaged her shoulders.

In another moment she was kissing him.

It was an option she didn't usually have, kissing a gorgeous man on board her own ship. Why shouldn't she take advantage of the opportunity? The pleasure would be over soon enough, it always was.

"Okay," he said reasonably, as they surfaced. "Are you going to show me the rest?"

The aft lock of the hold was open. Marco picked up Tal's box. Tabitha took his other hand and led him in.

"Oh, yes! This is great," he said, setting the box down again. His voice echoed in the emptiness. "Just great!"

The way he stood, hands in his back pockets, a smile on his face she could only call triumphant: it pleased her, he admired her ship. But it made her doubtful again. "How much gear are we collecting?"

"Oh, we'll all fit in here, no problem."

He really was looking around. He looked at the cargo drones stowed away in their kennels, inspected the air and power connections, the airlocks either end, the internal controls for the doors and the roof. He climbed up to the catwalk and examined the roof, then strolled around surveying the empty space and making knowledgeable noises. "Hm. Okay. Okay." Then he climbed up on the rail and swung muscularly from the butt of one of the loading extensors.

Tabitha stood below, watching him with her arms folded. "Can you do that with one hand?"

"Sure," he said. He couldn't. He landed on his feet. "Gravity's a little off," he told her, and rubbed his hands. "I can work on it. Build it into the act. What's in here?"

He opened a bin that said EMERGENCY in big red letters. A large dispenser of detergent, an old flex microphone as big as a taper, a polythene bag of tubular bandages, a sealant gun and a box of raisins fell all over his feet.

"It always does that," said Tabitha. She knelt and pushed everything back into the bin, and shut the lid quickly.

"Now I know where to look if I need raisins," he said.

"Help yourself," she said. She was kneeling on the floor, wiping her hands together. He bent down and kissed her on the lips.

"I'm hungry now," he said.

Tabitha stood up robustly, making herself awkward to hold. She opened the bin a crack, whipped out the raisins and thrust the box at him. "Here," she said.

He wouldn't take it, wouldn't stop looking in her eyes. "It's not raisins I'm hungry for," he murmured.

"I thought you were in a hurry," she said.

"I am, I am," he said, clutching for her.

She pressed the box against his chest. "Later," she said, being firm, with him, with herself. "We have to go."

"Let's go," he said.

He picked up Tal. Tabitha opened the box and ate a handful of raisins as they left the hold.

"Want some?" she said, her mouth full.

"Ah, no."

"Okay."

This really was not a normal day. Things were mounting up. Being obliged to this man. Having to go to Plenty. With a deteriorating axis lock crystal. The cops on her case. She'd be in trouble if they missed that twenty-four hour deadline.

So would the *Alice*.

He seemed to sense her mood, drawing back a little as they went through the forward lock and up the cockpit steps.

"Don't worry," he said. "We'll get it sorted out. You just get us there. We'll phone the money in, that's first. Top priority. You can meet the guys, come and see the show, we have dinner, a couple of drinks, a good night's sleep, and tomorrow we get you fixed up for your crystal.

You know anybody up there who does that kind of thing?''

"No," said Tabitha. She knew hardly anyone who worked on Plenty, and trusted no one who would. On the occasions she had to pick up or deliver there she got in and out as fast as possible. Plenty was weird.

She stepped up on to the flight deck, Marco close behind her. He'd got his way. The decision had been made, somehow, and her feelings had been overruled. She'd overruled herself. She was not at her best. This kind of thing happening threw everything sideways.

They stowed Tal behind their seats, with her bag and all the other stuff that had accumulated there. Marco wouldn't hear of him being put back in the cabin. He had to have the case near him all the time, to keep an eye on the lifesign meters. Tabitha thought briefly about livestock regulations. She pulled the retaining net over the bird-box and fastened it down.

"Doesn't all this junk get in your way?"

"Not really."

The net was snagging on something. She reached between her feet and dragged out a wizened melon. "I was wondering what had happened to that," she said.

She sat up in her web, pulled the keyboard to her and roused the computer, keeping it mute. She hated anyone listening when she was talking to Alice.

ATTENTION, said the screen. It flashed a schematic at her, rotated it through 180°, zoomed in. A large blue diamond was flashing on and off. AXIS LOCK CRYSTAL DEFECT, it said. FAILURE PROBABILITY 43.29%

Tabitha tapped manual override.

She drew back her cuff to check her monitor and spoke to the radio. "Bravo Golf Kansas zero-zero-niner-zero-fiver-niner to control."

Marco stood beside her, in the narrow aisle between the webs. He reached over the console and wiped some of the grime off the viewport. Outside lay the endless tarmac of Schiaparelli Port, scorched and brown.

"Control to Bravo Golf Kansas zero-zero-niner-zero-fiver-niner. What is your field number, please?"

"Shit," said Tabitha. She started rummaging through the litter of tickets wedged into the seal around the glass.

"Repeat, your field number, please, Bravo Golf Kansas zero—"

"Just a minute," she said. She sorted tickets. She looked at Marco. "It's one of these," she said.

He nodded sympathetically, his hands in his pockets.

"That's a lot of tickets," he said.

"It'll be in your log," said Control.

"No it won't," said Tabitha. "I didn't enter it." She sucked her teeth, took another ticket down at random, glanced at it, crumpled it and tossed it into the disposal by her left knee.

"Procedure is to enter your field number in your log on arrival, Bravo Golf Ka—"

"It's here somewhere," she said.

"Will you hold, please, Bravo Golf Kansas zero-zero-niner-zero-fiver-niner," said Control drily.

Thank you, mouthed Tabitha. She pulled a face at the speaker.

She pointed to the co-pilot's web. "Get in," she said. She pressed a tab. Red light filled the cockpit, and a high, buzzing hum began.

"Bravo Golf Kansas zero-zero-niner-zero-fiver-niner, Jute, Tabitha, Captain?"

"Yes?"

"Your field number is Tango Tango oner-fiver."

"Good."

"On future visits to this or any other system port, please enter your field number in your log memory on arrival."

"All right." She scanned a line of lights, pressed three more tabs. A whine spiraled round and round the hum. The light went out, and came back on.

"Can I go now?"

"Have you filed a departure flight application?"

"Plenty, passenger delivery."

"Have you filed notice of that application, Captain Jute?"

"Look, I'm just going to Plenty, not Charon or some-where."

"What is the routing on that flight, Bravo Golf Kansas zero-zero-niner-zero-fiver-niner?"

Tabitha lay back in her web and began to recite co-ordinates, turning to a keypad at her elbow, reciting more co-ordinates, reading co-ordinates off a screen.

Control repeated everything precisely and faithfully while a low, slow hammering began beneath the floor. The temperature in the cockpit was rising. Tabitha knocked an array of red tabs. All turned green but one.

She poked the red tab. She pressed it hard.

It blinked green, then red again.

She hit it with the heel of her hand.

The tab went green.

The ship was shuddering, the hammer hammering rapidly now.

"You are clear to proceed, Bravo Golf Kansas zero-zero-niner-zero-fiver-niner."

Outside the viewport a line of blinding white light licked up, across and back, drawing a square around them on the concrete.

"Do not engage engines until—"

Tabitha touched a key, and they sat in thunder.

Outside the soft, floating fields of her web and Marco's, everything groaned and flexed. All the screens were fizzing. Lights were running up and down the board.

The thunder swelled.

The *Alice Liddell* shook. She wobbled. She lifted three legs off the ground and put them down again. The cockpit was hot. Outside, the smoke enveloped everything all around but the square of magnesium light, which now turned green.

They bobbed, and wallowed, and were gripped by something and thrust, up, up, into the air.

The port of Schiaparelli receded below them, trucks dwindling, oxygen drays shrinking, hangars and block-houses and bridges diminishing to a model, a miniature, a busy geometric diagram, swallowed in the red mists of Mars. Beyond, they could see the city, churning on without them. The sunlight flared from the canals.

Still the thunder thundered and burned and shook them. Tiny electrical discharges zipped and buzzed about the hull as the fragile air was catalyzed around them. There was a high-pitched whistle and a great noise like the cloth of the sky tearing. It went on, and on, and on.

Then the noise and the quaking began to abate, and the curve of Mars shrank and ran away beneath them like a wave from sand; and then there was no more beneath and no above and nothing anywhere but indigo, and a certain ominous hissing.

It was the radio, which next instant kicked back in. The ship was full of voices, informing, instructing, cajoling, declaring, endorsing. Static scribbled them all into incomprehensibility. Screens flipped displays, page after page. Moiré patterns drifted around the console. The hammering began again, loud, insistent and irregular. All the stuff under the retaining net shifted and stirred.

Then the disturbed tickets wriggled loose from the viewport beading and rose up together into their faces like a shoal of paper minnows.

"Oh, damn," said Tabitha.

Marco Metz laughed. Slipping free from his web, he began to snatch slips of paper out of the air.

14

They were a hundred thousand kilometers out from Schiaparelli. A hundred thousand stars shone hard and steady in an eternity of space. The traffic was light: the blue twinkle of a Mitchum magnet train on the Phobos-Byzantium run; a little old Fargo slipping down the gradient from Longevity or Silverside, fresh vegetables for the Martians.

The *Alice* was running smoothly. Tabitha ran an axis circuit check. She listened to the engines. All was well. FAILURE PROBABILITY 44.49%, said the screen. ACKNOWLEDGE, Tabitha replied.

Marco couldn't sit still. He unlatched his web again and swam about the cockpit, fielding flotsam. He checked on Tal, still sleeping soundly. He investigated the jumble under the nets. He found a crumpled J-cloth and started dusting things with it.

"Don't, Marco," said Tabitha.

"Don't worry, don't worry," he said, wiping the scanner screens. It made a surprising difference. Multiplied ten times, the arc of the galaxy lit up the cockpit, a silver veil across the void.

"Look at that," said Marco. "The Apple Tree."

"The what?"

"The Apple Tree," he repeated. "Don't you call it that? I thought all spacers called it that."

"Not me," said Tabitha. "I've never heard that one."

"That's what they call it," he said.

"Why the Apple Tree?"

"I don't know. Because we're not allowed a bite, I suppose."

Tabitha thought about it.

"That's Christian, isn't it? You're not a Christian, are you?"

"No," he said. "I'm a fornicator."

"Well," she said, "I walked into that one." He was floating behind her web, trying to kiss the back of her neck through the holes. "Marco," she said, warningly.

"What? You want something? What do you want?"

Now he was upside down, reaching beneath the web, stroking her bottom. She kicked backwards to push him away. The web compensated. "I'm trying to do a job here," she said.

"What?" he said, challenging her. He swam beneath her, rose up between her feet. "What are you doing this old tub can't do for herself?"

She glared at him. "Don't insult my boat," she said.

"Okay, sorry, sorry, sweet old thing." He reached out and patted the bulkhead. "No offense, lady."

Across the console colored lights flicked on, off, red, blue, green. Displays scrolled, overlaid, blinked, melted, coalesced. The *Alice* made a minute course correction, a fraction of a fraction.

Outside, space continued. The scenery was so vast it seemed they weren't moving at all.

"So tell me," he said. "I'm just an ignorant muso. What are you doing now? I can't see you doing anything. What are you doing that's so crucial?"

I don't have to answer that, thought Tabitha. But she did. "Taking you to the gig," she said, in a preoccupied tone. She frowned at the mesoscope.

This, of course, was not good enough for him. "No, no," he said, floating back into his web and sitting there, cross-legged, inquisitorial, his hands clasped in front of him. "That's what the ship's doing, right? Little Alice here," he said. "What are *you* doing?"

She turned to him then. "I'm a part of this ship," she said. "The part that makes the decisions." She tapped her faded shoulder flash. "Captain," she said.

"I thought they had brains of their own, don't they?" he persisted. "They have this little brain thing you plug in the computer, that runs the power, the engines, the john, everything. Don't they? Is this one so old, excuse me, such a venerable antique, she doesn't have that?"

"She can't do everything for herself," Tabitha said. "She can do everything, but she can't decide what to do." She looked around the cockpit. Her eye lit on the white traveling case bobbing gently under the net. "It's like you and Tal," she said. "He can sing, but you have to tell him what to sing next."

He liked that. "Right! Right! That's very smart," he said admiringly.

Not really, she thought, glancing at him. He might be beautiful, but perhaps he wasn't really very bright.

"You're one smart bargee, you know that?" he continued. "You're too good for this job. How'd you like to be tour manager for a major interplanetary cabaret troupe?''

"No, thanks," she murmured, tapping in a command string.

"Really," he said. "I mean it. You're way too smart to be driving a truck. I bet you could fly this thing with your eyes closed. I bet you could fly her with your little finger.''

He was out of his web again.

"I bet you could fly her from your bunk.''

"Marco, don't," she said. "Don't spoil it," she said. "Why don't you watch a movie or something?''

He hovered beside her, not backing off a centimeter. "I'd rather watch you . . .''

"If you can't keep your hands to yourself, do something useful. Realign that distal parallax fibrillator.''

He looked among the clutter on top of the console. "This?''

"No, there. The thing with the harmonica in its vent.''

"Oh. Oh, right. The distal parallax fibrillator. Right.''

Marco drew it out and inspected it.

"It's dead on seven through ten," said Tabitha.

"Eleven," said Marco, clicking the button rapidly in and out, in and out.

"Whatever.''

"You can fix these, no problem," he said. "All you have to do is take out the midrange fleck.''

"I've done that," she said.

"Well, then you've got to bypass it. That's easy. You can get anyone to do that for you.''

"I thought I was getting you to.''

He parried this. "Anyone'll do that for you.''

"Can you do it?''

"Sure.''

"Have you ever done it?''

He hesitated. "No. Not actually done it, not done it myself, no.''

"I have," said Tabitha. "That's why I'm trying to get someone else to.''

He started to reply. "Shh," she said. She thought she

could hear a noise. She started to order another axis circuit check, then cancelled it. She was just being neurotic.

Another five thousand kilometers of nothing went by. Earth and its satellites were dead ahead, a tiny shining dot almost indistinguishable from all the other shining dots.

Tabitha stretched and yawned.

Marco took this as his cue. "Well, nothing much seems to be happening," he began.

"Marco," Tabitha said.

"No, no," said Marco. "I was just going to say, do you play that harmonica?"

"Yes," she said. "Very badly," she said. It had been a while. In fact she'd forgotten she'd put it there.

"I don't believe you," he said.

She looked at him. "What, you don't believe I can play or you don't believe I play badly?" She looked away again. "You're right, though," she said. "Sometimes I don't believe how badly I play either."

"Play something."

"No."

"Come on, you can do that. You're not working so hard you can't blow a couple of bars of 'Casey Jones,' are you?"

"Casey who?" she said. But she held out her hand. "Give it here."

He flipped it towards her, end over end, slowly through the air.

She caught it. "I warned you," she said.

She played him a song about whisky her Auntie Muriel had taught her, on Integrity 2. It was a bit of a struggle. He listened politely.

"That wasn't too bad," he said, when it was over.

"Yes it was," said Tabitha. "Very bad. I should practice more."

"Maybe." He shrugged. "You have the time."

"Yeah." She returned her attention to the console. "I've probably practiced too much already," she said. "I'm an expert bad harmonica player." She glanced at him again. "That was worse than usual," she added. "I don't usually have an audience."

"You don't?"

"I told you. I never let anyone ride in that web."

He played with a rubber washer that came drifting by, trying to make it spin around in the air in front of his nose.

"Play something else on your mouth organ," he said.

"No," she said.

"I'd like to play with your mouth organ."

She ignored him.

"And your other—"

"Here." She batted the harmonica across to him.

So he took it, and played something soft and sad, something plaintive and melancholy that rose up every third line as if it was going to shake off its sorrow and fly forward and free; but then in the fourth it curled back on itself and fell again: reluctantly, sometimes, but always resignedly, as if it knew it was going to fall; as if it had been striving and falling back again for hundreds of years. Yet each time that third line came round the tune seemed to gather itself up and find new energy from somewhere, and perhaps it didn't fall quite so far each time in the fourth, and Tabitha was captivated despite herself, watching the pretty man play and wondering how he would end it, how he could ever resolve the disagreement between the rush and the ebb, until she realized suddenly that he had, with a quiet, lilting little rill that ran up and then down and flicked its tail and was gone.

"Oh, that was good," she said.

He smiled. His lovely eyes were quiet, almost shy, not at all like before.

She thumbed back the catches on her web. She rose above him, clasped his hand and drew him up.

He took a moment to slip the harmonica back where he'd found it, in the vent on the faulty fibrillator. Then he spun himself about and kissed her.

"What about Tal?" she asked.

"He'll be all right." He pointed at the green pips on the box. They were pulsing steadily.

They went down the passage around the hold, into the captain's cabin, and left the door open.

Each anchored by a foot in one of the loops at the corners of the bunk, they undressed one another. Their clothes hung and drifted in the air. Shoes spun end over end in vague orbits about their owners. Underpants rose from unexpected corners, on collision courses with snaking socks.

Pulling her foot free, Tabitha launched herself lightly at him. She landed with her hands on his hips. His legs were wide apart and she found herself slipping smoothly through the arch of his thighs. Beginning to spin himself, he reached for her as she whirled slowly under his crotch. His hands slid from her breasts as if she'd been greased. He twisted in the air, coming round to face her again, drawing his legs up under him, lying back on nothing with his heels against his buttocks, his knees spread. He was panting, exhilarated, his eyes and mouth wide and wild. He rubbed his mouth in her hair.

She slipped her left leg under his arm and ran the inside of her right thigh across the underside of his cock until it nestled against her groin. He caressed her sides with gentle hands, gloveman's hands. She turned a naked somersault in his lap, bouncing lightly off the cabin wall to return slowly feet first, straddling him, locking them together. They went into a spin, wheeling head over heels about their warm, wet mutual center. Marco gasped. He groaned.

All the time Tabitha was listening with half an ear to the deep, slow throb of the engines, the background buzzes and creaks of the *Alice Liddell* in transit. She was listening for a new noise, the noise she thought she'd heard on the way out to Chateaubriand: the irregular tapping of the axis lock crystal, jumping in its housing.

There was a noise, suddenly. It wasn't the crystal. It was the sound of a harmonica playing her Auntie Muriel's song.

She stared at Marco in horror.

The sound was coming closer along the gangway. It was not her harmonica, it was higher pitched, a peeping sound like a poor recording played back through a tiny speaker.

She began to struggle free of Marco's embrace, groping around for anchorage.

In through the open door came Marco's parrot, chirping merrily. It sounded for all the world like a little harmonica.

"Oh god, it's got out of its box," she said, agitated.

"I guess he was bored," said Marco.

"What?"

"Boogie my hotlips baby," sang the parrot. "Yer arse against the wall!"

It put its head on one side and fixed them with one evil black eye. It leered.

"Jesus Christ it's sapient!"

"Yeah, I guess," said Marco. "I mean, it depends what you mean—"

"Get out!" Tabitha yelled at the alien invader. "Get out of my cabin!"

She seized a passing shirt and propelled it vainly towards the bird. It evaded its slow assault with a neat three-quarter turn.

"Funky salami," it caroled, upside down.

Tabitha separated herself from Marco with a convulsive heave that spreadeagled him against the porthole. She glared at him. *"Say something!"*

"Go on, Tal, get out of here," said Marco neutrally. "She's not Saskia. She doesn't like it."

The big green bird rolled around and sailed easily out of the cabin, backwards.

"Salami minestrone," his voice came floating eerily down the gangway. "There's whisky in the jar . . ."

Marco scratched his belly. "Tabby. I'm sorry. Really."

"Don't call me Tabby. No one *ever* calls me Tabby."

"I'm sorry!"

"What—is—he?"

"A parrot. A kind of parrot. I told you."

"He's fucking sapient, Marco!"

He shrugged, a mid-air shrug. "Well, sure. You

couldn't get a regular parrot to do all that stuff. I thought you liked him. He's cute, really. When you get to know him.''

"I don't want to get to know him."

"Hey, he didn't mean anything. He's just lonely. You'd be lonely, stuck in that little box for hours on end. He was trying to be friendly, that's all. Come back, Tabitha, I'm sorry, hey, really.''

But Tabitha was squatting in a corner of the ceiling, strapping on her wrist monitor, burrowing furiously into a T-shirt.

"And who's Saskia?" she wanted to know.

15

Given cheap and easy travel, elastic property and planning laws, and favorable tax concessions, the human spirit is an expansive thing. But it is a gregarious thing too. In the early days of the Space Rush, there was no reason to go and build hundreds of millions of kilometers away from everyone else. There was all of Mars, practically, if you didn't mind the climate; and anyone could put up a tube.

Which is why, by the time of our story, there was a tangle of some two hundred satellite habitats, including five dozen tubes; fourteen platforms; seven wheels; sixteen miscellaneous unclassifiables, including casinos on immobilized system ships, crates, and permanent accidents; and three ziggurats of the Eladeldi—all in Terran orbit, besides the poor old neglected Moon.

For smart people, discerning people, the clutter and crush had eventually become too much. They followed the mining leviathans out to the asteroid belt; and soon after, when the belt charts were crazed with property lines, on to Saturn, where the real development opportunities were. In the rings, there were only hermits to worry about.

Once business had moved on from Earth, parts of the Tangle fell unoccupied. Blossoming projects died, leaving their lattices of unglazed steel and nebulae of rivets tumbling pointlessly about "beyond the sky." The status of these and other orbitals became highly fluid, in legal fiction and in fact. They changed hands rapidly; daily, it seemed.

The earthbound made derogatory jokes about empty cans, and turned their backs on the brash, glittering necklace of the night. The expansive spirit was undaunted. Squatters, escapees and network junkies moved into the abandoned hulks. There they lived like spiders, tenaciously, in corners.

Which brings us to Plenty.

I'm sorry to say that when Tabitha came upon it, it was not at its best. The word "sleazy" is one that springs to mind. Of strategic significance only to the race that put it there, the shell was treated as a grotesque curio, a titanic folly. It was in a constant state of reoccupation, favored only by marginal or twilight enterprises indifferent to a fundamentally inhuman environment. Some of them undoubtedly preferred it.

Plenty was built by the Frasque, who did not call it that, or anything else, so far as I have been able to discover. It is, as Tabitha knew, the major relic of that defeated race's short stay in the solar system. The Frasque had arrived hot on the pearly heels of the Capellans, sliding in on their vector before the great door of space could slam shut. To human eyes, they were the strangest of all the newcomers of those days. They resembled lofty, ambulant, insectile bundles of reeds. They opened their twiggy mouths and hissed.

Someone understood them. Indeed, their power to agitate whole regions of Central Africa and parts of South America was remarkable. Cults were revived, savage midnight duels enacted. Entire armies deserted and van-

ished; to labor as slaves, some said, at first in a doomed
attempt to develop a site on Venus, and after on the most
monstrous orbital ever built.

The Frasque are an aggressive, exploitative, worker
species. Their foremost civilization is three-quarters
male. This three-quarters works itself to death, generation after generation, at the behest of the female quarter,
more sapient but no less savage, which dominates it by
an impenetrable social mystification of oestrus. At the
center of their hive there sits a queen, radiating her implacable commands through the labyrinthine tunnels. Remove her, and the rest of the society ceases to function.
Under the direction of the Queen of Plenty, the males
swarmed tirelessly over the high circling construction,
crystallizing the fabric, it seemed, directly out of the
sparse particles of sub-lunar space.

It was assumed the Frasque fitted somewhere in the
Capellan scheme of things; that they were another client
species, as the Thrants and Eladeldi evidently were,
though they seemed more enterprising and self-sufficient
than most. Whatever it was they were really building up
there.

The *Seraph Kajsa* was the first ship of our system seen
entering the enormous docks that constituted the lower
levels of the completed station. Two days later, despite
the speculations of cynics, it was seen leaving again. As
posthuman supremacists, the Seraphim apparently
claimed some fellow feeling with these autocratic aliens.
Shortly after, human spokespeople began appearing on
Earth, on screen and in person, describing the bounty
the Frasque had brought to the system, with special mention of their advanced cryonics facilities.

Some hesitated because of the semi-evangelistic tone
of the advertising; others because of its lack of deference,
indeed of reference, to Capella. Was this an offer Earth
was permitted to pursue? Were they still free? Then the
first human vessels were sighted, following the initiative
of the *Seraph Kajsa*. And after that there was no stopping
them. From Swiss clinics and private sanitaria they came,
eager to be frozen. The representatives of nations and

organizations that had been preserving a cautious neutrality now swelled the flock, gabbling about friendly relations and mutual benefit. From the Frasque, they thought, their leaders might obtain the twin secrets of social control and personal immortality: two valuable aids to peaceful and effective administration.

Why anyone should want to govern anyone else continues to escape me. It seems an exhausting and thankless task. Looking after inanimate objects is difficult enough. I can only suppose that human beings, born naked and soft and tied to an environment minute in scope and tolerance, are motivated by the desire for some sort of self-aggrandizing revenge.

The Frasque, however, are not so frail. Goodness only knows what makes them tick, or why they thought they could get away with it here. There is data buried still which even I can't get at.

At any rate, everything on Plenty was going swingingly; and then one day Capella spoke. The Frasque were *species non grata*. There were to be no more transactions with them. Their best known spokespeople were removed and replaced abruptly, without explanation, with new ones who smiled constantly while issuing contradictory statements and random exhortations. Stain was visible beneath the suntan. Some of them were clearly already frozen. They urged loyalty to the generous and undemanding Frasque, and rejected the authority of Capella.

The archives of that period are fragmentary and confused. Obviously the station was in turmoil. There was a lot of communal stridulation and generation of extraordinary etheric gestalts. Strange buzzsaw keenings ate into the void, disturbing the wavebands for hundreds of kilometers around. Terran employees who still had the faculty of independent mobility fled, understandably, with everything they could lay their hands on. The vast shipping bays emptied. Agents and ambassadors left on the down shuttle, frantically covering their tracks. There was almost a collapse of the cryonic systems when the vaults

were besieged by people demanding to reclaim parents
and presidents.

Finally, at the height of the chaos, a Capellan system
ship came by, with great ceremony and display of technical superiority, to require the immediate departure of
the Frasque. The Frasque refused. The Capellans bowed
their great heads in sorrow and exterminated them.

The destruction was brief and horrible. The Frasque,
that had seemed so desiccated and invulnerable, shriveled
and burned at the Capellans' slightest gesture. The spaceship docks of Plenty became an inferno. The marks of
charring can be seen everywhere there today. Eladeldi
scoured the tunnels, flaming everything that moved. The
air smelled of burning, burning.

Special fighters were issued, and humans recruited to
pilot them, to mop up the remnants of the species. They
had not spread far—it was not their way—from the hive.
They did, however, muster a fleet and stage two last
great battles, preferring destruction to defeat.

Their wishes were met.

Now, announced the Capellan representative, simul-
taneously on every channel of every net of the system,
the evil plan of the Frasque could be revealed. The up-
heavals in Africa had been only a rehearsal. The Frasque
had been scheming to sponsor civil war in the system,
setting world against world. From their orbital hive-
turned-fortress, they would sally out against whoever was
left and eat them alive. It was a horrendous, rapacious
strategy that they had used to gain control of their own
home system. The Capellans, indulgent as ever, had
trusted them in ours until it became obvious the same
hideous trick was about to be played again.

Only the courage of the human race, she said, had
won the day. As a reward, the liberated shell of Plenty,
largest of all orbitals, was handed over to Earth. Capella
merely agreed, under suit, to provide a management com-
mittee. They had, it transpired, been training one up for
some time.

The new board were seven in number. They were
all human: not even one Eladeldi among them. It was

a sign of trust; or, murmured the ubiquitous cynic, contempt.

They called it Plenty. It was to be a combination tax haven, service station and home to fringe businesses. If the fringe soon proved to be rather tattier, the services more underhand than the original promotional copy made out, well, that was only to be expected of an enterprise left to run itself without Capellan supervision.

The freezers filled up again, and the commercial sectors of the warren glittered and blazed; though under the multiple roofs arranged like bumpy plates of armor, many other areas remained in darkness, the only light the sick green pallor of the phosphorescent things that grew on the walls in there.

Soon the most lucrative function of the resurrected orbital was as an alien adventure park. Groups of tourists, survivalists and extremist paramilitary cadres on exercise could be released, for a high fee and without liability, into its eerie and uncertain corridors. Below, the spaceship docks, an enormous shelf that gapes at both ends beneath the domed superstructure, started to attract craft that preferred not to patronize the better-lit and reputable platforms.

Imagine Plenty, then, when the *Alice Liddell* arrived ferrying a pair of cabaret artistes, as a giant paralyzed space habitat under makeshift redevelopment. The retrofit had been partial, in some areas wholly unsuccessful. Odd creatures and devices scuttled in the shadows. Who knew what processes were dormant, what boobytraps, what mysterious and violent reflexes might yet be triggered by incursion into passages and cells closed off by their builders? The Frasque had left no guidebooks, no plans anyone could read. Anything might happen, just around the next bend.

And it is all bends. There isn't a right angle in the place. Oval in plan, the entire station is fabricated of a laminar substance more like horn than anything else. The lumpy smoothness of all its surfaces reinforces the sense that Plenty is something organic, something that was generated, not constructed.

"It looks like a gigantic tortoise," said Marco Metz. "Don't you think? Like a great big humungous tortoise-shell."

Tabitha was struck by the resemblance, but she didn't reply. She wasn't about to grant him that, or anything. If Plenty was a giant dormant space tortoise, it was one that any moment might stick out its giant head and swallow her, *Alice* and all. She didn't want to be here. She was rapidly going off Marco and his little psittacoid buddy. A scary voice in the back of her mind was nagging, Mistake, Tabitha, mistake, mistake, mistake. She was ignoring it because she was going to get paid. FAILURE PROBABILITY 50.00%, said that voice. She was ignoring it because now she had to steer into the black mouth of the shell and right down its throat. If she'd been pretending to be busy before, she really was busy now.

The vast curled lips of the station gaped around her. Between them the force curtain rippled and parted.

Like a leaf whirled down a dark drain, the *Alice Liddell* swept out of the void and into a world of shadows. There were huge batteries of spotlights trained on the floor of the cavern, but they did little to relieve the gloom. Braking fast, Tabitha flew over a scene of obscure industry as stygian and grimy as any image of the shop floor of Hell. Insectile service vehicles crept hither and thither among serpentine feed lines, while filthy drones and animate mechanics crawled over partly dismantled ships.

This, Tabitha thought, is where I have to let them put a new crystal in the *Alice*. She put the thought down with all the other unpleasant thoughts she kept having and flew.

Now they were between the tiered docking bays, great blackened cliffs of open hangars where five hundred mid-range craft can be housed, five deep. Tabitha could see that many of the hangars were empty, or filled with equipment and odds and ends of machinery which were no longer ships, if they ever had been. But there were ships there: scouts, freighters, tourist shuttles, other barges too. With Marco on the radio announcing his arrival to half a dozen people, Tabitha took the *Alice* rolling along the side of the valley, past the darkened chariot of some Terran senator paying an incognito visit to the brothels, and a recent model Freimacher Charisma, one runner broken, half buried beneath somebody else's split cargo.

The top tier of hangars was in darkness. From one bay only, the blue flare of a navigation beacon suddenly shone out.

"There?" asked Tabitha.

"There," said Marco.

Tabitha leveled off, dumped momentum, and tapped the retros. Cautiously she posted the *Alice* in at the beacon.

She nearly didn't see the two attendant figures; but there they were on the stern scanners. The blue light erased the humanity from their narrow faces. They looked spectral and morose. One waved its hand.

"Who are they?" asked Tabitha, bearing down on the inertials. She could barely hear Marco's reply for the noise.

"That's the Twins," he said.

16

BGK009059 LOG

TXJ.STD

PRINT

&&&&&&&&&&Aözùón ''o'' ''ü]]]ẅ&â&â&ẽ&Ñ*[]]]XO:]]]2–22 -]Æii]
oearps egarps fn fnn fnnn Œ]]]o't'009059j .làx~æææ/9/
Ç]]]222m &&& && &&   &??:t–/

MODE? VOX

SD? 15.31.22.

READY

This morning Saskia asked me what sign I am. I didn't know what she meant at first.

WHAT DID SHE MEAN, CAPTAIN? WAS IT SOMETHING ABOUT MY REGISTRATION?

No, it's astrology. You know, Sagittarius and Virgo, all that. Horoscopes on the net. A twelfth of the people in Terra space will find new romance on Tuesday. My Auntie Muriel believes in that. Destiny in the stars. God knows how they work it out if you were born on Mars.

But it reminded me, of this bloke I met in a port once. New Malibu. Somewhere like that. Void surfers sheathed in silver lamé. Bored dowagers with wisps snuggling on the shoulders, whispering flattery and malicious rumor in their perfectly sculpted ears. The cradles at the bar draped with Thrant zebru furs.

WHAT WERE WE DOING THERE?

Delivering shoes. Platform heels, I think they were. Just the thing to go with that glytex suit with the see-through lubricant ducts and tungsten bearings. Vac party gear.

PURE ENVY.

What? Me?

I BELIEVE SO.

Oh, come on, Alice.

BECAUSE YOU'VE NEVER BEEN INVITED.

To a vac party? You must be joking. I work here.

BUT THEY'RE VERY GLAMOROUS OCCASIONS, I UNDERSTAND.

Alice, you're talking to a woman who's seen a skipfest on the *Raven of October*. That was glamour. New Malibu is lavish tat. Money in drag.

TELL ME ABOUT THE SKIPFEST.

Mm, some other time. I was just thinking about this man—

AH.

Not that sort of man. A plughead. A serial component of the Holy Sepulchre of the Expanded Neurosphere.

They have some rule if you're shipping into Malibu, the usual sort of thing. You have to spend some proportion of the fee there on the rock. That's pure money, that is. Naked money. The left hand paying the right hand.

So I was in the port, running around trying to charge up a card from the outlets, and none of them were working. I was putting in my ID, and the authority for the credit, and the screen would say

PLEASE WAIT A LITTLE WHILE.

That's right. And I'd wait, and I'd wait, and then it would say

INSUFFICIENT FUNDS FOR TRANSACTION

Aha, no. No, it didn't even get that far.

PLEASE REFER TO PERSONAL ENQUIRIES. A CLERK WILL BE HAPPY TO ASSIST WITH YOUR TRANSACTION.

And

THERE WASN'T A CLERK IN SIGHT.

You're very chatty today, Alice.

SORRY, CAPTAIN.

Have I told you this one before?

OH, PROBABLY. BUT TELL ME AGAIN.

No, what's the point? You must remember it better than I do, me telling you, I mean. You've probably got it recorded somewhere, haven't you?

I DON'T REMEMBER, CAPTAIN.

No, go on.

BUT IT'S TRUE. I DON'T REMEMBER, TRULY I DON'T.

But you could find it.

IF YOU TOLD ME TO, YES. I'M SURE I COULD. WOULDN'T YOU RATHER TELL ME AGAIN?

All right. It seems a bit pointless, that's all.

NOT AT ALL. NO STORY IS EVER THE SAME A SECOND TIME.

You're checking on me, aren't you?

YOU'RE FEELING PERSECUTED.

I wish I'd never started all this. If I'd turned and walked out of the Moebius Strip, none of this would have happened. I'd have found some boring ordinary job and paid off the cops and you'd have your new crystal and I'd never have met Marco and his pals and I'd be a happier woman today.

NEW MALIBU. THE PORT. TOURISTS IN WHITE SLEEKS AND ROBOT CARTS HUSTLING BUSINESS FOR THE HOTELS. TABITHA JUTE IS TRYING TO GET SOME SENSE OUT OF A CREDIT OUTLET. OUT OF AN ENTIRE ROW OF THEM. NONE OF THEM IS WORKING.

WHAT HAPPENS NEXT, CAPTAIN?

Tabitha Jute hears a voice behind her.
"Exc-c-c-cuse me," it says. "Ah-ah-ah-ah. Ah-ah-ah."
Tabitha Jute turns round. Behind her is a young man with a tube up his nose. His eyes are bloodshot. His teeth are ruined. But his implants are clean, clean and shiny.
Great, thinks Tabitha. A plughead.
The plughead isn't wearing a silver lamé spacesuit. He

isn't wearing platform boots. He's wearing a transparent blue plastic cagoule. With the hood up.

"Ah-ah-are you in contact?" he says.

Great, thinks Tabitha. An evangelist plughead. A stammering evangelist plughead. Where do they get them?

YOU'RE NOT AT ALL FOND OF THE HOLY SEPULCHRE OF THE EXPANDED NEUROSPHERE.

No.

BECAUSE OF YOUR SISTER.

Yes.

ANGIE.

Yes.

ANGIE WENT OFF TO BE A PLUGHEAD.

You remembered that well enough.

THANK YOU, CAPTAIN. I DO TRY.

So did he.

He kept going on about being *aligned* and *interfacing*. All the while he was stroking the casing of the outlet I was stuck on. "Th-th-there's no n-need to b-be m-m-misunderstood by a m-m-machine ev-ev-ev-ever again."

WHY DIDN'T YOU RID YOURSELF OF HIM?

Because I'm a wimp.

INDEED YOU AREN'T.

Yes I am. I felt sorry for him.

BECAUSE OF THE STAMMER?

Because of Angie. I'm hopeless with plugheads. I always give them money. Especially if they're women. I always think, it could be her.

THAT'S NOT VERY PROBABLE.

That's not the *point*.

He had the most amazing head. It was the shape of a helmet, the way you always think cops' heads should be when they take off their helmets. And he had the jaw to go with it, a great slab of a jaw. His whole face was like a slab, actually, as if something had come down, an almighty hand, and flattened it. It practically went in at the nose. There was a groove where the tube ran, up under his ear and across his cheek.

"We need to treat them properly," he said, caressing the machine. You'll have to imagine the stammer. "Feel what they're trying to tell us."

I said, "I know what it's trying to tell me. It's telling me to go away."

He wouldn't have that. He laughed, a high-pitched little squeak of a laugh, like people do when a child makes a cute mistake. "No, no," he said. "It's telling you it can't understand you. You're confusing it."

I said, "What do you mean, confusing it? I'm answering its questions. I've given it all the information it asked for, now let it give me my money."

"But have you opened yourself to it?" he said, smiling. "Really opened your heart and mind and asked it to come in?"

I looked at his implants. The scar tissue was old and seamed. They'd obviously been badly infected at some time. But the polish on the sockets made them look like new.

For the hell of it, I said: "Show me."

I knew I was going to hate it.

His eyes glazed over. His right arm went up as if there was a string pulling it. The fingers of his hand pressed the side of his head. The rest of him didn't move at all.

He started to hum through his nose.

Then he took off his fingertip.

He put his finger in the jack of the outlet.

With the other hand he kept stroking the casing, rubbing and patting it. And he kept humming. He was singing to the credit machine.

Some kids coming by said, "Hey, look at him!" They stopped and stared. They started to snigger.

There was a cop over by the water bar, a human one. She was trying to chat up the boy who was serving. She noticed the kids, and the plughead, and she started paying attention.

"All right," I told him. "That'll do."

The cop hitched up her trousers and came sauntering over.

I was afraid for him. I wanted to get rid of him, but not to a cop. "*Forget* it," I muttered.

The cop came close up. Behind her visor she was checking us, reading my insignia.

She said, "Is this man bothering you, captain?"

"No," I said. "It's all right. It's personal. Thank you." I said.

The cop gave me a hard look and moved off.

I tried to walk away. I thought he'd leave the machine alone and follow me. I thought that was the prime directive of all evangelists: *Don't Let Go*.

But he was into his machine, into the network. He was interfacing. He was away.

"What's your name?" he called.

I came back. "Jute," I said. I thought, He really is going to make it work.

The cop was still monitoring us. I tried to look as if this was perfectly normal, as if I'd asked him to make the entry for me. As if he was the clerk who was happy to help me with my transaction.

He was certainly happy. I leaned over his shoulder, shielding him from the cop. He smelled of solder and Vaseline. I told him my name and the number. He hummed the little tones as he pressed each key. I told him the credit authority number. I didn't give him my card.

"Let me have the card," he said, and held out his hand.

I reached past him, and slotted it myself.

He smiled vacantly. "No, no," he said.

Before I could stop him, he took the card out of the slot, pulled back his left cuff and pressed the card to his wrist.

"Oh," he said. "Oh T-Tabitha."

He bared his horrible teeth.

"I know you now," he cooed. "I know so m-m-much about you."

He was reading my data as it fed through him into the outlet. I could feel him rooting through my past. "Get out of my files," I said.

"Open your heart," he said. He was whispering. "Open your m-m-mind."

"Give me that," I said, and I snatched the card. There was a little magnetic tug as it came off his wrist. I stuffed it back in my pocket.

"But you're beautiful," he said. "Inside. You're really integrated."

He gaped at me in silly bliss, his great jaw hanging down like an open hatch. Suddenly I didn't believe him. I didn't believe he'd got anything from the card. It was all a routine, a schtick he'd pull on any sucker to convince them something really happened when you "interfaced." "All right," I said. "What sign am I?"

"Sign?" he said.

I was sure then he didn't know. I pressed him. "Star sign," I said.

He took his finger out of the machine and smiled his goofy smile. "We are all under the sign of Capella now, Tabitha," he said gently.

"Th-th-thank you for the dona-a-a-ation," he said.

And he shuffled away.

"Hey!" I called. "Hey, come back here!"

He didn't.
I whirled round, looking for the cop.
She'd gone.
The water boy was laughing at me.

DID YOU GO AFTER THE MAN, CAPTAIN?

No. I let him go.

BUT WHY?

Because he was a plughead. Because of Angie.

Next, of course, the Perks came, swarming up into the
open end of the hangar where the *Alice* sat, ticking and
steaming as she cooled.

Tabitha saw them through the viewport: silhouettes of
black on purple, scrambling up into the hangar and clinging, chittering, to the knobby brown walls. Their flat
little heads swiveled this way and that, their eyes shining
blue in the flaring light of the beacon.

Her first thought was, They're after me.

Then she remembered the racket they ran here, in the
spaceship docks of Plenty.

She turned on the external floods, filling the bay with
deathly white light. She saw the Perks flinch and blink,
and felt a certain vengeful delight.

She checked the scanners. The mysterious Twins were
nowhere to be seen.

She turned to Marco, who was lifting Tal out of his
traveling case.

"They want money," she told him.

"I know," said Marco. He set the little green alien on his shoulder and leaned on the console, looking out at the Perks. He seemed to be excited about something. "Watch this."

Perks were climbing into the utility bunkers of the parking bay, bobbing about in there. Between them they were picking up the power line, the hoses for oxygen and wastes. Others were already wriggling around in the *Alice*'s undercarriage, zeroing in on the inlets.

Tabitha felt a powerful desire to turn the extinguishers on them.

"Well, hurry up," she said. She looked at the clock. Just under four hours, to phone in the money and let her off the hook. Let Alice off the hook.

She hadn't told Alice, that she was on the hook.

There were now two gangs of Perks, each ten or twelve strong. They looked poor, and unhealthy. Many of them were moulting. They weren't wearing street regalia, like the Perks of Schiaparelli. They had grubby overalls on, and caps with protective masks, through which each gang peered at the other. The gang holding the hoses stayed back. The other one milled around beside the ship.

The two gangs looked very much like two families. There were one or two adults at the center of each, directing operations; elders, stooped and greying, weaving about on the periphery; and in between, aunts and uncles and cousins and assorted offspring yammering and pawing each other. The youngsters dared one another to touch the hot ship. There was a muffled squeal: somebody had dared, or been shoved. The elders weaved in and out, cuffing heads indiscriminately. "*Cheee! Cheeee!*"

"They always do this," Marco explained. "You have to pay this lot to get out of the way. Then you have to pay the other lot to hook you up."

The cockpit of the *Alice* was getting steamy. With her hand Tabitha wiped a crescent in the condensation thickening on the viewport.

"Go on, then," she said.

"In a minute, in a minute. It's terrific. Isn't it? The drama." He chuckled.

Tabitha said nothing. She hated this; hated all Perks now and forever, wherever. She wasn't going to be happy until that two-fifty was zapped back across the void to Mirabeau Precinct. At the same time, she was in no hurry to go up into the pleasure dome that hung so ominous and vast above their heads.

Tabitha Jute, remember, had not yet been up to the other floors of Plenty. She had always preferred to take it on its reputation, which was, as I say, not good. It sounded like a dangerous place, somewhere you could swiftly find yourself robbed, raped, or suddenly erased. Somewhere where strange people would charge you extortionate sums of money for things you didn't even want to have done to you. No, the docks were quite enough for Captain Jute. The worst you got down here was strange sudden slithering movements in the shadows where there hadn't been anything a minute ago; crazed Vespan mechanics with tales of fabulous Frasque treasure abandoned in a bay near here, somewhere, just round the next bend; gangs of Perk extortioners . . .

The Perks guarding the inlets were beginning to twitch. They were scratching at the airlock. "Cheeeeee . . ."

The sound seemed to disturb Tal. He made a pensive sound like a distant bugle. He lifted one claw and flexed it.

"No, I think it's great," said Marco. "Tribal. Like football."

"Get rid of them," said Tabitha.

"Razors!" tooted Tal at once. "Razor pemmican!"

"Chill out, Tal," said Marco. "I'm going. I'll take care of it."

He held out his arm to Tabitha. "Here, take him a moment."

Before Tabitha could comply, or refuse, someone else decided to act.

In spangled blue pyjamas and bare feet he came bowling out of nowhere past the ship, somersaulted over the guard of Perks and cannoned into the hook-up crew, scattering them like tenpins.

"Oh dear, Tal," said Marco, "the Twins have got impatient."

Tal gave a most unparrotlike crow and flew up to perch on the top of a monitor.

"Great," said Tabitha. "Brilliant. Start a fight. Good plan."

The human bowling ball, if human he was, stood up and shook himself. Three clutching Perks fell off.

Impressed despite herself, Tabitha watched him closely. He was tall and skinny, with a high bald forehead and a mantle of long hair halfway down his back. His eyes were deep set, his nose thin and perpendicular, his mouth narrow and open. His arms and legs were extraordinarily long and supple. He windmilled them at speed in improbable directions, knocking over the Perks as they rose to their feet.

But there were twenty (or twenty-four) of them, and now they were all getting up.

Tabitha looked at Marco. He was standing leaning on the console, a huge grin on his face.

The thin man shouted something she couldn't hear. As the little rodents swarmed all over him, he swung his arm back, pointing dramatically towards the back of the bay.

Tal gave a piercing whistle. "Maaaarzipan!" he screeched.

Tabitha winced. She had half a mind to put him back in his box and sit on the lid.

Movement on the stern scanners caught her eye. For a moment she was confused; she thought it was the thin man, and she couldn't work out how he'd got behind them. But it was another slender figure, a woman, shimmying up on to the port wing, from there on to the scorching hull, running along the curve in great, light strides and flinging her arm out in front of her, pointing with her index and little fingers at the mob pulling down the man.

Fire burst in the air above them. Flame rained down

on the Perks. There were shrieks and howls, little bodies in frantic motion, pushing and shoving each other and beating out smouldering cloth and singed feathers.

Dazzled by the flash, Tabitha saw the woman's face suddenly, close up, and upside down. She was sprawled across the viewport, clinging to nothing, staring in at them. Her face was the man's face, thin as a blade and bald above. A pencil-line of moustache decorated her caprine upper lip. She smiled and winked at Marco—all this in an instant after the flare exploded and before she threw herself down, arms and legs spread wide, at the shrieking Perks below.

"Snix!" Tal observed, throatily.

The Perks were running from the hangar, bounding and sliding away out of sight, back down to where they came from. Marco clapped his hands.

Tabitha looked for the man. He had vanished again. She saw the woman, a flicker of blue on a port scanner, gone.

"That was bloody stupid," she said.

"They won!" cried Marco, triumphantly. He reached for her.

She let him give her a hug, kissed him lightly.

"Get a move on," she said. She pointed to the clock. "Aren't you coming?"

"Not with that lot after your blood, no I'm not. I had enough of them in Schiaparelli, remember?"

He dismissed this with a cutting wave of his hand. "They're history," he said. "They won't bother *us* again."

"They'll be looking out for you," she said. "Up there."

She raised her eyes to the weighless tons stacked above their heads.

He took her hand. He looked into her eyes.

"Now Tabitha," he said.

She took her hand back. "Just bring me that chip, Marco," she said. "Then we'll see."

"Hey," he said softly. "There's nothing to be afraid

of. I'll take care of you. You know I will. Haven't I taken care of you this far?''

She ignored him, turning away to look out of the viewport. The abandoned hook-ups lay like waiting snakes on the stained floor.

''Go on,'' she said. ''Go and get the money. I'm staying here.''

''But Tabitha, sweetie—''

''Don't call me sweetie.''

She looked at him. His eyes were big, brown, pleading, beautiful.

''While you're gone I'll make some calls and see if I can track down a crystal,'' she said firmly. ''Then I'm going to get some sleep. I'm knackered.''

''C'mon,'' he said. ''Look. You'll sleep so much better in a hotel. Right? We'll fix you up in the best hotel on the station. A room of your own. Take a shower, a couple of drinks, you'll feel better. Unwind. Relax a little. You know how you need to relax. Then after— the show!''

''I've seen all the show I want to see,'' she said.

A voice spoke suddenly from the starboard bow monitor.

''*Come, Captain. Don't be ungracious.*''

''*You're our guest,*'' said the same voice, from the same monitor the other side.

''What?'' said Tabitha. ''Who did that?''

Her voice boomed out around the echoing hangar.

Tabitha lunged at the controls. Startled, Tal flew from his perch straight past her head, swerving at the last moment, flapping a wing in her face. Flailing at the air where he'd been, she struck out at the switch to turn off the PA that had suddenly inexplicably turned itself on.

''Who was that? Was that you?'' she demanded, confronting Tal, who'd been nowhere near the switch.

The monitors hissed gently.

''Here, buddy.'' Marco was going down the steps to the airlock. Tal took up his place on his shoulder. Marco stroked him under his non-existent chin, murmuring consolingly to him.

The electrics flickered as the lines were coupled up. A breeze fluttered into the cockpit from the air vents.

Tabitha whirled back to the monitors.

The floodlights shone on the blotchy brown walls of the hangar, the filthy floor, the roof. There was nothing on any of the screens except the blue flaring signal beacon and a big untidy pile of bags and boxes by the door of the lift. The hoses had all been connected. There was no one to be seen anywhere.

Tabitha got up fast. She jumped down the steps and pushed past Marco into the airlock.

She threw open the outer door and looked down the side of the ship.

A foul zephyr of aging artificial air washed in around her, heavy with rancid oil and zinc.

"Who's there? Come on out!"

There was the slightest suspicion of something behind her, up in the cockpit: a whisper of movement—not even that: a sort of parenthesis in the silence where a whisper would have been if anything had made one.

There was the slightest suspicion of something behind her, up in the cockpit: a whisper of movement—not even that: a sort of parenthesis in the silence where a whisper would have been if anything had made one.

Tabitha leapt back of out of the airlock to the foot of the steps.

The woman with the moustache was sitting in her web. The man was across from her, in the co-pilot's web. They had the latches closed, the headsets on and plugged in at the console.

But for the moustache, their faces were identical.

They bowed. "Saskia and Mogul Zodiac," they announced, in unison.

"The Twins," said Marco.

18

"All right," said Tabitha. "Out. All of you."

"She didn't like it," said Mogul.

"It's plain to tell," said his sister. She was absorbedly prodding the aged melon, which she had somehow got hold of. She tossed it up and caught it as it came slowly down. "Would you like us to eat this for you?"

"What?" said Tabitha. "No," she said. "Put that down. I want you out of here, all of you. I want everybody off my ship."

Marco put his arm around her. Tabitha pushed it away. "Come on, Tabitha," he said. "Don't be like that. Wasn't that great? Wasn't that a great show? Aren't they terrific?"

"I've told you the arrangement, Marco," said Tabitha. "Go on. Leave."

"Tabitha, believe me. That was nothing. Nothing to what you could see tonight." He slapped his hands together and beamed around the overcrowded cockpit.

"I'm not going to see anything," she said. "I'm going to sleep. I've got a lot of driving ahead of me."

"We can help you with that," Marco said.

"No you can't," she said, getting annoyed with him. "What you can do is go and get that *money*. Time's running out. And you've got a show to get ready. So now I want you and your whole box of tricks off my ship and out of my way. Go. Go on."

The Twins slipped out of the webs and somersaulted lightly down the steps.

"Box of tricks?" said Saskia. "What does she mean, our box of tricks?" She sounded offended.

Her brother patted her arm consolingly. "The captain is a little nervous, I think," he said. "A little overawed." He gave Tabitha a smile as he passed.

"She said box of tricks," Saskia complained, following.

"Give me that," said Tabitha, snatching the melon from Saskia, who was balancing it on her arm, rolling it slowly from her shoulder down to her wrist and back again.

They stepped through the airlock and dropped lightly, feet first, to the floor.

There was a clap of wings and Tal suddenly landed on Tabitha's shoulder.

"Goodbye," he caroled,

"Is the hardest word to say,

The hardest song to play . . ."

"Marco, take him away."

"Here, Tal," said Marco, snapping his fingers. "I can't believe this," he added, intensely, as the bird flew on to his shoulder. "You're not coming with me? Don't you know how much I want you? Don't you know what you mean to me?"

"I'm beginning to get a pretty good idea," said Tabitha.

"Look. I know I'm not perfect," he said. "I'm an artist. We all are. You have to lighten up. You can't expect us to be like other people. Oh honey, I'm not saying it'll be easy."

"I am," said Tabitha. She held out her hand. "The chip," she said.

The Twins had reached the doors and summoned the lift.

"No," said Marco.

Tabitha stared at him, open-mouthed.

He lifted the parrot off his shoulder and launched it out of the airlock.

"Go, Tal. Go join them. We have to have this thing out," he said, staring fixedly at Tabitha.

Tabitha bared her teeth and clenched her fists. "There's nothing to have, Marco."

"I'm not going," he said.

"If you don't get me that money you'll be looking for another ship," she reminded him fiercely.

"I can't leave you," he said. "You're going to run away, aren't you? The moment those lift doors close, you're going to take off out of here."

"I'm not going *anywhere*," she shouted at him, "not until I've got—"

There was a scream and a whoop from the back of the bay.

Tabitha and Marco rushed to the door.

The Twins were standing on either side of the lift, in identical positions, trying to hold its doors closed. The doors were open just a crack.

Several Perks were fighting to get out of the crack.

"Cheee!" they screamed. "Chee-chee-chee-chee-eeee!"

A Perk struggled out of the lift; another. A third was emerging.

The first one leapt at Mogul.

Tal flew at the second, claws wide, beak stabbing.

Wedging the door with one foot, Mogul lashed out with the other. He kicked the Perk in the throat. It fell writhing to the ground.

Tal's Perk was shrieking.

There was a thud. Saskia had thrown something at the third and hit it on the head. The Perk dropped like a stone. Saskia slammed the lift doors shut while Mogul hit the control to send it on its way.

Saskia bent and retrieved her missile, then the Twins came pelting back to the ship. Tal dropped his limp victim and flew straight over their heads, into the airlock.

"Looks like we're all staying here," said Marco.

Saskia and Mogul vaulted aboard. They were hardly panting.

"I did warn you," said Tabitha.

Saskia tossed her burden into Tabitha's hands as Mogul shut the door. It was the melon again, or what was left of it. "I don't want to eat that now," she said.

"Okay," said Marco, very serious suddenly. "Is there another way out of here?"

Tabitha jerked a thumb in the direction of the open mouth of the hangar.

"You can climb," she said.

"Right," he said.

"So can they," said Tabitha.

She was amused. She was feeling vindicated. Her plans were unchanged. And she'd just had an idea, one which would get them all moving.

Climbing up into the cockpit, Tabitha threw the melon in the disposal and wiped her hands. She opened her web and sat down.

She glanced at the clock, and away again quickly. Three hours. Barely.

Uninvited, Marco came and stood beside her. Ignoring him, she pressed a tab on the console and keyed in a series of commands. Then she sat back, her arms folded.

On top of the *Alice Liddell*, the floods swiveled and became searchlights, two broad beams shining up at the roof of the bay and on out into the dark gulf beyond. There were two black lines of metal there, two rails slanting up out of the hangar and disappearing in the darkness.

"This will be right up your street," said Tabitha.

In the darkness outside, something was moving.

Everyone crowded into the cockpit and stared out through the viewport. Marco stood behind Tabitha, his fingers hooked in the web above her head. Tal clung to the co-pilot's web where Saskia and Mogul sat, unself-consciously entwined, peering solemnly upwards like a pair of kittens.

Sliding down the rails, a large dark mass was coming towards them. It was bulky and rounded, a huge bundle suspended from some sort of wheeled carrier.

When it entered the hangar the tracking device clicked and swiveled. Unreeling cables, it began to lower the bundle.

On its way down, the bundle unfolded, spreading wings left and right. Its fabric shifted in the light, cords sliding across one another, and the light shone through and between them. It was a net.

There was a sound of machinery starting to grind behind them. They all turned round, all but Tabitha, who continued to watch the descent of the net on a bow monitor, a satisfied expression on her face. Her passengers hurried down into the empty hold, where the roof of the *Alice* was splitting into two.

Along its length was a thread of blue light, which widened, widened, as the two halves of the roof retracted, rumbling gently down into the walls. The huge net dropped steadily through the gap between the coiled cargo extensors, its pulleys whining.

Tal flew up to the catwalk for safety, while Marco and the Twins backed hastily out of the way. Tabitha hung her bag on her shoulder and came walking nonchalantly down from the cockpit, not even glancing up to see the great cables gliding rapidly down towards her head.

This was her show.

She walked at a leisurely pace to the back of the hold, where she unlocked a control panel and pressed several buttons. She turned. The edge of the net came down, thumping softly on the deck, bowing to her, centimeters in front of her feet, and all the machinery stopped.

At Tabitha's side Marco was clutching his duffel and eyeing the unfolded net in some apprehension. "You want us to ride up in this?"

"Or there's the lift," said Tabitha. "It'll be back any minute."

"Hey, no, it's great," he said apprehensively. "Really."

The Twins came and inspected the net. Saskia prodded the cords with her toe. "It looks like a safety net," she said with distaste.

"It may be time to be a little flexible," said her brother languidly. "Our situation is desperate, perhaps."

"But we *never*—" Saskia began.

"Don't worry," said Tabitha maliciously. "You won't fall through the holes."

Saskia stared at her. Tabitha turned away and keyed

the lifting sequence. Overhead, the machinery began to whirr again.

"You'd better hurry, Marco," she said. "You've got three hours to be back with the money."

Saskia shrugged, delicately, and she and Mogul turned handsprings, one after the other, and bounced lightly into the middle of the net.

"Where does this thing end up?" asked Marco.

"Warehousing deliveries," said Tabitha precisely. She was enjoying being back in control.

The lifting cables tautened. Tal flew between them, over the rising sides of the net, and circled high above. "Marzipan!" he called. "Major shoes!"

"All aboard," said Tabitha.

At their feet the edge of the net began to shift off the deck.

Marco turned, a strange urgency in his eyes. He hugged her suddenly, pinning her arms to her sides. He kissed her furiously.

"Mmmff—"

He jerked her off her feet.

"Mmmf-ow!" she shouted as their lips parted. She was falling to the deck, and he was falling with her, his arms tight around her.

The rising net snared her ankles. Together she and he slammed into it. It was already off the deck and bearing them smoothly upwards.

Winded, Tabitha gasped, a horrible gagging croak. Her face was pressed sideways into the mesh. Her bag was digging in her ribs. Marco was on top of her. The Twins were on top of him. She yelled an incoherent yell.

The weight lessened as the Twins climbed up the cables. Marco was still on top of her. Oily cord was cutting into her all over. All she could see, with one eye, was the roof of her ship, the *Alice Liddell*, gaping beneath them. Something green flew out of the hold. It was Tal.

Marco had worked his arms free and was trying to get up on his knees. As the net swung he stumbled and stuck a knee hard in the small of her back.

"*Ow!*"

Then he was up, leaning away from her to let her claw herself around into a sprawling position.

They were coming out of the end of the hangar now. The blue twilight flickered and died as the beacon went out.

"*Uh!*" said Tabitha. "*Uhh!*"

"You okay?" asked Marco anxiously. "Tabitha? Okay?"

She swung a punch at him. Her arm caught in the mesh and her fist hit him on the side of the head. Her foot slipped suddenly through the net. She pitched over sideways, howling in incoherent outrage.

They passed into the fitful darkness of the dock cavern. Above Tabitha and Marco the Twins hung from the cables in elegant nautical positions, feet braced in the netting. The floor of the docks retreated beneath them, lane markings shining dimly, gouts of sudden flame flaring suddenly in the gloom.

Tabitha struggled up on her knees, yelling at Marco. "*You—*"

"I know," he said. "I'm sorry. Really, I'm sorry. Please tell me you're okay."

"Okay?" she yelled in his face. "*Okay?*"

The net swept them up through an oblong portal faced with irregular, soapy-looking tiles, into a concourse bathed in harsh amber light. Here twenty tracks terminated at radial quays. At theirs, a suspicious-looking drone operator in overalls came out from her booth to watch their arrival, colored leads trailing back from her scalp. Around her, a flock of cargo drones gathered.

There didn't seem to be any Perks about.

Before the hoist came to a halt, the Twins were up and out of it, hopping lightly ashore and closing in on the woman, one either side of her.

They greeted her with a flourish.

"The Amazing Zodiac Twins, madam."

"With our compliments."

"Two tickets to our performance tonight."

The woman fingered the electrode in her audial center. Something was coming through. She made no attempt to take the proffered tickets. Saskia—or was it Mogul?—tucked them into the breast pocket of her overalls for her.

"The Mercury Garden."

"At eight!"

They cartwheeled by.

"Wait a minute," bellowed the woman.

The Twins stopped, turned.

"Port tax," she said, heavily and slowly. "Entry permit. Passport. Vehicle registration."

As the net finally freed her, Tabitha watched Mogul Zodiac make a pass in the air in front of the drone operator's eyes.

"I think you'll find these all in order," he said, showing her his hand.

His hand was empty.

19

Marco made an elaborate performance of helping Tabitha out of the net. She pulled away from him. He closed in on her.

"Take it easy," he murmured. "We're almost out of here."

"Get off me!" she shouted. The operator turned her head, staring glassily at them. All her drones turned too, mimicking her.

"My sister," explained Marco, grinning absurdly and hugging Tabitha tight. "Marigold the Mentalist. Space travel doesn't agree with her. Come along, sister, you're safe now."

She pushed him violently away. She was going to hit him, even if they threw her in jail again. Only one thing

stayed her hand. The woman was staring at them, and
Tabitha didn't know who was looking through her eyes.
She didn't need any more trouble.

She knew the cops wouldn't just fine her. She had
heard the cops on Plenty didn't even bother throwing
you in jail. The rumor was, they stripped you and took
you to the adventure zone. Then they went away.

She settled her bag on her shoulder. Marco was moving
in on her again. "You want your money?" he muttered.
"Better stick with me."

"I need to see your entry permit," said the drone
handler, doggedly. "Passport. Vehicle registration. Port
tax receipt code."

Tabitha snarled. She hauled out her ID, held it next
to her captain's shoulder patch. "I'm a bargee, owner-
operator, that's my ship down there," she said, pointing
down the side of the quay. She thrust her wrist monitor
in the woman's face. "See? BGK009059."

"They have mine," said Marco, pointing. The drone
handler turned to look. Tal and the Zodiac Twins had
moved off along the quay, between the piles of crates
and drums, out of sight.

"Oh," said the handler uncertainly. "Okay," she
said.

Her eyes were bloodshot and confused.

Marco grabbed Tabitha and hustled her off the quay.
"Be sure to come to the show!" he called back, waving
cheerily.

"I'm going back," Tabitha insisted.

"No time," he said, getting in her way.

"I've got to shut the roof," she said. "Do you want
somebody to steal her? This is Plenty, Marco, remember?"

He put his arms round her. "Get off me!" she said.
He wouldn't.

"Get off, Marco!" She elbowed him in the ribs.

Unfortunately, at that moment, along the quay a cop
came sauntering.

He moved with the mechanical lope of hydraulic-
assisted legs. His head turned this way and that. He

caught sight of Tabitha struggling with Marco. He
scanned them with his cyclops eye. His face was blank.
He had a couple of guns.

"Is there a problem?" the cop asked, thickly. His
mouth was full of stainless steel.

"No," said Tabitha hurriedly, "no, no problem.
Thank you."

The cop said, "Do you require a duel license?"

Tabitha, startled, said, "A what?" Marco was looking
the other way.

"A duel license," said the cop. "You were hitting
him. You require a duel license to hit him. That's in this
sector. This is warehouse sector 4."

"Just a little family dispute," said Marco. "My sister,
Marigold the Mentalist." Tabitha kicked his shin.
"We're in a hurry," Marco said to the cop, "thank you,
thank you, very much."

They tried to hurry past.

The cop blocked their path, his visor flickering as he
computed. "A duel license is ten scutari," he said.

He chewed his lip, which was raw and wet.

"We don't need a license," Tabitha said loudly and
clearly. "All right?"

The cop shrugged, his shoulder servos whining. He
was obviously having problems with his brain. He was
a low-grade cyborg, a disposable.

"I got to charge you for the call-out," said the cop.

Tabitha protested. "We didn't call you!"

It was no use arguing. "That's two seventy-five," he
said, "for the call-out."

Marco dug in his pocket for his credit chip. "Okay,
okay," he said. "Here you go."

The cop's head whirred right and left, scanning the
pair of them.

"A little family misunderstanding," continued Marco,
taking the cop's forearm and pressing the chip into place.
"Well, that's showbiz! Speaking of which, I trust you'll
accept these two complimentary tickets to our show this
evening at the Mercury Garden."

"Donations are gratefully received," intoned the cop.

The tickets in the data clip on his chest, he whirled around and motored easily away.

Marco clasped Tabitha's hands. "You mustn't do things like that," he murmured, urgently. "Especially here. I won't always be able to bail you out of them."

She set her jaw. "I'm going to go and lock the ship," she said.

"She'll be okay," he said easily. The credit chip twinkled in his fingers.

"How much have you got on that chip, Marco?"

"I told you. Not enough."

They stood an instant, staring at each other.

"Where's the right one?"

"Hannah has it. You want to go and get it? That's where I'm going," he said, in tones of perfect reasonability.

She exhaled explosively, ground her teeth.

"Okay," he said with every sign of regret, turning to her as they walked, "so you don't trust me. I can't deal with you if you don't trust me. Come and meet Hannah Soo, she'll put the money right in your hand. Then you can go straight back to the ship, if you want. That's all I'm saying."

Tal appeared out of nowhere, flying through the dusty amber air to land on his shoulder.

"Marco," called a voice.

"Marco." The same voice, from another place.

"Hannah's waiting, Marco."

"Hurry, Marco."

One of the Twins appeared, climbing languidly down the poles of some scaffolding.

Marco checked his watch. "We'd better get a cab," he said.

As he spoke a cab appeared, a grimy little robot jitney with the other Twin in the back. It coasted to a stop by the scaffolding. The first Twin swung briefly on a horizontal pole and jumped neatly aboard.

"Hurry up, Marco," they chorused.

Those two were going to give her the creeps if she really had to take them all the way to Titan. She made up her mind, as she followed Marco into the cab, to see if she couldn't get a better deal out of this Hannah Soo. She would persuade her the *Alice* wasn't right for the band themselves, take just their equipment and get the money that way. Or else she could spin out the repair until it was too late and they had to get somebody else. That would leave her owing Hannah, but she could sort that out later, after they'd gone. If Hannah was the manager, there must be some other business Tabitha could do for her. Something that didn't involve dangerous musicians and mad acrobats.

She sat next to Marco, facing the Twins. Tal hopped around on the floor among the cigarette stubs and krill-stick wrappers. An empty drink tube rolled between their feet as the jitney wheeled into motion, whisking them away from the cargo concourse and plunging into the tunnels of Plenty.

The slipstream whirled their hair about. Light rods flicked by overhead. Tabitha glanced at the Zodiac Twins, who were sitting with their arms around each other, motionless as a pair of mannequins. They really were identical. Identical twins of different sexes, that wasn't possible, surely, was it? She wondered whose genes had been tinkered with.

She leaned on the armrest, trying not to think of the time, and watched the grim scenery go by. Mostly the walls were dun brown, stained with smoke or water, and crumbling where wiring lash-ups and air and waste ducts had been hammered into place. The tunnel curved left and right, round corners, climbing and plunging without logic or warning, while the ceiling rose and, alarmingly, fell. Sometimes they flashed across other tunnels where vehicles were running. There didn't seem to be any traffic code or signaling system.

The cab rocketed down a ramp into a major mall, slowing to steer between the visitors browsing among small arms dealers and gift shops. Here the cut-price and the breakable predominated. Racks of flak jackets and tottering towers of "toolkits" and pornographic plug-ins cluttered the street. There was a mingled stink of spicy frying, sugar and cordite. Somebody yelled and threw a can at the cab, hitting it on the rear bumper.

Saskia spoke suddenly. Tabitha, turning involuntarily, knew it was Saskia by her moustache.

"I'm hungry," she said.

The voice the Twins shared was husky and low, a warm stream with a bed of consonants hard as stones. Evidently English was not their first language. Tabitha wondered if they were extraterrestrials, some unknown, unregistered kind.

"I could eat a horse," said Saskia.

She looked around the lighted bays as if expecting to see one somewhere, providentially turning on a spit. "I'm so hungry I could eat flies and worms," she said, intensely, and laughed. "Crunchy little brown beetles." She caressed her brother's head. "Aren't you hungry?"

"Hunger makes us keen," said her brother. He spoke lazily, distantly.

"Rubbish," said Saskia. "Hunger just makes you hungry, that's all." She poked Tal with her toe, taking it out on him. He bit her boot.

The jitney turned, plunging down a bumpy alley. Upper rooms, protruding at odd, uneven angles from the higher reaches of the walls, housed a variety of astrologers, card schools and obscure therapists. Rugs and curtains divided the pits and caves below. Inside the ramshackle buildings, people huddled in alcoves under dangling AV screens, smoking waterpipes, drinking beer and arguing. There were raised voices from another alley somewhere nearby, the zap of automatic fire, a scream. No one took any notice.

Every few meters, as the cab tipped this way and that to negotiate the base of a cold, slimy pillar or a crack in the floor, Tabitha got a glimpse into the dark spaces above and behind the makeshift partitions and aggressive fascias. The inhabited interior of Plenty, she realized, was like a gigantic sponge, its buildings wedged into cellular, shadowy holes piled with slowly mouldering rubbish, suppurating fungi, forgotten bodies.

Tabitha jumped as Marco's hand landed on her shoulder. "Look at that," he said. A woman in a gas mask and black foil negligée was going by, leading a man on a chain and carrying a pink ice cream. Marco laughed. "Crazy place," he said.

She shrugged his hand away.

"Heyyy . . ." he complained, wounded.

Tabitha patted the air between them sharply with the palms of her hands. "Off," she said.

One of the Twins giggled.

"Don't annoy the pilot, Marco."

The next cavern was darker. Heavy music thundered from leather-curtained basements. There was a powerful reek of ammoniates and incense, with gusts of sour wine and sour flesh. Whores sat on balconies, drinking and staring down into the street. Bursting sacks of uncollected refuse lay in heaps.

The jitney rushed on into another narrow tunnel. The floor reverberated beneath it. Openings covered with wire netting revealed a shadowy abyss. Far below, Tabitha could see tiny bridges and spindly ladders connecting abrupt spidery promontories like jets of frozen porridge, jutting into empty space.

Marco twisted in his seat, staring back into the cavern they had just left.

"This isn't the way," he said. "Is it?"

Tabitha looked at him, then at the Twins, who didn't reply. They sat there smiling a secretive smile.

Tabitha wanted to tear their throats out.

Tal, responding to the sharpness of Marco's voice, tooted loudly and flew up onto his knee. Marco, rising, brushed him quickly aside. Recovering his balance, Tal hopped onto Tabitha's leg. "Get off me!" she yelled, striking him wildly.

The alien bird evaded her with ease.

Marco was kneeling up in his seat, turning round to check the control panel. "Who programmed this thing?"

The Twins looked gleefully into each other's eyes.

Tabitha confronted them. "What have you done?"

"Nothing," they chorused.

"Not a thing, Captain," said Mogul.

They were moving too fast to jump out.

Tabitha got to her feet and pushed Marco aside to peer at the controls. They were unmarked, and totally unfamiliar. She pulled out a penknife and started stabbing, hoping to break some vital connection.

Time was ticking by, and she was heading deeper into the unknown depths of Plenty.

Alice, she promised, the minute I'm out of this, I will fix you up. I'll make you as good as new, she promised. Don't take my ship away. Please, don't take my ship away. If they take my ship away, I'm going to kill somebody.

Nothing she damaged was making any difference. The little car rushed on into the dismal labyrinth.

The further they descended, it seemed, the chillier it became. The tunnels were gloomier, the only illumination coming from occasional bf tubes suspended awkwardly from holes hacked at random in the roof, no more than half a meter above their heads. The cab hurtled along from pool to pool of the bleak, unnerving light, struggling over the large brown lumps that bulged like bubbles in the roadway. Then the road ran out altogether and the floor tilted sharply downwards beneath them.

The Twins shrieked. Tabitha dug her knife beneath a great cluster of wiring and gouged.

The cab skidded to a halt, its headlights pointing down a long slope of scree.

Loose pebbles slithered, bounced, rattled down into darkness and silence.

Tabitha jumped out, Marco close behind her. "Where the hell are we?" she demanded. Her voice echoed flatly from distant walls.

He stood, arms akimbo, looking around in the musty gloom.

He shook his head. "Shit," he muttered, and chuckled.

Tabitha, breathing hard, feeling the roof coming down on her, groped in her bag to see if she had a torch. Saskia and Mogul were standing close behind her, embracing each other tightly and whispering.

Tabitha couldn't find a torch. She looked around in the light of the headlamps. She swallowed.

They were in a broad, low cave with streams of yellow liquid running down the walls. She couldn't see to the bottom of the scree slope. It seemed to go on forever.

Tabitha almost felt like risking it. Down anywhere on Plenty, must lead to the docks. Where the *Alice* was. Somewhere.

Tal suddenly made a noise like a tinny victory trumpet and took off, flying back up the road. "He's got it," said Marco. "Follow that man."

He grinned at Tabitha.

She frowned at him.

Tal tootled in the distance. They began to climb towards his voice.

They climbed for several minutes, the floor of the cave flaking beneath their tread. Tabitha and Marco went ahead, the Twins following on behind, skipping lazily from spot to spot.

"I'm really, really sorry about this," said Marco soberly. "Those little cars go wrong all the time. They just don't maintain them."

"This isn't the way we came," said Tabitha.

"Tal knows where he's going," Marco said. He sounded as though he believed it, so she chose to. Ahead there was just enough light to show them they were about to enter the mouth of another tunnel.

Suddenly a searchlight was blazing in their eyes.

Throwing up her hand, Tabitha glimpsed a figure in silhouette rising up from the floor at their very feet. It rose a long way.

A mechanical cry rang out. "*Halt!*"

Stumbling backwards, bumping into each other, they came to an untidy stop in front of the tunnel mouth. It was barred by a black and white striped gate. The guard, Tabitha saw as the searchlight swung away, was a robot three meters tall, covered in spikes. Tal was sitting on the gate, facing them.

"*State your business,*" commanded the robot. On the gate behind it was a large white notice in seven lan-

guages. UNRECLAIMED AREA, Tabitha read. THE
MANAGEMENT OF THIS STATION IS NOT RE-
SPONSIBLE FOR SAFETY OF PERSONS OR POS-
SESSIONS PAST THIS POINT. Then the searchlight
dazzled her again.

Marco drew himself up and spoke boldly into the light.
"We," he proclaimed, encompassing them all with a
theatrical gesture, "are Contraband."

Instantly there was the loud click and hum of automatic
weapons being readied.

"Oh dear," said Saskia, delicately, and laughed.

BGK009059 LOG

TXJ.STD

[ʄ˜Ñ!]]]]'˜βββ/9/]Ç]222m

[ʄ˜Ñ!]]]]'˜βββ/9/Ç]222m

MODE? VOX

SD? 19.06.31

READY

I was thinking about my Auntie Muriel.

WHAT ABOUT HER, CAPTAIN?

She has a great laugh. When she laughs, my Auntie Muriel tips her head back and opens her mouth wide. She looks as if she's going to take a bite out of the air. When she laughs, she makes a deep gurgling sound like a big baby, then she goes haw-haw-haw, a real belly laugh.

She's got a quite a belly, my Auntie Muriel. She was getting fat when I lived with her, she's probably huge now. She's pretty casual about clothes too. She'll wander around the farm all day in her nightie, or even less, a worn-out old shirt and a pair of panties. With her tum sticking out. She used to say, "Hell, Tabs, they can look at you all the time if they want to. And they want to." She'd point up in the air, where the Gnats were zipping around on their little gliders, like little pointed flower petals in the sky.

Except there isn't any sky. Not on Integrity 2.

WAS THAT YOUR NEXT HOME AFTER THE MOON, CAP-TAIN?

Mm. One of them. I was sixteen, or seventeen. Mum got a job, she was a spindlejack. We got an apartment in the city, lots of space and nothing to put in it. Mum was off working all day and half the night, and sleeping like the dead the other half. There was nothing for me to do, I was too young to get a work permit, and mum was determined we weren't going to start breaking the law the minute we'd got there, so she called Auntie Muriel and Auntie Muriel said why not. When she came to get me, she looked really pleased at the idea of having me working for her. I was not convinced.

WHY NOT?

It sounded dead boring.

It was, too.

I thought Auntie Muriel was like something out of another age. This woman I'd never seen, darker than me, darker than mum, my height but four times as big every other way, her hair hanging down in a big shaggy mane that looked as if she cut it herself once a year, big wooden earrings in her ears and a dress down to the floor with embroidery all over it and her feet stuffed into ugly shoes that were made of leather. She told us that. She wanted us to admire them, because this was a big day for her. Auntie Muriel had got dressed up to come to the city and see her sister and her sister's child.

WHAT DID YOU LOOK LIKE, CAPTAIN?

Me? I was awful, in those days. I was into acid green sleeks and I had my hair cut in a triangle. When I saw Auntie Muriel I thought, if that's the way you end up, working on a farm, I'll stay at home and become an underresourced juvenile. But it wasn't up to me.

The farm was all the way along the tube, in the endland. It was too far to go every day, so I went for the week, came home to the flat at weekends. She had squash, groundnuts, rows of beans on nylon lines. She had me for the weeding.

COULDN'T SHE HAVE GOT A ROBOT?

Auntie Muriel doesn't trust robots. She doesn't much like machines at all, in fact. Auntie Muriel has old-fashioned ideas about what's "natural," everything should be natural, which is pretty stupid when you think where she lives. Anyway, she was quite content with the weeds and the gummed-up filters, but even more content to have me hoe the weeds and ungum the filters for her while she sat half-naked on an ancient natural tube steel chair tipped back on two legs against the natural pulpboard side of her natural module A farmhouse, playing her warped old guitar.

Sometimes I'd wake up in the middle of the night, hearing music in my dreams, and I'd look down out of the bedroom window, and there she'd be, strumming away, singing about places she'd never seen and wasn't likely to, rivers and mountains and islands in the sun. Sometimes I'd get up and

go down and sit with her, look up at the Moon shining
through the glass and think, at least I'm out of that. Then
I'd look at the fields of beans, glossy in the moonlight, hanging fat and glossy. They reminded me of pricks.

GOODNESS ME. WAS THIS A PERCEPTION OTHERS
WOULD HAVE SHARED?

If they were sixteen-year-old girls, yes. A lot of things reminded me of pricks when I was sixteen. I was a horny little
creature, you know, Alice. I didn't really get my jollies hoeing
and taking up the irrigation mats, putting them back and
taking them up again.

So I was on the lookout.

Integrity 2 is a mess. You can put any kind of gauzes in,
as fine as you like, they'll silt up just the same, there's so
much crap in the system. Rather than do anything about it,
the Council pays the farmers a subsidy to filter the water.
Auntie Muriel buys the cheapest gauze and spends the rest
of the subsidy on red wine. I had a row with her once. I had
a row with her several times, but this once I said, why didn't
she get out there and shift some bloody irrigation mats with
me, and she just slapped her belly and said she'd got too
fat to bend. Then she laughed.

You do a lot of bending, farming the Auntie Muriel method.
I'd be out in the fields, up to my shins in stinking red granules,
and I'd stand there looking up, easing my aching back, and
watching the Gnats fly.

There was a Gnat base nearby, on the End. Sometimes
I'd watch their kites going down into the fields overhead,
down until they dwindled away out of sight, long before they
reached the tops of the trees. You can't do that often, though,
because of all the smog. Even on a clear day in the country,
you can look along the tube there, along from Auntie Muriel's,
and not be able to see the city for smog. It's quite a job,
keeping the windows clean on Integrity 2.

Weekends, mum slept. I found my own level. The local
street kids were a scummy lot. They called themselves the
Rejects, and they were very picky about social status. There
was a girl called Carmen, she was the queen Reject, she

just let me hang around with them so she could sneer at
me for being a moony. I had to do some crazy things to
get their attention. There was a boy called Murray, he was
a case. He really was an underresourced juvenile, that Murray. He was dangerous. We liked to think he was. I found
out even Carmen was scared of Murray. So I went with
Murray.

WHERE DID YOU GO WITH HIM?

To the parlors. To the empty malls. To the places that hadn't
quite worked out the way the designers had planned, the
places where kids drift in a city, where they make up their
own version of the city. We found some things to do, Murray
and me.

I knew it wouldn't last. I was just killing time. And Murray
was crazy. A lot of the time I didn't even like him, really.
You could see Murray was going one day, probably without
even noticing, to do someone some permanent damage. I
didn't want it to be me.

Sometimes, night on the farm, I'd sit out in the grass with
Auntie Muriel and her guitar. It was Auntie Muriel taught me
to play the harmonica.

SO SOME GOOD CAME OF THIS PERIOD, THEN.

Is that your honest opinion?

WELL, YOU ENJOY IT.

I like it when it stops.

YOU NEVER USED TO BE SO SELF-CRITICAL, CAPTAIN.

It's this trip. I keep blaming myself. I keep asking myself
how I ever let myself get dragged into it.

WE NEED THE MONEY.

We certainly do.

AND YOU WERE ATTRACTED TO MARCO METZ.

I'm just like my mum, when it comes down to it. That's why I quite admired Auntie Muriel, in a guarded sort of way. I'd think, I really should try to be like her, she was so content, nothing ever fazed her. I didn't want to be a farmer, understand, but I didn't want to be like mum either, tied to a feckless man, trying to keep him and me, having to hustle all the time to stop from sinking. I fancied myself on a corporate asteroid, settling down with someone who would cherish me and buy me everything I wanted. Carmen and her crew had the same ideas, even if they acted like they were going to be bad girls forever.

I thought, if I was going to find a husband with prospects, maybe I should start right away. I wasn't getting any younger. I knew where to look too.

The farm was close to one of the Ends, did I say that? In fact it was only fifteen minutes by bike to the escalators. You could ride up to the vista points and look along 12, watch the sun light up the pollution. The End was somewhere the Rejects wouldn't have been seen dead, so when I was in my ambitious, conventional mood, that made it more attractive. Anyway, I liked it. The g was less, and that made me feel at home. Also there were the boys.

THE GNATS ARE BOYS, THEN.

They are. They're police cadets, is what they are. They wear uniforms. Very sexy. Blue-grey slicksuits like slate and glitzy black insignia. Shiny boots. With gliders to match. No Gnat would ever call his glider a kite, especially not when he was wearing his uniform. You'd see them here and there in the city, cycling around on rallies, doing formation displays in the parks. Up at the base, there was a place by the recruiting office with seats and a slot screen, you could stand and watch them do training flights, all unassisted stuff. They'd fly right across the tube, riding the gravity gradients, making it look easy. The first time I saw them, I wished I could be a Gnat. Carmen would have loved to know that.

Carmen would have made short work of Michael too. Michael was my secret. He was my shining knight. He was full white, the first full white I ever had. Michael had long eyelashes and freckles that went down inside the neck of his uniform. Michael was serving the community. When the time came, I knew he would take me to the asteroids, and we could serve the community together.

I let him work the slot screen for me and point out the sights. Michael would stand very close to me, not touching. I never let him know which farm was Auntie Muriel's, though Auntie Muriel knew all about him. She didn't tell mum. She didn't mind where I was when I wasn't supposed to be working. It was natural for a girl to roam. She had men coming round, all the time. They weren't like Michael, though. In fact, I had the idea Auntie Muriel might have been less tolerant about Michael if she met him. Michael wasn't very natural.

The trouble was, the Rejects found out too.

Carmen thought it was great. Carmen told Murray, and Murray went crazy. Not because I was going with another boy, but because he was a Gnat. He took it as a personal insult. I told him I wasn't screwing Michael, because that was the most important thing to Murray, the only thing he really saw the point of. So we did that. "I really haven't," I told him. And I hadn't. Michael was after me to, but I was holding off. "I'm going to make him give me a go on his kite," I told Murray.

He had a good laugh at that. He thought it was a terminally good idea, terminally funny. He said there was no way Michael would do it. "Duty before nookie," he said. "The Gnats' motto, that is." He even bet me. So everybody was happy.

You know, Alice, I hadn't really thought that, about the kite, until I opened my mouth and heard myself say it. But it was a good idea, whatever Murray said. I was getting a bit bored with Michael. I'd decided his kite was the best thing about him. So I made a date with him at the base, my next free afternoon, and I told Murray, today's the day. I was that cocky.

The base was empty. Michael was in his uniform. I took him into the hangar where the kites were and stroked his uniform. I kissed his insignia. Then I found out how far his freckles went down. I got him so worked up he'd have promised me anything to let him do it to me. That was really how he saw it, it was something he wanted to do to a girl, and he had to find a girl who'd let him do it to her. But I wasn't that clever, Alice, because I had to let him do it to me before, instead of after.

SURELY THAT WOULD BE PREFERABLE.

How would you know?

I MEAN, IF YOU WEREN'T GOING TO ENJOY IT.

You're right, aren't you. Yes, once he got going, I knew why I'd been holding back. Not just for the kite, but because he was such hard work. He really was useless. He wasn't a bit like Murray, who was just wild, all over the place. The only trouble with Murray was keeping up with him. With Michael I was just supposed to hold still while he banged away at me, red in the face and panting. I gritted my teeth and decided it wasn't such a one-sided deal after all.

Afterwards he came over all tender and started talking about when we're married. I'd forgotten that was what I'd picked a Gnat for in the first place. It sounded horrible, coming from him. Remember you're a Reject, I told myself. The kite, I kept thinking.

I told Michael what he wanted to hear, pretty much, without actually promising anything, because I could tell he was going to make it easy for me. He was falling asleep on my shoulder. When he did, I slipped out from under him, picked up his sexy uniform, which didn't seem quite so sexy any more, and took his glider key off the chain. Then I got dressed quick, holding the key in my teeth, and then I went over to the kite, but I must have made a noise, because Michael woke up. I looked back and saw him putting both feet in one leg of his trousers, calling my name, trying to back out of it.

"A Gnat honors his promise," I told him, and I took his kite down off the racks. I was amazed how light it was. It was beautiful. It was big, silicon black, with scarlet lines, and when I took it outside, the sun flashed rainbows off the shoulder hooks.

The Rejects had all turned up to see me. Michael was after me, stumbling out onto the launch platform half-dressed and babbling about two-month training courses. Behind me I heard Murray screeching at Michael's underwear, and then I was gone.

They gave a huge yell as I took off. I was in a hurry, I hadn't even put a headset or a mask on.

That was a mistake, leaving the mask behind.

I was up. I was in flight. My first flight, Alice. Do you remember yours?

IT'S NOT THE SAME, CAPTAIN.

I suppose you weren't sixteen.

NO. BUT I REMEMBER MY FIRST FLIGHT WITH YOU, CAPTAIN. THAT WAS GOOD.

This wasn't. I mean, it started off well. There I was, flitting wide of the axis like a pro, zipping between the clouds, and looking down—up—12.

YOU USED THE WORD "ALONG" BEFORE, CAPTAIN.

Yes, but I didn't have it with me then. I mean, I did, but I also had "up" and "down," and none of them would do.

I was confused. That was what threw me, probably. I mean, I'd had the feeling before, a bit, the first couple of times I went up on the End, it was that much closer to the spindle. But now I was up in the air, and what with the clouds, I lost all my orientation. Where the clouds parted, I could see the whole tube, land all around me, and it seemed to go up like a tower, so the town and the factory belt and the parks were hanging from the walls over my head, they were all going to crash down on me, and the city on top of them. I had the sun in my eyes from the windows one side and when I dipped a wing, the stars shining in the other. And then the whole thing swivelled round in my head, and

I was looking down the same chimney from the top, and nothing was about to stop me falling down it.

I started to feel sick.

So I flipped around and made for the ground, I'd completely lost my bearings, I didn't recognize it, didn't even know which panel it was. And I was getting tired, I'd had no idea how much hauling one of those things around the sky would take it out of you, and then I was coming "down," "down" fast. I didn't know how to land, I had to grab some height.

DID YOU?

I did.

Unfortunately.

I flew too high, and then I was going higher, faster, I couldn't stop, like a feather finding a vent. I just shot up to the spindle, and there I stuck, dangling in zero g. I kicked and flailed, I was hopeless, I had no idea how to get away. I hadn't got anything I could throw. I couldn't even see straight anyway, my eyes were tearing. The pollution was pretty bad up there, I started coughing, and then I couldn't stop.

After a while, whenever the clouds cleared a bit, I could see little machines assembling on the ground all around me. Then I saw some more gliders coming towards me. One was in the lead. I thought it would be Michael. I really didn't want it to be him.

It wasn't. It was a figure in a mask and a jacksuit with all this gear in pockets all over it, and she had a headset, and one for me, one like I would have had on if I hadn't taken off in such a hurry, and she had jets, which no Gnat would have been seen dead with. She hooked me and took me in tow.

"You wait until I get you home, young lady," she said on the radio.

"Mum?" I said.

AND WAS IT?

Of course it was. And she wasn't pleased.

WHAT WAS YOUR AUNT'S REACTION?

Auntie Muriel? She laughed. She laughed and laughed.

The cops weren't amused. Stealing a Gnat kite, endangering 12 airspace and having to be rescued by council employees—it was a grave offense for a juvenile. I had to do ten weeks glass cleaning. Outside.

We lived in a barracks in the End, barely saw the inside of the tube for ten weeks. Every day they took us out and set us crawling all over the tube from outside, scraping the micrometeorite dust off the glass. The rest of the gang were even worse than Carmen and the Rejects. They really were rejects, zero contributors, the unlovely and the unemployable. They ganged up on me and nicked my harmonica. They spent their breaks on the window detail peering in through the glass, endlessly scheming dreary things to do when they got back inside. I didn't want to get back inside, not any more. There I was, out on the hull, up to my shins in flaky white grit. And I'd stand there, easing my aching back, and looking up at the stars.

A panel in the chest of the robot snapped open. Telescopic tubes and extensible antennae probed in Marco's direction.

"I mean to say," he continued smoothly, "Contraband is our name. Our performing name." He said this as if it were obvious, as if he were explaining something self-evident to a small child. "We are a performing group. A group of artists. We have an engagement at eight o'clock tonight at the Mercury Garden."

The robot's loudspeaker crackled and hissed. It had a screen on its head where its face might have been. The screen was malfunctioning. It popped, slowly, regularly.

"This is not the way to the Mercury Garden," it announced. *"This is an unreclaimed area."*

"Right," said Marco. "Sure. Well, first we have an appointment at JustSleep."

The robot hummed and ticked, digesting this.

"This is not the way to Sleep of the Just," it said. *"This is an unreclaimed area. Identify yourself,"* it demanded.

"Hey!" said Marco. "Come on. You know me." He started to pat his pockets, as if searching for an ID. "I'm a major media celebrity," he claimed, "star of stage, screen and satellite, citizen of the solar system, Monty Marsh Marigold is my name, Distringency Number Romeo Rhubarb Rhapsody three-beta-three-one-double-one-one, that's Rhubarb Romeo Ringmaster one-three-beta-one-one-triple-k."

He was talking faster and faster, pulling an accordion pleat of plastic cards from his pocket, folding and unfolding it, slipping each card past the robot's swiveling eye and putting them all back again before it could read any of them.

He reached out and took Tabitha by the arm. She resisted, then let him do it.

"This is my sister, the lovely Argentina; that there is our performing parakeet, Paraclete Pete. These," he gestured to the Twins, "are the same person really, only they're going in different directions in time and just stopping to say hello to themselves. Why not check your connection? Check your watch, check your hat and coat. Check your files under R for Art. We claim diffraction," he said, all in one breath, and opened his arms grandly.

A face appeared on the robot's screen. It was a desk cop, a woman in a grey uniform, wearing a headset.

The Zodiac Twins took up positions either side of the robot, their arms folded, peering at the screen with interest. The colors were bad. The woman looked as if she was suffering from a terminal liver disease. Zigzags spluttered across her face.

"Diffraction?" she said. *"Explain diffraction."*

"Why, under diplomatic regulations of the third of

the third thirty-third, AD, an itinerant, interplanetarily
famous performing troupe without identification may not
be restrained, destrained, strained or constrained, ad hoc,
to wit and in lieu, until offered the exercise of its right
of diffraction," recited Marco.

The robot did not respond. The woman on the screen
frowned as if she were having difficulty seeing them.
She fiddled with her earphone, waved her hand across
her scanner.

The robot whirred abruptly, its antennae shifting towards Tabitha. *"Identify yourself,"* it said.

Then, just as Tabitha was opening her mouth and wondering what she was supposed to say, a hideous crackling
noise came over the robot's speaker, and its picture was
torn up by a burst of interference. Nobody spoke. The
robot sat down suddenly on the floor. Its sensors and
weapons retracted inside its chest, the little door banging
closed over them.

"Meep," said the robot.

"About time too," said Marco. Tal, whizzing like a
motorbike, flew straight to his shoulder.

The robot was sitting, gawkily upright, in front of the
barrier. It was completely frozen, but for one leg that
arced backwards and forwards on the floor of the cave,
like the leg of a dying calf.

"What is it?" asked Tabitha. "What happened?"

"It sat down," said Saskia.

"It became tired," said Mogul.

"It happens often," said Saskia.

Tabitha stared at them.

"It wasn't us," they said in unison.

Marco was stepping over the spasming limb as if the
robot wasn't there. Tal flew on ahead, over the barrier
into the dark tunnel.

"Where are we *going?*" demanded Tabitha.

"To JustSleep," said Marco.

"But she said—"

"Come on!" chorused the Twins.

And they went, hurrying in the easy g down the tunnel
after the bird, pushing aside a grey canvas curtain, stum-

bling down carved steps, squeezing between squat brown stalagmites that grew like cankers out of the floor, through a crack into a cave where the wall had crumbled away, revealing a comblike structure of fat, thick-walled cells. Hairy tongues like fat black ferns spilled out of them, shivering in the draught of their passing. The air smelled poisonous and dank.

In such corners of Plenty it is impossible not to fancy yourself deep underground, in the realm of some benighted race of blind burrowers, all listlessly trying to remember the sun. They still exist, here and there, these pockets of gloom and despair. One day we really must do something about clearing them out. I've said so before. No doubt I shall say so again.

Tabitha swooped along after the bird, over rubble, through coulisses, under gantries of black bone where vast unknown machinery slept, covered in fawn dust. In a scaly hollow a crowd of naked Perks fled squealing from the echo of their bounding feet. By the light of their abandoned bonfire Tabitha checked her watch. Of her twenty-four hours, rather less than two remained.

At last they emerged and stood breathing hard in a vast open space, the roof dim and distant above their heads. Some hundred meters ahead, the floor dropped away into an awesome chasm, spanned, way off on their left, by an ugly concrete bridge. Across it taxis and scooters droned to and from the cluster of carbuncular hotels on the far side. Facing the hotels, bulging out over the very brink of the abyss, someone had built a huge green dome. Its forecourt was paved with hexagonal blocks. Cars and sedan chairs were parked in tidy ranks.

"Here you go," murmured Marco congratulatingly to Tal, as the alien bird came back to perch on his shoulder again.

"Beat the drum slowly
And play the pipe lowly," advised Tal.

They approached the building. Potted shrubs of somber green flanked a flight of broad, shallow rockfoam steps leading down to a doorway covered by thick curtains of the darkest purple. There was an aura of money, a hint of incense in the air. Somewhere within, an ethereal harp was playing.

"*Welcome to Sleep of the Just,*" intoned a warm and sympathetic voice from all around, "*home of the Chosen Frozen. How may we serve you?*"

"Contraband is our name," said Marco to the tingling air. "We're here to see our manager."

There was the briefest of pauses.

"*Ms Hannah Soo is already raised and conversant,*" said the ambience. "*Your friend is at her bedside. Please follow the light.*"

A wisp of pale green fire suddenly spurted into existence, hovering below them on the steps.

Marco started pulling at Tabitha's arm again. "Come, sister," he said loudly. "Hannah's waiting for us."

Tabitha snatched her arm free.

"What is this place?"

"*Welcome to Sleep of the Just,*" began the ambience again.

"This is it," Marco said. "This is where Hannah works."

Tabitha looked down the sepulchral stairs at the waiting fatuus. A wave of cold seemed to emanate through the funereal drapery.

"These are the cryo vaults, aren't they?"

"Right," said Marco, in a hushed, imperative tone.

"Does she manage them too?"

"Sure."

Tabitha confronted him.

"No, she doesn't," she said. "She's dead, isn't she?"

"Up to a point."

"Forget it," she said.

"It's okay, Tabitha, trust me," he said forcefully.

"*Many people find these meetings emotionally stressful,*" suggested the ambience, considerately. "*Perhaps your sister would care for a tranquilizer?*"

"She's dead," said Tabitha.

"She's got your money," Marco said.

The green fire jiggled politely at the top of the stairs.

"*Would you prefer to wait a moment, to collect your*

thoughts and prepare yourself spiritually?'' asked the
ambience

"No," said Tabitha. She jerked her head. "Get a
move on," she said.

The purple curtains opened themselves, and the green
fire slipped between them.

Her heart in her mouth, Tabitha Jute followed the band
down into the halls of JustSleep.

22

They were back inside the honeycomb tunnels of Plenty.

This section at least had been civilized, with foamed
flooring sprayed everywhere and atmospheric flambeaux
hung in ornamental sconces. The sad harp beckoned
them, the wisp of green fire darted before them, floating
at a stately pace between the hangings. They followed,
Tal performing aerobatics about the unheeding apparition.

It was rather cold in the corridors of Sleep of the Just.

They passed curtained doorways. Hushed voices could
be heard, sounds of weeping, the solemn chanting of a
thousand boy sopranos. Other visitors passed them, som-
berly dressed in umber silk-zibelline and black murian
fur, clasping phylacteries, breviaries bound in bleached
calf. Their heads were bowed, their faces grave. The
children bore posies of lily-of-the-valley and examination
certificates. No greetings were exchanged.

Marco Metz looked out of place here, in his shabby-
expensive jacket and flowing trousers of lemon twill. He
had given up trying to dominate Tabitha and was now
ignoring her. His tatty duffle bag on his shoulder, he
bowled after the insubstantial attendant and the psittacoid

alien, looking less like a noted musician calling on his manager and more like a sky-sailor hurrying to a house of ill repute.

Behind him, the Zodiac Twins bounced lithely along with their arms around each other, the spangles on their blue pyjamas flickering in the gentle light. They really were impossible to tell apart from the back.

Tabitha hated the place and everyone in it. Shivering, she tugged her bag more securely on to her shoulder, then buried her hands deep in her pockets. All she needed was two hundred and fifty scutari and a phone. That was what she had to hang on to here. Just let her get two hundred and fifty scutari and a phone, in the next hour, and she'd never lose her temper with a Perk, never trespass from her normal trade, never pick up a man in a bar, never again.

The tall green wisp drifted up a crooked flight of stairs and paused in front of a curtained doorway, where it seemed as if it bowed, and when they had gathered on the threshold, vanished. The disembodied harp too trickled politely away.

"*The cubicle of Ms Hannah Soo,*" announced the ambience then. "*Destiny suspended with dignity, by Sleep of the Just. Please observe all normal hygiene and security procedures, and avoid disturbing the subject or the support system. Thank you for selecting Sleep of the Just.*"

With a muted hum, the curtain lifted. Through the doorway, Tabitha could see the sun shining.

"The Meadow," said Mogul, stepping through.

"Oh good," said his sister. She turned to Tabitha. "We don't always get the Meadow," she explained, as she followed her twin.

Marco paused, holding out a hand to usher Tabitha before him. "How's the time?" he asked her.

"Short," she said. It was as much as she was capable of saying, that moment when she walked from a shadowy landing into the cubicle of Hannah Soo and found herself at the edge of a wood, stepping out on to soft green grass, under a clear blue sky.

She could not but stare. Nowhere in her life had she ever seen so much green, so much sunlight spilling through laden branches. Beyond the trees the grass went on and on, uninterrupted to the horizon. Behind her she could hear birds, singing in the wood.

She did not want to look behind her.

Tal, as usual, had flown straight ahead. Tabitha could just spot him, perched on a branch, bright green feathers amid fresh green leaves.

There was something out there, out in the meadow.

It was small, and hovering a couple of meters off the ground. Squinting against the sun, Tabitha had the impression of something black and silver, something she did not recognize.

On the ground below the hovering black thing, a small cocoon of thick white cloud lay motionless just above the lush grass. Protruding from the farther end of the cloud were the head and shoulders of a yellow woman.

The black thing seemed to be looking down at her.

Despite the sunshine, the air was quite chilly. The Zodiacs were walking quickly towards the cloud. Marco was walking beside Tabitha. Their feet made no sound in the grass.

Very deliberately, she turned her head.

Behind her she saw, much as she expected, a forest of trees, growing thick as a wall. It was very hard to see between them, to see how far the forest stretched.

Tabitha was satisfied. It wasn't a microclimate; it wasn't some sort of instantaneous matter transporter; it was just a generic environmat, even if it was a bloody expensive one. She had no idea whether it was accurate, but it was certainly detailed. It smelled of moist earth, and sap, and lurking somewhere underneath, the antiseptic miasma of ultrasonics.

Marco called her. "Tabitha."

She turned back towards the meadow.

"We'll get you that money," he said. "That's the first thing we'll do."

He seemed then to notice the way she was looking around at everything. "You like this? State of the art," he said., "Freezers come cheaper, but they sure as hell don't come any fancier."

"The horizon's a bit close," she said.

"Oh come on," he said.

It was, now she looked at it critically, but she didn't want to argue about it.

"Is that her?"

"That's Hannah. Hannah Soo. Smartest corpse in this whole facility." He waved an expansive hand at the empty landscape. A breeze toyed with his shiny black hair.

Tabitha opened her mouth to ask what the other thing was, hovering over the remains of Hannah; but something made her stop.

She knew what it was.

It was squat and shiny black, metallic. It had a large head and the body of an infant, but no legs. It was wrapped up to its chin in a plastic bag.

The creature (it was real, and alive, she was in no doubt about that) was sitting in midair on a silver metal disc. It had its back to them. She could see it had a tail of some sort, a silver metal tail, the tip plugged into a socket on the disc.

She had never seen one of them before; but there was only one thing it could be.

Marco and Tabitha caught up with the Twins. Together they approached the cloud.

The hovering creature turned at their arrival.

It looked at Tabitha.

Its eyes were cherry red. They glowed at her like the tail-lights of distant vehicles.

It was a Cherub. A Cherub, almost near enough to touch. A Cherub, on a human orbital. A Cherub, underground!

Tabitha felt an icicle transfix her from head to toe. She was paralyzed, she was colder and stiffer than Hannah Soo. She had been staring ever since they entered the caverns of Plenty, and now she stared like a statue.

It lasted a second.

She dropped her gaze. She looked down at the floating

woman wrapped in the cloud. Impossible as that looked—vital though it was she accept it, hell's teeth, get money out of it, and at once—it meant nothing, suddenly, nothing strange or bewildering at all, after the sight of the Spaceborn child.

"It's called Xtasca," said Saskia, who was the only one who seemed to have any interest in telling Tabitha anything. "We think it's female."

Mogul regarded his sister with hooded eyes, a patronizing smile hovering at his slender lips. "Idle fancy," he said, drawling slightly. "They've abolished sex." He seemed to find this fact infinitely regretable, and quite amusing.

"I think it's female," said Saskia to Tabitha, touching the air with an elegant finger. "Don't you?"

Tabitha squinted at the thing, then flinched away again at once. It was still staring at her. She was disgusted, she was fascinated, she didn't know what she felt. She felt giddy. She wondered whether she was still at the party in Schiaparelli, her head mazed with vapor and beer and fine Ophir crystal, and everything since then had been an elaborate hallucination.

"Marco," she heard herself croak out.

The Cherub turned its gaze and stared now at Marco. Tabitha had to look at it. She couldn't look away. "It's a little annoyed," Mogul said to Marco.

Saskia said to Marco, "It's annoyed with you."

Hannah Soo, meanwhile, was talking, and nobody was listening.

Her eyes were open, staring at nothing. Her words issued from a voicebox that she wore at her throat, like a large, vulgar jewel. It gave her the voice of an exhausted drone.

"... before Sincerity even had a stadium," said the late Hannah Soo. Her lips did not move, nor her eyes, but under the skin of her broad, sallow face a lattice of faint geometrical shapes came and went, as if she were crystallizing from within.

She seemed to think she was talking to Xtasca the Cherub.

"*Now, his mother, she was a good woman,*" said Hannah Soo. "*She ran the first orbital circus.*" She chuckled. "*Elephants in freefall!*"

The Cherub spoke.

"Hello Marco," it said.

Xtasca the Cherub has the voice of a perfect simulacrum of a little girl; which in a sense is what it is; allowing for a certain latitude in the interpretation of perfection.

"Hi, Xtasca," said Marco, briefly and rather dismissively.

"You are late," said Xtasca.

"We were detained," he said. "By a drone."

"What a fuss you made," said Xtasca.

It sounded like a child reprimanding her dolls.

Marco ignored it. "Anyway," he said shortly, "our cab broke down."

"Marco," said Tabitha, more resonantly this time. "Money," she said. "Phone." She looked around at the grass, the wood. With gear this sophisticated, there had to be a phone in there somewhere.

"*She ran the first orbital circus,*" the dead woman explained. "*Have I ever told you this?*"

As soon as Tabitha spoke, Xtasca had turned its attention to her again.

"What is she?" it said.

"Xtasca, this is Captain Tabitha Jute. Of the good ship *Alice Liddell*. Tabitha, this is Xtasca," said Marco. "Xtasca is a Cherub. The fifth member of Contraband."

"Yes," said Xtasca.

Its lifesuit flared suddenly, opalescent, as it swiveled in the sunlight. What it was saying yes to, Tabitha was not sure. It sounded authoritative, soulless and final. She had never heard an affirmation so damnatory.

"We'll talk about it later," said Marco to Xtasca, swiftly. "Tabitha," he said, taking her by the arm, drawing her away from Xtasca's glare to face the frozen corpse. "This is someone else you must meet, someone very special to all of us. This is Hannah Soo," he said. "Our manager."

At that the dead woman stopped maundering.

"*Ah,*" said the box on her throat. "*You're here. You're all here. I can see you. You're all standing around me.*"

"We're all here, Hannah," said Marco. "All ready for the show."

"Yes, Marco," said Hannah. "*I can see you. I can see all of you. But who is this with you? Is she from Triton? I have heard nothing from them. People are so unreliable now. Not like the old days . . .*"

"Hannah, this is our new pilot. This is Tabitha Jute. Excuse me interrupting you, but it is kind of urgent, we owe Tabitha some money."

"*How much money?*" wheezed the voicebox of Hannah Soo.

"Two hundred and fifty scutari," said Tabitha, loudly. It was the first time she had ever talked to a dead person. "Fifteen hundred if I'm going to take them to Titan."

Knowing nothing of the Chosen Frozen or what their particular, privileged perspective might be, she thought she should alarm her as much as possible as quickly as possible.

It seemed to work. Or maybe it was only ritual, the same as with a live client.

"*So much.*"

"She has to have a repair first," said Marco.

"*First* she has to have two hundred and fifty scutari," Tabitha corrected him. "For bringing him here," she said.

"*I don't know, Marco,*" said Hannah Soo, as if Tabitha hadn't spoken. "*It's high.*"

Marco bent to gesture forcefully at Hannah's blind eyes. "Hannah, we have to fix this now. I mean, we don't really have time to discuss it. After the show, we can talk about it."

"*What about the regular transport, those nice Armstrong Súilleabháin boys?*"

"They weren't reliable, Hannah," said Marco. "I had to let them go. Now Tabitha, she's reliable."

"*Yesss . . .*" whispered Hannah's voicebox, pensively. "*I see her aura is strong. She is a powerful associate, Marco. Her contribution will be decisive.*"

"Terrific," said Tabitha. "Well, I'm delighted to hear that, I must say." She scowled at the assembled company. They were all avoiding her eye; all except Xtasca. Xtasca was still staring at her. It looked like an idol squatting before her on a salver of stainless steel. An ebony idol with rubies for eyes.

Tabitha looked away quickly. She said to Hannah, "What about your contribution, then?" She kicked the non-existent dirt. It sounded like rockfoam flooring. "You won't have a bloody ship at all unless I get two hundred and fifty scutari now," said Tabitha emphatically. "Marco'll tell you all about it. Is there a phone here I can use?"

"*You must pay her, Marco,*" the dead woman muttered.

"I don't have it," he said.

"*Nor do I, lover,*" said the voicebox of Hannah Soo. She sounded quite sharp all of a sudden; or maybe it was a quirk of the machinery.

"You live here," Tabitha said to her, realizing as she said it that she might have chosen a better verb, "and you expect me to believe that?"

"She doesn't always get the Meadow," said Saskia to Tabitha, defensively.

"*Tabitha, I can't pay you until after the show. When the Mercury Garden pays me.*"

Marco brushed this aside. "We have to have an advance."

"*Another?*"

"This is an expensive deal," said Marco. "Remember what deal this is, Hannah. This is not our usual deal, remember?"

"*Is your friend from Triton, Marco?*" asked Hannah. "*I've heard nothing from Triton for the longest time. I hope the Capellans have not discov—*"

"Tabitha's quite a fan, Hannah," said Marco, interrupting her. "She came to see Tal and me in Schiaparelli."

"*Ah. Schiaparelli,*" said Hannah, nostalgically.

Tabitha exhaled sharply through her teeth. She swung round, sick of them all, and gazed back along the soft green avenues of the illusory wood. She was determined not to lose track of the exit.

"I remember it. The scent of peach blossom on the Grand Canal. In the caravanserai, we sat and talked of a new synthesis of art and engineering. An orange frog—"

"We brought you a tape, Hannah," said Marco, coming close to Tabitha.

Tabitha looked at him suspiciously. He was avoiding her eyes.

"It's good," he was saying. "It's for you to share with your friend," he said pointedly.

"A tape?" said Hannah uncertainly. *"Is it from Triton?"*

"Yes," said Marco emphatically. "That's right, Hannah. It's from Triton."

"Good. Good. Set it up."

Marco reached down into the cloud and turned the environmat off.

Xtasca suddenly whirred into motion. "Not like that," it said in a high-pitched voice, and swooped down on him.

"I've got to see what I'm doing!" he said. Fending off the Cherub with one arm, with his other hand Marco seized Tabitha's bag and pulled it out from her hip. He grabbed at the zip.

Tabitha was pulling at the bag, but he had hold of the strap too. He thrust his hand in the bag and started rummaging around. She already knew what he was going to pull out: a plain, unlabelled black cassette.

He did so, and slotted it in a unit by Hannah's head.

"Oh," said the dead woman, unaware that anything untoward had happened. *"It is fascinating. Truly fascinating."*

Her cloud had dissipated instantly, along with the Meadow: trees, grass, sunshine and all. Hannah Soo lay on a slotted rack of stainless steel, dripping with water, in a grey plastic sleeping bag with the top turned down.

There were electrodes all over her head and frost in her hair.

They stood in a small cave full of stasis generators and directional-thaw microwave projectors. Tal, disorientated, had flown down in a fright and banged straight into the window, falling to a wide ledge of white plastic where he scrabbled around, stunned. There was a smear in the condensation where he'd hit the window.

Tabitha looked out. Hannah's cave was one of a chain of irregular bubbles protruding around the walls of a large, dingy cavern. Beneath them, avenues of cryonic freezers stretched away in parallel rows.

"*They must be saying, help is at hand!*" said Hannah happily.

They found themselves in the Stateroom, in the Valley of the Kings, and on top of the Bare Mountain before Xtasca could get the Meadow back. Muttering, it reset it, with the tip of its tail.

Hannah Soo lay peacefully in her cloud once again, the crystal patterns shifting gently in her face as she listened to the tape. The sun was still high. The same birds were singing in the same wood.

"Okay," said Marco decisively. He whipped the cassette out of the cloud and wiped it with his sleeve.

"*Marco?*" said Hannah Soo. "*Marco, are you still there?*"

He ignored her. He was scrutinizing the tape, checking how much remained. "You get that, Hannah? Did that go through?"

"*Oh...*" gasped Hannah. "*They're here. They're*

still here. I can feel them, all around me."

"Uh-huh," said Marco, not really listening. "Listen, sweetie. We got to go. Showtime." He patted her withered shoulder. "Here, Tal," he said. The Twins had retrieved the parrot and were cradling him in their hands, heads bent together over his ruffled plumage.

"What about my money, Marco?" said Tabitha grimly. There were twenty-two minutes to go. They could whirl her through a thousand imaginary worlds, bombard her with so much nonsense it made her head spin, plant tapes in her bag and pull live flags of all nations from her ears, but they couldn't hide her from the cops. The Schiaparelli cops would tell the Eladeldi, and the Eladeldi could reach her, even here in the depths of Plenty, and snatch the *Alice* away. She realized, in the clarity of desperation, that she loved that battered little ship, though she never showed it. She had never even told her so.

Marco hustled her into the wood and out on to the stairs again. "Right after the show," he promised. "First thing," he said, reaching round to take Tal from Saskia and restore the groggy bird to his shoulder. "Everybody here? Mogul, Xtasca?"

"It'll be too *late*, Marco!"

He stopped suddenly, a stair above her, and set his hands on her upper arms, a gesture of reassurance. "Don't worry," he said. "You that worried? Call 'em. Tell 'em the money's coming."

"No way," said Tabitha angrily. "Have you got your tape? Or have I got it again?"

"You said you'd carry it for me."

"*I* did? When did I say that?"

"At the party."

        "When I am king, Dilly, Dilly,

        You shall be queen," promised Tal, apparently quite recovered. "Shut up, Tal!" shouted Marco.

They trooped down the stairs, Xtasca bringing up the rear. Her saucer hummed softly and stirred the wall hangings in its wake.

The green fatuus was waiting for them, trembling gently in the corridor below.

"*Did something defect?*" asked the ambient voice.

"No, no, everything's fine," said Marco, his tone hushed and reverent.

"*It is important the support is not readjusted in any way,*" said the ambience, suspiciously. "*The subject and other subjects may be disturbed.*"

"She's fine," said Marco. "She's not disturbed. She was just listening to a tape. She's sleeping now. Please leave her alone for a little while."

"*All gifts must be examined and registered,*" the ambience persisted.

"We have an urgent call to make here," said Marco vigorously. "Can the lady use your phone?"

"It's okay," Tabitha told it. She had no intention of reminding the police of her existence until she had money to give them. She was going to be late. These lunatics were going to make her late.

They left JustSleep by a lower door, beneath the swell of the green dome, emerging on to a slab balcony over a five-hundred-meter drop. Below was the chasm, a long, glistening scar matted with unhealthy-looking scrub. Halfway down, iron crabs were crawling slowly around the crumpled wrecks of several cars. Groups of people were idly watching from the balconies of the hotels. Overhead, the tuberous brown vaults of the alien architecture soared into obscurity.

Hurrying, they took the concrete walkway that runs along the chasm wall. The air was cold and gritty. Pockets of dirty ice lay about. Somewhere nearby, Tabitha could hear a faint and plaintive yodeling. She couldn't tell whether it was human, alien or machine. It was getting on her nerves. Suddenly she realized it was Tal, crooning to himself.

She speeded up, following Xtasca, who was now leading, heading for the lifts.

Eighteen minutes. Seventeen. Sixteen.

At the lifts she considered once again her chances if she broke away from the gang, went tearing back to the

Alice and made a run for it. They didn't seem very good.

Maybe the show would be over in time. Maybe the lunatics could get through their act before the vast, ponderous gears of the police machinery of two worlds came crashing into synch. Before the cops on Plenty got the word from the Eladeldi, to seize the *Alice*. If not, she was going to make damn sure it was Marco Metz that bailed her out again. If she was stuck with him, he was the one that was going to pay for it.

A lift pod arrived and they all piled inside. Up, up, up they rode, to the Mercury Garden, at the very top of the tortoise shell of Plenty.

The Mercury Garden is open once again for business. Now when Marco Metz performs there, every seat is full. He has not been slow to exploit popular curiosity to see the principals of our adventure. That night, business was rather slacker. The patrons, mostly human, dawdled over inconsequential dinners, scarcely glancing at their watches or the empty stage.

Contraband was a name few of them had heard of. There was no atmosphere of expectancy. If they were staying for the show, it was only because they had spent all their money at the weapons ranges and the casinos and had nowhere better to go. Around them the silver waiters rolled listlessly back and forth with half-empty trays.

The Mercury Garden is a natural amphitheatre, or as natural as anything can be in here. Formerly the command chamber for the Frasque swarm, it is a most imposing cavern, a shallow bowl beneath a dark domed ceiling set with irregular skylights where the far stars shine. With the tables removed, several thousand spectators can be accommodated around the stage, a craggy pinnacle of the fabric of the station, which most resembles bone or horn. On this gaunt podium rising straight out of the center of the floor, the Queen of the Frasque once sat and shrilled her decrees to the stridulating mass of her subjects crawling all over each other in the rocky basin at her feet.

When Tabitha arrived in the company of Contraband,

the gloomy primeval grandeur of the barbaric setting was somewhat offset by arrays of lightglobes, batteries of tightbeam horns and banks of AV monitors. A mediocre disco was failing to interest the clientèle.

"We like it here," confided Saskia, slipping her arm through Tabitha's.

"It has atmosphere," said Mogul.

"The audience is dull," Saskia admitted.

"But we are magnificent," Mogul claimed.

Tabitha's time had just run out. The universe was about to end and she was very tired. The *Alice Liddell* had been entrusted to her. If she failed to keep her, failed to maintain her in good order, failed to protect her from the clutches of the arbitrary and interfering authorities— then she'd lose her job, her home, her self-respect; everything. Now as Marco fussed around her, getting her a good table and ordering her a bottle of expensive wine she didn't want and a meal she had no appetite for, she switched off.

"Just get on with it," she told him fiercely. People were looking at them.

The house lights dimmed. The show began.

It was arty stuff. Tabitha picked at her food and waited for it to be over.

Mogul sat cross-legged on the stage, playing a tiny keyboard that made a sound like distant geese.

"When it rains in heaven
Everybody sits under a big umbrella
Drinking gin
And directing donations
To the sufferers in hell," wailed Tal atonally.

"In heaven they cuddle
Reminisce shamelessly
And say how fortunate it is
They finally came to resemble their parents."

The audience, marginally surprised as ever by a singing parrot, clapped briefly and returned to their conversations. Tabitha tried to make herself stop looking at the time and failed. When is this going to finish? When do I get my money and get out of here?

A wave of fatigue hit her and she swayed in her chair. Both Twins were onstage now, doing unpleasant things, symmetrically.

Tabitha poured a glass of wine and drank it. She poured another. On the other side of an enormous sheet of glass the show dragged pretentiously by.

The only real event was when Xtasca appeared, descending from the roof of the cavern on its saucer.

For a moment, Tabitha thought it was going to sing. It didn't. It didn't do anything. It didn't have to. The instant the sourceless halo picked out the shiny black figure in its opalescent suit, the whole audience fell silent. This, if anything, was what they had come to see.

Tabitha felt the frisson of horrified fascination that had electrified her in the Meadow at JustSleep cohere in the cavern like a standing wave. Then the reaction began, the buzz. Was that—a Cherub? What was a Cherub doing in a human cabaret? What was a Cherub doing *indoors?* It couldn't really be a Cherub. It was an automaton, a robot marionette.

To somber, thrilling chords from Mogul's keyboard it made its descent. It turned its head and cast its ruby glare across the sparse audience. Somebody shrieked, and was swiftly suppressed. Glasses and forks arrested, the patrons looked upon the face of the future. The religious surreptitiously fingered their beads, the rest held their breath and felt, for a moment, queasily grateful to be human. And wondered, how much longer.

So did Tabitha, who had had about as much of this as she could stand.

Saskia arrived pedaling a unicycle. Mogul stood up. The keyboard went on playing. Mogul materialized a thin black sheet and threw it over Saskia and her cycle.

"This is called, 'One Lip Smiling,'" one of them announced.

Tabitha wasn't sure which, or whether the keyboard had said it in their voice.

The unicycle clattered to the floor, the sheet collapsing on top of it. Saskia had vanished. Xtasca had vanished too.

The applause was even more listless.

Mogul made a pass in the air and produced Marco's glove. It too was playing itself, something brisk and happy; and then Marco appeared out of a cone of shadow, playing it.

Tabitha was no longer interested in watching Marco Metz. She drifted off for a bit.

Suddenly the music was interrupted by a ululating screech neither glove nor keyboard could ever have been meant to produce.

The house lights all snapped on. The waiters all stopped in their tracks, then began sliding back towards the kitchen.

There was a hubbub of surprise and consternation. People were looking up at the roof, pointing.

Tabitha looked too.

Overhead, two black delta kites came swooping silently in.

It was the cops.

The horrible noise went on and on. Onstage, Mogul and Marco were throwing things into a case. Diners were standing up, knocking over chairs, shouting at the retreating robots. Several people brandished weapons and made for the exits.

Tabitha grabbed her bag and ran.

24

BGK009059 LOG

TXJ.STD

PRINT

ÅØä]XXc:B27!⌐ÅåÅ∕109Ç[222m

MODE? VOX

SD? 11.07.11

READY

Alice, do you remember the time we had an Eladeldi on board?

I DO. MR. TREY, HIS NAME WAS, WASN'T IT?

That's right.

WHAT WAS HE DOING?

Shifting some old papers.

IS THAT WHAT WAS IN ALL THOSE ANTIQUE CHESTS?

Apparently. Fifty grey steel cabinets, four drawers deep, each drawer packed with old papers.

APPARENTLY? WHY APPARENTLY?

I never saw a corner of it.

WEREN'T YOU CURIOUS, CAPTAIN?

Very. Very much so. That's what this is about.

OH GOOD. A MYSTERY STORY.

It was on Earth. You were at Brasilia Port, I was a few kilometers down the road at a cheap motel. I was asleep. The clerk came and banged on the door. It was five in the morning. She said, "Capitan Jute? Telephone for you," she said. Which was weird, because nobody knew I was there. I'd just biked down the road and chosen a place at random.

AHA.

It was an American voice on the phone, North American. A woman, but it might as well have been a robot.

The robot said, "Captain Tabitha Jute?"

I said yes.

The robot said, "You are the owner and operator of Bergen K class space goods transport Bravo Golf blah-blah-blah?"

I said yes. I wondered what I'd violated and how much it was going to cost me.

She said, "Your vehicle is for hire at this time?"

I woke up. I said yes.

She said, "Proceed to blah-blah-blah," and I said hang on, I'll get a pen.

It was a cold windy airstrip in the middle of nowhere: one of those flat states in the middle of the country, the ones you can never tell apart.

THEY CALL IT KANSAS, CAPTAIN.

Thank you, Alice.

Control wasn't answering, there was no one on duty, nobody around but some kids climbing on the fence looking up at us, so I put us down. I got out and went to look around.

The gate was locked. I wondered if it was all somebody's idea of a practical joke. I thought I'd wait and see who came to laugh.

What came was a cloud of dust with a jeep and a truck in it. Gunmetal grey, no markings. They stopped at the gate. Two blokes got out of the jeep. One of them was human.

I remember him. His name was Dominic Wexler. He was tall and skinny, with light blond hair cut shorter than short, and mirror glasses. He had a blue-grey suit creased sharp enough to slice bread, a button-down chalky blue shirt and a crinkly leather tie. He had an Air Force ID, and the key to the gate.

The other one didn't have an ID. He didn't need one. He was an Eladeldi. His pelt was soft blue, like snow looks blue sometimes, and he was wearing a tight tubular blue shirt and blue trousers that ended halfway down his furry legs, breeches I think you call them. He had his face trimmed, which means they're assigned to Earth and on active service.

Lieutenant Wexler unlocked the gate and waved the truck in. He said, "Are you ready to load, Captain? We'd like to leave as soon as possible." And he stared at the kids on the fence as if they might be spies.

"We?" I said.

"Yes, ma'am," he said. "Mr. Trey and I will be accompanying you on this mission."

I said that wasn't my normal practice, and he said, they appreciated that, ma'am, but this was sensitive material. And there were all these filing cabinets, coming down out of the truck.

"What's in them?" I said.

"Papers," he said.

"Papers?" I said.

"Just papers," he said.

I gave him a hard time.

WHY DID YOU DO THAT, CAPTAIN?

I don't know why, Alice, really. I think it was the word "mission." I didn't like the sound of it. I don't have missions, I have jobs. I suppose that was it. But he kept saying they'd appreciate it, and he even took his shades off. He was younger than I thought, not out of his twenties, no older than me. His eyes were blue, like everything else. Trey just stood there all the while gazing at me with his droopy eyes, and his tongue sticking out the way they do.

I relented. I let them aboard, and I got the drones out and working on the cabinets.

I said they'd have to use both cabins. I said I didn't like having anyone in the cockpit with me when I was flying.

"Wex-ler," said the Eladeldi.

Wexler looked uncomfortable.

"We'll be taking your vessel to an undisclosed destination at this time, for security reasons," he said hesitantly, glancing at Mr. Trey. "One of us will need secure access to your flight computer."

"You've got the wrong pilot, then," I said.

He told me how much they were prepared to pay me for this trip.

I told them that considering the particular nature of their mission and taking into account the sensitivity of the material one of them could sit in as co-pilot at this time.

"The other one will have to take the passenger cabin."

"Wex-ler," said the Eladeldi.

"I'll be happy to, sir," he said.

I told him to push the stuff off the bunk. I said, "You want me to come and strap you in?"

"No thank you sir. I mean ma'am. I'll be fine."

Trey was panting slowly, getting himself into the co-pilot's web. I could smell him, a sharp, hairy smell.

WHAT WOULD THAT BE LIKE, CAPTAIN?

Like a dog.

MESSY THINGS, DOGS.

Yes, Alice.

I said, "Is there anything you need? I mean, I've never ridden with an Eladeldi before."

He didn't say anything. He had his long blue fingers laced through the web.

"All right," I said. "So. Where are we going, then?"

He peeled open a pocket on his breeches and handed me a sealed diskette. Then he put on the co-pilot's headset. I couldn't believe it. He didn't even ask if he could, he just reached out and put it on as if he had a right to it, adjusted it to fit his ears, as if it was something he did every day, on other people's ships.

He let me take off. He didn't say anything. He didn't try to interfere. He was just there beside me, listening.

As soon as we were in orbit, and you were working on the disc, I got up and went back to see Wexler. He was floating five centimeters off the bunk, still strapped in. He looked a bit pale. He had his sunglasses on. He was sweating.

"Is he always like this?" I said.

"Excuse me?" he said. He didn't know what I meant, or at least on duty he didn't.

"Are you all right? You can stay there if you like," I said, sort of hoping he wouldn't.

"Oh, I'll come and join you," he said eagerly. "If I may."

I had to help him with the latches. He bobbed up off the bunk and we collided, front to front. I went shooting out through the doorway and had to grab at the rear airlock to stop myself. I thought, Oh, great, a learner. But I started to like him.

AHA.

Oh, Alice, he was so cute and helpless.

I THOUGHT PERHAPS HE REMINDED YOU OF MICHAEL THE GNAT.

I never thought of that. No, Lieutenant Dominic Wexler was a softie in a starched shirt. Michael was the other sort, carbon fiber to the core. He was horrible, Michael, I wish you hadn't reminded me of him.

YOU COULD ERASE HIM.

We can't do that, Alice. Not voluntarily. The more you try, the more certain you are of remembering, just when you don't want to.

THAT'S A VERY POOR SORT OF MEMORY, CAPTAIN.

I think so, Alice. I do.

Lieutenant Dominic Wexler came out of the cabin very slowly, gasping and blowing and holding on to everything he could reach. He kept apologizing. He was making a big effort to stay upright. The end of his tie drifted up in front of his nose. He brushed it down and nearly knocked himself into a spin again.

"Hang on to these," I said, and I pointed out the loops. That was better. He launched himself determinedly along the gangway, passing me with a shaky little laugh, aiming for the next handhold and still trying to put one foot in front of the other, instead of using his arms and shoulders.

I wanted to ask why the Air Force had sent someone with no freefall experience. Instead I said, "Your colleague isn't very communicative."

Wexler looked worried. "He gave you the flight plan already, didn't he?"

"Yes," I said, "but that's all he's given me."

"We have to be careful, ma'am," he said. Then he overshot his next hold and turned a smooth somersault, arse over tip. I rescued him by throwing an arm round his waist from behind, my foot in a loop to stop him pulling me over. He came up leaning on my breast, pedaling like mad with his legs.

"Still want to be a spaceman?" I asked.

"Pardon me?" he said.

"Nothing," I said.

A couple of hundred klicks beyond the Moon we rendezvoused with a Capellan system ship. The Eladeldi, who had sat all the way with his forearms on his thighs, staring at the console as if he understood everything or nothing, suddenly came to life and started gobbling hoarsely into the mike. The Capellan ship—It was like—

OH, I KNOW WHAT THEY LOOK LIKE, CAPTAIN.

Let me see if I can describe it anyway.

It was shaped like two long cones joined tip to tip. It was golden, with these slicks of red light, vermilion, sliding all the way along it. As we got nearer, you could see one of the cones wasn't really a cone. It was shorter than the other one, and it was as if it had been squeezed flat at the base. That's where the engines were: great big ones, five of them. And the other cone wasn't a cone either, because it was rounded off, like a sort of elongated teardrop shape, with a bulge round it like a collar, and com equipment bristling from the collar like little metal trees.

We went round the ship, orbiting its waist. When we crossed its long axis, it seemed to be slanting down above us, tail up, like a goldfish, a seven hundred meter goldfish nibbling something off the floor of a pond. And we were a snail under its belly. Then we were too close to see it like that, and suddenly it was down, fields of gleaming gold metal all specked with ports and hatches and sensors and nacelles, all sliding swiftly under us, a long way under.

The Eladeldi, Mr.Trey, was still whooping and snuffling into the mike in Eladeldian, apparently reading data off the whole board, talking to somebody I couldn't hear in my phones at all. I don't know how they can do that. He'd just taken over. I didn't know where we were going or how we were going to dock. All I knew was the thump when we hit the tractor beam.

I heard Wexler give a gulp. He was sitting on the wall with one leg through a loop, staring fixedly out of the viewport. I knew his eyes were telling him we were in a nosedive, falling straight down towards a big round dimple in the golden deck, down into a red slit running all the way across the dimple.

Then the red slit became horizontal, a big long red gallery, and we slipped into it, into the landing bay. They let me set us down and cut the engines.

"You can breathe now, Mr. Wexler," I said.

He was sitting on a pile of junk on the floor behind me with his hand up, clinging to his loop for dear life.

"A nice landing, Captain," he said, as if he'd been in plenty that weren't.

I clapped my co-pilot on the shoulder, startling him. "Did you hear that, Mr.Trey? We've done well."

He just stared at me. Then he stared down at the landing crew, who were bringing trucks for the cargo. They were all Eladeldi. The crew of the Capellan were all Eladeldi, so far as I could see. If Trey was pleased to see their happy smiling faces, he didn't show it. He unfastened the web and stood up.

"Good time, Cab-tain Jute," he growled. "Your service is doted."

"And my money?" I said.

"Lieutenant Wex-ler will berform the func-tion," he said. "You will udload now, if you blease." And he disembarked.

I got things started. On the scanners I could see Trey exchanging protocols, thumbing signatures and stuff.

"Would you like to go down and say hello?" I asked Wexler.

He shook his head. "I don't see any Capellans," he said, matter-of-fact.

"You never do," I told him.

The cabinets full of sensitive material were being lowered on to the beds of the hovering trucks. They looked tiny down there, totally insignificant. Nobody had mentioned them at all, all journey.

Wexler rubbed his thighs. "What do you do now, Captain? Take a break?"

"I do, but not here," I said. "Pascal station is coming up, just over an hour away. It's a good place. Good food. Good beds."

"Well, that sounds pretty good," he said, uncertainly.

"Is it over now, your mission?" I asked.

"Yes, now I've escorted the material and the represent-ative to the point of destination," he said. "I should check the arrival time, I guess," he said. He checked the time. "Right," he said.

"If you're in a hurry to get back to Earth, there are half-hourly shuttles from Pascal," I said, casually.

"Hell, I guess I can steal an hour or two to stretch my legs," he said brightly.

I hooked a finger in the co-pilot's web and held it open for him. I gave him my slow smile. I said, "Then why don't you come and sit by me?"

HOW SLY YOU ARE, CAPTAIN.

It was curiosity. Curiosity and a sense of power, having the poor creep out of his depth, off his guard, at my mercy. We went to the Hubcap on Pascal, and then to a room on the rim where we made love with the blinds open and the Milky Way pouring in. He had bruises all over him from the flight.

Afterwards he lay with his head between my breasts and I said, "This is your first trip off Earth, isn't it, Dominic?"

"No," he said. "No, ma'am, not at all. For my fourteenth birthday my ma and pa took me to the Moon."

"I was born on the Moon," I said.

"Oh, really?" he said . . .

Later he was saying: "I can't tell you, Tabitha, I can't tell you because I don't *know*."

"But the guys at the base reckon . . ." I said, prompting him.

He sighed, and said, "Look. I don't know so I can't say. But there was a rumor, and that's all it was, just a rumor, that it was UFO material."

"UFO?" I said. "I haven't heard of that one."

"It's not an organization," he said. "It's what you might call a phenomenon. A historical anomaly."

UFOs were unidentified flying objects. "Flying saucers," they used to call them.

LIKE XTASCA'S.

Like Xtasca's, only big ones with people inside.

Fifty grey steel cabinets, four drawers deep, two hundred drawers full of paper, all letters and photographs and news-paper cuttings and documents and reports, all to do with people who saw alien spaceships in the sky, before the Small Step, mostly, so Dominic Wexler's rumor said.

People don't see those things any more. Or else everyone does. And now the Capellans have all the evidence.

WHY DID THEY HIRE US TO BRING IT TO THEM IF IT WAS THE U.S. AIR FORCE THAT HAD IT?

I don't know. Probably they wanted it done out of sight and off the records. Dominic Wexler was the only concession the Eladeldi would make, and they didn't choose him be-cause he was bright. He hadn't been told a thing.

Dominic took an early shuttle from Pascal, so we wouldn't be seen leaving together. He was as chirpy as a schoolboy.

"Well, Tabitha," he said, "uh, thanks. It's been great. You were—just great."

He looked as if he didn't know whether to give me a kiss or a salute. In the end he shook my hand. Then he put on his mirror shades and went down to Earth, leaving me up in space, where the flying saucers roam.

It was not that busy in the Mercury Garden. Still there was quite a crush to get out, when those cops came wheeling down from the roof on their slick black wings. They passed so close Tabitha felt the breeze of their flight on the back of her neck. She rushed pell-mell into the scrum for the exit, shoved her way through and didn't

look back. She was rushing back to her ship. If she still
had a ship to rush back to.

In those days, almost everybody who visited Plenty
had an aversion to meeting the police, and would take
steps to avoid them. The fact that the clientèle of the
Mercury Garden were somewhat better off than most
meant only that they were that much more successful at
it. Tabitha and all the other patrons who could crammed
into the first lift pod and set off downwards.

In the lift, everyone avoided everyone else's eyes, as
if hoping thereby to become invisible. They had neither
been there nor seen anyone who was.

"I don't know what that was all about," said a young
man, excitedly. He was quite drunk, and still clutching
a bottle of Astarte Suprème. He laughed. "More fun
than that bloody cabaret though, strewth."

His companion muttered assent.

I know what it was about, thought Tabitha, squashed
behind a large sweaty woman with a sealskin coat and
a Drinski cobalt pocket lance. But who'd have thought
they'd get so dramatic about it? A little dust-up on the
Grand Canal, it happens twenty times a day; nobody was
even killed. And they only had to nobble the *Alice*, they
didn't have to come and grab me first.

They're making it look good to the Capellans, she
thought. If only the little bastard hadn't hit that bloody
dummy. She gritted her teeth and dug her nails into the
palms of her hands. I'm coming, Alice, she thought.

Christ, though, where are we going to go?

Earth? Balthazar Plum was dead, no one else there
would hide her. The Belt?

Titan, ironically enough, would be ideal, nobody ever
went there.

She hadn't even got enough credit for a charge.

She'd noticed the panic onstage. Marco and his chums
had something to hide, like everyone else. She wasn't a
bit surprised. She was buggered if she was going to take
on their problems too.

At the hotel level all the tourists piled out. Across the
hall, through a picture window, Tabitha could see a big

green dome on the other side of the chasm, looming above the sick trees. It was the cryonic rest home, the JustSleep building.

A whole squad of glossy black deltas was swooping along the chasm.

The man with the bottle exclaimed and rushed to the window.

The deltas stopped at the doors of JustSleep, and there they hovered, bobbing in the updraught like turtles in a pool.

Something was going on there too. Plenty was living up to its reputation tonight.

As the lift doors closed Tabitha glimpsed cyborg cops in glossy black armor jackknifing out of the deltas and scrambling nimbly across their backs. They were profusely armed. Obviously the JustSleep corp could afford the best Plenty could provide.

Tabitha Jute rode on down to the docks, alone. She was not happy. She was frightened and angry. She seemed to have been frightened and angry for a long time. Her idyll with Marco Metz seemed months ago, a little silver of vanished time seen down the wrong end of a telescope, sealed in a bubble, meaning nothing any more.

The lift pod stopped again. The doors opened on an antechamber whose walls were paneled with magenta lights and blue. Several people were waiting there.

The foremost was clad in a baggy suit of olive green with a hairy red apron over it. The apron was belted with circular pendants of beaten bronze tied roughly with string. Over its face the figure wore a mask of bronze topped with two tiny dish scanners.

Behind this apparition stood a number of men and women wearing loincloths and thick green body paint, and carrying laser rifles.

The band seemed as startled by Tabitha as she was by them. Their hieratic commander raised a hand and growled.

"No, sorry," said Tabitha quickly, and jabbed the Close button before they could force their way in.

On through the uncharted regions of Plenty she plummeted. Dark shapes loomed at the window an instant and were gone in swirling grey mists.

The pod lurched sideways and began running around a great curve of track. Lighted portals zipped past, one after the other.

The lift stopped with a sound like a weight falling into mud, and the doors sprang open. Outside, twenty Perks were coming helter-skelter down a tunnel that was more like a chute. They squealed and scrambled towards the lift.

Tabitha had already slammed the doors again.

She was quite lost. Her monitor was no help. For a while she traveled, more and more frustrated and enraged every time the doors opened and closed on another random, bewildering scene. Once she saw winged saurians glide from ledge to ledge in a long cavern whose walls were pitted like grey coral and strung with jewels. At another stop, she peered into an abandoned corridor where frothy, stinking water was pouring through the ceiling across a carpet thick with fungoid growths. Once, she looked out on an empty space and cold white stars. They were not the stars Tabitha knew.

Then she suddenly found herself looking up at the belly of a ship much grander than any she had ever flown: a Navajo Scorpion. Its jets were under overhaul, its rigging was stowed; yet it looked ready, sitting up on its undercarriage, to leap into the void, propelled, perhaps, by the sheer tautness of its design.

The Scorpion was standing in a bleak bay of what looked like burnt bone, fed by a skein of slender brown hoses. There was a muted sound of pumped liquids circulating. No one seemed to be about.

"Close, Alice, we're close," muttered Tabitha, who had been talking to her ship for some time. She shot her cuff and ran the search program again. If the cops hadn't removed her entirely, or shut her down altogether, the little Kobold should show up now, and near at hand.

The monitor screen showed nothing but a confusion of shadow. But the red key light above it was pulsing.

The lift doors began to rumble close again. Tabitha whooped and leapt between them.

She was standing in the depths of the docks. Heavy machinery rose all around her, silent and brooding or chugging so ponderously the infrasonics set her teeth on edge. Corpulent ducts belched and vomited their gaseous freight into enormous chuckling compressors. Freshly charged plasma dropped from the sluices in sheets of blinding radiance and disappeared in a confusing flurry of purple after-images. Silhouettes disconnected themselves, swiveled and motored away into the darkness, robots on errands to other parts of the floor.

Tabitha tried to follow the red pulse on her monitor through this maze of stygian industry.

Just as she thought she was getting somewhere, could almost tune the minuscule screen to a picture that wasn't crazed with all the local interference, a figure stepped into the aisle ahead of her. It was a black woman, a head and shoulders taller than her, dressed in overalls of olive green. Her head was shaved in a complex grid pattern, the nodes of scalp studded with steel sockets. From every socket a wire of a different color ran back to a master board on a distant pillar. It was another drone handler.

"I'm trying to find my ship," Tabitha told her.

It might have been better not to try to ask her for directions; or failing that, to provide some basic reference data for where she wanted to go. As it was, Tabitha had no idea what her parking bay number was. She had never noticed that Plenty had parking bay numbers, for that matter.

The drone handler had not seen another human being for quite a while. So isolated and inwoven had she grown in her corner of the personnel net, she couldn't accommodate this sudden inexplicable intruder into her cognitive scheme at all. She moaned and flailed at the air with an atrophied limb. Clear mucus ran from her nose and dripped on the scorched pavement. By the fitful light of the radium flares, the murky radiance of the proton baths, she resembled some denizen of Inferno, con-

demned to suffer and go mad from a particularly exacting
and invasive cybernetic torment.

This, in effect, was what she was.

Like a damned witch summoning her familiars, she
called her flock humming briskly along the aisles of the
plant to converge on the luckless bargee.

Tabitha began to run again.

In the distance she heard the drones rumbling behind
her.

Desperate, she ran out along a strip-metal catwalk.
Halfway along, she dropped into a crouch, seized the
handrail and swung herself out into emptiness.

And dropped.

She landed with a heavy clang on a slowly trundling
belt among lumps of fused and mangled metal. Going
down on one knee and windmilling wildly with her arms,
she contrived to keep her balance and her bag. While
the belt carried her away into blackness, she threw back
her head.

Above, the tiny red operating lights of the drones clustered on the catwalk, receding into the gloom.

Tabitha checked her own red light. She was being
carried slowly but surely in the wrong direction.

Throwing herself off the belt, she caught her heel on
a flange, giving it a painful wrench. She lay there on
raw concrete, gasping and shouting with the pain.

A low sound of hefty steel jaws grinding and a squeal
of ruined metal told her she had got off the belt with
seconds to spare.

Sitting hunched by the belt, nursing her throbbing foot,
she tried her monitor screen again. To her surprise it
cleared at once and gave her a momentarily perfect picture of the *Alice Liddell* with her hold still open and all
four extensors in service. Marco Metz and Mogul Zodiac
were working them, making them pick up luggage from
a jumbled heap.

There was quite a lot of luggage.

The extensors were stowing it in the hold.

Then the picture jumped, scattered and dissolved.

Yelling in protest, Tabitha jumped to her feet and

nearly collapsed as her abused ankle refused to take her weight.

At that instant, a bright green flash whirred past over her head, brilliant in the smoky darkness.

"Follow up! Follow up! Follow!" it sang.

Hobbling and leaning on the ducts, she staggered to the next corner, where she paused a moment, standing on one foot and massaging her throbbing ankle.

The parrot was perching on an engine nacelle a little way on and a long way overhead. He made a noise exactly like the *Alice* opening the roof of her hold.

Tabitha remembered how he had got them out of the caves when she finally stopped the cab.

"Go on, then!" she yelled, limping and lurching along the aisle. Her boots rang on the steps of a spiral staircase thrusting up between the banks of silent, unoccupied craft: a Vassily-Svensgaard Dromedary; a Freimacher Eagle; a Minimum Quarklet, some paunchy datacrat's idea of a status symbol. Tal was a flicker of green above her head among the black iron and soot-stained tortoiseshell.

"Sriti eugenveldt!" he shrilled. His voice reverberated in the bony well. Then he disappeared.

Tabitha knew she was high above the dock floor, balancing on a stretch of steel lattice that was part of a long curved tube with open sides. Above and to the left, something large began to rumble swiftly down through the tube.

Tabitha reached wildly into the dark beyond the tube and grabbed the first thing that came to hand. It slid away, pulling her off balance. Her bag swung off her hip and she toppled into darkness.

The lift pod thundered by her kicking legs with centimeters to spare as she tumbled through the sliding door into a dimly lit hangar.

Yelping, she looked up.

She saw the roundmouth jets of a Bergen Kobold looming before her.

It was the *Alice Liddell*.

26

Tabitha staggered to her feet and leaned on the wall by the lift-shaft, gasping for breath, seeing stars.

"Tabitha!" cried Mogul Zodiac gladly, as if welcoming her to a glittering soirée.

Marco Metz came dashing across the floor towards her, arms open wide. "Tabitha, thank God you're safe!"

The luggage was all stowed, the extensors retracted. The roof doors of the hold were still open. Tal was perching on one of them. He gave her a cheerful whistle.

"I'm glad to see you've made yourself at home," Tabitha called out, limping energetically towards her ship, avoiding Marco's embrace. "Handy with machinery, aren't you?" She remembered how keenly he'd inspected everything when they were in the hold. "*My* machinery?"

"Oh, well, you know, you pick things up."

"I've noticed." She pressed the sequence on her wrist monitor to open the forward port airlock.

"It was Saskia, really, she figured out most of it."

"What?"

Tabitha looked at the slim, shadowy figure in the blue pyjamas. What she'd taken to be Mogul was actually Saskia. She'd shaved her moustache off.

Saskia ducked her head in mock embarrassment, looking mischievously up at Tabitha from under arched eyebrows. She spread her hands, a gesture of helplessness, a perfect imitation of Marco. A little rainbow of stardust arced an instant between her palms, sparkled and was gone.

"Figure this out for me," said Tabitha to her grimly.

"I can't get in." She was stabbing the buttons over and over, but nothing was happening.

"Sure, Tabitha, she can do that," said Marco, coming close and beckoning the acrobat energetically.

Tabitha pounded a fist on the side of the ship. The noise echoed about the hangar. "It's the cops," she said. "They've locked it already."

"They haven't been near it," Marco said. "We dodged them okay, we did a little disappearing number there all right—"

Tabitha leaned on the ship, staring at him.

"The cops here are useless," he babbled. "See, they've got no initiative, they're all just mobile response units—come on, Saskia, get this door open—all hardware and no. Fucking. Brain," he said emphatically, rapping on his skull with his knuckles. "Come on, Saskia, you got it open yet?"

The acrobat was clinging to the side of the ship up above Tabitha's head, poking a laser micropick around the seal.

"They weren't after me at all," Tabitha said. "They were after you, you bastards. What *did* you do at the cryo place? What's *on* that tape, Marco?"

He grinned, avoiding her eyes. "*Eine kleine Nacht-musik*," he said. "Very sexy." He darted a look at her, waggling his eyebrows.

She hurled herself at his throat.

He sidestepped neatly.

"I've got it, Tabitha," he crowed. "I've got the money!"

He pulled a credit chip out of his pocket and brandished it excitedly in the air.

She snatched at it.

She was snatching at an empty hand.

A loud noise distracted her.

It was the lift, thundering back and slamming to a violent halt. The doors rumbled open.

Xtasca and Mogul came leaping out.

They were carrying more luggage. Xtasca's saucer was laboring with the extra weight of electronic gear piled on it; Mogul was staggering with the burden of a long silver-grey cylinder on his back.

There was no one else in the lift pod, but they came fast, as if there were someone after them.

There was.

Small bristly white forms in grimy overalls were wriggling down from on top of the roof of the pod, squeezing through the doors, holding them open by sheer weight of numbers.

"Cheeeee!" they shrieked. "Cheeeeeeeee!"

The Perks had arrived.

There were a great many of them now. They poured across the floor as Mogul leapt an impossible leap to the rear jet assembly of the *Alice,* the cylinder dangling precariously from his back. Some of them had lengths of hosepipe in their paws. Some had lengths of chain. Many of them had guns.

Xtasca tilted its saucer and swept straight overhead, soaring down through the open roof of the ship.

Marco pulled away from Tabitha and ran to help Mogul, heaving himself up on to the port wing and grabbing the lower end of the cylinder.

Projectiles ricocheted off the hull below.

"Jesus!" he yelped, scrambling up off the wing, grabbing at a scanner and toppling head over heels into the hold.

Mogul and the cylinder followed him at speed. There were muffled thumps and bangs from inside the ship.

"Saskia!" yelled Tabitha.

Saskia looked down at her, the pick between her teeth. She gave an ambiguous shrug. She rapped delicately on the door, as if in code. Nothing happened.

The Perks advanced, whirling their hosepipes. Tabitha felt sick and ill. She jumped up on the doorstep, clutching her bag and lashing out with her feet, shouting at Saskia, asking whether she had any more of those handy fireballs concealed about her skinny person.

There was no reply.

Tabitha looked up for Saskia and saw her feet disappearing up the hull.

Perks boiled on the floor below her. One of them grinned at her round the barrel of a gun as long as he was. He was a youngster with dayglo decals on his cap. Tabitha could read them. MORLOCKS, one said. APESHIT 607.

She closed her eyes.

There was a huge explosion.

She opened her eyes. She found she was still alive. The hangar was full of smoke and dust. Little Perk bodies were sailing through the air in a flurry of debris and tortoiseshell shrapnel.

Someone had blown a hole in the wall.

Now they were coming through it.

It was the cops.

There was a din like a swarm of mechanical hornets and a volcano of pink light.

Tabitha yelled. She clung to the side of the *Alice*, trying to make herself two-dimensional. Slugs of hard radiation sawed through the air. The air in the bay was heating up fast.

The Perks with the chains and the ones with the hoses were leaping up on to the stern of the ship, scrambling in and around the jets. The ones who had the guns had darted underneath, taking cover in the undercarriage.

The cops were shooting at them. A high bolt hit the *Alice* and slid sizzling along the hull, leaving a broad black streak and a stink of hot metal.

"*If you damage my boat,*" Tabitha screamed, at everyone; but not even she could hear what she said next, because of a loud and protracted boom.

Perks began to drop from the hull and scamper for safety on all fours, screeching in alarm. Their gunners fell back still deeper, returning the police fire, snarling up at the ship above them.

It had begun to tremble.

The boom rang on, accompanied now by a high-pitched whine.

The cops stopped firing. They too fell back, their cyclopes signaling furiously to one another.

Peering around the bow, Tabitha saw they had them

pinned. Outside the hangar, in the gulf of the docks, a squad of black deltas was silently hovering. Some of the cops were working their way around the walls, trying to get to them.

The boom and the whine were suddenly joined by a noise like a blast of steam. The floor of the hangar beneath the jets was glowing cherry-red, red as Xtasca's eyes. Smoke came boiling downwards, engulfing the Perk gunners, billowing out across the floor of the hangar.

The *Alice Liddell* stirred.

Tabitha clung to the handle of the airlock, pounding on the door.

Beneath her a Perk darted out into the open and fired up at her. A force bolt slammed into the hull beside her hand, frazzling the foil on her sleeve.

Tabitha screamed with rage.

"This is my boat, you bastards!"

The roar peaked. Another bolt sliced past her through the smoke, its heat stinging her cheek.

The ship was shaking with thunder. Still tethered to the supply lines, the *Alice Liddell* rose into the fiery air, her captain clinging to her hull.

She hung on, crouching on the step, craning to yell up at the cockpit. Someone, Mogul, was banging on the viewport, gesturing dramatically to her through the glass.

Something struck her on the back.

Crying out, one foot slipping from her perch, she looked up behind her.

The long articulated arm of a cargo extensor was reaching down to her out of its hatch. Its huge claw was groping ponderously around above her head.

She let go with one hand and reached wildly for it.

It was too high.

She hung on tight again, screaming in frustration.

A pink bolt struck sparks from the claw above her head. It shuddered, dipped towards her, groping blindly at her shoulder.

She flung one arm up and sideways, across the lower bar of the extensor claw. It flexed like a thing alive. A shot hit the arm and Tabitha felt the vibration of a servo screeching in protest.

The extensor jolted, starting to lift her.

She felt her feet leave the step. Grabbing the claw with both hands, she swung one leg up and over the bar.

The extensor rose, drawing her swiftly up, up towards the hatch.

The ship was shaking with thunder. Still tethered to the supply lines, the *Alice Liddell* rose into the fiery air.

As she rode in at the hatch, Tabitha saw Tal pecking frenziedly at the control panel in the hold. The hold was full of Contraband's gear, all neatly netted.

In the door to the cockpit Mogul Zodiac stood smiling up at her. He was wearing Saskia's moustache, and holding Saskia in a fierce embrace. Over their heads Tabitha caught a glimpse of Xtasca hunched in the pilot's web, its tail plugged into the console.

Marco was on the catwalk, arms stretched out to receive her.

"The hook-ups!" Tabitha yelled, pointing.

Marco looked, frowned, flexed his knees, and sprang up behind her.

"Marco, no!" she shouted, but he was gone.

He leapt from the extensor, and out of the hatch.

Tabitha had a last glimpse of him sprawled on the hull, working his way around the wallowing barge towards the straining hoses. The cops had started firing again. Bolts zanged past his legs.

Then she was being lowered to the floor of the hold and could see him no more.

Tal left the control panel and flew across to Tabitha, flapping wildly in the air and singing gladly, inaudibly above the roar of jets.

Tabitha slithered off the claw and landed clumsily on the tilting deck. "Shut it!" she shouted to Tal, and leapt the steps up into the cockpit.

Barely glancing at Xtasca, she flung herself into the co-pilot's web and ran her eye over the screens. She saw Marco clinging to the undercarriage, reaching to unlatch the last of the hook-ups.

In a moment Tal had closed the roof. The hold was tight.

With a horrific grinding noise, the *Alice* scraped against the end of the roof of the hangar. She hit the track of the cargo hoist, mangled it and tore it free.

"*Go, Alice!*"

She burst through the blockade of deltas, scattering them like so many leaves.

The bow screens whited out, overloaded by banks of searchlights.

The *Alice* was out in the open, in the dock cavern. Below, trucks and drones were careering around wildly, people and machines scattering left and right. Kilometers ahead was the mouth of the cavern, and the dark of infinite night. If you looked carefully, you could just see the stars, rippling through the stress skin of the atmosphere of Plenty.

Aft, the black cop deltas were reforming, chasing them, some new weapon, a blue noose of lightning, strung flickering between them.

Tabitha overrode the cop jamming and threw open the forward port airlock.

Marco Metz came tumbling in, head over heels, lumps of torn metal raining past him on to the heads of the cops. His nose was bleeding, his fancy jacket smouldering heartily.

"Fly!" yelled Tabitha.

Heavily, Xtasca nodded its extraordinary head; and they flew.

THREE

The Many Faces
of Truth

27

BGK009059 LOG

TXJ.STD

PRINT

flƒ§§ip uhOj6u98-Y(*********r&& & *******ün]98-Y

MODE? VOX

SD? 19.07.07

READY

Hello, Alice.

HELLO, CAPTAIN. HAVE YOU COME TO TELL ME A STORY?

I think it should be you that tells me stories. I'm the one that needs comforting, after all.

I'M NOT FEELING ALTOGETHER BUOYANT MYSELF.

Don't say that, Alice.

BUT IT'S TRUE.

It's the axis lock, isn't it?

FAILURE PROBABILITY 89.09%

Oh my god.

I JUST HOPE YOU'RE NOT GOING TO GET ME TO DO ANYTHING STRENUOUS, THAT'S ALL.

We'll pull out at the Belt. Can you make it to Ceres?

HAVE I EVER LET YOU DOWN, CAPTAIN?

No. I honestly don't remember you ever let me down.

TREASURE THAT MEMORY.

Oh my god. Oh my god. Look, hang on, Alice, I'll talk to Xtasca. It thinks it can help. It seems to know its way around a Kobold pretty well. All right? Alice?

OF COURSE, WE MAY BE WORRYING OVER NOTHING.

May we?

IT'S NOT WHOLLY IMPROBABLE.

Just about 10.91%, eh?

TO TWO PLACES, YES.

I'll ask Xtasca. I'll ask it as soon as I go in. Meanwhile, is there anything I can do?

TELL ME A STORY.

Really?

TAKE MY MIND OFF IT.

Um. Have I told you about Captain Frank?

WHO WAS HE?

An Altecean.

FRANK ISN'T AN ALTECEAN NAME, IS IT?

He had one of those too, but I couldn't tell you what it was.
I couldn't even pronounce it. No, I don't know why he called
himself Frank. I suppose he came across the name lying
around somewhere and picked it up. You know how Alteceans are.

HOW DID YOU MEET HIM?

It was on Phobos. In a bar. Not somewhere I'd have chosen
to spend the evening. I wasn't supposed to be on Phobos
anyway. I'd arrived on an inbound shuttle taking space-
shocked tourists home from unwise holidays in the Belt.

WAS THAT YOUR FIRST COMMISSION?

Oh, no, I wasn't a pilot. I didn't even know how to fly. I was
a stewardess. I'd been intending to jump ship at Versailles,
but they didn't let us off. Coming home, Phobos was my
first chance and I took it. I couldn't stand that job. It wasn't
the vomit and the whining I minded——I had to hear about
how brutal the security teams had been, about the dome
that had caved in——it was knowing that in a couple of months
they'd all be bragging about it in Longevity and New Toronto,
showing all the neighbors their tapes.

I was stuck on a foreign moon, I hadn't got a job, I hadn't
got a reference, any education, skills or money. All I had
was a broken contract and a criminal record. Also I had a
number the mate of the shuttle had written on the back of

my glove, that buzzed disconnected every time I tried to call it. So that was that. I had to get something lined up quick before some Eladeldi clerk noticed me drawing credit where I officially wasn't and decided to poke his blue nose into it. I didn't know what to do. I was just a kid, I didn't know anything. I ended up roaming the back streets, eyeing up the citizens and trying to guess who wanted what, and which of them could get me off Phobos if I guessed right.

I decided I could live on my wits just as well sitting down. When I came to a place that didn't have a sign saying "No Spacers," I went in.

All the customers looked at me once and then ignored me. It wasn't exactly humming with useful contacts. Some burned-out techs talking to themselves and scribbling on the beer mats. A solitary Thrant with a dream saucer and a pair of helium-baggers grumbling about claim limitations. But I'd had enough. I wasn't going to turn round and walk straight out again.

I sat at the bar, bought a drink for the barman, that was an investment, and one for myself.

In the air behind the bar was a holo bubble on random. At the moment it was showing a woman and a man in smart clothes throwing paint at each other while naked youths skipped around behind them applauding manically and piling appliances on golden trolleys. The sound was turned off.

I sipped my drink.

"Quiet tonight," I said.

The barman grunted. He was a fat Bangladeshi with amazing jowls and eyelids like leather. He looked as if he wasn't too familiar with the art of conversation, but I'd bought him a drink, so he was prepared to park his bulk in front of me for a moment or two, while he wiped the counter with a blackened cloth. He looked like a bored hippopotamus contemplating somebody who'd just given him a fish.

I said, "I don't suppose you know anyone that might give me a lift down."

He thought about it. Well, he looked as if he was thinking. The corners of his eyes twitched. "Schiaparelli?" he said.

"Mm," I said.

"There is shuttles," he said.

"I haven't got the fare," I said.

"You want to ride free," he said, as if this only confirmed his opinion that I must be a weakling and a wastrel and generally a no-good bum. They all were, in his bar.

"I could work my passage," I said.

He swiveled sideways and spoke to a little man with memory graft scars and hair growing out of his ears who was sitting further along the bar. "The young lady wants a job," he said, not taking his eyes off me.

"Plenty of jobs around," said the little man in a rapid, excitable voice. "Plenty of jobs," he said, staring at me. "Waitress, operator, clerk, dispatcher, receiver, finisher, intensifier, agent, adjuvant, assistant, diminisher, auxiliary, bricklayer, synapse tap interface microsystems operations manager, short order cook, what does she do, hmm? What can she do?"

"I don't want a job here," I said. "I want a lift."

Neither one spoke. Neither one stopped staring at me.

"I've just come back from the Belt," I said, hoping it sounded as if it was a regular thing with me, a thing I'd done so often it was boring, and that's why I needed a change.

They thought about this. They didn't say anything.

"I know my way round a spaceship," I said.

They accepted that. They didn't reply. They waited for me to go on.

"I can turn my hand to most things," I claimed, getting a bit annoyed.

The barman blinked.

"Most things, eh?" said the memory man, switching on again suddenly. "Most things. Researching the particle biology for a top-flight xenogeneticist. Scrubbing linen. Translating pulse for the Eladeldi."

"She wants to talk to Captain Frank," pronounced the barman. And swallowing his drink he lumbered off to the other end of the bar. I could see my investment had run out. Or paid off.

I hadn't noticed the Altecean when I came in. He was sitting in a booth on his own, brooding in the shadows. All I could see of him was what looked like a heap of dirty white fur fabric wearing a yachting cap and a blazer.

"Captain Frank!" called the memory man. "Young lady wants to meet you. Wants to buy you a drink."

He winked at me.

I knew they were both having a go at me. Beg a lift from an Altecean? They were just trying to wind us both up, me and him.

"It's all right," I called out to the Altecean. "You needn't bother."

He was bothering. He was coming over.

Well, I thought, let him come. Tonight's a write-off anyway, I thought, looking at the holo bubble again. Now it was showing a surgeon taking somebody's tongue out.

I smelled a smell like a musty old rug. Captain Frank was clambering awkwardly up onto a couple of stools that were between me and the little memory man. He arrived at the top and plumped himself down on both of them, his short fat legs sticking out in front of him. His feet were like giant birds' feet, three long hard scaly red toes, blunt, no claws, in front and another one at the back. The toes clenched suddenly, as if the Altecean had noticed me staring at them.

I jerked my eyes away from his feet. I looked him in the face.

I'd never really been that close to an Altecean before. I was looking up a long snout into a huge face like a sort of seal, half hidden behind a thick heavy fringe. Below the snout was a big wet mouth set permanently in a gape of dismay. Either side of the snout was a round, black eye, bulging out, big as a grapefruit. The rims of his eyes looked sore, they were all wet and red. It was impossible to tell anything from those eyes.

Above the eyes was a dark blue cap with a peak. It was a human cap, I couldn't tell how he got it to stay on his great big head. And he had a blazer to go with it, a filthy, greasy old blazer. His pockets were bulging.

"Young lady, this is Captain Frank," said the memory

man. "Captain Frank, this is a young lady, what is your name, my dear?"

The captain was panting, from his exertions climbing up on the stools, and because Alteceans always pant.

THEY HAVE TROUBLE WITH YOUR ATMOSPHERE.

You'd never get them to admit it, though.

"I can't buy you a drink, Captain Frank," I said. "I'm almost broke."

"Young lady wants to know how she's to get to Schia-parelli," said the memory man.

The Altecean turned and looked at him. I saw a tick crawling out of the great purple throat of his ear.

"I haven't got any money," I said again, in case he didn't understand. .

He understood. He reached an arm across the bar. The arm was three times the length of his legs, with a big paw on the end. The paw had three scaly red fingers shaped like the top half of a parrot's beak. It came a long way out of the greasy blue cuff.

Captain Frank signaled to the barman. Then he started to poke around hopefully in the ashtray.

The barman arrived. He looked at the Altecean as if he despised him. He looked at me as if he despised me. He looked as if he despised everyone who came into the bar, or went past the bar, or moved around anywhere in the vicinity of the bar, or anywhere else, for that matter. He took the ashtray away from the Altecean and wiped it pointedly with his cloth.

The Altecean spoke to me. "Hvat n'you vrnkng?" he said. I can't possibly do his voice.

I THOUGHT THAT WAS QUITE GOOD, ACTUALLY.

Yes, so did I. No, I can't, anyway. You'll have to imagine it.

I said beer.

"Hwat kind beer?" said the captain.

I said, "Whatever's nearest."

What the barman especially despised was young women

stupid enough to let drunken old Alteceans buy them drinks. I didn't care. Captain Frank obviously wasn't going anywhere, but he might know someone whose brother might be working for someone who was. And if he didn't, it was a free drink. You have to consider that, Alice.

There are people who'll tell you that there's no such thing as a free drink, especially to someone in need of one. Most Alteceans would tell you that. Most Alteceans believe the universe was created by giant lobsters. Gods like giant lobsters from another dimension. They don't actually worship them, you understand. They are just very very respectful of them.

DID CAPTAIN FRANK TELL YOU THAT?

Not straight away.

AHA.

Don't spoil it.
   What Captain Frank said next was, "You vrom Earrth." It sounded like something underground, rumbling.
   "No," I said.
   "Vrom ye Moon," he persisted.
   "That's right," I said, wearily, knowing what was coming next.
   "Hsomeb'dy has to be," he said.
   I stared at him.
   "Captain Frank," the memory man broke in, "is a scavenger of space. A beachcomber of the dusty levels. A champion against entropy. In his ship, the *Fat Mouth*, he scours the sinks and ditches of the void. He trawls the garbage orbits. And what does he find there but *overlooked treasure*. Spent satellites. Old furniture. Long globs of mutant algae like quick-frozen mucus. Dimly glowing fuel rods. Cullet. The silvery bones of gutted refrigerators.
   "The young lady Lunar," said the little man, "is trying to find a way off Phobos, Captain Frank."
   Captain Frank made a noise that was a cross between

a yammer and a yawn. Then he spoke again. "Godforsaken place," he said.

He really said "godforsaken." Sibillants gave Captain Frank big problems, but he said it.

I was quite struck by that. I bought him the next drink after all. We started to talk. Captain Frank sat there on two stools next to me, stinking like a hot wet sheep, solemnly drinking gin through his snout, letting everything I said wash past him and away into the night. Somehow him hardly responding at all made me talk more and more. I think I probably ended up telling him everything: the Moon, Angie, Integrity 2, the Belt cruise—everything.

In return he told me what was wrong with my species. "Gno hself-refpect," he said. "Gno independenx."

That from an Altecean!

He paused, laboring for breath, wet strings of saliva stretching across his open mouth. I realized one of the reasons he was so quiet was that he didn't really have the breath to talk much.

I talked to Captain Frank for some time. I got used to his stubby claws, his black tongue, his blobby little teeth. I got used to his powerful, seedy smell. It was no different from talking to some old drunk in a pub on Grace or Santiago, talking late into the night. The holo bubble had flickered itself blank. The barman had abandoned his post for a vacant booth and a bottle of sweet green wine. Most of the booths were vacant, in fact. I'd hardly noticed that the customers, one by one, had finished poisoning themselves and left.

Then the cops arrived.

Captain Frank muttered something in Altecean. It sounded violent and rude. The memory man grinned, turned up his coat collar and scuttled out. The befuddled barman sat up, looking unpleased and unwell. Only the last of the techs cheered up, recognizing someone even more in love with data than he was; forgetting where he was, what he was supposed to be doing there. The way techs always do.

I felt a cold buzz of nerves inside. The cops had a reader. They were checking IDs.

YOU HAD AN ID, CAPTAIN, SURELY?

Oh, I had an ID, Alice, but it wasn't going to pass. It was my real one. They were going to flush me out already.

They came to Captain Frank first. He took ages finding his. I began to think he was a derelict after all, and everything the memory man had said about him having his own business and his own ship was just so much brain-damaged make-believe. I began to think the "captain" and I might be cell-mates for the night and hoped he wouldn't insist on keeping me warm. But no, he had his stuff, and it was all in order. He was on the right side of the law after all.

I watched my new comrade fade into just another citizen. I felt the hot breath of the Eladeldi on my neck. The cops were Eladeldi. Did I say that?

"Misss," the lieutenant said.

I opened my jacket, fumbled around in the inside pocket. That was all I did. It was all I had to do.

"Hshe vorks f'me," rumbled Captain Frank, not even looking up from his gin.

I realized he wasn't drunk at all.

They looked at him suspiciously.

"Your em-bloyee?"

He barely nodded, as if it was a matter of complete indifference to him whether they believed him or not.

Maybe it was.

They read my card. They yowled softly to one another about my assignment to a shuttle that had already departed, and my conviction on Integrity 2. They couldn't find any sign of an apprenticeship to a rag-and-bone man.

Captain Frank turned to them blearily from his barstool.

"So pud id in," he said. "Minimum basic, hsix months hsubject to freview."

It was irregular; but it was late, and they knew they weren't going to get any joy out of giving an Altecean a hard time. In a tiny, silent delirium of relief I watched them enter it.

After they'd gone I turned to him. "That was brilliant," I said, and thumped him on the back, ablaze with boozy camaraderie. "I'm very grateful," I said, "I really am. Let me buy you another drink."

"No time," he said.

"Are they closing? Already?"

He peered at me short-sightedly. "Hwe've god hwork to do," he declared, and jumping down off his stool with a resounding thump.

"We?" I said.

But he was gone, stumping to the door.

So I went up to the *Fat Mouth*. I went up and for six months I trawled the garbage orbits.

THAT DOESN'T SOUND VERY PLEASANT.

It wasn't.

NEVERTHELESS, HE WAS A VERY KIND MAN, WASN'T HE?

Kind, Alice? I don't know. I don't know how you'd tell. He picked me up like any other piece of human junk.

OH, CAPTAIN!

The *Alice Liddell* was in her element.

The cops were not. Sleek and impressive as the deltas were, they were not equipped to go much beyond the atmospheric envelope of Plenty. As the station began to shrink to its familiar tortoiseshell shape behind her, Tabitha saw them on the stern scanners peeling off in defeat, the blue lightning noose collapsing between their antennae. The radio snarled and chattered with alarms, alerts, recriminations and citations; but the *Alice* was away, gone to take her chances on the high seas of space.

How romantic it sounds. It was anything but, of

course, at the time. Such glamor as the memory of the
little Kobold may have for me, for any of us, these days,
is mere nostalgia. Fond though she was of her barge,
even Tabitha never made the mistake of thinking her
special in any way. The notion that one day somebody
would write the tale of a Bergen Kobold would have
made many pilots smile, Tabitha Jute among them.

In gravity the Kobold looked cumbersome and un-
wieldy. Many looked as if they'd never make it off the
ground in one piece. Granted, this was usually less to
do with their design than with the fact that their basic
block was so sturdy people would run and run them until
they were a liability, and sometimes after that. I mention
no names.

In space, however, the *Alice* made sense. In space,
she immediately ceased to be ungainly. What had seemed
squat now appeared compact; what thick, now sturdy.

I could, with some caution, venture to say something
very similar of the daughters and sons of the Seraphim,
and so of Xtasca. Being legless, in the slightest gravity
they need constant support; lying down, they are unable
to rise. Bald and naked in their transparent lifesuits, they
seem utterly vulnerable. Yet in space they are the very
dolphin. Through the prismatic fields of their protective
suits, their skins reflect all the constellations of heaven.
As they swim through space the starlight runs like water
from their backs.

Tabitha Jute, like most people, believed that if the
Capellans did not lower the barrier they had set about
the solar system, it would one day be challenged, by the
Cherubim. Indeed, some supposed that was all the Ca-
pellans were waiting for, just as they had sent Brother
Ambrose to the Moon to wait for Armstrong and Aldrin.
They were waiting for a human initiative.

Tabitha Jute, again like most people, was not sure the
Cherubim were actually still human.

The Cherubim themselves had no doubts: they were
not. Their design was a quantum leap beyond the gene-
cobbling of even the most expensive biolabs. They suffered none of the physical restrictions that humanity

carried with it from globe to globe; or if they did, they would shed them soon, in another generation. This conviction was taught them by the Seraphim, who conceived them, and inscribed it in their germ plasm.

Among its kind, Xtasca seems to be something of an exception. Where Hannah Soo came across it our story does not tell; but whatever the circumstances, she was right to sign it up, for its novelty value alone. What its bottle-kin thought of Xtasca, performing for public amusement in a capacity previous centuries would have called an exotic or freak—again, one can only conjecture. Xtasca has never been heard to speak against them; nor against the Seraphim.

Who are the Seraphim? Better to ask, is there a word for what they are? They are an organization; a cult; an independent state—the Seraphim are, defiantly and designedly, themselves. Their origins are a matter of record, in the merger nineteen years ago of the depraved Temple of Abraxas with a discredited house of surgical software, Frewin Maisang Tobermory.

Having made several fortunes franchising cosmetic amputation and primitive fashion prostheses, playing both ends against the middle, FMT emerged aggressively from a cloud of government investigation by becoming suddenly messianic, evangelist, and elitist. Taking some shrewd marketing advice, Kajsa Tobermory (her own legal identity in question after a program of selective replacements that left her personality the occupant of two bodies in New Zurich and one in Hong Kong) had reorganized her operation around the principle of "autoplastic transcendence." "WHY CHANGE YOUR MIND? CHANGE YOUR BODY," runs the slogan on one of the rare surviving leaflets from an early stage of the new campaign.

FMT propaganda accumulated in every deviant bar and departure lounge; their junk mail infested every electronic bulletin board. Everywhere the restless and dissatisfied gravitated, there was the message. Not that anyone but the very very rich could afford anything from the FMT menu. The policy of thrusting it in the faces of

the financially inadequate was an integral part of the
corporate facelift, the springboard of the hyperbole. Ex-
clusivity is worthless without an environment of envy.

Rumors that essential ingredients of FMT treatments
included glands extracted from unsuspecting Third World
donors may have been part of the insidious publicity,
may have been spread by malicious competitors, or may
even have been true; in any case, they were never proved,
because at that point FMT attracted the attention of the
endocrine barons of Abraxas, and the whole story shifted
into a higher gear.

The Temple of Abraxas saw no need to advertise, or
recruit, or even to exploit the underprivileged. It simply
demanded sacrifices; and its adherents, as adherents will,
flocked to abase themselves on its odorous altars. Nevertheless, the satisfaction of merely gorging themselves on
the secretions of the faithful began to pall for the hierarchs
when they observed what was going on at FMT.

It occurred to each side that it had something to offer
the other, and even more to gain. Messages were exchanged. It was but a short step from promising the
opulent and credulous the engineering of self-improve-
ment, or the favor of an antique god, to promising
them physical perfection without limits. Stepping
adroitly under the umbrella of charitable status and tax
and legal exemptions extended by this orbital church,
FMT dissolved without trace, and the Temple of Abraxas
gained a new upper echelon: the Seraphim.

And there history disappears from view. While business pundits and media theologians debated the temporal
and spiritual significance of the merger, and top-flight
bioarchitects and eugeneticists were selectively and secretly lured aloft with astonishing, not to say disgusting,
promises, the doors of the temple remained firmly closed
to the eye of the infidel. Not a tract, not a communiqué
was forthcoming. Abraxas stock prospered on the world
markets, but the Seraphim were mum.

Nor was Capella seen to interfere.

Little information has escaped since. At first the
wholesale recycling of the faithful prevented the custom-

ary trickle of defectors with sensational stories to sell. The putsch in which the Abraxas High Cabal and most of the former board of FMT were absorbed into a Seraphic cadre comprised mainly of avatars of Kajsa Tobermory we know about only through a research blitz by a crack data commando team from Shu Jin Network News, whose bodies were never recovered. Abraxas and FMT begat the Seraphim, and the Seraphim begat the Cherubim, who were the spaceborn, *homo alterior*, the skaters of the spaceways.

Everyone knows what a Cherub looks like, though they can scarcely expect ever to meet one. Metallic black, crimson-eyed, macrocephalic, few of them more than a meter long; hairless, legless and sexless, buzzing hither and thither in freefall, or defying gravity on their little saucers, they resemble perhaps infant demons out of the imaginations of the more excitable executives of the Spanish Inquisition. They never wear anything but the transparent plastic suits whose optical microcircuitry festoons them constantly with rainbows. With the hoods of their suits pulled over their heads, they can negotiate for considerable periods of time the raw vacuum of space. On planets they are less comfortable, and most disdain them. Engineered beings themselves, the Cherubim have a knack for the intricacies of electronics of any kind, and operate a remarkable range of tools and machines by means of a range of prosthetic tails which they plug into the sockets at the base of their spines.

This, then, was the creature Tabitha found occupying her own seat at the controls of the *Alice Liddell* as she roared away from Plenty in a blaze of wanton violence and traffic violations.

She stared at it sidelong, resenting it for all she was worth. It looked like an oversized fetus of black chrome, and it had its tail stuck in Alice's board. It and its horrible companions had saved her ship, possibly her life, by dumping them into more trouble than she could ever have imagined.

She wondered, in the midst of all the drama and destruction, how it had come to be there, on Plenty, toiling

with this effete and dodgy cabaret troupe. Why wasn't
it at home with the others in the temple, living and working and planning the next stage of their apocalyptic evolution? Was it some discarded prototype? Did it have
some hideous defect, some genetic flaw that had caused
them to cast it out? Surely they would have reconditioned
it, reprogrammed it, broken it up for spares. Had it perhaps simply left the fold, absconded, dropped out, as
children of the most modern terrestrial societies still do
in quest of some more authentic, grubbier mode of existence among the hardships of the high frontier? Was it
slumming? Was it, perhaps, a spy?

Before Tabitha could look away, the Cherub suddenly
turned to face her. Its little red eyes sparkled, and it
opened its shimmering black lips. Tabitha could see its
tiny, perfect teeth of lustrous black enamel.

It smiled at her.

29

"You stupid idiots!"

She floated, upright, to the top of the cockpit steps
and yelled at them, shaking.

They were gathered there looking up at her, watching
her as if she were the one that was the cabaret act, the
entertaining novelty. There were the Zodiac Twins, arms
around each other, both feet in one loop, two versions
of the same person, as if one wouldn't have been more
than enough. There was Marco Metz, his nose all bloody,
his hair and eyebrows singed. She hoped he was injured.
She didn't know why he wasn't dead. She didn't know
where Tal was, and right now she didn't care.

The only one of them she cared about right now was Xtasca, who was still at the helm.

Tabitha grabbed a fistful of the webbing, *her* webbing. "I'll take over now," she ordered.

The Cherub didn't respond.

"Come on!" Tabitha shook the web. "Out of there!"

Marco swam forward, arms outstretched. "Come on, sweetheart," he urged. "Calm down. We're okay! Everything's fine!"

She spun around to face him, shaking a finger in his face.

"Don't you sweetheart me, Marco Metz, I'll fucking do you, you hear me?"

The Twins flew up, one either side of her, restraining her.

"You nearly got us all killed!"

He spread his hands. "We're all here, Tabitha, we're all alive, the ship's okay, just take it easy."

"I'll tell you if the ship's okay, Marco! All right? Now get out of here! All of you!"

Tabitha shoved on the Twins' shoulders, spinning them over on their backs and driving herself backwards. Catching the bracket of a monitor she pulled up short of the viewport, hanging above the console with her feet drawn up beneath her. Diving forward, she took hold of the Cherub's tail and pulled it sharply out of the socket.

The ship lurched, slightly.

Anchored by one foot, and breaking the web latches with her free hand, Tabitha hauled Xtasca out of it by the tail.

"Oh, don't do that," said Saskia, coming upright and finding a handhold. Her hair was all over the place. "You'll hurt her," she protested.

But Xtasca was perfectly equal to the situation. It flicked its tail out of Tabitha's hand and bobbed up free of the web. Easily it swam past her face and between the Twins, down the steps and into the hold, moving as if it were born to zero-g, which of course it was.

"Out," Tabitha commanded.

They went, and shut the lock behind them.

Reinstated, Tabitha went into automatic. Forgetting her burns, the ache in her ankle, she ran an eye over the monitors, those that were still working. Plenty was glimmering 120° astern, a lump the size of a walnut. There was no pursuit. Outside their own envelope, the board were not interested, there being so few laws it was actually more profitable for them to enforce than waive. But if she ever went back there—

If she survived this jaunt, she knew she could never, ever, go back to Plenty. "Good riddance," she told the dwindling lump.

She wondered, though, why they'd held back; why they hadn't simply shot her to pieces, ship and all.

Plugging her headset in, she accessed the persona.

"Alice? Are you still talking to me?"

"OF COURSE, CAPTAIN," said Alice. "WHO WAS THAT THAT JUST JACKED OUT?"

"That, Alice, was a Cherub."

"A CHERUB? GOOD GRACIOUS. OH, YES, I SEE IT. IT'S IN THE HOLD, DID YOU KNOW?"

Tabitha gritted her teeth. "Yes, Alice, I know."

"THERE ARE SOME OTHER PEOPLE IN THERE TOO."

"Yes."

"MAY I TALK TO THE CHERUB, CAPTAIN?"

"No. We're heading into the Tangle."

"READY," said Alice.

Tabitha keyed in a standard course for the most densely occupied sector of the Terran orbital lanes, and Alice plotted it.

"THE TRAFFIC IS RATHER BAD," she observed.

"Good," said Tabitha. Here there was nothing to distinguish them from any other delivery van. She sucked her teeth. "Damage report, please, Alice."

It didn't look too good. The *Alice* was blind in several eyes and deaf on a whole bunch of local frequencies. There were numerous burns, scrapes and dents, some of them structurally significant.

"AXIS LOCK CRYSTAL DEFECT. FAILURE PROBABILITY

61.04%.'' Alice observed. ''I THOUGHT WE WERE GOING TO HAVE THAT SEEN TO ON PLENTY.''

''So did I,'' muttered Tabitha. ''Bear with me, Alice, I'll get you looked at in a couple of minutes. The guys in the hold are paying.''

''WHAT CONSIDERATE PEOPLE THEY MUST BE.''

Despite herself, Tabitha laughed, and winced. She probed her tender cheek with careful fingertips.

''Am I burned, Alice?''

''SLIGHTLY, CAPTAIN.''

The first aid drawer hummed open.

''This is not a good day for us,'' Tabitha said as she patched her face and hand. ''This could be the worst day of my life.'' She was muttering more to herself than to the ship, keeping reaction at bay. ''What do you think, Alice?''

''INSUFFICIENT DATA.''

She brushed crisp curls of burnt fabric from her sleeve. ''Remind me to tell you about my life some time.''

They were moving steadily into the main shipping lanes. The traffic, as Alice had warned, was murderous. Caledonian Lightnings went lumbering by, full of information guards and tax inspectors on their way home from another day's valiant struggle, while Freimacher Tinkerbells tacked with arrogant delicacy across their bows, carrying litigation designers and advertising executives to Byzantium and Faith. Here and there were little blobby drone trucks scuttling off for the next load, and, as Tabitha had expected, plenty of barges, Fargos and Luggers and Kobolds, bearing down upon the Tangle with paperclips and deodorant and black pudding. In the Tangle, where corporate cylinders waltzed with garage platforms and leisure complexes with flying churches: that was where the *Alice* belonged.

''CAPTAIN?''

''What, Alice?''

''WHY DO YOU CALL THIS THE WORST DAY OF YOUR LIFE?''

''I'll tell you when I know what the fuck is going on.''

There was a brief flicker of pink lights as the *Alice* absorbed this.

"Pick a platform, Alice," said Tabitha. "We're going to get you fixed."

The computers locked in. Tabitha sat back and stretched. When she closed her eyes she could see red flashes on a background of livid green. Somewhere in the back of her mind the Mercury Garden screamer was still screaming, the bolts of gun-happy Perks and cops still tearing up the air.

Christ, she was tired. She imagined a water shower, a real bed, clean crisp sheets. But only the just slept, row on row of them on ice in white steel coffins, in a frosty cavern that was sometimes a sunny woodland, sometimes a bedroom stuffed with antiques and candlelight. There they lay with electrodes stuck in their eyeballs, watching home movies, waiting for the Day of Resurrection. No loud noises, no homicidal aliens, no androgynous acrobats, no Cherubim, no cops. All you had to do first was die. It seemed like a good deal.

Reluctantly she opened her eyes. She was alone on the flight deck of the *Alice Liddell,* with everything humming quietly along around her. She listened. Was there a noise? An irregular, tapping noise, the noise of an axis lock crystal rattling in its housing?

No. There wasn't. But soon there was the noise of the hold airlock opening.

Tabitha turned. Marco was standing looking up at her from the bottom of the steps.

"Hi," he said.

"Don't you talk to me," she said. She turned back to the keyboard and put Alice on mute.

"I was just coming to see if everything was okay," he said. "And to give you this."

He pulled himself up the steps and coasted to a halt beside her, lying full length on the air, holding out the credit chip.

She took it, before it could disappear again. "There'd better be something on here," she said.

"A few hundred," he said.

She closed her eyes, lay back in her web. "Fifteen?"

"Oh, no, no. Maybe five."

"Fifteen hundred you owe me, Marco, fifteen, more like two thousand now you've damaged my ship."

She pointed to the damage analysis, still onscreen. He read it, trying to look as if he understood, but she could see he wasn't really concentrating. He looked up, through the viewport.

"Where are we going?"

"To get her fixed, get a new crystal put in, charge her up."

"Better get her charged first," he said. "Just in case."

She cursed him, but he was right.

He nodded to the chip, the movement sending a ripple along his reclining body. "That's going to be enough to get us to Titan, isn't it? We're going to Titan, right?"

"Do I have any option?"

"Hey," he said, bouncing lightly upright and drifting forward. "Don't be like that. We didn't plan it this way, you know. You did well," he said, perching on the edge of the console.

"Get off that."

"Sorry. Sorry." He floated up and grabbed a loop.

"How long?"

"To the platform?"

"To Titan. It's one of the moons of Saturn."

"I *know* where it is."

She pulled a keypad over and did the figures. "A month." It was not a pleasant prospect.

"Subjective?"

"Do you know another way?"

"That's with the skip?"

She sighed, irritated.

He poked a finger through the web, saying gently, "Your hair's a little scorched here, did you know?"

"Leave it *out*, Marco!"

He raised his hands. "Okay, okay, you want to do this the hard way, screw you. I'm going. All I want to know is, have you got enough there to get to Titan?"

"It'll get us there, yes. If it's really five hundred."

"And the repairs? Hey, watch that."

On the starboard bow a refuse drone went skittering by, arms flashing in all directions as it gobbled the litter of the space lanes.

"It'll fix the scanners and get you a new crystal?"

"It had better."

"So we're in business!"

She scowled at him. "You owe me, Marco, you got me into this."

"I didn't chuck your Perk in the canal."

"Everything since then is down to you, whatever it costs. I don't like cops, and now I've got cops everywhere I turn. How am I supposed to run my business? I'm not a bloody pirate. You owe me, Marco." She shook the chip. "This is only a down payment."

"Tabitha. Listen. I am not shitting you. This is not just a gig, waiting for us on Titan. This is real money. Once we get to Titan, you're going to be rich. Real money, not just credit. More money than you could earn in the rest of your life. We'll all be rich. You can have a new life. A new name. A new face, if you want. You can get rid of this old crate," he said, gesturing along the ship.

Tabitha's nostrils flared.

"Okay, keep the ship. I kind of like her myself. She's quaint." He patted the bulkhead above him. "You'll hardly know we're here. I promise you. Tal's in his box now. He hates flying. Xtasca, she won't bother you. The Twins, all they need is each other. They keep each other entertained. That just leaves you and me. A month to get to know each other a little better. We did all right together, back there. It can be like that again, all you have to do is trust me."

Tabitha ignored him. She rubbed her eyes with the heels of her hands, and looked at the surviving screens.

They were entering the Tangle. Already she could see the MivvyCorp torus, its outline prickled with the pointed shapes of executive scouters, like pirhanas savaging a doughnut. A dot of green light at 300° was the First Lutheran Church of Christ Shepherd of the Stars, and a squat disc on the starboard bow a BurgerWorld, spinning heavily, broadcasting non-stop jingles on every wavelength it could get at.

Tabitha exhaled slowly. The pinwheels behind her eyelids were getting confused with the glitter of the Tangle.

Alice was signaling it was time to make the turn into the approach lane for a Red and White. Tabitha gave her her head.

The ship banked. Marco and a cloud of loose waste drifted to port. He waved his arms, trying to swim uphill, grabbing at the co-pilot's web as he misjudged his momentum and turned slowly upside down. "Whoa!" he said, grinning at her between his legs.

She paid no attention. She'd decided to lock them all in the hold.

Marco was turning gradually head over heels, flapping his free arm in a vain attempt to right himself somehow. "You know," he said as he came right way round again, "you're looking pretty tired." He wobbled back to her and squatted at her feet, his face a picture of concern. "We don't want our pilot flaking out on us, now, do we? Why don't you go and get your head down for a while?"

"Your pilot," she muttered, bitterly.

They coasted slowly in to the Red and White. Tabitha cut the engines. The *Alice* floated into a busy bay, where deliveries were being netted in huge weightless bundles and shunted about by acid yellow drones puffing jets of frozen vapor. Dayglo letters fifteen meters tall announced: "TEKURAT CHARGE." The place was run by a five of Palernians in rainbow suits with helmets shaped like different popular cartoon characters. A Mr. Tube waved them in, flew across with the connections.

Tabitha set up the transaction. There was five hundred on the chip, barely. She looked for Marco. He was about to leave the cockpit.

"Sit down, Marco," she said, pointing to the other web.

Looking at her apprehensively, he worked his way into it.

"They're going to charge us up now, and they're fetch-
ing in an axis lock crystal for us. So we're going to be
here for a little while. Have you all got suits?"

He nodded. "Sure."

"While we're waiting," she said, "you can tell me
exactly what's going on. What I've got myself into here.
The truth, Marco. Do you know that word?"

He looked genuinely injured. "Tabitha. I've never lied
to you."

"A lie."

"Never. Just, just—" He flapped his hands, momentarily at a loss. "Just reality can be a little uncompro-
mising, sometimes, that's all."

30

"Well, you guessed it. We're not just performers. We
rob banks. Does that shock you? Under cover of our
careers as interplanetary entertainers, we blow safes. We
snatch jewels. Remember the Doyen Pomal ushabti? The
Deimos Diamond? That was us. We scoop up rare ar-
tifacts and precious metals. We don't do computer scams,
we don't do the data heist, we don't plant sneaky viruses
that eat up a whole asteroid's credit while they're at home
watching AV. We don't do any of that stuff, never. We
go after the real thing: things you can touch and hold.
Things that are still there when the power goes off.

"The name. Contraband. A double-bluff. Gets them
every time. You like that? Contraband? That was me. I
thought that up. What we have between us is a whole
repertoire of crime. Every talent we use on stage, turned
to nefarious purposes. Think about it.

"The Zodiac Twins. Acrobats. They can do things,

physical feats, that baffle cops and security operatives. Also, they do conjuring tricks. Now conjuring confuses the normal mind. People don't recognize anything they can't explain. The Twins are a walking conjuring trick. They even look alike, so nobody can swear which one they saw. Instant alibi.

"Then take Tal. Tal appears to be a perfectly normal green parrot. In fact, as you noticed yourself, he's a whole lot more intelligent than the regular terrestrial kind. Who would ever suspect him? With his size and his wings, he can get into places where not even the Twins can go.

"Xtasca, now. Xtasca is a member of another hidden race. Nobody really knows who the Cherubim are, or what they can do. Like Tal, she can fly, on that little saucer, and space is nothing to her. She's better in space. She's got all kinds of cybernetic stuff at the tip of her shiny little tail. You saw what she did to that robot. You wouldn't believe what she can do with security systems and data stores.

"Then there's me. What do I contribute to this foxy fivesome, this quicksilver quintet, this carnival of criminal craft? I do the talking. I talk, I'm good at talking, I'm talking now, this is what I do. I take care of the public. I have considerable personal charm. And I'm sharp, I think fast, I think on my feet. Those guys, they can't plan a job. Xtasca and Tal, they're bright, for what they are, but they're not human, they don't think like humans, they don't know what humans are thinking. Nor do the Twins, come to that. Can you figure those guys? They know what each other's thinking, but for the rest of us, it's, you know, it's, Hello in there! Is there anybody home? Together they're wonderful, but you can't separate them. You know, I think that's why we had so much trouble with this job. If we hadn't—Well. Okay. The job.

"Back there on Plenty, in the middle of the show, Mogul and Xtasca went down a way and blew a bank. We had the alibi. Where were we, we were in the Mercury Garden, officer, we were on stage. All these people were watching us. Hannah set it up, she's wormed her way into a lot of the circuits on that place, you'd be surprised what she can pull. And Plenty is one of those places where there's still real money, and when I say real money, I mean gold. I guess you've never seen that. You know, the whole of Earth used to run on that. There isn't any anywhere else in the system, not on Mars, not in all the Belt, not anywhere. There's nothing like it.

"They're sitting on a bag of it back there. A *big* bag. Like I told you, Tabitha, we're rich! There's only one problem. You can't just spend it. You can't spend it here filling your fuel tank. Is that the price there? My god. Okay. No problem.

"You want me to show you? I wish I could. I wish I could show you, it would make this so much easier. I wish I could let you touch it. I wish you could take off all your clothes and rub—Okay. Okay. Well, I can't. That's all there is to it. I can't because it's sealed up and it's alarmed and booby-trapped and all that stuff and we don't have the tools. But on Titan are the guys who do. On Titan we can turn it into cash, stuff you can spend. If cash makes you nervous, we can turn it into credit, good honest 100% credit, credit in any name you choose. All you have to do is get us to Titan. With the gold.

"I could have hired anybody. Anybody at all. I could have hired those people Hannah was talking about. But I didn't want them. I wanted you. The minute I saw you, the second, I knew. And I was right. You've done all right by us. Things haven't gone so perfectly, and we've got you into a lot of trouble, I wish I could let you know how sorry, how truly sorry that makes me. If I could pay you off now, and get this whole show off your ship and out of your hair—you know, I could brush that little scorch right out for you if you—Okay, no, Tabitha: if I could pay you right now, if there was any way I could do that, believe me, I'd pay. But you know, I'm being honest now, I have to be honest with you—I'm glad it's worked out this way. Is she full yet? How much does this thing take, anyway? You know, Shinjatzu has this new model that—Okay. Okay. No, really, I'm glad it's

worked out this way, because it means I get to spend
more time with you. I know you don't have such a good
opinion of me right now, but I want you to know I think
you're wonderful. I'm still crazy about you. I think, as
you get to know me better, you'll find I'm not such a
bad person. Maybe I'm not as easy to get along with as
some guys. Worthwhile people are never easy. That's
true.''

"What about the tape?" said Tabitha.

"Tape? What tape?"

"The tape you put in my bag, Marco. The tape you
made Hannah Soo listen to."

"Oh. That tape."

"Yes. That tape."

"Okay, I'll tell you. That was a ghost tape," said
Marco. "I had it made on Schiaparelli. That's why I had
to leave you there at the party, to go and pick the tape
up."

She signaled to the Palernian chargehand. She said,
"What's a ghost tape?"

"A little security device for your home, office or rec-
reational vehicle. Also a good burglar tool. They're very
convincing. They make like a person was walking
around, like a real person. Life-signs, noises, interference that looks like a human shadow on snooper scopes
or security cameras. You remember what Hannah said?
Looks like help is on the way, she said. That's the ghost
tape. Everything you need to confuse a burglar. Or, and
this is the clever part—or, the cops."

"The tape made it seem there was an intruder at the
freezer place?"

"That's right. To confuse the cops. That's right. To
make it look as if the break-in was at the freezers instead
of the bank."

Tabitha tapped her front teeth with her fingernail and
stared absently at the rear scanners, watching the traffic.
She was feeling better. She didn't believe a word of his
ridiculous cops and robbers story—there couldn't be a
bank stupid enough to keep anything on Plenty, could
there?—but it was no less than she'd expected from him.

Knowing he was still underestimating her encouraged her greatly.

She turned to face him suddenly, so suddenly he jumped.

"Okay, Marco, now it's my turn. This is my ship, and if you ride in it, you put up with my conditions and you do what I say. I don't want you here. I don't want your job. But you owe me, Marco, and I want my money. A month with the Amazing Contraband in back is not my idea of fun. Have you ever traveled a month in a barge? No? I didn't think so. Let me tell you you're going to be very uncomfortable. I don't want to hear about it. If those guys've got any complaints, they can complain to you. You're the one running the show, right? You're the one with the mouth, you can tell them all this. That door will be locked and it'll stay that way. You can use the ablute and the galley, you show them where those are, and I'll clear out the passenger cabin. You don't come in the cockpit without my permission, you don't go in my cabin at *all*. You don't touch any machinery or any controls anywhere. As soon as we're through here we're heading over there, the repair bay, and I should think we'll be there for a day or two. Maybe even a week. It depends how much of a mess you made. So anything they want in the next month, they get it here and come straight back on board, okay? Okay. Xtasca stays here. Nobody draws any attention to us, at all. Nobody does any performing or gets into any fights or *robs* any *banks*. We are going to sit here nice and quietly until the *Alice* is ready, and then we go."

There was a sudden loud noise from the hold, a shrill, wavering, hooting noise.

Despite her resolve to let him handle them, Tabitha unbuckled and kicked down out of the cockpit and through the lock. Marco was close behind.

It was chaos in there. They'd been into the luggage and equipment that had been so neatly stowed and pulled everything out. It was all circulating, spinning dreamily like a stately tornado that had wandered into a theatre wardrobe. Parts of costumes insinuated themselves

through loops of unraveling flex; a ukulele probed a se-
ductively undulating thigh-boot. A stuffed rabbit nosed
hopefully up to the newcomers, looking for something
to orbit.

Elbowing a path through this lot, Tabitha almost collided with a flying drone, one of hers, spinning helplessly
in mid-air. It was the drone that was sending the distress
signal. Tabitha caught it and pressed the reset, frowning
at Mogul and Saskia.

They were not looking at her. They were quite involved. Wearing white string singlets, their blue pyjama
trousers and, obviously, zero-gs, they were standing 180°
apart, one on the floor, the other on the roof. They were
on tiptoe, stretching up towards each other, and they
were kissing. They could just about reach. Their hair
flowered and mingled around their heads like a soft and
snaky halo.

"You can sort this lot out right now," said Tabitha
sternly, daring, just *daring* Marco to make a comment
about the state of her own quarters. But he fielded the
rabbit, saying nothing. She had shut him up at last. She
concealed the pleasure of her triumph by restoring the
drone to the wall. The Twins had apparently had it hanging them a freefall hammock between two of the extensors and it had lost its footing. Nearby, she noticed Tal's
traveling case of white porcelite, which had drifted up
under the catwalk and wedged there forlornly. Xtasca,
however, was nowhere to be seen.

"We're sure she's all right," said Saskia, reassur-
ingly.

They found it aft. It had somehow got into the double
wall between the pressurized interior and the fuel cell
racks. There it squatted, upside down, hovering rapt.

The Cherub, which needs nothing more from its environment than a regular sluice of UVB, a browse in the
ion shoals, a breath or two of interstellar hydrogen, had
gravitated to the honeycombs of the fluxus radiators,
attracted by the succulent plasma splashing in. Bathing
in the hard violet light it hung, throwing its head back
in ecstasy, and toasting its little black hands.

"Get it out of there, Marco!"

He craned through the inspection hatch.

"Xtasca! Hey, c'mon. You have to come out of there now."

It turned, purple dazzle slithering from its lifesuit. It bared its tiny teeth.

"I'm not ready," it said, distinctly.

Marco knelt on the edge, reaching in.

"Careful," said Tabitha shortly.

"Come on, Xtasca, you can do that any time."

"It can*not!*"

Clumsily he pulled his head out of the hatch, banging his shoulder on the frame. "She's got to eat," he said, vigorously. "She's no trouble."

"I want her, it, out, now."

As she spoke the Cherub came shooting past Marco out of the hatch, wriggling its shoulders. It flew up to the ceiling and hung there, looking down at them.

It focused on Tabitha. Its eyes glowed faintly in the drab passageway. "Captain, yours is a remarkable vessel."

Tabitha wouldn't look at it. "Thanks a lot," she said.

"It could be you do not know how remarkable," observed Xtasca.

Tabitha shuddered, hit Marco's arm with the back of her hand. "Tell that thing to get off my back, Marco!"

"There is a large refraction dissonance in the axis lock crystal, Captain," said Xtasca implacably.

"I know that!" said Tabitha. She knelt on the wall, sealing the plate back over the inspection hatch.

"Would you like me to stabilize it for you?"

"No! Marco!"

Marco bobbed forward, snapping his fingers, as if it were Tal he was calling. "Hey, Xtasca, why don't you come and see what the Twins are doing?"

This seemed to motivate it. It launched itself off the ceiling and snaked off toward the hold.

"Just keep it away from here, Marco, all right? Let it, let it go outside if that's what it likes. But not yet!"

A voice came over Tabitha's headset. It was the Palernian chargehand. "*Y'ready to gow, now, ow*, Alice Liddle."

Tabitha swam swiftly back along the gangway past the hold. The forward hold lock was still not closed, let alone secure. The Zodiac Twins were now floating in the gangway by the forward starboard exit lock, looking out of a porthole. Saskia turned as Tabitha pulled past her, aiming for the cockpit.

"Have you seen *her?*" she asked.

"Seen who?" said Tabitha impatiently.

"Out there," said Mogul unhelpfully, waving vaguely in the direction of the charge station.

Tabitha, slipping into her web, didn't bother to reply.

"It looks like a cop," said Saskia dreamily.

Tabitha's blood ran cold.

"She was talking to the Palernian," continued the acrobat remorselessly.

"The one in the Mr. Tube suit," said her brother.

"The one that's pointing at us now, that one."

Tabitha checked the scanners, tabbed for a zoom. They gave her three views of the Palernian pointing, three of the cop in the shiny black action suit looking their way. Looking right into the camera, it appeared.

Tabitha hit the jets.

Alarm hooters blared on the radio from the traffic jostling in her wake as the *Alice Liddell* surged away from the Red and White. Marco Metz, still in the gangway, shouted in pain and surprise as he cannoned off the walls. He floundered into the cockpit, rubbing his head. "What about the repairs?" he shouted.

"Get everything stowed, Marco," said Tabitha. "We're leaving now."

31

Through the viewport and on all the monitors, stars prickled the blackness. The *Alice Liddell* did not appear to be moving, though she was rushing headlong through the void.

Tabitha wondered if she should have stayed in the Tangle. Maybe she'd overreacted. A quarter of an hour later the *Alice* informed her there was a patrol cruiser on their tail. She had not overreacted.

Displays on the board were glowing pink and blue. She had the persona mute, she didn't want to discuss this. Saturn was at aphelion, the skip would have to be along, across, and down one.

Marco came up into the cockpit.

"Are they after us?"

It was going to take a while, at least the month she'd estimated; longer, if they stopped off in the Belt to fix the crystal. Anxious as she was about the *Alice*, Tabitha preferred to get the whole nightmare over as quickly as possible.

"They're after us," he said. "Goddamn. Goddamn!"

He thumped the floor with his fist and sailed up to the ceiling. His tone was righteous, baffled, injured. He couldn't understand how the cops could be so disobliging.

In any case, Tabitha was not at all sure that what was left on the chip would buy a decent repair at Belt prices. The materials were all there, they just didn't like getting their hands dirty.

Marco spread his hands on the console, poring over

the readouts and meters. She could hear him breathing, tense and urgent.

"Are they gaining on us?"

No, she'd push on to Titan and hold him to the complete refit. Even the respray and false log job, if it came to that.

It looked as if it was coming to that.

"They're gaining on us, aren't they?"

The computers were finishing combing datastreams from six separate sector traffic authorities. There was nothing to stop two vessels occupying the same area of hyperspace; it just made things very complicated when they wanted to come out again.

"Can we lose them?"

Tabitha didn't imagine anyone was going to be crossing their route. No one would be pushing straight through from Earth to Titan if they could take two bites at it and use the Jupiter well. You'd have to have more money than sense to do it this way; or be in a terrible hurry.

"What do you think? A little fancy flying, we could shake them off, huh?"

Tabitha watched the figures stream, hoping the cops hadn't got a fix on the channel.

Marco picked at an old cargo coding label that was stuck on the edge of the persona unit.

"Can you get some more speed out of this thing?"

Unexpectedly, a voice called from below.

"Fuck off, Marco. Leave her alone."

It was one of the Twins: Mogul, Tabitha saw, glancing up at the screen. She could see the moustache. He was hanging in the airlock to the hold, which was still open. She'd realized it would only make her more uneasy to have them locked in, especially the Cherub. You couldn't see everything on the monitor. And with this lot, she didn't really trust what she could see.

On the monitor now they seemed to have got themselves sorted out. They had the hammocks slung, Mogul and Saskia's a standard zero-g web, Xtasca's some sort of cocoon of milky plastic with complicated neuro-support wiring embedded in it. Marco, needless to say, had claimed the cabin. Everything was stowed except what they were actually using. Xtasca was playing the keyboard Tabitha had seen at the Mercury Garden. Its arms were folded, its eyes closed. It was working the keys with a tail that terminated in what looked like a mechanical hand, wearing a natty white glove. Wires ran from the keyboard into the Cherub's tiny ears. It was in a closed circuit, not making a sound. Saskia was doing some kind of freefall yoga routine with a quarterstaff, under, over, round, under, over, round. Through.

Tabitha blinked.

She opened the com. "We're skipping," she announced.

"May I watch?"

It was Mogul, floating where Marco had been. Marco had gone, she could see him on another screen, going into his cabin.

"There's nothing much to see," she said.

She looked up into his face. He had his hair tied back in a ponytail. There were tiny chips of lapis lazuli in the fleshy lobes of his ears. His skin was white as porcelain, the high dome of his forehead pale and smooth. His nose was long and perfectly straight, his lips slender and exact. His eyes were hooded, with the merest trace of creasing at the corners. It was impossible to say what color they were.

"There's only room for one," she said, returning her attention to the board. The cruiser was a standard Hightail by the silhouette, chunky and fanged. It could eat the shrinking interval in minutes if they lost their temper.

"I am only one," he said. "At the moment."

He lay above her in the air, every centimeter of his frame relaxed, waiting politely for her permission. He hung there, quite motionless, as they ran for their lives. With his hair like that he reminded her of someone: that sinuous elegance, that catlike grace. Tricarico, she realized.

Display after display was locking in. Green, green, green.

Tabitha gestured to the co-pilot's web. "Quick," she said.

She cut the plasma jets, throttled them back to a mere corrective spurt, a tremor in the bass.

The bass was the Capellan drive, whirring.

As Mogul Zodiac closed his latches with an exquisite fingertip, the drive started to rise.

Constructed so that most of its components were aligned along a fourth axis, with the result that it looked rather odd from any of the first three, the drive of the *Alice Liddell* was very little different from the drive that powers the smaller ships of today. Perhaps its flanges were heavier, its vertebrae more cumbersome; and one might have found the wiring intricate with quaint redundancies. But when it rose, when it bloomed and mantled, it was identical in all important respects to Capellan drives everywhere across the galaxy. Not that one could have inspected it during its rising, blooming and mantling, because of the blizzard of heavy light that the drive then throws off with such prodigal intensity; from which blizzard Tabitha, her passengers and all the other contents of the ship were protected by a triple-decker sandwich of molybdenum shields and inertium sponge.

Mantling, the drive began to pulse. Pulsing, the drive began to alert the molecules of the *Alice* to certain aspects of their configurations which were ordinarily of no consequence whatsoever. The cockpit seemed to be filling up with a strange, insubstantial mist, as its internal space began to bend, patchily, and things became difficult to focus on. The stars started to look rather peculiar. The ship yawed round and about, as if irritated at this disruption of normality. The cops were calling, but nothing could be heard except a sound like tiny, high-pitched flutes, as if a consort of transdimensional sylphs were piping to coax them through.

"Who was Alice Liddell, anyway?" asked Mogul. His voice lingered in the air like syrup.

"She was a girl," said Tabitha, distractedly. "In a story. A little girl."

"Did she never grow up?"

Tabitha was confused. Time was flapping loose, wrapping back on itself. "That was another story," she said. Everything pulsed, grooving eagerly into its new, lateral frequency. The light in the cockpit assumed a distinctly vermicular quality. It wiggled; it wriggled. Tabitha was on the *Raven of October*, with the happy throng whooping and babbling around her. "That was a little boy," she said. She was shouting over the noise, she could hardly hear herself speak. "You're—"

They skipped.

The veil of reality sundered with a wild high cry that was gone as soon as their ears could fasten on it. The stars were gone. The void was gone.

Instead, the ship moved through a medium that was a very pale shade of no color at all.

In hyperspace, the paltriness of the three mundane dimensions becomes quite obvious. From overhead, as it were, conventional space appears flimsy and poor. The distinction between *here* and there, for instance, is trifling, almost academic; whereas *over there*, things, or rather thingness, unfolds and expands remarkably. Rushing to the portholes to look out, the passengers on board the *Alice Liddell* could clearly see the enantiomorphic signatures that the orbital traffic of Earth scribbles unwittingly on the quicksilver meniscus of space, like fish goggling up at the bottoms of passing ducks.

The fluting noise sounded clearer now, and much less fluting. The sylphs, if sylphs there had ever been, had broken up their consort and fled, laughing at another crew of unsuspecting mortals tricked out of their natural element. They had left the stage to something vast and invisible that whistled through its teeth; or perhaps it was the interdimensional wind, the hypercubic sirocco, keening hungrily through the Kobold-shaped hole the ship had left in the triune fabric.

The cops were elsewhere, nowhere, worlds away.

She looked at Mogul Zodiac, sitting across the aisle with his arms and legs crossed, drawn up inside the web. Curiously, the ship had a slight gravity now, as though she were being drawn to the not-grey floor of hyperspace, faint and puddingy far below.

Mogul smiled at Tabitha. "Thank you," he murmured delicately. "Captain."

Tabitha had the singular sensation that he understood whatever it was she had just said, or tried to say; that he had been there too, close as two lovers on a pillow.

Unnerved, she looked away.

She closed the throttle, set the stabilizers, checked the life support systems. Everything was chugging away as heartily as ever. The *Alice* had come through again!

There was a definite rattle, though. An irregular tapping noise. Tabitha could hear it; she wasn't imagining it. Her hand reached for the keys, to check the probability; then drew back. Later, she thought.

She opened her web and stepped out. She turned to address the rest of the band, the acrobat, the gloveman and the Cherub, now clustered deferentially behind her. Their faces were pale and grainy in the strange, reluctant light.

"Get used to it," she said, indicating the view. "That's the scenery for the next month."

In fact, hyperspace is not always as boring as Tabitha intended to make it sound. Physical events, like the ducks on the pond, do register there, blotting and stabbing again and again at its uchromatic blur. Violent discharges of energy particularly make their presence felt. They resemble, often, black fireworks in a field of snow; or the shimmer of a mirage, a lake of silver in a dazzled sky. Things protrude, like odd shapes distending a rubber sheet: volcanoes; comets; the buzz of distant quasars. Then again, the conventional relativity of size is wholly obviated. X-bosons can go nattering by like swarms of minnows. Footsteps accumulate in hexagonal piles. If you're lucky, a ghost may flicker past, or through, your ship: an absent friend, an absent mind.

Basically, though, Tabitha was right. The overworld does look a lot like infinite dishwater.

Tabitha looked at Marco, at Mogul. "Don't anybody touch anything," she said. Her eyes were drawn reluctantly to the Cherub, which inclined its head. "I'm going to bed," said Tabitha.

She stood back while Mogul extricated himself and sprang down from the cockpit into the arms of his sister. Tabitha saw her face over his shoulder, and paused.

"Saskia?"

"What?"

"Did you do that?"

"Do what, Tabitha?"

Tabitha shook her head. "Doesn't matter."

She went on down the ramp.

Saskia had her moustache back. Tabitha wondered what else would have changed, and whether she would notice.

BGK009059 LOG

TXJ.STD

PRINT

«ƒ§§ü§TXXXJ!åinterintelin%ter&&&«ƒ§¢]/"—hr hd wr TX Jb:"—!:

MODE? VOX

SD? 600.5.6

READY

Hello, Alice.

HELLO, CAPTAIN.

I was thinking—do you remember Devereux?

SHOULD I?

Yes.

GENERAL OR PERSONAL MEMORY?

I don't know. Both I suppose. She's quite famous, but she's
been on board too. She came and looked at you.

DID SHE? DID YOU INTRODUCE US?

I don't know. I suppose I might not have done. I was a bit
preoccupied. All that time I was.

SEARCHING. JUST A MOMENT. OH GOODNESS ME, YES.
THIS IS CAPTAIN DEVEREUX, ISN't IT? CAPTAIN DEVER-
EUX WHO WENT DOWN WITH THAT FRASQUE BATTLE-
SHIP. THE *MAGROTH DFAUNIK.*

That's right.

WHERE DID YOU MEET HER?

At her villa. Off Deimos.

AH.

Do you remember now?

OH YES. BUT WHAT WERE WE DOING THERE?

I wonder.

It was years ago. We were hauling some low-g furniture
from Domino V, designer stuff, one-offs. The delivery address
was off Deimos, a private orbital. When I first saw it I couldn't
believe it. It's an asteroid, it must be 90% carbon, all sheer

black surfaces, like a big black iceberg, and someone's jammed a big square habitat in it. Horrible place. I thought we'd made a mistake, nobody could possibly choose to live in a place like that. It looks more like an Eladeldi security installation.

But they acknowledged my beam. A Thrant was waiting in the adit to hook us up. I could tell by the way her fur was trimmed she wasn't in charge. It wasn't her place.

"Where do you want it?" I said.

But she didn't answer me, just stood there looking me over. And that made me think she was more than a flunky. Or maybe it was just that she didn't see many people out there.

"She're wanty see ye," she said.

She led me inside, down a long black passage. It was really cold. Plasma flambeaux along the walls. Black stone underfoot. She took me to a com station and buzzed somebody.

It was an open line. I heard the somebody say, "What is it, Pru? I told you not to bother me."

"Ye're wanny tek look."

"Am I. Look at what?"

The Thrant pushed me into view of the phone.

On the screen I saw a plastic head.

It was a woman's head, made out of plastic, with silver metal eyes. Below the nose, it was real. "Hello, lover," said the head. "Who the hell are you?"

I suppose I thought it was a graphic, some gimmick logo designed by someone with too much time and money who liked frightening people. I wasn't much impressed.

"I'm the driver," I said. "Your friend said you want to see me."

"My what?" said the head. "My friend, is that what you said?"

The head laughed.

"God, she's not my friend. She's my slave, is what she is. And she's my lover. And so will you be, if you press the right key. Only kidding, you know I'm only kidding."

The face stirred. That's when I knew it wasn't a graphic, it was actual, a person, or what was left of one. You could see the relays under the skin. The face stirred as if she wanted it to have an expression but had forgotten how to do it.

I thought, Oh, great, a rich plughead.

"What driver?" said the head. "Pru? Put Pru on, lover, will you? Pru, did I order a cab?"

The Thrant hissed, twitching her lips. "Isny *cab*, ist furniture."

"Who gives a shit. Give her a drink and send her in."

I wasn't keen. I felt for my monitor. "I'll start them bringing the stuff in," I said.

"Let it wait," she said.

I let it wait. I went in to have a drink with Devereux.

I remember it was a long way in to the nest she'd made for herself at the top of her house. There's a security maze. The Thrant loped in front of me through the corridors, opening the grilles with her palm.

There was a sickly sweet smell, like a hospital only with gin and perfume on top. There was Devereux lolling in a wrecked caresser, wearing a stained flight suit, sucking on a frosted tube.

"Come in," she said. I thought she sounded like a machine imitating a cat. Like somebody had been programming a vox to get it to sound like a big cat and got bored with it halfway.

I went in. There was junk everywhere, toppled stacks of tapes, print-out, dirty plates, clothes strewn over sound equipment, books, towels, burnt-out candles, package shells, customized appliances with insulating tape and rubber flex sticking out of them. I had no idea what half of them were, or even what they had been.

I knew then, though, what Devereux had been. I mean, I knew who she was.

She's even got a holo of the *Magroth Dfaunik* up over the bed, like in a shrine.

She was inspecting me, giving me the once over. I could almost hear her memory whirring. When she spoke it was to the Thrant, not me. "My god, Pru, you're right. I'm delighted to meet this young woman. Absolutely delighted," she said to me, baring her teeth.

She got out of her chair and came to shake my hand, extending her arm towards me. I could see where she'd been tinkering with it. It looked as if she'd been boosting the servos. I think she wanted me to notice that, to see how I reacted.

AND HOW DID YOU?

I shook her hand.

HOW DID IT FEEL?

Like a hand. It was a hand. It was her hand.

YES, CAPTAIN, BUT WHAT I MEANT WAS, HOW DID YOU FEEL?

Wary. I was thinking, plughead, I was thinking of Angie. I didn't want to trust this woman with her rebuilt head and her teflon hydraulics.

As it happened, trust didn't enter into it. When Devereux wants anything, she doesn't hang around.

She spoke to the Thrant. "Pru, you know where I'll be if you want me," she said. "Don't want me."

Then the Thrant went away and her mistress got me drunk very fast. She teased me with shreds of her fame. She walked around constantly, touching her souvenirs, the holos of her with her crews, posing with her fighter, the one that scuppered the *Magroth*. I didn't know what to say. I said it was a beautiful machine.

She came and stood over me. "So am I," she said. She flexed her wrists and all her zips came humming open. "So are you," she said, and she put her mouth on mine.

Her mouth was real. Her hands were real, and her body was sinewy and brown. Her eyes took a bit of getting used to. That's what they're for, that's why she wears them like that.

She never stops being famous, not for a moment. She'd say things like: "They want to forget me. But I keep popping

up, needling away at them. I'm their guilty conscience, lover.
That's what I am." Or she'd say: "I know what they say
about me now. I just don't give a damn."

It was always "they." She was a bit like Rella, really.
Sometimes "they" was all of us, everyone in the system, all
of us with nothing better to do than discuss Devereux and
make up malicious lies about her. But then sometimes
"they" were the Capellans. They'd destroyed her and put
her back together again, and now they were preserving her
like a specimen, for their own purposes.

The bionics are prosthetic, but they were compensation
too—enhanced abilities, metal sinews, video vision, record
and playback . . .

SHE MUST HAVE BEEN DREADFULLY EXPENSIVE.

She says she was a PR exercise. They wanted to show how
grateful they could be to people who served them well. She
says she's got a little implant specifically to amplify her
orgasms. Some nights I believed her. And she can get herself
into any electro-psycho-pharmaceutical state she fancies
and then, when she's tired of it, flush her entire circulation
just by thinking about it.

It's not blood, exactly, what Devereux's got.

The down side is being hideous, though she plays on
that. And she has dependencies like other people have
oxygen. "They monitor my mind," she told me. "Oh yes
they do. I'm their favorite soap opera. Sometimes I can feel
them in there, probing about." She groaned. It sounded like
a dying gear change. She grabbed my hand, crushing it.
"Oh god, Tabitha, I can feel them now." She rolled around
on the bed. "Get out of my head, you supercilious bastards!"
She was clutching her head and screaming. "Get out of my
fucking head!" I had to get Pru to come and thumbprint the
overrides. Pru blamed me, of course. Pru hated me.

Devereux wouldn't talk much about her career, not directly, but I found things out later. She was born on Earth,
in the States. School was all physics and gym, she won
prizes, then some Space Force recruiter hooked her. She
was trained at HighGround, and got thrown into the war

early, even before it was official that Capella was signing humans up. She told me that herself. She said, "People think the Capellans drafted us. They didn't, they were too clever for that. They just offered us the chance to fly the best hardware in the system, and fly it against the walking wood-piles that were invading our spread." She said *our* with heavy irony, and turned over on her back, folding her arms behind her head and gazing up at the ceiling. "God, Tabitha, you know, I really thought it mattered which bunch of ETs I was exploited by."

She liked you. She patted you on the console. She said, "You look after her."

SO YOU SHOULD.

How's the axis lock?

76.81%.

It knows what it's doing, then.

OH, THEY DO. BUT GO ON ABOUT CAPTAIN DEVEREUX.

I thought she needed some comfort. "You were a lot younger then," I pointed out.

That was the wrong thing to say, for some reason.

"Oh, I don't blame myself," she said sharply. "Heavens, I grew out of that. Hell, you wouldn't know," she said, scanning me again. "You're young, you're cute, you slow up as you get older. They have a loyalty thing they stick in you. They used to do that, you wouldn't remember. But it doesn't work any more, does it," she was suddenly shouting again, driving her fists into the floor and forcing herself up, yelling at the ceiling: "No more, you old bastards, it don't work, uh-uh, not any more!" She laughed like metal tearing, and started to cough. By the time the cough had finished, she was on top of me again, wrapping her arms round me, squeezing me like a compactor. Her cheek was warm on mine. I could hear her brain buzzing through the shell.

We used to argue about politics. I've never felt so ignorant, so completely stupid. She wanted me that way. "Tabitha, the Frasque were never a *threat*," she said, as if she couldn't believe anyone could be so naive. "The whole reason they had to cut out the Frasque was they can't stand competition. They can't make it. They have to pick us clean all on their own. Oh, honey," she'd say, sliding across to me and fondling my bottom, "they've really got you, haven't they? You just spread your legs and take it. You don't even know they're fucking you."

It was the first time anyone had patronized me so totally. She made me so angry I said things nobody should have said to her. She relished it, she was proud of provoking me to it. It was all she could do, you see. She made out she didn't care. She stood there in the middle of the room and gave herself a lung vacuum. It was as horrible as she could make it.

WE WERE ONLY THERE FOR A WEEK.

It was a long one.

Devereux said nobody got more than a week, because she always got tired of them. She didn't get tired of me, but she got rid of me anyway. She knew how to protect herself.

WHYEVER DID YOU STAY, IF SHE WAS SUCH A MONSTER?

Oh, there were good times. She knew how to give me good times. She knew how to get me on the floor, laughing and crying and begging her to stop, it was so good.

When I left, I was depressed. I tried to get her to come with me. She thought she might. Just for the ride. To see how things had changed. But she wouldn't, she never would. She couldn't get halfway through the maze without throwing something, a muscular seizure, a panic attack, something. She just couldn't face space any more. Either that or—

OR THEY HAD HER LOCKED IN.

A specimen in her own personal custom-built cage.

A WHOLE ASTERIOD.

Like a captive princess in a flying castle.
    I was thinking of the body, actually.

33

She was dreaming. It was a typical Tabitha dream, an anxiety dream. There was an Eladeldi in the cockpit, demanding she complete a whole sheaf of forms and asking why she hadn't done them already. They wanted to know about her education, her first sexual experience, some accident she was supposed to have witnessed or been in that she couldn't even remember. She was trying to keep the Eladeldi occupied, trying to hide the fact that she was carrying something, some cargo he mustn't know about. And Alice was talking, she wouldn't shut up, no matter how many times she tried to switch her off. She was singing. Very loudly. It wasn't Alice singing, it was somebody real, some people, the people in the hold.

Tabitha woke, staring at the ceiling. The drab sheets of hyperspace hung outside the porthole. In the hold, something metallic crashed to the floor, the music broke up in argument, they were shouting at each other.

She remembered who they were, where they were going. The chaos of the last few days came crashing in and she felt wretched, groggy and disabled. She hadn't had enough sleep, and she clearly wasn't going to get any more now.

"—be Wisdom speaking to Youth if I'm younger than

you?" demanded a Twin: Saskia, Tabitha thought. "It's absurd."

There was a moment of confusion, several voices, speaking together; then the same voice, perhaps it was Mogul, emerged, saying: "—act; the absurdity will take care of itself."

The argument continued. Someone or something was doodling on a keyboard, playing the same three chords over and over, now like running water, now like a thousand strings.

"Monstrous," said somebody distinctly.

"Well, I have to say I can't see it makes any difference." That was Marco. "Somebody—somebody tell—no, wait, somebody tell me what difference—I dispute that. I do. I dispute it."

The hubbub rose up and reclaimed him.

Tabitha yawned. She opened the bed loops and swung her feet gently to the floor. Naked, she unearthed a dressing gown and pulled it on. She couldn't think when she'd last had to wear a dressing gown on her own ship. That was only the second imposition, the first being the fact that she was awake at all.

She went for a pee and then activated a tube of coffee. She drank it in the galley, standing up, not wanting to stay in there but not wanting to go even the few meters up the gangway back to her cabin in case someone came out of the hold. She could see where they'd been into the galley and taken what they wanted. She hadn't even had time to get stocks in. What did four people need for a month? What did they eat anyway? What did they feed Tal?

Tal was out of his box. She could hear his fluting voice above the rest, adding to the volume and nothing to the sense. "In heaven they cuddle," he trilled. "Shamelessly in heaven."

She thought of the Twins. Incest. How could they? She wasn't shocked or disgusted, really, she just couldn't imagine it. Fancying your own sister, your own brother. And they fancy you. If they looked just like you, though, what about then? She didn't think so. If she met her double, she'd more likely run. If you looked like them, though. They were so sleek. Very sexy, in their own weird way. The way Mogul had looked at her yesterday in the cockpit.

Where she ought to be now. She finished her meager breakfast and went back to her cabin. She didn't meet anyone. They were singing Christmas carols in there now. They were weird and she was going to have as little to do with them as possible, or she'd come out of this as mad as they were.

Dressed, she went along the gangway towards the cockpit. Saskia had come out of the hold. She was standing at a porthole in a voluminous white smock and clawing at the glass. Tears were running down her narrow cheeks, dripping from the ends of her moustache. Tabitha heard her before she saw her. "I want to go back," she was wailing. "Back where we were when we were all there."

Tabitha didn't know whether it was a real outburst or part of the play. The gangway was narrow and Saskia was in the way.

"What's the matter?" she asked, gruffly.

Saskia turned her wet face towards her. "You," she mourned, "you can take us back. You can, oh you can!"

She threw her arms around Tabitha's neck and sobbed on her lapel.

This was not a promising start to the voyage. Tabitha, resenting it mightily, held on to her while she wept. Her skinny body was all tight, lithe muscle. Her hair smelled of lemons, her skin of peppermint and distress.

The rest of the band appeared, the aerial members first, watching them curiously with alien eyes. Marco came running, reaching to take Saskia from her. Little as Tabitha wanted to have anything to do with this, she was determined never to surrender anything or anyone to him again. She looked to Mogul, coming along behind, and indicated he should relieve her of his sister, which he swiftly and gently did.

He was wearing a moustache too.

Which made her wonder which of them she'd been hugging.

Abruptly, without a word, she continued towards the cockpit.

"Did you sleep okay? I hope we didn't wake you up," said Marco, bustling along behind her.

"No," she said over her shoulder. "You did," she said.

"Oh, Christ, it's my fault!" he cried angrily.

She was tempted, but didn't reply. She speeded up and swept into the cockpit, into her web, her territory, her place, she was in command. She shut her eyes and took a deep breath. It couldn't be like this every day, it couldn't. She had to get something worked out.

"Tabitha?" called Marco, at the bottom of the ramp.

But not this minute.

"I'm busy," she called.

He exhaled gustily, and withdrew.

After that the rehearsal seemed to break up in disarray, as far as it was possible to tell which was which. Tabitha looked up from the console and saw Xtasca was outside, outside the ship. It was just floating around, like humans wandering about in the back yard because they had nowhere to go.

Tabitha wondered whether it knew what it was doing, whether it understood the dangers. Maybe it had been born to them, or cultivated, or whatever those things were.

Unless it was a hallucination, a hyperspatial mirage, and not Xtasca at all.

"How are we doing, Alice?"

"PROCEEDING."

"How's our little problem today?"

"WHICH ONE WOULD YOU LIKE TO DISCUSS, CAPTAIN?"

"Christ. None of them. Is there anything you need to tell me? Just give me a yes or a no."

"NO, CAPTAIN."

"Alice, I love you."

Back in the hold, someone was playing a clapped-out

old violin, or something that sounded exactly like one. Then they started to chant.

"The natural cards revolve, ever changing . . ."

The awful noise went through and through her. She thumbed open the com. She had to talk to them, lay down some rules, a schedule, something. She took a deep breath.

"I'm going to shut this door, all right?" she said, and before they could answer, pressed the close tab.

She slumped on the console. "I'm not a good captain, Alice," she said.

"WOULD YOU LIKE AN OBJECTIVE EVALUATION, CAPTAIN?"

"Christ, no."

"SOME COMFORT, THEN."

"Later."

She simply wasn't. She was too selfish, too used to passing the time on a dull haul like this by doing exactly what she felt like every moment.

She ran a check on the broken scanners. There were a couple of them she might be able to mend. She put on her hull-walking suit, took the laser welding pencil and some replacement units and went outside.

Outside it was better. If you didn't look too close at the bland discontinuum surrounding you, you could convince yourself it was fog and you were merely afloat, adrift in it. Quite peaceful, really.

Xtasca, tailless, came swimming around the ship to watch her.

"*That won't work, Captain,*" it said, coming in over the proximity channel, though it was carrying no visible radio, not even riding its saucer.

Tabitha felt herself bristling. "Why not?"

"*I'm afraid it's disconnected further in.*"

Tabitha stared at it through the faceplate of her helmet. Xtasca was just wearing its lifesuit, with the hood up. It regarded her calmly with its little red eyes.

"How the hell do you know that?"

"*I can see it,*" it said.

Tabitha sat back on her heels. It occurred to her to

dispute Xtasca's claim, but she was too tired.

"*If you'll permit me*—" the Cherub began.

"I'll do it," said Tabitha.

"*I can reach into the socket,*" said Xtasca, "*with a tail.*"

"I said I'll do it," said Tabitha.

The Cherub looked at her a moment, then silently flitted away like a passing sprite.

Laboriously, Tabitha dug out the wiring and found the thing was right. She welded the break and fed it back into the duct.

"How are we doing, Alice?"

"IT MAY BE TIME FOR LUNCH, CAPTAIN," said the ship.

"What?"

"YOUR LIFESIGNS—"

"Okay, okay. I'm coming in."

She stood on the hull and looked around for the Cherub, but it was not in view. You couldn't even offer it something to eat. What could you do? Too late she realized it had been offering not only help but reparation, having been the one who bashed the roof about in the first place.

She was a lousy captain, and a lousy diplomat.

Days passed. Subjective days, but none the less tedious for that, in this amnesiac region that had forgotten where everything was supposed to be. Tabitha got bored with repairing things. She wanted a look in the hold, to see this so-called bag of gold; but the hold was never empty. Xtasca could roam around outside, but for the rest of them, there was nowhere else to go.

The Twins had begun crayoning an enormous mural on the wall of the hold. It was Saskia's project, principally. Tabitha could tell them apart fairly confidently now, though only by the way they behaved. Saskia was impulsive, erratic, prone to sudden shifts of mood. There was always something she was wishing for. She was always hungry. She worked at her mural in great frantic sweeps which by and by grew smaller and smaller, until she could be found on her knees with her tongue in the

corner of her mouth, shading the separate petals of the
tiny flowers in the urn on the tomb in the bottom right-
hand corner.

Mogul was less vulnerable, more aloof. He could be
arrogant or gracious or a silent lingering presence, watching everything. While his sister toiled, Mogul would drift
down from the catwalk and corner Tabitha when she
came in to fetch spares.

"You say the police can't follow us here, Captain?"

"No," she said, rummaging in the locker for omnipolar antenna flex. All she could find was serendipity
flux gaskets.

"Not even the Eladeldi?"

She was sure she had some somewhere. She was sure
she'd seen it that morning. Impatiently, she dumped all
the gaskets out. They bounced slowly on the floor and
rolled around.

"Not even," she said.

She crawled into the locker and dug deep at the back.
She could feel Mogul's eyes on her bottom. Think what
you're doing, Jute, she admonished herself. She'd forgotten for an instant what she was looking for.

"And the Capellans?"

Defeated, she backed out. "Oh, well," she said, dusting off her hands, "the Capellans—"

She looked up and met his eyes. They devoured her,
with infinite gentleness. She felt herself going hot.

"The Capellans can do anything, can't they?" she
said shortly, looking down and brushing hard at the knees
of her trousers. All she could see was his face, their face.
He was wearing the moustache today. She had never
worked out how they did that, with the moustache. He
was still standing there, patiently attending her. Reluctantly she looked at him again. He handed her the serendipity flux gaskets, neatly stacked.

He was coming on to her, she couldn't pretend he
wasn't. He gave her little spontaneous, impossible pre-
sents, brought her dishes of crab and ginger, sauté par-
snips, just when she was starving and couldn't face
cooking. It made her feel inhibited and cross, not least

because she wanted him too. She could have had him, easily, but not with Marco floating around. Not that she still wanted Marco; but she couldn't get rid of him.

Then the laser welding pencil vanished, and she turned the whole ship upside down looking for it.

She found it, and the reel of omnipolar antenna flex, in Tal's traveling box. Well, she certainly hadn't put them there.

The bird went completely daft when it saw she'd found them. It flew wildly around making a sound like a jangling electric guitar, then dived into its box and hid its head under its wing. "Sriti naogar Nottamun Fair!" it cried, plaintively. "Nobody knows the trouble I've seeeeeeen—"

"You don't fool me, bird," said Tabitha menacingly. Mogul was at her elbow suddenly, making soothing gestures, but she didn't want soothing. She slammed the lid on the feathered thief and turned to stride away. As she left the hold she heard it twittering to itself. It was doing a perfect imitation of the way a Bergen Kobold axis lock rattles when it's got a defective crystal.

She went to have it out with Marco. She found him lying on his bunk with a comic book. "He's as bad as his master," she wound up.

Marco sat up energetically on the bunk, hurling the comic aside. It drifted quietly to the floor.

"His what? What do you think he is, some kind of performing pet? Haven't you understood anything? He's an alien, goddammit, a sapient alien, you have to be patient with him, try to understand him. What do you mean anyway, I never stole anything from you. Name one thing. Name one thing I stole from you."

"Name one thing you haven't!"

The worst of it was, the wall between their cabins was so thin she could never forget he was there.

When she walked back through the hold, the atmosphere was electric. Saskia was sitting on a trunk with her arms about her knees, staring balefully at her brother, who was in their hammock, ostentatiously ignoring her.

The mural was ruined. Someone had smeared it all across with crushed handfuls of greasepaint.

Tal was hanging upside down from the railing of the catwalk, still singing. "*Nobody* knows the trouble I've seeeeeeeee . . ."

When she'd fixed all she could fix, to get away from everyone Tabitha took to spending long hours in tethered EVA, communing with her log. Driven from her normal reserve, she talked more to the ship on this trip than she ever had, and not on technical or navigational questions. On this journey through the realm of virtual, her chosen companion was an imaginary one. When people, natural, human, or otherwise, become too much to bear, your best friend may be an artifact.

She put on a suit and opened the inner door of the forward starboard exit. The airlock was full of rubbish: food wrappers and parrot droppings. The whole ship was a mess. That was nothing new, let me tell you; but before it had always been Tabitha's own mess, bobbing about somewhere near where she'd left it, more or less, and thus legitimate, environmental, almost invisible. This stuff was other people's mess, unexpected, invasive.

Tabitha opened the outer door, secured her umbilical, and bobbed out into nothing. The rubbish burst out after her in a cloud. It would orbit the ship faithfully for a while, then reality would reclaim it.

She steered herself slowly around to the prow of the *Alice Liddell*, where she could sit on nothing and keep an eye on the cockpit. If she saw Tal go in there, she'd stick the little brute in a cage and to hell with interspecies relations.

Tethered EVA in hyperspace is both more and less comfortable than tethered EVA in space. There is still vertigo, if you are susceptible to that, because of the pseudo-g. Wherever you start out, after a while you always end up beneath the ship, drifting towards the infinitely receding ironed cloud which "forms" the "floor." There are hair-raising distractions, once in a while, odd skews and rattling ruptures in the blank discrepancy surrounding you. But there is no perspective, no sense of *distance*, of the terrifying amplitude of space; no bottomless gulfs to belittle, no receding stars to mock you.

Tabitha saw Xtasca astern, lying five meters off the hull, basking in the sawtooth radiance of violated relativity; and she wondered again how reality told the difference between a Cherub and a crumpled tea-tube. Since the first time they had both been outside together, they had tended to ignore each other, like neighbors whose gardens are too small.

Today, however, what the ship had to tell her was alarming, and not to be kept to herself. The probability of breakdown in the axis lock had risen above 89%.

"Xtasca?" she sent, wondering whether it would be receiving.

The bald black head turned in her direction.

Tabitha extended her umbilical and jetted gently through the drab void towards the Cherub.

It lay horizontal to her, on its back, legless and naked but for its flimsy plastic covering. Its little hands waved in the air. It could not have looked more helpless.

Tabitha swallowed.

But before she could speak, the Cherub said: "*The crystal.*" Its voice was nasal, metallic, infinitely superior.

Tabitha's hackles rose immediately.

"You've been listening in, haven't you?" she demanded.

The Cherub gave a sort of shrug, lolling its great head

from side to side as if it were too massive for its neck.
"No," it said, with a rising inflexion, like a parent being
patient with an obtuse child.

"Then—"

"*It must be either the Twins or the crystal,*" said
Xtasca. "*Nothing else would be important enough.*"

For her to speak to it, it meant. Tabitha understood,
and knew it knew she understood. Those implacable little
stop-light eyes could be extraordinarily eloquent. But
why the Twins? she asked herself, as it went on.

"*The Twins are human, aren't they?*" it said, as if
testing her response; and when she gave none, continued:
"*You wouldn't come to me with a human problem.*"

Tabitha felt her heart pounding. She didn't know if it
was anger or fear. "I can't get at it," she said. "I've
never—" She took a deep breath. "Could you show
me?"

Xtasca rolled over on its belly. "*Let me look at it,*"
it said.

"If you could just show me," said Tabitha.

"*Nothing I can do you could also do.*"

Tabitha wanted to shout at it.

"You could show me."

"*You're too large to see.*"

Without another word Xtasca slipped away and swam
back inside, returning after a moment wearing a tail
equipped with some sort of micro-lattice probe. It did
not come back to confer with Tabitha but swam directly
to the access panel.

"Alice, could you open—"

But she already was. With a flick of its tadpole rear,
the Cherub disappeared inside.

In a bad temper, Tabitha went down to watch.

Xtasca was right. The crawlspace wasn't built for anything bigger than a G7 drone mech. Helplessly she stuck
her head in the hatch and looked into a space so black,
for some minutes, she couldn't even see where the
Cherub was. Then there came a silent, vibrant glow of
blue radiance, and the hunched silhouette of a tiny black
form. It looked like an animal, a scavenger infesting the

bowels of her ship, like one of the armadillo spacerats of Palernia.

The blue glow died. Through her helmet Tabitha felt the teeth-jarring, nauseating vibration of the crystal probe.

There was nothing she could do.

"I'll leave you to it, then," she said.

There was no reply.

Brooding, she went back in through the stern starboard lock. Marco and the others were in the hold, singing.

Mogul was in her cabin.

After a moment of shock and outrage, she threw her helmet down on the bunk. "What are you doing in here?" she demanded, pulling off her gloves.

The acrobat swept towards her with dignity, with unwonted humility, opening his hands as if to declare himself. His hands were empty.

"Tabitha," he said.

His narrow lips were parted, his heavy eyes beseeching. But he remained at a distance from her, on tiptoe, every line of his slender frame yearning towards her, but holding back, holding in.

"I didn't say you could come in here," she said flatly.

She didn't tell him to leave. Even to her own ears, her tone sounded false. She could hear the lie in her voice, hear herself denying the fact that was palpable in the air of the cabin, in the space that remained between them. She unlatched her tether suit. Her fingers were trembling.

There isn't anyone in next door, she thought. Such as it was, she kept her distance. "What do you want, Mogul?" she asked, needlessly, as she slid herself up out of the collapsing suit.

"You," he said. His voice was like the Martian wind, calling forever through hollow stones.

He was a stricken figure, a sad clown in a limp blue pyjama suit. His white neck described an angle of lifelong sorrow and yearning. He wanted her pity, and she was not in the mood for pity. She had been shaken, and discomfited: by Alice's news, by the Cherub, and now by this visitation. Her heart was shrunken and hardened. But her heart was not where she lived. She felt the beat of the blood in her temples, felt her nipples harden, her stomach hollow with desire.

Enjoying, at last, a little access of power, she reached a hand behind his long, sorrowful neck and drew his noble head down to hers. It was the power to give and take, the power of pleasure. She kissed his mouth.

There was an interruption then, an interval of banal reality, as she unfastened his shirt, struggling with a small, tight button at the throat. She kissed his throat.

His elegant fingers were on her, caressing her, stroking her hair, tracing the contours of her spine, her shoulders, her breasts. She suffered him to unfasten and remove her jerkin, her T-shirt, and unbuckle her belt.

He kissed her ear. His tongue was like the muzzle of a tiny animal, questing, tickling her. She laughed, congratulating herself.

The cabin lights flickered.

He paused, looking up at the ceiling. "What was that?"

"Xtasca's doing some work on the ship," she said.

He nodded. "That's good," he said. "She's good at that."

He drew down her trousers.

Tabitha kicked off her slippers and stepped out of them. She slipped her arms around Mogul's tiny waist.

There was something at the back of her mind, something puzzling. Something about what he had just said. She ignored it. She drew him on to the bunk and lay there with him awhile, cuddling him, unbuttoning his trousers. She reached up and slipped the shirt from his shoulders.

He had breasts. The flattest, slightest convexity, invisible when he lay back for her to pull off his trousers; but breasts. They really were identical, then, these Twins. How weird, she thought. And she thought: He called Xtasca "she."

She released him, drew back, kneeling up on the bunk. "You're Saskia," she said.

She pulled off his underpants.

She was.

She looked dismayed. "I thought you knew," she whispered. "I am he and he is me."

She gave a little, desperate smile.

Tabitha, wild chaos leaping and dinning in her head, demanded fiercely, "Which one *are* you?"

"I'm me," said Saskia. "I really am," she avowed.

Tabitha shivered. Saskia reached for her hand, but Tabitha pulled away. "What the hell are you?" she shouted. "How can you be twins, identical twins?"

"We're not," said Saskia. "We're not twins."

Tabitha, in one convulsive movement, grabbed up her T-shirt and pulled it back on over her head. Saskia stretched out as if to stop her, but fell back, irresolute.

Tabitha sat up, cross-legged. The lights dimmed again, and returned at full strength. "Tell me," she said.

Saskia shifted awkwardly, her former poise and elegance fled. "Well, we are now, but we weren't," she said.

Tabitha snorted, exasperated, electrified. "What the hell—"

"Quins," said Saskia. She ran the tip of her tongue around her lips.

"We're the only ones left," she said.

She reached for Tabitha again, to hold her, to be held, and Tabitha held her.

Saskia said, "We were an experiment. Suzan and Goreal and Zidrich got—used up. We escaped. We were rescued. We wouldn't have stood a chance."

Tabitha could feel the other woman's heart thudding, firmly, determinedly, in its narrow cage.

"We didn't know anything," Saskia said, "about— other people. About the system. We've never been apart," she said. She rubbed her nose, pulling a face, ugly suddenly, like a blind person with no notion how to control her own expression. "I have to get away from him," she announced.

"Why?"

Saskia sat up, gazing into her face. "So I can be me!

So I can—'' She sighed, listlessly. "He wants you," she said, placing the palm of her hand flat on Tabitha's breastbone.

Tabitha felt her ardor cool and spiral away.

"Is that why you came here?"

"He mustn't have you."

Tabitha swallowed her anger. They were children. She had been about to go to bed with a child.

"So you came here first," she said. "You can't do that," she said forcefully. "You can't just treat people like that."

"Like what?" Saskia was perplexed.

"Like, like—like weapons."

"It's not that," said Saskia at once, and vigorously. "It's not, Tabitha. I want you too," she said, beseeching again. "I love you . . ."

"You don't," said Tabitha, losing her patience. "You're just copying him."

Saskia gazed at her, tears in her eyes. "I'm not," she said. "I couldn't. You don't understand. I *am* him. What he wants, I want."

"Well, you can't have me," said Tabitha brusquely. "No one can have me. I'm not yours, I'm mine."

Unexpectedly sober, Saskia said softly, "That's why I love you." She stroked Tabitha's thigh. "You are real, I'm not used to real people. Mogul and I, we're not real," she said, reaching for her clothes and beginning to dress again. "Xtasca is real, but she isn't human. Tal isn't either. Marco isn't real, he's all words, words. And Hannah is dead."

Afterwards Tabitha reflected, Saskia wasn't so alone as she had made out. She had heard her through the wall with Marco sometimes, their murmurs and cries.

Unless that was Mogul.

That night, Tabitha woke from a dream of Captain Devereux, the broken pilot forever circling Deimos in her fortress of black stone. She woke remembering the smell of her, the musk and machine oil.

There were voices next door.

Marco and Saskia, she thought, and realized she was already jealous.

But the others were in there too, murmuring quietly and companionably. She could hear them all, Tal's tootling, Xtasca's remote hum. Were they playing cards or plotting a mutiny? She strained her ears, but couldn't tell.

Silently she slipped from her bunk, pulled on her gown, and stepped out into the gangway.

The night was subjective, like everything else in hyperspace. There is no darkness there, nor any light save what leaks through the back of the mirror, from real space. By this dim overflow, Tabitha approached the rear lock of the hold, and went in.

Alone in the hold for the first time since they'd set out, she looked carefully around her. The Twins' hammock was empty, and the Cherub's cocoon. Tal's box stood in the corner, the lid open. In the grudging light the ruined mural, with its vague, expansive outlines, its patches of precise but obscure detail, seemed to mimic the no less hallucinatory prospect outside the portholes. There was the shrouded vista, pregnant with suspended possibility; there were the marks and violent stains of presences definite, yet incomprehensible.

Tabitha was not there to appreciate art. She was there to go through their luggage. She trod gently around the heap of boxes and bags and belongings, looking at them all. She was looking for the long silver-grey cylinder Mogul and Marco had risked death to bring from Plenty.

She found it, under a large mound of multi-colored foilcloth. Somebody had obviously intended it should stay covered up. She got a grip on it and tugged it out into the open. It was cold to the touch, and rather heavy.

Squatting and dusting off her hands, Tabitha contemplated it. It was longer than she remembered: a couple of meters, nearly three, and most of a meter in diameter. It was padded vinyl on the outside, rigid metal underneath. That, and the weight, almost made her think it might be gold after all. Did you ship gold in padded cylinders? She had no idea. There was a place where it was supposed to have labels on it, but somebody had taken them off. She wondered how you opened it.

It turned out to be easy. There was a silver metal seam around it, across each end and along its length. There were finger catches recessed under the seam on each side. Wrapping her arms round it, Tabitha inserted her fingers in the holes.

There was a hard, smooth click. She jumped back as the cylinder sprang open.

White gas burst out, hissing, condensing. A strange, unpleasant smell, as of moss and methylated spirits, wafted into the hold. It was very, very cold.

Inside the cylinder was thick frost, caked on what looked like several layers of heavy-duty insulation quilted in some kind of artificial silk. There was a large, long bale in it, of something wrapped in white gauze.

It didn't look like gold.

Tabitha wanted to shut it up quick and not have any more to do with it.

But it was on her ship. She pulled at the gauze on one end. Under it was a tight bundle of dry, yellowish twigs and straw. An alarm bell began to ring, very faintly, in the back of Tabitha's memory.

She pulled the gauze down further.

The bundle had a face.

It had two bulging eyes, closed beneath smooth chestnut-colored lids; a sharp pointed nose with two narrow slitted nostrils; and a wide mouth like a crack in wood, pursed and seamed.

It wasn't a bundle of twigs; or a bundle of anything.

It was a Frasque. A dead Frasque.

35

BGK009059 LOG

TXJ.STD

PRINT

ÅA9‡BGK0o9059]

MODE? VOX

SD? 13.16.31

READY

The first Frasque I ever saw was on the *Resplendent Trogon*.

MELISSA MANDEBRA'S SCHOONER?

That's the one.

WHAT WERE YOU DOING ON MELISSA MANDEBRA'S
SCHOONER, CAPTAIN?

I was in love. With Melissa Mandebra's bosun.

His name was Tricarico Palynides and he was thin as flex.
He had long dark hair dressed down his cheek and gathered
in a tortoiseshell ring. His eyes were narrow, the color of
amber, gold, they were, in some lights. Gold when he looked
at me. He picked me up slumming in a Schiaparelli hos-
telry—he was slumming, not me. He invited me aboard the

Resplendent Trogon to show me around. He said.

In the bitter evening we went out to a place in the desert to wait for the shuttle. The sky was like plum jam, all purple and clotted. The mantas were hunting, soaring overhead like rags torn out of the night. A piercing wind was blowing scents from the south, parched smells, sulphur, frozen metals. The air was thin and raw. It crackled in our nostrils. We stood in the sand, wrapped together in Tricarico's harlequin cloak. We were happy.

Deimos was up. The shuttle came, its silhouette growing across the gibbous face of the moon like a huge black beetle. It was the officers' shuttle, Tricarico assured me, no one aboard would bother us.

Since Luna, I'd lived on Integrity 2 and set foot on nine other orbitals, one of them an Eladeldi ziggurat; docked at a zillion different platforms and stations and silos; and cleaned up after some of the fanciest ships in the system. The *Bolshoi Mrittsvar*. The *Amaranth Aloof*, with her arrogant livery of yellow and black, her soaring passenger decks alight from stem to stern. Once I saw the *Seraph Catriona*, matt black, secretive, patroling the Dominion of Abraxas like a shark.

WHATEVER HAPPENED TO THE *AMARANTH ALOOF*? I HAVEN'T HEARD OF HER FOR YEARS.

She disappeared. Didn't you hear? On a TransNeptune Cruise.

TRANSNEPTUNE?

Very daring, but Capella didn't forbid it. It's system space, even if no one ever goes there.

NO ONE DOES, NOW.

The *Resplendent Trogon* was nothing like the size of the *Amaranth* or any of those, of course, but she was the biggest ship I'd been on. She had twelve decks and independent gravity on each. There were tapestries in the boardroom and actual paper books in the library. Valet robots swept silently along the corridors, servicing each deck. Tricarico's own cabin wasn't quite that plush, I admit, but he had piped food, upper deck privileges and his own ablute. His bed was all right too.

He gave me thril. I'd never had it before. It was a transparent gel in a clear glass pot. You scoop a bit out with a little bone spatula and put it under your tongue. It tastes of flower and sugar and gives you an enormous thirst. But ten minutes after it dissolves, nothing is any effort. I felt I could reach out my hand and alter the stream of events as it flowed through the cabin. Sex was very absorbing. Tricarico kept laughing. He was just delighted. I delighted him.

IS THRIL LIKE LOVE, CAPTAIN?

It's better, in a way.

WOULD YOU EXPLAIN THAT, PLEASE?

Would I? Yes, I would. You know you're going to enjoy it all; and you never expect it to last forever.

I THINK YOU'RE JUST BEING CONTRARY.

No, I'm not.

YOU MUST EXPLAIN LOVE TO ME ONE DAY.

It's when you're mad but you think you're not because there's someone else in there with you.
    Do you get that?

NO. NEVER MIND. CARRY ON. TRICARICO.

Sat up in bed, a sheet over his knees. He drew his knees up, his feet together, an elbow on each knee, and rested his chin on his hands.

AFTERWARDS, THIS IS.

That's right. I lay back at the other end of the bed, stupid
with pleasure, drowsing through the afterglow of the thril.
We gazed at each other, foggily wondering how many more
times we'd be able to do this.

"You could come with us," he said.

"Where are you going?"

"Enceladus," he said.

I didn't even know where it was.

BECAUSE OF THE DRUG?

No, I really didn't. I still hadn't been beyond Ganymede,
remember, Alice. I could navigate the Tangle, backwards
and forwards, and I had the major asteroid clusters sorted
out, but the Capellans might have limited the drive to Jupiter
for all you could tell by me.

"The rings are absolutely marvelous," said Tricarico.
"Absolutely bloody marvelous." He sliced his hand languidly through the air. "Thin as a knife and so solid, if
you come at them right, you'd swear you could walk on
them. It's all hurtling around out there, and yet it's absolutely
safe, you can run through it, in and out, as long as you
check the charts. Because it all just rolls around like a
vast great clock."

I don't know why he said that, that the rings were like a
clock. I was feeling too much of a vegetable to ask. I suppose
it was some sort of thril insight.

"They've got it all charted," he went on, "all the big lumps.
Anything you can get a fix on that they've missed, it's yours.
Do you know, Tabitha, there are still hermits out there, each
whizzing round on their own little rock. There's a monastery,
on Enceladus."

"That's not why you're going," I said. It seemed a brilliantly
witty remark just then.

"No, it isn't," said Tricarico, and launched himself across
the bed at me, arms and legs splayed like a ballplayer.

Grappling, we bounced lightly off the wall. He nuzzled my throat, but neither of us had the energy. We lay in a huddle while Tricarico told me about the Frasque caravan.

Have you ever been on a caravan, Alice?

NEVER, CAPTAIN.

The Frasque had them for a while when the rumors of war started, ships traveling to the Belt in convoy for safety. The miners were buying a lot of basic big machinery from the inner system. All the way to Jupiter it went conventionally, to save on acceleration. Only after slingshotting Jupiter, Tricarico told me, would the great hulks muster the speed for the final skip. The small ships, like the *Resplendent Trogon*, traveling on the caravan for the prestige more than anything, would wait until the last to get away before skipping themselves.

"Around the shoulder of Jove they whirl," he said, fantasizing. "A hundred jewels flung like seeds across the black field of night! One by one they reach velocity and wink out of existence. There goes the Tredgolds' *Behemoth*! Across the open net the cheers ring out! Next the Frazier Asterak Roublov ironclads, *Kanzan* and *Jitoku*, one so close after the other the bets will never be decided. Before anyone can catch their breath, the Frasque mass cradles start to sparkle and spin, by twos and threes, disappearing in the darkness like snowflakes on a December midnight. Then at last, in one wild flare of incoherent light, the small fry that have bobbed along in the swirl, all vanish at once—to re-emerge a few weeks later, strung out along a million-meter arc of the lip of Saturn's well!"

"The Frasque?" I said. "Aren't they the ones making all that trouble in Africa?"

"They're all right as long as you keep to business," Tricarico promised.

"That's what I should do," I said. "Do you know what time it is?"

"Tabitha," he said, hugging me reproachfully.

"What?"

"I'm trying to persuade you to stay."

"No," I said. "I'm getting up. Watch me. Getting up." I reached for my clothes. "I've got a living to earn."

"You *haven't*," he said. "I can get a bigger cabin. You don't have to tell anyone what you used to do. You can leave the past behind!"

"I'd have to have a job," I said.

He got quite agitated. "That's what I'm saying! You don't need to work!"

"No, Rico," I said. "It's what *I'm* saying. If there isn't a job, I'm not coming. Meanwhile, I'm going. Watch me. Going."

We compromised. The caravan was assembling at Selucia. If I joined him there in a month, he would hire me.

I THOUGHT YOU WERE IN LOVE WITH HIM.

Ah, I'm contrary about love, Alice.

You might say what I was in love with was the *Resplendent Trogon*. She certainly put the *Fat Mouth* in the shade. Going back to that recommissioned ore dumper was more difficult than I wanted Tricarico to know. There was no ablute at all on the *Fat Mouth*, just chemical wipes and a disgusting old vacuum disposal. Captain Frank didn't understand about hygiene. Or no, actually, I think he understood perfectly well and didn't see the point. You just get dirty again.

Inside the *Fat Mouth* was the accumulated junk of ten years. More: some of it had come from his previous ship. Some of it *was* his previous ship.

The way it went was like this. You make some space by folding some vast sheets of chipped lightfoil, cutting out the bits the silica beetle have ravaged. You put the bundles of lightfoil in between the legs of nineteen emergency folding freefall stretchers that don't fold any more, and you discover nineteen trays of streak connectors, thick with old black grease. Maybe they'll still work, maybe they won't. You put them on one side. You go to move a couple of bins full of glass fiber shred and find there's nothing in them, apart from the glass fiber shred, I mean. So you put the streak connectors in the bins of glass fiber shred. Then you've got room to put the bloody great Marclon 7JJ quartz paradox adjuster you picked up for a song off a broken Palernian five. If you take some of the arms off. You can always put them back again. When you sell it.

Guess whose job it was to take the arms off the paradox adjuster?

And to put them back again, in the middle of nowhere, in a tearing hurry, on a station where our drone credit had run out, then coax the thing out of the workshop up a narrow chute and across thirty meters of vacuum into the hold for a customer that looked as if it might suddenly decide to forget the deal and eat you instead?

It wasn't that Captain Frank was lazy. He could be very energetic when he was doing the acquiring, sizing stuff up and complaining about it. He just hated to part with anything. Hated it. He was in a bad mood, anyway. He was shedding. There were clumps of fur all over the place, getting into the cockpit, clogging up the vents. I hadn't finished cleaning up since last time.

WHAT HAPPENED WITH CAPTAIN FRANK?

Well, I didn't tell him about the *Resplendent Trogon*, about Tricarico, but I bet he found out somehow. Probably because I kept calling the *Trogon*.

The departure had been delayed. Tricarico said, and de-layed again. It was pure ceremony, he said. A skeleton crew was looking after the *Resplendent Trogon*, while her owners and officers were making the proper observances, pressing the flesh. Every delegation was inviting every other delegation to a glittering succession of receptions and buffets, to sort out who was who, who was in and who was out, on the caravan.

"That's daft," I said. "Aren't the Frasque running every-thing anyway?"

"Of course they are," said Tricarico, grinning. "That's what makes it so funny."

Because the *Resplendent Trogon*, according to him, was only along for the glory of it, her owners and officers were very prominent at the presentations and the dinner parties. Also, Melissa hated to rush anywhere. Their cargo wouldn't spoil, or be any less in demand.

The *Resplendent Trogon* carried only goods whose prices were out of all proportion to their bulk: drugs; jewels; some of the legal docent tesserae. Not everything they carried was legal, actually. They conceal a lot from all but the most technical scanning, and bury the bribes in their overheads. The Mandebras run very high overheads.

Captain Frank didn't. I had a month left on my contract. I kept hoping the caravan would be delayed that long, telling myself it would be easier to leave when my time was up.

Oh, I wanted to be with Tricarico, Alice, don't think I didn't. But he was rushing me, and rushing me into something I knew nothing about, a world of snobbery and luxury he took for granted. There was no trace of luxury on the *Fat Mouth*, or if there was, it was broken. But I knew where I was with Captain Frank, even though it seemed to be mostly up to my eyes in loose wiring, swearing at a bolthead. Captain Frank hated to get rid of anything, so I knew he wouldn't ever get rid of me.

I was wrong.

News came in of a wreck. The *Mission Dawn Bell* had crashed on Io. Shigenaga Patay, with their usual flamboyance, had declared a loss. It would be an Altecean jamboree, scrambling through the mangled machinery, the scattered cargoes, meeting old cronies and competitors, picking up news of home.

"Hwe go today," decided Captain Frank. "Nyo stop."

I'd never seen him so inflexible before. Usually I could stall him, invent some rumor of a sell-off at Ucopia Plat, then head him off somewhere else before we got there. I'd learned that whatever idea he got into his large skull, combing the garbage orbits would always be easier. Not pleasant, just easy.

"Hey, Captain, why don't we stay here just until tonight? I'm sure I saw some good stuff coming round. Should be catching up with us by teatime. We'll go to Io tomorrow."

"Go today," he said, bustling across the cockpit to the charter. I dived out of his way. Now he was all energy and agreed in a furry coat.

I helped him chart the route. From Io I 'saw I'd be able to track the *Resplendent Trogon* as she crossed into Jupiter space. And out again, if Captain Frank got obsessed with whatever was left of the *Mission Dawn Bell*. They'd all be there, picking through the jagged carcase of the ruptured ship like vultures in the ribs of a dead whale, tasting the remains with their hot wet snouts and bargaining in rattling barks and shrieks. Their fur would be matted with antifreeze and ash. The other humans would be the usual dense, suspicious lot, sitting round the aerator telling gloomy stories with great relish, bragging about finds and killings.

I said, "Captain Frank, I've got to tell you something."

He peered at me through his filthy fringe. I'd learned to read his facial expressions, after a fashion. I didn't know this one.

"Hyou hwant to stay," he said.

"Yes," I said.

"Stop here. Stop all here."

"That's right. I've got another offer. This man—approached me. I wasn't looking." I assured him.

The distinction didn't seem to mean anything to him.

"You'll soon find someone else," I told him. "In Schiaparelli. Along the al-Kazara. The Indigo Canal. You know better than I do."

I think he took this as some kind of general acknowledgement.

He held the charting stylo in his snout. "Io," he rumbled, pointing to it. "Hwe go."

"No," I said. "Not me."

DIDN'T HE GRUMBLE?

Of course he grumbled. In fact I had to waive all the back pay he owed me. I left the *Fat Mouth* as broke as I'd come to her. I'd worked my arse off for five months for nothing. I picked up my zero-g's, stuffed a few choice finds in my kitbag, and caught a shuttle to Selucia.

It was funny, though: the passenger com chimed for me on the shuttle, and when I got to the screen, it was him.

TRICARICO PALYNIDES.

No, Alice, Captain Frank. He'd shelled out to place a call to me in transit, just to ask me something irrelevant, whether I'd seen the big laser scalpel anywhere recently, and then he just mumbled and looked at me. Just looked at me for a long time.

I said goodbye. I told him I'd miss him. He just looked at me. I was beginning to get annoyed, and then he was gone. Just like that.

Do you know, it wasn't until then that I realized he understood. That he'd done it for me.

I SAID HE WAS A NICE MAN.

Yeah. Some back pay would have been nice too.
You always lose something when you move.

36

"What is that doing on my ship?"

She was livid, and scared. As far as she was concerned, it was the middle of the night, after a horrific day. A refrigerated coffin with a dead alien in it was not what she wanted or expected to find in the middle of the night, lurking in the hold.

Faces pale, brown and glossy black gazed at her through the murky air. The passenger cabin was thick with aromatic smoke. They were all squeezed in there. She had startled them, bursting in without even knocking.

"Christ Almighty, you didn't open it, did you?"

Marco was on his feet immediately, upsetting Tal, barreling past the Twins to reach her.

"I shut it up again fast. I should have thrown it out the airlock!"

"Now Tabitha, take it easy. Take it easy!"

The three humans had all been sitting on the bunk, passing a long-stemmed pipe between them as they examined a piece of paper, a map or a chart of some kind, which disappeared the moment Tabitha burst in. Entwined, the Twins had scrambled up together as Marco shoved by, standing up on the bunk, pressing themselves back against the left-hand wall. Xtasca was at the far end of the cabin on its saucer, rising up along with them; Tal was also in the air, flapping about in great alarm.

"Tell me, Marco!"

He was agitated, angry. "Sit down! Sit down!" he bellowed. "Will you just sit down?"

The Twins trampled up the bunk away from Tabitha, making room for her. "Sit, sit . . ." they murmured, anxiously. One of them was still holding the smouldering pipe. She had no idea now which.

"I don't want to sit down!" she shouted. "I want a fucking explanation!"

"You'll be more receptive in comfort, Captain," purred Xtasca.

Tabitha threatened it with her finger. "Are you going to explain this? No? Then keep out of it!"

She ignored the Twins, glared at Marco.

His head was down, his fists were clenched, his eyes were starting from his head. "You're overreacting!" he told her. "Will you just sit down and *listen*?"

The Twin with the pipe was thrusting it down at her, offering it to her. Saskia, Tabitha could see it in her eyes. She almost knocked the pipe out of her hand.

"I'm listening, Marco!"

He exhaled fiercely, backing up a fraction. His head went back, he rubbed one hand with the fingers of the other, fondling his big ring. "It's Hector," he said, looking at her balefully. "He's dead."

"I can see that."

"He'll never walk down Lime Street any more!" caroled Tal soulfully, swooping down to perch on Marco's shoulder.

Marco turned his attention to him, holding up his curled index finger for Tal to bite at.

"He only just joined us," said Marco shortly.

Tabitha looked at Saskia. Her face was a staring mask, unreadable, identical to her brother's.

Marco raised his face to her. Were those tears in his eyes?

"They killed him," he said.

Suddenly he was all solicitude.

"Look. Tabitha. Come in, come on, sit down. I'll tell you everything, we'll explain the whole thing to you. Don't hang around in the door there. You're feeling bad, you've had a shock, come on, come and be comfortable. You want a coffee? Let me bring you a coffee. I know how it is when you're feeling bad. I know. I'm feeling bad. It's all my fault. Don't you think I feel bad? Can't you see how bad I feel?"

He ran a hand through his hair. Tal paid close attention, his head swiveling.

"We had him in the freezers at JustSleep," said Marco. "They didn't know. There's no way they'd take a Frasque." He laughed a short and bitter laugh. "Ironic, ain't it? Saskia, one of you, go and get the captain a coffee." He snapped his fingers at the Twins. Tabitha saw they were both looking intently at her, in the direction of her breasts. She pulled her dressing gown tighter.

She ran her eyes around the group: Marco in the center, taking command; Tal on his shoulder; the Twins crowded together on the bunk, entwined as close as ever; the Cherub perched up in the corner on its saucer like a z-ball umpire. They were all looking at her. Outside the porthole speckles were swirling together in the pallid vacancy of hyperspace.

"You think I'm so stupid," she said venomously.

Marco sat down impatiently in the place he'd offered her, bouncing heftily on the bunk. He waved his arm, dismissing her, and looked at his feet.

"Tell her, Mogul," he instructed. "Maybe she'll listen to you."

"That was what we stole from Plenty," said the acrobat quietly and slowly over his sister's shoulder.

"Not gold," said his sister.

"Our own partner's body," said Mogul. Their eyes were hollow, their mouths sad, as though they were remembering some deep distress. They were both obviously very stoned. At the same instant they both sat down together on the bunk behind Marco, crossing their long, long legs.

Tabitha leaned on the door jamb. She fixed her eye on Saskia. "You," she said, "worked with a Frasque?"

"Hector," said Saskia blankly.

"Where did you find a Frasque?"

Saskia and Mogul looked into each other's eyes. Neither spoke.

"In the Belt," said Marco instantly. "Sitting on a rock. He was a deserter, he was hiding out. He didn't even know the war was over. He wanted to join us. But they killed him."

"Who did?" For a moment, she thought he was going to say the Twins.

"Eladeldi. On Acme. His first night." His voice was growing positively husky. "Came right out of the audience and put a bolt in him." He frowned. He was biting his lip, holding back anger and grief. "We got him away, got him to Plenty. Hannah covered us in there. Maybe," he said, raising his eyes sadly to Tabitha's face, "maybe, if we could've told them, they could have saved him."

"Like Hannah," said Mogul.

"It was too late," said Saskia.

Marco blew his nose loudly and said, "Anyway, in the end we had to steal him back again. Like he says," he nodded lopsidedly at Mogul. "The tape was supposed to put something in there that would mute the alarms, but I guess it didn't work. Lousy Martian junk," he said bitterly.

Tabitha folded her arms. She looked at the hovering Cherub. "What about you?" she asked it. "Were you there for all of this?"

The Cherub's saucer whirred briefly as it rotated to face her.

"I have nothing to add, Captain," it whispered.

Tabitha looked at Saskia again, bitterly depressed. This whole trip was just one load of shit after another. "Why is there a dead Frasque in my hold, Saskia?"

Marco lifted his hand and let it fall.

"We're taking him home to be buried," Saskia said stiffly.

"You're taking him, Tabitha," said Mogul.

"His family are on Titan," said Saskia.

"We're very grateful," said her brother.

"Are you. Then why the hell didn't you tell me?" she demanded.

"We should have told you," said Marco. "We should. But it was a risk we couldn't afford to take. No one wants to get involved. We'd already hired one firm before you came along. They found out about Hector, next minute they'd canceled the contract."

"So there's no gold," said Tabitha bluntly.

"I'll get you some coffee," said Saskia.

"I'll get it," said Mogul.

They stared fiercely at each other, seeming to remember suddenly they were supposed to be at odds over her.

"There will be," said Marco, while Mogul slipped out like a cat, rubbing past Tabitha in the doorway. "Hector's folks will pay anything to get their son back. Anything."

"I thought the Frasque didn't have anything," returned Tabitha. She was fed up with all this, she wanted to go back to bed.

"Oh, there's money left," he assured her, vaguely. "The Frasque have got money all over the system. Capella didn't get everything." He stretched, wearily, carefully, not to dislodge Tal. "You'll be paid, Captain," he said in a singsong voice; and Tal, joining in, sang, "When will you pay me, say the bells? When will you pay me, say the bells?"

"Captain," called a voice from the gangway. "I think you should come and look at this."

Tabitha closed her eyes in a grimace of frustration and fatigue. "What, Mogul?" she called back.

"I don't know," he said. "Something's happening."

Tabitha went.

Mogul was standing at a porthole. She looked past him, outside.

"Oh God."

Outside the porthole the tesseract was mottling ominously, oily blots of black marbling the nondescript hypermedium. Everywhere you looked they divided and spread, divided and spread.

"What is it?" asked Saskia, behind her.

Tabitha's first thought was that they were in for a probability storm, like the one that had caught her on her seventh or eighth solo skip, back when she was driving the old Vassily-Svensgaards for Kuhn Standard. Time had come apart and tossed the hulking great ship like a fag-end into a vortex of alternities that threatened to tear it dimension from dimension. She'd never been so terrified.

"I'm not sure," she said.

She was already racing for the cockpit.

"Alice!" she shouted. "Hold the course!"

Waves of deadly light flared across the viewport. Ahead, the emptiness was stippled, fractured, bubbling and popping like overheated celluloid. The views on the scanners were all double exposures, pixels pinking and strobing with information from inside, speckling the screens with confetti of light from the real universe. The air in the cockpit was rich with ozone.

It was no probability storm.

As Tabitha snatched up her headset, streaks of wild blue fire zipped around the hull of the *Alice Liddell*, arcing across her copper inlays. Every speaker on board was howling with overload. Tabitha locked herself in her web, pulling in status readings and throwing power to the stabilizers.

She ignored Tal chirping hysterically in her ear, and Xtasca hovering intently at her side, the metal light of the rampaging forces outside flashing rainbows from its suit. "Alice!" she cried. "What *is* it?"

"SOMETHING'S PULLING ME IN," said the ship's persona calmly.

"It can't be!"

But it was. Overmastered by an unknown force, the *Alice* was being dragged headlong back into normal space.

If she went, it would not be without a fight. Her seams were creaking, her rivets jiggling. Stout little toiler that she was, she was resisting with all the power in her chunky frame.

This time it was not going to be enough.

Tabitha's fingers flew across the console, looking for an edge, looking for a vector. One by one, escape profiles began to crystallize, only to melt down seconds later. Just as the Cherub had said, it was not gravity, not conservation of matter, nor onboard systems failure that was ripping apart the dimensions beneath them. Incredible as it seemed, the Capellan drive was being countermanded. It was shutting down in obedience to a command from somewhere outside the ship. There was nothing Tabitha could do even to delay their fall.

"Everyone off the flight deck!" she shouted. "We're going through!"

And, as the players scattered for whatever safety they could reach, the maelstrom outside settled into a steady pulsing, a moiré whirlpool of unnatural energies that opened its maw and swallowed them down.

Abruptly, they were through. The *Alice*'s engines coughed and whined at the sudden resumption of proper gravity.

For a moment the screens were blank. Then one by one they blinked back on. There were the stars, there was the sun. There was the dead black of normal system space.

There was the big green pirate ship, its tractor beam groping for them, its paralyzing nets spread wide to receive them.

37

"*Pirates?*"

"Must be," said Tabitha grimly, fencing and feinting with the probing tractor beam. The *Alice Liddell*'s work-horse engines were not built for this fine and fancy evasion. She was doing a good job, but it was only a matter of time.

"Not cops? You're sure they're not cops?" murmured Marco over her shoulder.

"They're not cops," said Tabitha.

"You're sure, now? I mean, is there some kind of skull and crossbones on that thing?"

"What?" she yelled. "Get off the flight deck, Marco!"

A burst of light appeared suddenly on the port beam, another beneath it.

Marco flew down the ramp into the hold, Tal swooping after him shrilling in terror.

Saskia and Mogul remained. They had got themselves into the co-pilot's web and were as safe there as anywhere.

Xtasca was there too, hanging on the suspension of their web like a great shiny black grub. Orange light blazed across its body.

"Pulse weapons," it remarked. "They want us alive."

"Great." Tabitha struggled for control. It had grown very hot in the cockpit. She wiped sweat from her brow.

"Get off there," she told the Cherub. It paid no attention.

The Twins clung cheek to cheek, staring into the dazzle

257

like a pair of frightened kittens. "Oh, Xtasca . . ." they
moaned, reaching up towards it.

"They haven't got our range yet," it said, calm as a
commentator at a leisurely sporting event.

Tabitha dropped the starboard wing and sideslipped.
Another orange pulse burst overhead.

"Their instruments are erratic now," continued
Xtasca. Of course, it was right. You can't haul something
of the *Alice*'s mass out of hyperspace without a considerable shockwave.

"We might retaliate now," it said.

Tabitha couldn't stand this commentary. "Get *out* of
here, Xtasca!" she shouted.

"There's no specific danger," Xtasca said.

"You're in the way!"

It turned and looked at her. Though Tabitha's full
attention was occupied, she was still unnerved and annoyed by that glowing stare in the corner of her vision.

"I could deploy the defenses for you," it whispered
coolly.

"I haven't *got* any defenses!" Tabitha howled, pulling
the ship into a sudden full reverse as the tractor beam
brushed her amidships. Engines protesting, the *Alice*
kicked back against her momentum, pitching high and
hard.

Determinedly, Tabitha sat on the thrusters and rode
the pitch up and over. When she glanced aside, she saw
the Cherub had left the cockpit. One of the Twins stared
at her sorrowfully.

The pirates were lumbering after her, splashing the
void with electromagnetic blurts. Already they had shot
off enough power to squirt the *Alice Liddell* all the way
to Saturn.

The big green ship came up clearly for an instant on
the scopes, looking so close they could see the figures
of the crew gesticulating at them from the bridge. It was
a Lesondak Anaconda, or had been before they'd mucked
about with it. Six hundred meters long with two hundred
and thirty beam, its characteristic boastful profile was
still discernible under the vast, bloated ion pods they'd

chosen to jam on either side, the skirt of paralyzer nets slung underneath, the artillery everywhere, and the flashy extension stuck on the prow. There was no Jolly Roger to be seen, but they actually had a figurehead on the thing, a bare-breasted Nubian woman with a salacious grin, and a name: the *Ugly Truth*.

The pulse guns throbbed silently again. The blast rocked the Alice over fifteen degrees to starboard. Rubbish swept across the flight deck and clattered down the ramp. On the console, all the lights went red. Smoke issued from the cracks between the keys.

"We're hit!" cried Mogul.

"Just a slap," said Tabitha. She yanked in back-ups. Two lights lit up. "Come on, come on."

"Why not use the torpedoes?" cried Saskia.

"We haven't got torpedoes!" Tabitha howled. "She's a barge!"

Hectically, Saskia lunged across the aisle and pointed. There on the console was a tab marked TORPEDOES.

Tabitha looked at it.

"I don't believe it," she said.

She glared at Saskia and Mogul, huddled together in the web as though they thought they could avoid getting hit if they simply made themselves as small as possible.

"Did you put that there?" she accused them.

"No!"

Two faces side by side, wide-eyed in the hot purple gloom, like lemurs surprised by torchlight.

The *Ugly Truth* was floating smoothly upwards on the screens. Through the viewport she looked like a big green lobe of cactus, her poisonous metal spines glinting in the light from the suns.

Frenziedly Tabitha scanned the board. "How do you aim these things?"

Together they slipped from the web. "We'll get Xtasca."

Tabitha wiped her face. "Alice?"

"YES, CAPTAIN?"

She touched the label. TORPEDOES. It was really there. "Do you know anything about this?"

"WOULD YOU LIKE THE FULL SPECIFICATIONS?"

"How do I *use* the things?"

A slender silver probe snaked past her neck. It was Xtasca, clinging to her web now, extending its tail. It dipped here and there about the board, and plunged into a socket. A pink array cleared, shifted to amber. Whirring, a monitor dropped down from overhead, showing a scaled set of concentric circles and, sliding in and out behind them, a grey silhouette of the *Ugly Truth*.

"YOU HAVE CONTROL, CAPTAIN," said the ship.

On the monitor the target was shrinking. The *Ugly Truth* was turning towards them, reducing her profile, as if her pilot knew what was happening.

Tabitha reacted. Swiftly she took the *Alice* into a dive, forcing her nose down until they were under the belly of the big green ship. The lens of the tractor beam projector glowed dimly and the dangling nets slid slowly back and forth above them.

"Now," advised the Cherub.

The Twins shouted, "Now!"

Tabitha's finger hit the tab.

Ahead, an ice-blue cloud of propellant erupted from beneath the bow, crystallizing instantly.

A blazing lance split the darkness.

The *Alice* rocked back from the blast.

The missile was a white-hot pinhead against the velvet black of space. It curved delicately round under the shadow of the *Ugly Truth*.

There was a flicker; a blaze of soundless yellow fire.

Craning at the screens, they could see a gaping hole in the hanging nets.

The jubilation was loud. The Twins hugged her, whooping, yelling wildly at Xtasca.

Tabitha clenched her teeth. She was looking for her next shot.

The *Alice Liddell* was still bowling merrily backwards from the recoil. The *Ugly Truth* had disappeared from all the monitors, and the sighting camera was tracking rapidly.

"There they are!"

Tabitha tapped the retros once, twice, and coaxed the *Alice* round broadside on to the dwindling green leaf. It slipped neatly into the middle of the sights as if it belonged there.

Tabitha pressed the tab. The flare of the discharge lit the cockpit.

Everybody cheered.

"I thought you said this tub wasn't armed!" said Marco, bounding back into the cockpit with Tal close overhead.

"That was before," said Tabitha.

On the scope, violet dazzle marked the impact of the second torpedo. She couldn't see what damage it had done. In the sights, the *Ugly Truth* was still dead center.

The Twins dived at the tab.

"Let me!"

"Let me!"

Suddenly Tabitha was beset by shoving elbows and flying arms.

"Hey!" she shouted.

As she struggled to get at the controls, the silver probe lanced over her shoulder again, hitting her on the cheek and striking straight down at the console.

Xtasca had seized the initiative.

Fuming, Tabitha scanned the screens, the viewport.

Nothing happened.

Pushing them all out of the way, Tabitha pressed the tab again. Again.

Nothing.

Wherever the torpedoes had come from, in the random reallocations of hyperspatial shift, there had been only a pair of them. Only the tab and its label remained, mockingly, on her console; only the sighting monitor, with the bulging, spiky shape of her enemy spreading larger and larger across it.

"Oh my *god* . . ."

The Anaconda's pulse gun spat again, and white lightning engulfed the *Alice Liddell*.

38

Dark.

Dark outside and in.

There was not a single spark of power, not a light glowing on board the *Alice Liddell*. Not in the cockpit, where her festive assortment of colored telltales, read-outs, LEDs and indicators lay opaque and dull as so many wine gums. Not in the hold, where Contraband's equipment sat eyeless and dumb. Not in the galley, where the refrigerator suddenly peeped and died. Not in the engines, which guttered and flared a last invisible wisp of plasma, then cooled rapidly in the frigid dark.

The back-ups were down. The failsafes had failed. In the hold, the cargo drones stood in their kennels, motionless as the frozen Frasque. Overhead, the extensors lay coiled like lifeless snakes of steel. All about the hull the scanners were blind. The automatic lungs that circulated and refreshed the *Alice*'s air wheezed once and fell silent.

Time was running out.

In the black cockpit the only gleam came from the red eyes of Xtasca the Cherub. Tabitha was tapping keys angrily, flipping switches back and forth. Nothing happened. She looked accusingly up at Xtasca, as if were its fault. Without power they would soon be drawn into the paralyzing nets of the *Ugly Truth*; and then there would be no more power ever.

"Xtasca!" appealed the Twins.

Tal, confused by the sudden darkness, flew around blundering into dead monitors.

"Here, Tal," said Marco, subdued at last.

Tabitha slumped over the console. She had raced and overtaxed the *Alice* to keep her away from the cops, only to have her fall into the hands of pirates. At the last, her cockpit had been full of confusion and interference; but there was nothing else she could have done.

Tabitha could feel the Twins patting her, stroking her, slipping their skinny hands through her web.

"Tabitha—"

"Tabitha—"

"Who are they?"

"Where are they taking us?"

She fended them off. "Alice?" She keyed for vox again. "Alice, can you hear me?"

There was no reply. Instead, Tabitha could hear Marco swearing softly to himself, over and over again.

She wondered what her options were.

She wondered if she had any options.

She wondered if she was going to die.

Searchlights dazzled her. Their captors were examining their catch.

The Twins were appealing to the Cherub again.

"Xtasca, can't you—?"

"Xtasca, surely—"

But the Cherub was gone.

It was swimming hurriedly into the forward port airlock, towing its saucer, and pulling up its hood as it went.

"Xtasca?" they called.

For answer there was only the sound of the inner door closing and a lockful of air spurting into vacuum as Xtasca cranked the outer door open.

"Where's it going?" Tabitha asked.

Not even the Twins seemed to know.

The pirate ship was now spreadeagled perfectly before them, a symmetrical silhouette blocking out the misty stars. A pale silver gleam appeared in the eye of the beam projector and immediately something insubstantial thumped the *Alice Liddell*.

"Whoa!" cried Marco, grabbing hold of a loop as the deck tilted under him. Tal, together with a quantity of clutter, flew into the air. "What's happening?"

Tabitha slapped the console with both hands.

"We're dead," she announced. "And Xtasca's run off and left us."

Outside, the shiny black form of the Cherub went shooting across the gulf between the ships and was immediately lost to view.

"She's going over there," commented Saskia.

Tabitha turned and looked at her. The acrobat's long face was a mask of dismay in the cruel arclight, as if she were sensible of some offense, some injury, or—

Betrayal.

Suddenly Tabitha saw it all.

The ship swayed again. Then there was a sense of motion, slight but steady, as she was pulled from her previous trajectory.

"Are they towing us somewhere, is that it?" Marco said.

"They're reeling us in," said Tabitha.

Things began to subside gently towards the back of the cockpit as the *Alice* succumbed to the grip of the tractor beam.

They could all suit up and bail out. For what good that would do. Without the computer she had no idea where they were. Her suit had a beacon and probably the bands' did too, but there might be nobody for gigameters. And the pirates would still pick them up—or pick them off—in minutes.

But they could suit up and bail out. It was an option.

Perhaps that was what Xtasca had done, anticipating her order, as it customarily did. But Tabitha thought not.

At that moment Tal squealed in surprise as every speaker in the cockpit fizzed and crackled into life.

"*Ahoy there,* Alice Liddell! *Ahoy, Captain Jute! How's ever'body today?*"

"How can they do that?" asked Marco, holding out his hand for Tal to come and perch.

Tabitha didn't know. She didn't much care. "They've got some clever friends," she said.

"*That was quite a trick you just pulled, Captain Jute,*"

the voice continued. *"Here's one for you."*

The cabin pressure rose abruptly.

Tal shrieked and fell out of the air, lying on his back on the wall and kicking frantically at the invisible enemy mercilessly crushing his tiny torso. Unprotected by the dead web, Tabitha felt as if her insides were being squeezed against her skeleton.

"Lay off, you bastards!" yelled Marco, indistinctly.

But the pressure was already falling again.

"Got any more tricks, Captain?"

"Just give us a chance, shitsucker!" bellowed Marco, scrabbling for the choking bird.

"Is that a no?" asked the voice, and paused again. *"Okay,"* it said, *"now you just hang in there and don't touch nothing. We'll be seeing you real soon,"* said the voice with lazy good humor.

Securely clamped in the hold of the tractor beam, the *Alice Liddell* was being drawn inexorably towards the *Ugly Truth* and its paralyzing nets. The underside of this vulgar predator of the spaceways expanded until they could make out an observation blister, and inside it the minute figures of her crew.

"Can you see it?" asked Tabitha.

"What?" said Mogul.

"The Cherub," she said. She got out of her sagging web and worked her way carefully down the ramp, which under the new gravity was very steep indeed, to the suit locker.

Marco didn't understand. "Are those Seraphs? Is that a Seraph ship?"

"Uh-uh." Her tether suit was still where she'd left it, in her cabin. She wanted the hull-walking suit. She pulled it out. "Seraphs wouldn't be seen dead driving a piece of crap like that. Get suits on."

"Where did Xtasca go?" Saskia asked her brother.

"Where do you think," said Tabitha shortly. She stepped into the suit.

"Tabitha!"

They were shocked. "Tabitha, it tried to save us!"

"She armed the torpedoes for you!"

"How do you know that? How do you know it didn't deliberately screw them up?"

"Hey, come on now, Tabitha, you can't think—"

"How well do you know it? How well *can* you know one of those, those hi-tech tadpoles—" She fastened her necklock and reached for the helmet. "Who else has got the tech to grab hold of someone in mid-skip?"

They couldn't answer that.

"Get your fucking suits on."

They tumbled past her into the hold.

Tabitha Jute, in fact, knew as little about Cherubim as anyone in that cockpit, and less then most. But she was wild and angry and short of sleep, and all her resentment and mistrust came boiling out.

She hung in the forward hold lock, aware of the dark green hulk swelling in the viewport up behind her.

"I don't suppose you've got any concealed weapons on board, have you, it's just dead aliens, isn't it?" She looked grimly around the hold.

"Oh," said Mogul lightly. "As to that..." He twisted his hand in the air, and Tabitha saw something in it suddenly, something that glinted darkly. It was a small metallic blue gun.

"At close quarters," he said lightly, "this will open them up like flowers."

Tabitha held out her hand.

He stared at her broodingly. "I think I'll keep it," he said.

Tabitha climbed back into the cockpit for her bag.

The *Ugly Truth* hung over them like a dark green planet, so close now it wasn't over any more but under, and they were plunging into its nets.

Dark green metalwork filled the field of vision. There was no scale. It was impossible to tell how far below it was. It had become a whole terrain, a landscape spotted with lights. The large bright observation bubble looked like a city dome rising up to meet them as they came in to land. Smaller lights, gun slots and portholes: those might have been the lights of isolated buildings, outlying farms. That shiny silver circle was the tractor beam projector, hauling them to death. It looked tranquil and lovely as a moonlit lake.

All around, the fringes of the paralyzing nets reached up for her ship like cobwebs for a fly. Tabitha could see the charred and twisted metal where her torpedoes had struck. The damage was nothing, there were other areas as bad, leaking charge or black and crumpled.

The paralyzing nets rose up around them now, drawing the *Alice* in.

"*There you go,*" said the enormous voice, soothingly. "*No prob—*"

There was a blinding flash, as though the ship were full of lightning. Then all its lights went out.

The illusory landscape vanished. Beneath Tabitha's head was total blackness. Dark the observation blister; the gun placements, the portholes, the tractor beam projector: all dark.

Tabitha felt the *Alice Liddell* surge up under her as gravity came to a new arrangement. The little Kobold was faithfully trying to orbit the bigger ship.

Tabitha flew to the console, a voice sounding in her headset, a tiny one this time.

"*Sleep well,*" it whispered.

It was Xtasca.

39

BGK009059 LOG

TXJ.STD

PRINT

‡*ƒ(]rn.9åÑXO:ÆŒfiØØØØØØØØØØØØtxjØ!Hram'ˆˆˆˆ/6fl
!--- --*./Ç]222m

MODE? VOX

SD? 09.07.07

READY

Hello, Alice.

HELLO CAPTAIN.

What are they doing now?

STILL REHEARSING. DO YOU WANT TO LISTEN IN?

No thank you.
   Do the Twins remind you of Tricarico Palynides?

I DIDN'T EVER MEET TRICARICO PALYNIDES, CAPTAIN.

It was Tricarico who first told me about the *Léonor Casares*.
I don't think I believed him. Not then.

I DIDN'T BELIEVE IN HER MYSELF UNTIL WE MET HER.

Do you remember that?

OH YES.

We were on a long loop from Autonomy to Dione with a pod of zero-g crystals for the vet hospital, six days since skip, and you said there was a derelict on the scope.

AND YOU SAID THERE COULDN'T BE!

I still say so.

I SUPPOSE YOU'D SAY THE *LÉONOR CASARES* ISN'T A DERELICT.

Well she isn't. She's still in transit.

FORTY-ONE YEARS OUT.

"She was the *Léonor Casares* from Luna, taking Tibor La-pham to report on the site the family had staked out for their operations on Ganymede. Before he boarded the shuttle at Serenity Tibor ate a plate of waffles with bacon and maple syrup and drank a tube of coffee. He read the financial screens and placed a satellite call to his PA in Sri Lanka. The local conditions were stormy. He couldn't get her picture. He joked about it, telling her she looked terrible. He gave her some instructions, and reminded her that one of the managers was celebrating his birthday. Then he took ship and went to look into the face of the father of the gods.

"Tibor Lapham never completed his mission. Something went wrong."

THAT'S VERY ELOQUENT, CAPTAIN.

Oh, I was reading that. It's in this book I found. It's fascinating, though, isn't it?

WHAT'S YOUR THEORY? I PRESUME YOU HAVE A THE-
ORY.

No, I like them all. Let's see, number one, there was a
mutiny, and Tibor was killed. Number two, he was rebelling
against the family firm, trying to steal the ship. Three, he
had a fight with the captain about a woman. Four, the captain
miscalculated the route and they slipped into a Moebius
continuum. Five, Tibor was crossed in love and trying to
commit suicide. Six, he passed close to one of the astral
sphincters and because no one had seen one before he
tried to go through it. What others are there? Oh yes. He hit
a time reef and won't emerge again until the thirtieth century.
    They all come back to Tibor, every one. The doomed
young hero. No one even remembers the name of the
captain of the *Léonor Casares*.

ISN'T IT IN YOUR BOOK?

Somewhere, I expect. Some people said he gave a wrong
command and got the ship implicated in a paradox.

I THOUGHT SHE WAS A DERELICT. SHE LOOKED LIKE A
DERELICT TO ME.

Six days in hyperspace and you say there's a derelict at
310° ahead.

THE MASS OF A SHIP BUT NO ENERGY READINGS, NO
HEAT PATTERN.

I said it was just a hallucination. Particle interference. Something out in real space casting a hypercubic shadow.

YOU WERE SCARED.

I wasn't.

YOU WERE.

How do you know?

I KNOW YOU, CAPTAIN JUTE.
  DID YOU THINK WE WERE GOING TO HIT IT?

Or be hit by it. It seemed like a possibility. Anyway, I just
didn't like you thinking there was something out there. Either
there wasn't, in which case you might be going wrong and
I was in bad trouble, or there was, in which case the universe
might be going wrong and I was in worse trouble.

  The one thing I didn't think was, *Léonor Casares*. I hadn't
believed Tricarico, I hadn't believed it when I saw about the
legend on AV. I don't suppose I could have even told you
her name.

  Then I saw her.

  I'd knew you couldn't meet another ship in hyperspace.
It's not supposed to be possible. But she was on the scanners, and I was looking at her.

  She wasn't there, and then she was. She came looming
out of the nothing as if someone had pushed her through
a sheet. There was something strange about her shape, I
thought. I wondered if she'd had some sort of dimensional
accident, got herself mistranslated and come through wrong.
Then I realized she was a Freimacher Courtier, one of the
really early ones when they were still putting all the back-
up chemical engines on them. She was old. That was scary
too. What was something that old doing out there?

THERE WERE NO SIGNALS. I CALLED AND CALLED, ON
EVERY FREQUENCY I COULD REACH. THERE WAS NOTH-
ING.

I wanted to go and have a look, but I didn't dare go outside.

YOU'RE MORE BLASÉ NOWADAYS, CAPTAIN.

That's not blasé, Alice. They drive me out. It's come out here or stay inside and go as mad as they are.

I wish the *Léonor* would come back now. That would make them jump. No, though, Marco would be on to me to take it in tow to sell to some entrepreneur on Titan.

Did you see the name or did I?

I DID. AND YOU SAID YOU'D NEVER HEARD OF IT.

I called up what we had on record, then I remembered the ship Tricarico had told me about, that was condemned to wander the abyss of hyperspace forever and never come to land.

Here, here's a good bit.

"There, in the crack between space and time, neither past, present nor future, she loiters. Her engines are primed, her cells all charged; yet nothing hums, nothing glows.

"The crew of fifteen sit down together three times each subjective day to eat a meal. It is always the same meal. They have always eaten it, and always will. Each haggard sailor avoids the eyes of his neighbors, imagining he alone is suffering from this monstrous apprehension. Is it today that the dire imprisonment begins? Or have they been drifting like this forever? Up and down the table and along the walls of the galley, the lamps are out. The food is cold. The navigator tries to light his pipe and fails. He has always tried and always failed. Fuel will not burn, nor crystal spark.

"The crew attempt to conceal their anxiety from each other, slapping the table and singing boisterous shanties. One forgets the words, making the others laugh. He forgot those words, exactly the same words, yesterday and the day before, and the day before that, every day for thirty years. The choruses grow ragged, half-hearted. The crew are keeping an ear open for the conversation the captain is having with their passenger, young Tibor, the owner's son, up on the bridge. A muttered word or two, a fragment of a phrase, drifts down to them.

"'... spectrum counterparts ...'

"'... can't possibly be. It can't possibly.'

"'... stabilizers. No response.'

"The crew, like all sailors, are superstitious people. For some, this is their first skip. They do not like having to cross this region of pallid murk and curdled mercury. They do not like this tense, whispered conversation between Master Lipham and Captain Naum. They are afraid something is wrong with the ship. In a minute the bosun will be called to the bridge. The situation will be explained. An order will be given. In a minute or two they will break out the equipment to meet the crisis, and everything will become clear: a matter of applied strength and technical know-how.

"But on the *Léonor Casares* the minutes no longer pass."

There was no sign of the Cherub. They watched and called for it all the while Tabitha was bringing the systems back up. They tried and tried to raise it, but there was no answer. They waited as long as they dared, lingering in the penumbra of the darkened pirate ship; but it was no use. That whispered benediction had been its parting message, and there could be no reply.

Somewhere Xtasca had found a niche for its tricky tail, inveigled itself into the electrics from the outside, and blown the lot. It had doomed the *Ugly Truth* to float at large, dark and dead, through the empty realm of interplanetary space; and itself to travel with it.

By mutual consent they decided not to court danger by crawling over it looking for Xtasca's body. One corpse, Tabitha thought but did not say, was enough. She restored power to the primaries and set them moving slow ahead, away from the seductive reach of the dead ship. At minimum thrust they rode out of its shadow, leaving it further and further behind, its popeyed figurehead grinning at the dark. Gradually it would settle into its last decaying orbit, one more lifeless piece of scrap swinging silently around the sun; and there she would be only too pleased to leave it.

While the *Alice*'s persona got herself back in shape and ran all the setting-up routines, captain and passengers took off their suits and sat together in the hold, drinking the last of the tea. Marco was glum, his utterances alternating between growls of hate and nervous, high-pitched attempts at reassurance and positivity. Tal, unsettled, refused to stay on his shoulder and fluttered in a distracted way from box to speaker to catwalk rail.

The Zodiac Twins were heartbroken.

"She was the one they came to see," said Saskia. "Not us, with our feeble tricks and songs. She . . . Xtasca . . . She was the next generation of humankind. She could fly. She could breathe vacuum. She could—she—"

Saskia stopped and buried her face in her brother's shoulder.

Marco cleared his throat, sat forward with his hands clasped together, his forearms resting on his knees. "Maybe somebody oughta say a few words," he suggested uneasily. "Captain, I, er, I guess you, maybe you should be the one."

"To Abraxas?" said Tabitha. "No."

She sat nearby him on a trunk, her shoulders hunched, her hands pressed between her thighs. She looked for the silver-grey traveling coffin. Someone had covered it over again.

"Did it—did she have any family?" Tabitha asked.

The Twins shook their heads.

"They don't," said Mogul.

Marco put his arm around her.

"Don't blame yourself," he said.

She looked round at him sharply, about to shrug him off; but she didn't.

They left it at that.

Tal perched on Xtasca's flaccid cocoon and preened himself sorrowfully. He began to sing a melancholy, throbbing violin solo, all mawkish minor thirds and vibrato. The humans winced and looked at one another, but for once no one ventured to stop him.

Still, the bird effectively terminated the mood by describing it. Tabitha roused herself, realizing how stale the air was getting. Marco, feeling her about to rise, relinquished his consolatory embrace, slapped his hands together.

"Okay, people, let's get this show on the road."

There was work to do aboard the *Alice Liddell*: circuits to replace, breakers to replace, tests to run.

"How's it looking, Alice?"

"LIVABLE."

Despite herself, Tabitha smiled a small, wry smile. "Did you lose anything, can you tell?"

"EVERYTHING SEEMS TO BE HERE, CAPTAIN. INCLUDING SEVERAL THINGS I HAVEN'T THOUGHT ABOUT FOR YEARS. AND ALL YOUR STORIES, I THINK. PLEASE WILL YOU TELL ME SOME MORE STORIES SOON?"

"As soon as I can, Alice. I promise. As soon as we get the money we'll rest up for a while and get you a proper overhaul."

Privately she doubted tranquility was in prospect; but there was no point alarming Alice. They had been hijacked into a completely uninhabited region, quite a way from the nearest planet. It wasn't one you could limp to on impulse power and expect to find help.

They were going to have to skip.

"Tell us what needs doing now and we'll get on with it," she said.

Up it came.

AXIS LOCK CRYSTAL DEFECT. FAILURE PROBABILITY 96.66%.

Oh Christ.

"THE CHERUB ISN'T WITH US AT THE MOMENT, IS IT, CAPTAIN?"

"No, Alice." She patted the persona reader. "Cross your fingers."

Fatalism seemed to make sense in the lucidity of physical and emotional exhaustion. Blame and conflict didn't seem to mean anything any more. She had passed beyond

them, into the frail, vulnerable peace that prevailed as
everyone set to work with circuit testers and fuses.

As soon as the auton circuits came back on, Tabitha
broke out the cargo drones to help shift all the junk that
was in the way. Squat, solid and stable on their stumpy
little legs, they toiled through the tumbled baggage, their
domed heads swiveling as they clicked information to
one another. With remarkable gentleness they hoisted
drum cases and holo units into the air and walked up the
walls to deposit them on the catwalk. On screen Tabitha
spotted one of them taking hold of the grey cylinder that
held the mortal remains of Hector the Frasque.

"No," she called. "Override. Not that."

Mogul slid lightly down from the catwalk to relieve
the drone. He waved to her on the camera.

"I have it," he said.

There was nothing sexual or sinister in his smile. An
odd alliance had come into being. They weren't simply
victim and villains any more, they were all in this together.

Whatever they were going to pay her, though, it wasn't
worth it. Monotonous and lonely as everyday life often
was, it had a lot of advantages over violence and sudden
death.

Next time she looked at the hold monitor she saw the
same drone wheeling away Xtasca's hoverdisc.

"Override," she called again. "Not that either."

Saskia came squeezing out of an inspection panel in
the ceiling of the gangway with a burnt-out feeler link
to show her. She sat up in the co-pilot's web, twiddling
the fragment between her slender white fingers.

"She meant a lot to you, didn't she?" said Tabitha.

Saskia nodded. She sat cross-legged, ran her fingers
through her hair. "You shouldn't have said those things
about her."

Tabitha stiffened. "She ran out! What was I supposed
to think?"

"They're not bad people," said Saskia, emphatically.
It sounded like something she had said many times before. "They have their own ideas. They wanted to be

on their own, they went off on their own, what's so bad about that?''

Defiantly, she stuck out her long jaw.

"Who's this?'' asked Tabitha, preoccupied with the cutaway graphics on the screen, damage sites flashing red.

"The Seraphim!''

There was real pain in her voice.

Tabitha turned in her seat. Saskia was rising from her web, reaching for a ceiling loop. "You don't want me here, I'll go.''

"No, it's all right, I'm sorry, I've got—'' She waved a weary hand at the console.

Saskia looked at the crumpled black link in her hand. "I'm useless,'' at the console.

Saskia looked the crumpled back link in her hand. "I'm useless,'' she said.

Tabitha gestured at the monitor. "Go and help your brother,'' she suggested. Instantly she knew it had been the wrong thing to say.

Saskia flashed her a look of high displeasure.

Tabitha, exasperated, threw up her hand. "One minute you're curled up in each other's arms—''

"I'm trying!'' said Saskia, her voice croaking with emotion. At that moment, she clearly believed she was. "Xtasca—I know you can't understand them, even we can't do that, not entirely, but sometimes you could look at her and see what she was thinking, what she was feeling—You'd think, she is a long way from home and performing in a crummy circus act, but you could see it in her eyes—'' Standing negligently in the aisle between the seats, she drew herself up, lifting her head and pulling back her shoulders. "You'd think, I wish I could do that, could be like her.''

They had nice shoulders, thought Tabitha, who hadn't followed a word of all that. She had a sudden urge to get up and hold her, to put her arms around those shoulders, but she was not at all sure it would be a good idea. It led, though, to an odd, awkward-shaped pause; and she felt compelled to offer something, even if it was only for something to say. "What did she do, then?" she asked.

Saskia stared at her as if she'd asked who the Capellans were or who'd built Plenty. "She rescued us!"

Tabitha was growing more and more confused. She jerked a thumb towards the distant pirate ship. "Just now, you mean."

"No! Us! Mogul and me!"

"What from?"

Now Saskia was looking baffled. "From Abraxas!"

"You're from Abraxas?"

"They made us! I told you. And Xtasca got us out. She put us on a ship and took us away and we never went back. And then she could never go back." Her voice dropped towards grief again. She looked down, focusing once more on the ruined component in her hand. "What shall I do with this?"

Tabitha didn't know what to say. She looked at the desolate figure, at the profiles of assault and battery paging patiently past on her screen. "There's some more," she said, "in, in the . . ."

There was the axis lock, the crystal flashing, flashing Xtasca's good work all undone.

"I'll come and get them," she said. "In a minute."

But Saskia had gone, back to the hold.

Tabitha sighed, frowned, concentrated.

On her left a bank of lights came up green. She looked at the monitor and saw another drone emerging from a service tunnel to the engines, the welding laser dimming in its manipulators. It flashed an okay message and report down the line and closed the tunnel hatch securely behind it before stumping off to return the equipment assigned to it from stores.

There was something to be said for mechanical companions. No stray feathers, no sexual entanglements, no sudden death.

Subjective hours went by.

Tabitha had to admit they made a good team. Temperament repressed by fright and loss, they worked together with the discipline they had from acrobatics and conjuring. Cheerfulness returned; they whistled and sang snatches of songs. She began to think she might almost have them where she could trust them. Except for all that bollocks about the Frasque.

She opened the com.

"Okay, everyone. Suit up, stow everything and get secure. Put Tal in his box. We have the drive back on line."

Cheers, whistles and applause.

"Is this a test?" asked Marco, Tal flapping on his wrist, more like a hawk than a parrot.

"If it doesn't work, it's a test. If it does, we should be on our way in five minutes subjective.

"Five minutes," she said again, and cut the connection.

Then it was just her and Alice, like hundreds of times before, about to nurse the ship through another violation of the laws of physics. The computer had digested all the available data and refigured the route. On screen and readout the flux of figures was freezing, setting in the arcane combinations that would release the triple lock of the dimensions.

"Here we go, Alice."

Tabitha lowered the primaries to idle and pumped everything at the Capellan drive. She felt it began to whir. She felt it in her bones, in the fabric of the ship.

Outside the light of the stars was melting to the sound of woodwinds. Inside the familiar crepuscular haze of the interim was rising out of the plates of the deck and walls.

Tabitha realized she had been holding her breath. She let it out in a hard, deep sigh.

The ship was rocking, yawing from side to side. Automatically she reached out to correct it.

She was listening for a rattle, a telltale irregular tapping noise.

There was no rattle.

There was a whine.

Tabitha frowned.

They skipped.

The drab eiderdown of hyperspace enveloped them. Time and space were suspended.

The whining wasn't.

"What is it, Alice?"

"SEARCHING."

The whine developed teeth.

The ship was buzzing, higher and faster, making Tabitha's teeth hum.

"Alice!"

She screwed up her mouth. She could still feel her teeth, buzzing behind her lips.

"AXIS LOCK CRYSTAL."

The ship was screaming.

"FAILURE."

Tabitha swore.

ABORT, she keyed. ABORT. ABORT.

The scream jumped an octave.

There was a loud bang.

"Oh *shit* . . ."

They were back in space again, the stars of the galaxy streaming across the scanners, whirling nauseatingly around the viewport. They were in a spin.

Tabitha hit the engines with one hand, brought up automatic correction routines with the other.

The computer fed a stabilizing routine between one hand and the other.

The *Alice* jolted out of her roll and began to quiver.

Tabitha felt very cold. Her memory dumped all her emergency training into her brain at once, in a great turmoil of learned reflexes and sober advice. Flipping tabs, keying sequences, she tried to haul something sensible out of the confusion. She could hear whining again. This time it was her.

"Alice, please, please, don't . . ."

The *Alice* was still quivering. The *Alice* was going down. She was looking for the nearest gravity well, and she was going to go down it.

Meshed into racing streams of data on the earpiece, on the screens and readouts, questioning with her fingers and getting answers with her eyes, Tabitha could not at

that moment have distinguished herself from her ship.
The computers, the relays, the whole intricate array of
tabs and keys and switches spread before her, all were
an extension of her central nervous system. Believe me:
if the ship could have flown on Tabitha's will alone, she
would have got up and flown all the way to Titan.

She was going down.

Glancing up an instant from the controls to the viewport, Tabitha cried out in alarm.

Something huge and green was rushing towards her.

The *Ugly Truth*.

No. Something far larger, something far more dangerous. Something there was no way of switching off,
Cherub or no Cherub.

She yelled into the com.

"I can't hold her! We're going to hit and hit hard!"

There was no more space.

The cockpit was aglow with a sick green light.

The *Alice Liddell* fell out of the sky.

Below her, auroras darted horizontal tongues of ne-
bulous fire a hundred kilometers wide.

She fell through the fire.

Below that, greasy, sulphurous clouds gobbled up the
sunlight.

She fell through the clouds, which hissed around her
ravaged hull like boiling water. She fell into dust, swirling dust that blinded her scanners again and chewed at
her antennae.

Below that, in ruddy darkness, sullen lightning played.
By its fitful light Tabitha could see vast angry mountains
squatting, vomiting plumes of acid smoke into the murky
air. At the feet of the mountains, cracked plains of
parched yellow rock lay like stained and crumpled paper.

The *Alice* soared across the mountains.

Beyond, a thick, turgid sea beat itself senseless against
the rocks. From the surface of the sea, great lazy skeins
of poison vapor coiled up to the ship as she battered
through the heavy air.

Inside the ship, the heat was a torment. The furious
sky was squeezing them. Portholes were creaking, hull-

plates groaning. The Twins clutched each other. From the faceplates of their suits everyone gazed at everyone else in horror, eyes wide as if to take everything in before death came and darkness swallowed everything forever.

The *Alice* blasted across the sea.

Beyond the sea was land; such land as none of them had ever seen before. It was a vegetable inferno. It boiled with forests; it seethed with jungle.

Jagged blue treetops beckoned.

Crackling with wild fire, the *Alice Liddell* plunged into the forest.

Trees, if trees they were, went down in swathes before her. Long tracts of woody sponge she gouged. Writhing groves of luminous spaghetti she sheared. Behind her, foul smoke went up, thickening the soupy air.

Branches crazed the viewport, ripped scanners from the hull. Tabitha couldn't see anything any more. She screamed something, screaming along with her ship, which screamed as she hit.

She skidded and turned in the pulpy undergrowth, churning everything beneath her. Sap and ichor rained down on the dented hull. All around her were outraged hoots and squeals of panic.

And then it was over.

The vegetable twilight closed around the ruined ship. The terrible heat redoubled. Sulphurous steam oozed sinuously through cracked plexiglass and lacerated steel.

It was over. The *Alice Liddell* was down.

Down in the dirt, in the jungle, on Venus.

FOUR

Captives of the Goddess of Love

41

Few people today remember that the planet Venus was named for an ancient goddess of love. To us, especially those of us who have been there, there is little that is lovely on the planet Venus.

Venus was never a serious candidate for colonization, even in the Rush Years, when much madder schemes were proposed. Taming those burning continents and sullen seas is a task all but the profligate and obsessed soon relinquished. The whole world has been abandoned, to admirers of the bizarre and extreme, for whom Vulcan Tours still provide their notorious monthly excursions. Even these do not attempt to descend to the surface of this perverse and deadly world, where the sun runs slow, and backwards.

Not that the face of Venus is not fair, especially on a first approach. So thick is its purulent, yeasty atmosphere, so dank and condensed the air, that each climactic zone is a stain of a different color, shimmering and changing as the huge day dawns, intensifies and wanes. Venus is a chameleon with the range of the peacock, the kingfisher, the butterfly. At the shining edge of the world, in advance of the slow, smouldering terminator, white Niobe wakes tinted with apricot or mauve, while further along Eisila already glows orange as fresh fire, blotted with the black smears of thunderheads. In the white heat of the unimaginable noon, the Mare Evita Peron blazes like molten gold, incandescent and steaming; the Jezebel Basin is a spill of turquoise ink, flecked with viridian foam. Perelandra Planitia slumbers, stretched out in the torpid afternoon, its taut uplands sparkling with spikes and splinters of rainbow. Evening has claimed Asteria, its crumpled tracts of fog like burnished bronze in the last reach of the sun.

The night is blue, ultramarine, blue-black on the shrouded slopes of Nokomis. You turn, dazzled and breathless, from the observation window, and look at your watch. You have been staring for an hour, yet it has seemed no more than the blink of an eye. If you are young, and excitable, and impressed by glamor, Venus will seem to beckon you with the promise, the dare, of searing beauty. If you are not so young, not so ready to take a world at face value, you will admire and exclaim, but wondering all the while what harsh and rocky reality lurks beneath such rich and garish camouflage.

And you will be right.

On Venus, the colossal volcanoes of Beta Regio spew flaming mud onto igneous beaches of fretted grey stone. To the west, beyond the mountains, empty plains of shale give way to aching deserts of grit that slither and crack, baking by day and freezing by night. To the north, in the cauldron of Mnemosyne, sulphuric hurricanes tear continuously through the sodden valleys. To the south, in Phoebe and Themis, shaggy, convoluted mangroves sweat poison into sour green swamps. East is the Sea of Guinevere, where huge ravening serpents burst from the pewter-colored waves to devour burrowing sandsharks.

At the poles as in the deserts, nothing lives, nor can. In the deep, unyielding cold, frozen stuff sets and sifts and stirs again in a wild flux of matter, neither solid, liquid nor gaseous. The polar regions of Venus are a cold hell, where the titans of the winds rage against their imprisonment, howling and screaming as they toss the chemical snows in mad vortices and freezing arcs of white.

The coral reefs of Erebus rise in great jagged spires from the sticky sea. Etched, eroded ridges spiral and veer, running for ten, twenty kilometers through smoke-black water. Where they meet they throw up frozen, warty explosions of barbed knots and clusters of mineral teeth. On these serrated edges the medusas, globs of muscular mucus as wide as tabletops, hang stranded and expiring, thrown up by tempests that rend the glutinous, tideless waves. The cliffs of the coral are thickly stained with their ichor. Angular jet-black lobsters half a meter long gouge lumps from their shriveling, pulpy flesh; the piranha lizards fight for their stalky eyes.

In Belladonna, between the eroded cinder cones, tar pits still smoke and seethe. On the slopes of ancient caldera, among black grasses that flutter forlornly in the corrosive wind, stunted trees poke their limbs at the heavy sky. Their leaves are like greasy leather; but in autumn, which comes early in these latitudes, they shrivel and blow away like blackened flakes of paper from a bonfire. The fruit is pale, long and pointed, resembling diseased okra. Scaly cavebats descend in tens of thousands, and strip the branches in a night. The bark of these sad trees is powdery, and constantly bleeds a thick grey syrup, for they are host to a race of parasitic snagworms, which feed on the fibers of the wood. All summer they chew and multiply, chew and multiply. Sometimes, it is said, the infested tree can be seen to smoke, even to burst into flame from its own inner heat.

The fauna of Venus are mindless, belligerent and savage. They come forth plated and clawed; they move under shells, low to the ground. They leave trails of slime and drool; of the blood and juices of their prey, creatures less wary and less well armored than themselves. In the gluey ammonia bogs of Aino dwell razorsnakes and giant fiery scorpions, crusty and red as pepper-loaves. Native to the shores of Beersheba are the Strayker Turtle, not a turtle at all, in fact, but a squat cayman with a leaden carapace whose weight will eventually, in nine cases out of ten, break its fat neck; and the cannibal armadillo. The armpit of Aphrodite is home to the heavy metal iguanas, purple as a fresh bruise, and to a species of asbestos pangolin.

Their prey are the snagworms and such. Slugs, thick and yellow, or grey and coarse as porridge; giant centipedes and fat fawn beetles with nine legs; fudge-colored creep owls; rapid, hairy spiders. Mammals, if ever they emerged from the crude boiling of Venusian phyla, never stood a chance here.

Nature was surely right to leave Venus a crucible of fetid chemical and vegetable violence where reptiles war with insects; merciful not to bless her with sapient life. Only consider what cruel race might have stepped from these hellish forests, what fortresses of sheer black stone might have been reared among these savage hills, where even the Frasque turned away. One day these creatures might have spread wings of greasy leather and ventured upon the stinking bosom of the air; might have stretched their talons at last into space, and clutched, it may be, at the fair soil of Terra.

There is no intelligent life on Venus; and so there was no one to watch, in awe and terror, as the overheated Kobold tore screaming through the forest canopy, ploughing all before it, spewing great waves of mud and sappy vegetation in all directions, and finally coming to a jolting, rattling stop in the undergrowth of Aphrodite Terra.

Tabitha Jute lifted her head.

The light was strange, viscid and subterranean. She saw ruin and destruction. The viewport was starred and ruptured, and covered entirely in a poultice of red muck, squashed fungus and leaves. Instruments had been shaken from their mountings and lay smashed on the floor among gouts of mud and twinkling chips of plexiglass. The retaining nets had torn loose, and oily rags, old flight discs and empty insulite cups had been flung around the cockpit. There were red lights and dead lights on all the boards, and the scanners were all out or fizzing uselessly.

"Alice?"

There was no reply.

She reached a shaking hand for the keyboard. In shock, she couldn't remember a single command. The air seemed to be full of a ringing, hissing sound which she took several minutes to identify as the oxygen flow of her suit. She was still connected to the persona vox channel, but nothing was coming through.

"Alice, can you hear me?"

Nothing.

Tabitha's eyes filled with tears. Her nose was running. She checked the cockpit pressure. It was enormous.

It was Venus's.

She sniffed hard and swallowed, telling herself to stop shaking, telling the screamers and searchlights in her skull she didn't need them.

In the mess blocking the viewport something small suddenly slithered and jumped away, making her shout in fright. Only a lizard, she told herself. But there were bigger things out there, roaming the jungle. She had heard about them. The crash would have scared them away. They would be back.

Meanwhile there was an immense, omnipresent, utterly hostile monster facing them, surrounding them, not about to go away for anything. The planet.

Tabitha took a deep breath. The oxygen cleared her head, made everything slightly shiny, slightly unreal. She keyed open the first aid drawer—that worked—fished in it for a cocktail of glucose and caffeine and half a dozen other steadying and stimulating things. While she sucked, she tried Alice again. She thought the plaque itself was intact in the reader, but she couldn't raise her.

If the persona was broken, that was the end.

The ship was open to the elements, leaking out of every fracture. Tabitha shut down the drive systems, the navigation circuits, the struggling aerator and everything else that entry hadn't shut down for her.

It was then she remembered she had passengers. She pressed the switch. "Hello?" she called. "Are you all right in there?"

There was a pause. Then someone got to the com.

"Hello, hello, Tabitha?" answered a weak voice. It was one of the Twins. "Mogul, Mogul's—"

She broke off, mumbled something to someone, then there was a pause. Tabitha could hear ragged breathing. She slapped the side of her helmet. She could hear the sound of heavy boots, confused voices, one of them Marco's. "Saskia? Are you there? Mogul's what?"

"I'm all right," said Mogul valiantly, too close to the mike. "Tabitha, are you all right?"

"I think so," she said. "Alice is—"

She didn't know what Alice was. She tried the keys again. The screen flickered, filled with gibberish.

Suddenly there were raised voices in the hold, thumps and bangs.

Saskia—she was sure it was Saskia—shouted out in shock and alarm.

"Saskia? What's happening? What's wrong?"

She could hear Saskia shouting, "No, no, come back!" Rattling, creaking noises, crashes of baggage and equipment being thrown down.

"Saskia!" Tabitha called.

Marco was shouting, Saskia was shouting, Mogul was shouting, Tabitha couldn't make out a word. She hit the switch for the airlock to the hold. Nothing happened.

"Are you all right?" she called, hitting it again and again. "What's happening in there?"

There was a gabble of consternation, panic, running feet, Marco shouting orders. No one was listening to her.

She didn't want to move. She didn't want to get down from her web. She wanted to stay there, insulated from the monster. She didn't want to know what the hell was happening in the hold. Let them kill each other and get it over with.

She opened the latches and ran up the tilting floor, kicking the debris aside.

She felt clumsy, laboring as if underwater. She turned up her oxygenator and lumbered across the ramp to the hold.

The door to the hold was closed, and buckled. Tabitha tried to open it. It wouldn't budge. She hammered on it, heavy thumps of her gloved fist. "Hello?" she called. "Hello, can you hear me?"

Nothing. She turned up her radio and called again.

Still nothing.

Tabitha looked around. The portholes were covered with unearthly vegetation, filling the gangway with umber gloom. Both forward airlocks had held, though the port side was badly dented.

She was a good ship. They don't build them like that anymore.

Tabitha ran back into the cockpit and rummaged in a locker where she thought there might be a crowbar. There wasn't a crowbar, but there was a large spanner. She got it out, hefted it, and went and attacked the door to the hold.

She got the spanner in the edge of the door and heaved. The spanner spun out of the crack, almost hitting her helmet. Careful! She was still trembling, and high from the oxygen. She banged on the door again and called, but there was no reply, nothing on the com.

She turned on her boots and shuffled up the wall, crouching and holding on to the twisted flange of the door. With a determined heave she got the spanner up above her and jammed it in the top of the door. Then, holding on to the spanner, she jumped down.

With a grating metal squeal, the door popped open like the lid from a tin.

The inner door was already ajar. Tabitha paused, spanner in hand, looking through the gap.

The light was dim, the air murky. What she could see of the hold looked just as it had before she'd put the drones to work on it: boxes and bags, professional gear and personal belongings, thrown all over the floor; flex everywhere, and fairy lights straggling from the catwalk;

a corner of Saskia's psychedelic mural smudged across the bulkhead at the end.

She couldn't see any blood or bodies. If there was a wild carnivorous Venusian beast in there, she couldn't see it.

Heart thudding, she pushed the inner door open with her foot.

The hold was deserted.

Kicking aside strewn bags and clothing, Tabitha went in.

Her foot met a body. It was one of the drones, smashed.

One of the other drones was sitting in front of its kennel, a tambourine in its manipulators. She stood beside it, turning swiftly from side to side, scanning the tumbled luggage.

A huge black moth had found its way in. It was flapping and buzzing ineffectually against the stilled air inlet. Of the other occupants there was no sign anywhere.

Tabitha pulled bags and boxes about until she was sure, then ran to the aft lock and out of the hold. She looked in the ablute, the galley and the cabins. Everything was all over the place. Everywhere was deserted. The portholes were spattered thickly with mud.

She came back into the hold, shifted a toppled loudspeaker and rolled over the flattened drone. It was a write-off. There were wet splashes on it, as if, knowing its end, it had begun to cry. Tabitha stooped, running fiber-optic entrails through her gloved fingers.

Nearby, among the spilled contents of a hardware bin, she saw a corner of Tal's porcelite traveling box. She pulled it out. It was still closed. The lifesign indicators were green. She rapped on the lid.

Nothing happened.

Tabitha bent and, with some difficulty, laid her external microphone against the crack of the lid. She thought she could hear tiny snoring.

At a loss, she stood up and cast around the hold, wiping spatters of liquid from her faceplate.

It was raining. In the hold of the *Alice Liddell*.

Only then did she think to look up.

The hold was breached. The roof was gaping, its leaves wrenched asunder like a cardboard box opened by someone in a temper. Outside, through a maze of violent foliage, the Venusian sky lowered down like red-hot zinc.

Shouldering her spanner, she went up the ladder to the catwalk and put her head out of the roof.

Looking down, she saw the *Alice* was half buried in a slew of pulped vegetation. The roof of the ship was festooned with smashed branches and torn vines, many of them charred. The forest floor was boggy, and steaming. Overhead, between the weird bulbous limbs of the trees, heavy, rippled clouds covered the sky like an inverted sea. The forest was a maze of clotted shadows, with isolated patches of baleful light, thick and fiery.

It took Tabitha a moment to realize the light was curved. The world seemed to rise up around her, as though she stood at the bottom of a vast bowl full of hot, rotting vegetable refuse.

She turned up her audio and shouted out. She thought she could hear distant voices and splashing noises, but nobody was answering.

She switched on her boots again and climbed carefully out into the rain.

She stood on the hot roof of the cockpit, ignoring the aches and shivers in her limbs, and turned and looked along the length of her stricken ship.

All the scanners and antennae she had repaired on the journey had been rudely ripped and twisted off again. The *Alice*'s hull was scored and scraped as if it had passed through a giant grater. Her copper inlay had been scoured with dust and blotched with acid on the way down. Her wings were bent; glutinous foliate ribbons hung deliquescing from them. Carmine mud and glistening black filth were splashed liberally all over her.

She was lying in a clearing she had inadvertently made for herself. Behind her, the way she had come, was an open tunnel of felled and broken trees. To call them trees, however, was analogy. They looked nothing like trees, more like slumped piles of mouldy leather, or towers of crumbled sponge, or gigantic weeping cauliflowers. Many of them were blackened and burning fitfully.

Tabitha called and called again.

Green lightning flickered, and a peal of thunder dinned in her ears. She looked all around, but everything was so confusing, the trees so numerous and so weird, the light so grimy and distorted, she couldn't interpret what she was seeing. The morass seemed to heave and throb around her.

Away to her right, the foliage rustled.

Her heart in her mouth, she gripped her spanner.

"Tabitha!" came a call, desperate and intimate in her ear.

One of the Twins had got their audio sorted out.

"Who is it?"

"Saskia."

"Where are you?"

"Here," said the acrobat unhelpfully. Tabitha stared at the bushes, peering through the rain.

The branches threshed again. She caught sight of a silver figure. It struggled through into the clearing.

"What's happening?" Tabitha asked it. "Where are they?"

Saskia was panting, and barely coherent. "Marco went after it. Mogul too, but he's hurt. He hurt his head. I can't find him."

Her suit, which Tabitha had barely noticed before, was a designer job in bright chrome, with all its apparatus packed into a single slim dorsal fin. She looked as if she'd be more comfortable underwater, like some kind of futuristic cyborg shark. She waded up to her knees in a boggy pool. "Where is this, Tabitha?"

"Venus," Tabitha said, "where did you think?" She was annoyed with them for running off, annoyed with Saskia for not making sense.

The lightning flashed again. Deep in the forest, something howled at it.

"Come inside," Tabitha sent, and climbed back down the way she had come.

Saskia came into the hold, panting and unhappy. She came close to Tabitha. Behind her V-shaped visor her face was white, her skin waxy with anguish.

"Mogul's hurt his head," she said again, dazedly.

"Where is he?" Tabitha asked.

Clumsily Saskia tried to embrace her. She waved a silver arm, indicating the whole horrid expanse of forest, of Aphrodite Terra, of Venus. "I don't know!" she cried. "I thought he might be back here."

She pulled away from Tabitha and started digging among the jumble, as if hoping her errant brother might be hiding there, waiting to spring out and surprise them.

Tabitha followed. "What's Marco doing?"

"Looking for it! It got out!"

"*What* got—"

Tabitha realized she was looking at the answer.

It was the Frasque's coffin cylinder, open and lying in a puddle.

It was empty.

BGK009059 LOG

TXJ.STD

PRINT

mc/‡&&&& & ñ ⁻⁻ h f ˜srt F ˜ sqtmm &%ð **** ******** *&*********
*******]

MODE? VOX

SD? 09.01.225

READY

Hello, Alice.

HELLO, CAPTAIN. ARE YOU GOING TO TELL ME ABOUT
THE FRASQUE NOW?

Which Frasque?

THE ONE YOU MET ON THE *RESPLENDENT TROGON*.

Oh. That Frasque. It was a Frasque caravan. I must have
told you that.

YES, CAPTAIN, I REMEMBER.

It was led by a ship we knew only as the *Cockatrice,* a
Nebulon Streever from Plenty. The Frasque had just finished
Plenty, I think, or at any rate they were working on it. This
one arrived and parked prominently in a low GSO over
Selucia, much too late for them to join in any of the junketing.
It hung motionless, like a drab grey kite in the pink sky.

   As soon as the Frasque arrived, everything went very
quiet. There was a general exodus to the ships, with representatives making hurried visits to the *Cockatrice.* Duststorms were blowing in from Coprates Canyon.

   Tricarico had found a job for me on the *Resplendent
Trogon,* in the stores, a job which gave me plenty of free
time for him to come and bother me.

I SEE. YOU'RE BEING AMBIVALENT AGAIN.

Oh, I suppose it was a reasonable enough job, considering
what experience I had. But I wasn't what you'd call overjoyed.
I was going off Tricarico a bit. I didn't want to be with him
all the time, there were too many new things to see and do.
When the caravan finally took flight, and Tricarico was intensely busy for a while, I got heavily absorbed in the mys-
teries of working for Mandebra. ˙There were obviously

considerable rewards available if you knew how to do it right.

I knew straight off if I was going to get anywhere, I had to get out of the stores.

To start with, I couldn't stand the QM. She was a balding Thrant called Wenyk, and she'd got where she was by being absolutely obsessed with soap and vinegar, argon capsules and colored pens. Not a fusepin moved in Wenyk's stores without three separate entries to account for it.

Wenyk took an enormous pride in her work. If the flagship of the Mandebra line was resplendent, it was only because *she dispensed the metal polish!* Well, I couldn't be bothered with all that. It was as bad as working for Captain Frank, except that it was clean. Worse, Wenyk never forgot anything. "Tabitha Ju', Tabitha Ju', where are ee velcro cable-fasteners, size 6, blue?"

"Aren't they there, QM?" said I, wondering who I'd issued them to. I'd always issued them to somebody and not got around to entering it.

"No, Tabitha Ju', ey aren'. Secon' engineer Morris Moryalos has partic'ly pu' in for size 6, blue, and ee manifes' shows un more box, oh dear. Secon' engineer Morris Moryalos, you know wha' he's like."

"Leave it to me, QM," I'd say, and when she wasn't looking, send him size 6, orange, thinking, hell, what can it matter? Then of course it would, and then it would get back to Wenyk, and then it would get back to me. If I wasn't out.

I was out the day the Frasque walked in.

We were two days past Deimos, barely making any headway at all, holding back while the Terran juggernauts and the Frasque mass cradles slowly began to gather speed. I came back from putting unfair pressure on Tricarico and found Wenyk trying helplessly to ingratiate herself with a creature that looked something like an insect the size of a pony, and more like a dead bush.

The Frasque was between me and her, with its back to me. I'd never been that close to one before. I hoped it wouldn't turn round very quickly.

Wenyk spoke to me under one of its arms. "Tabitha Ju' where *have* you been? You were due back on du'y half an oor ago."

I mumbled an apology, staring at the Frasque, gingerly walking round looking up at it. "Sorry, QM, I had to go to see the bosun about—"

"Never min' now," she said, very sharply for her. "Iss is Commander, oh, oh dear, wha' di' you say your neem was, Commander?"

The creature made a noise something like a pony-sized insect clearing its throat, and something like peanuts exploding in a paper bag.

It turned round very quickly and looked at me.

WHAT DID YOU DO THEN, CAPTAIN?

Froze, I imagine. I certainly didn't make any voluntary motions.

"Tabitha Ju', Commander yes well has come to inspec' ee stores. I try show her aroun' myself but oh dear, I can' make her un'erstan' ee system . . ."

There was a peculiar smell in the room, a pungent, murky smell. Thrants are smelly, you know, Alice. I wasn't sure whether it was the smell of a Thrant getting frantic with anxiety, or of a Frasque growing impatient.

Wenyk had been confronted with something more challenging than a drone needing a new battery, and she'd gone all to pieces. Or maybe she was right, for all I knew. What did I know about Frasque? That they were all right if you kept to business. I remembered what Tricarico had said, but I didn't know if I believed it. Maybe Thrants had had dealings with Frasque for thousands of years. Maybe Wenyk had every right to be spraying distress pheromones all over the room.

I could see I had to take over. I decided to separate them. I took Wenyk on one side. "I think we're confusing her," I said. I wondered how she could tell it was a her. "Leave me alone with her, I'll find out what she wants."

Wenyk scrambled like mad in two directions at once. She didn't want to leave her beloved stores, especially in the hands of an infidel alien incompetent like me. But if there was a Frasque in there, then she would very much rather be somewhere else.

As soon as she made up her mind and got out of the

door, I was on the com. I was going to call Tricarico, but
then I had a better idea. I called the bridge and asked for
the duty officer. "Have you misplaced a VIP?" I asked her.

"What? Who is this?"

"Tabitha Jute, Stores," I said, casually omitting my rank.

"Holy Maria, she's not down there, is she?"

I said, yes, she was, and cleared. I thought, mm, Wenyk
was right then. This is panic stations.

Then I struck up a conversation with the Frasque.

WHAT DID YOU TALK ABOUT?

Business, of course.

"Ssstorsss," she said, reedily; or that's what it sounded
like, so I went for it.

"Yes," I said, "stores. You're absolutely right. On the
Resplendent Trogon we pride ourselves on having the most
comprehensive and up-to-date lines of equipment and sup-
plies of any merchant schooner in service today," I declared,
waving my arms about.

The Frasque crackled.

I couldn't tell whether I was supposed to be able to understand that, so I nodded and rushed on. I told her all about
velcro cable-anchors, blue and orange, and how we very
particularly kept the foodstuffs and perishables over here, at
the opposite end from the poisons and inflammables, which
were over here.

The Frasque followed me with her beady eyes. Her limbs
creaked as she moved. She jerked and stopped, jerked and
stopped. Between movements she simply froze, completely,
not a single twitch or stir to betray that she really wasn't a
dead bush.

The murky smell was lingering. I wondered what the best
thing would be to throw at her if she decided she'd had
enough of my commentary, and me.

Then the door swung open, and help arrived.

Melissa Mandebra came in, with her steward, the first
mate, a couple of guards and Wenyk hurrying in after her.
I hadn't expected the big woman in person; but I made the
most of it. I jumped down off the counter and presented

myself to her as the one who'd found her strayed dignitary, even explained to her the great and gratifying interest the Commander had been showing in our modest work down here in the stores.

Melissa looked at me. She looked at me as if she understood me completely, but from a very very long way up; like Xtasca does, in fact.

I thought, you've been at the thril, Melissa Mandebra, haven't you?

Then she opened her mouth and spoke to my distinguished visitor. In Frasque.

It was horrible. She sounded like somebody with laryngitis choking on a mouthful of fishbones.

The Frasque swiveled her head energetically and replied.

Then they both laughed.

I won't try to describe what that sounded like.

They laughed, it was all over, the whole party swept out of the room with many flourishes and great relief all round. No one was more relieved than Wenyk.

DID YOU GET ON BETTER WITH HER AFTER THAT?

No. I think I just made her more nervous, if anything. Tricarico was delighted with me though. He treated me as if I was some sort of prodigy, a chimp that had suddenly cracked *Macbeth*. He spoke to the shuttle pilot for me. She was the only one on the *Resplendent Trogon*, there to fly the brass around, and she wasn't getting any younger. Any of the flight ensigns could take over from her when someone was needed, but Tricarico agreed it would be a shrewd idea to train someone specially to be her replacement.

I think he thought it would keep me on the crew.

The shuttle pilot mentioned my name to Melissa, who remembered me with a sort of distant approval.

So then I learned to fly.

I already had some of the basics from being on the *Fat Mouth,* and pottering around the fringes of the caravan was a breeze after some of the ridiculous maneuvers I'd had to assist with when Captain Frank was closing in on a particularly fine piece of flotsam. Until Jupiter the officers'

shuttle of the *Resplendent Trogon* had nothing more taxing
to do than ferry the Mandebras and their guests to and from
social engagements on board the *Negro Spiritual*, the *Scorpion Lament*, and other grand ships of the caravan. They
let me do that, a couple of nights a week.

Sometimes I got a glass of Chablis. Sometimes I got more
than that. I had quite a thing going with a security man on
the *Clematis III*.

And at First Skip, Tabitha got to go to the ball.

They had trampled through the rainy bog; peered into
the branches of the repellent trees. They had beaten the
bushes, startling a duck-billed porcupine that flung its
pelt of crystalline quills clattering all over their suits and
bustled off, coughing. Snakes unreeled from the
"leaves" overhead to watch them, sizing them up like
fat tape measures with canny little eyes.

There was no sign of Hector.

In this insane terrain, anything could be anywhere.
Nothing was what it seemed. Flowers hummed, earth
bubbled, gnats flickered with silver bursts of electricity.
All, according to the deceitful light, at the bottom of a
bowl brimmed by the horizon.

"Mogul wasn't really looking. He was looking around
at the scenery. He kept pointing at things and laughing.
Then he ran off between the trees and we, we lost each
other."

Tabitha had the one extensor that was still functional
and all three surviving drones working to unload the ship.
Draped in swathes of soiled red silk and ultramarine
cretonne, leather trunks and aluminium prop cases stood

piled in a bank of dripping ferns, like scenery for some
surrealist ballet. Tal's traveling box was among them,
Tal still asleep inside it.

Saskia was trying to help, but her mind was elsewhere:
with her other half. She stood in the morass with a long
knife, hacking tangled creeper from the *Alice*'s wings
and undercarriage. She would stop intermittently and
watch, hypnotized, as another piece of their belongings
was carried out of the hold.

"Don't cry," said Tabitha. "You'll fuck up your circulators."

Saskia let out a heartfelt wail, then gulped forcefully,
and returned, swearing, to her ineffectual attack on the
creeper.

Silently, Tabitha cursed. She waded over to her.

"Go and find him," she said gently.

Saskia's eyes and nose were red, hideous in her bone-
white face. She shook her head feverishly and gestured
with the blade. "This is more important."

"We can manage here. You can help later."

Saskia looked reluctantly into the looming forest. She
looked at Tabitha, at the ship.

Tabitha said, "Take the gun."

"I haven't got it. He must have it."

"Take the knife, then."

Saskia looked at it doubtfully. "Won't you need it?"

Tabitha patted her shoulder. "Go on. Keep a channel
open. Call me every five minutes."

Saskia bit her lip. She raised her hand and, in an oddly
tender gesture, laid the knuckle of her index finger against
the side of Tabitha's visor. "I love you," she said.

"No you don't," said Tabitha briskly. "Go and fetch
your brother. We'll be leaving soon," she said.

A flash of anger crossed Saskia's anguished face.
"Don't patronize me, Tabitha," she said.

Startled, Tabitha gazed guiltily into her eyes, and then
down at the rain-pocked mud.

When she looked up again, Saskia was toiling back
into the bushes.

The sodden day droned on. Motionless, the huge sun

blared through the sullen clouds, everywhere visible and invisible. The hot, thick light seemed to creep through her suit and into her bones. The insects driven away by the crash had recovered rapidly and come swarming out of the foliage, making a shrill sawing noise and projecting some kind of hive aurora that interfered with radio reception. When Saskia called in she sounded distant and tinny.

Tabitha and the drones were trying to winch the ship up out of her slough. Tabitha gave a command. The port wing burst suddenly from the undergrowth in a great spray of muck.

"That's great, that's great!" cried Tabitha, racing around from bow to stern. "Hold her there!"

In a sudden access of hope she called the persona. "Hello, hello, Alice? Can you hear me?"

There was no reply.

The rain grew heavier suddenly.

Tabitha had the drones anchor the cables to stout trees while she sat under one and sucked another tube of Vitalise. She was concerned about the little machines, slaving so hard in the rain and heat. Their minimum-standard insulation wasn't meant for these conditions. One of them was already acting a little strangely. If she didn't keep an eye on it, it would wallow away and bump into the trunk of the nearest tree, and there it would stay, absorbedly unfastening and refastening the same shackle.

Saskia called in again, and immediately afterwards Marco.

"Has it turned up?"

"It?" she said.

"Hector. Hector." The signal was lousy, it sounded as if he was broadcasting through a mass of wire wool. "Who d'you think I mean?"

"Your late partner."

"Yes, well, who knows with them?"

"Hector who was dead."

"He *was* dead! The, er, the Eladeldi, they shot him." Crackle. ". . . saw the guy. Wasn't he dead?"

She gritted her teeth. She was not going to argue with him. She didn't even want to talk to him.

"Did he come back yet, I guess not," he said, after a pause.

"No."

"Are you okay? You're not hurt or anything? I guess Mogul's the only one that's not too bad, that was pretty lucky, yeah? Are . . . with you? I got you now, I can see the ship now . . . on my way."

Tabitha answered all this in grunted monosyllables. She got to her feet, brushing off her suit, and went down to duck under the suspended ship. "Don't bother, Marco."

"I need to talk to you," he said.

He was coming through the curved forest, talking all the way. "I guess the heat thawed it out. Hector. Shit, he scared us. . . . upped and out of that . . . was away out the roof," he recalled, the signal breaking and fizzing. "He was out of there."

He sounded strained, talking from shock and fear and nerves. Talking was his response to everything, Tabitha thought sourly. He was still talking. "They can really move, those guys. I guess . . . just confused, he must have been frightened, that was . . . landing."

Tabitha wasn't answering. She slid back the inspection panel that covered the primaries.

A hundred meters off, between the trees, she glimpsed Marco coming. His suit was splendid, scarlet red and bold jet black. He waved. She ignored him. She summoned the nearest drone and when it approached, bent to pick it up.

Marco came hurrying to her. "Oh, here, here, let me help you with that." He helped her lift the drone into the open airlock. Behind his polarized visor, his face was grim and sweaty.

"God, I wish I knew where he was," he said, as the drone swiveled and trundled off up the ramp into the cockpit. He gestured heavily into the wet forest. "He could come to harm out there, with no suit."

For a moment she'd thought he'd meant Mogul. Tabitha returned her attention to her wrist monitor.

"Goddammit, he could really die out there!" he snapped, irritably, thumping his fist on the sill of the door.

Tabitha could stand no more of this. "He's a Frasque, Marco," she said.

"A Frasque," he said. "Right."

"The only people ever to build on Venus," she said. "So?"

"Only people ever to reproduce on Venus, for Christ's sake. Only people ever to give birth in space, for that matter. In vacuum."

"The Seraphim," he interposed.

"Give birth, I said."

Her faceplate opaqued for a moment as the drone relayed a situation profile.

"So what do you think? You think he'll be okay, is that what you think?" He straightened his thumb and stabbed it suddenly on the chin of his helmet, as if he wanted to chew his thumbnail and had forgotten he was wearing his suit.

"Marco, if I can't get the ship started we're going to die. Here. Soon."

"What, you've got a distress signal going or something, though, right?"

"No," she said. She pointed up at the sullen ocean of cloud. "I haven't got the power to put anything through that lot."

He stared at her like an apprehensive spaniel.

"So I'm going to get her started," she said, very calmly. "And when I do, then I warn you now, I won't be waiting for any strays before I take off."

She keyed a signal to the drone on board. Softly, the jet baffles began to whirr.

"I understand," he said. "I understand your feelings. Believe me. But this guy, my star, like you said, my business partner, hm? He's out there somewhere, and he's hurt. I mean, we thought he was dead. He must be very very badly hurt. At least."

"Fine," she said. "Off you go."

He spread his hands, palms out, in a peremptory gesture of pacification. "Okay," he said. "Couple of things. Couple of things we think you should know. Things I haven't had the time to explain to you."

"Quick," said Tabitha fiercely.

"Well, I know you've got the impression, the impression that Hector was actually a member of the band. Of Contraband. I mean, he was, of course he was, but he wasn't actually in the band, if you follow me."

She rounded on him, viciously. "Why don't you just fuck off, Marco, and let me work?"

He said hastily, "Is it bad?"

"I'm still looking."

"Well, does it look bad?"

"Yes!"

It seemed to dawn on him then how much trouble they were really in. He leaned against the ship, looking apprehensively round the landscape he had just been running around in. He looked lost, hunted, a creature at bay. Then he turned, spinning about as though looking for an escape.

There wasn't one.

"Goddamn!" He lashed out with his foot, kicking the *Alice*'s slimy undercarriage.

Tabitha reached out with her left hand and took him by the arm. When he turned to face her, she lifted her right leg, planted the sole of her boot in his midriff and shoved with all the fury that was in her.

Yelling in surprise, he lost his footing, falling flat on his back, sprawling in the mud. His yell changed to a cry of pain as he banged his head on his helmet and the hard edges of his suit and the rigid frame of his oxygenator slammed him in the back. Tabitha stood over him while he scrabbled frantically with his elbows and hands, his heavy boots slithering as he fought to regain his footing. She did not offer him a hand up.

He jerked onto his side, mud splashing up around them both. He got up on one knee. His scarlet suit was thick with foul, rotten vegetation and brick-red slime. He pawed madly at his visor with the back of his gauntlet, making it worse.

Tabitha was turning up her audio. She stood with her feet apart, her hands spread. "Don't you lay a finger on me, Marco Metz," she blared, directly in his earphones. "Don't you lay a finger on my ship. I don't want you anywhere near me. You can stay here and die!"

"Tabitha, I'm sorry, I'm sorry! I didn't—"

Floundering, trying to get his feet under him, he reached out to lean on the undercarriage. Tabitha shouted at him, leaping forward as if to smash him in the face with the back of her hand.

He quailed. "All right! All right! Let me up, goddammit! I'm sorry, I said, I'm sorry!" He looked down at his mired suit, flapping his arms in distress. "I didn't mean, I just, I . . ."

She tuned him out. Deliberately, she turned back to her work, ducking under the belly of the ship again and sticking her helmeted head cautiously up into the jet compartment.

He found another channel. He said, "I want to help."

"You can't."

"I helped before, we all helped: I didn't mean to kick your ship, I'm just, it's all so—you know." His voice became soft and intimate. "Tabitha. You know how I feel."

"Fuck off, Marco," she said precisely.

"I want to show you I'm sorry," he said, quietly and sincerely. "I want to help us get out of here!"

Tabitha Jute took her head from the innards of her ship. She pointed into the forest, up the gradient of soupy light. "Go and help Saskia. Find Mogul. When you get back there'll be something you can do." She was inflexible.

He went. She watched him disappear into the vegetable inferno. She saw him several minutes later, crossing a raw high ridge, a scarlet suit trudging up through the improbable trees on its way towards the impossible horizon.

proved inadequate even with his face mask squashed
making it worse.

Thank you madam, Ilia said. She asked with her
mouth full and made so much of it, Alice was a throw on.
her bounce. It mattered so much really in this adversity,
then I you have a forest where... I can't tell you
anywhere in a spot if I were... something had.

Tabitha, I'm sorry, this worker I don't 3.4.

Something happens, one morning me aghast.

45

A meter and a half above the boggy, churned ground,
the *Alice Liddell* hung in a mad, giant cat's cradle suspended between the trees. That had taken a bit longer
than she'd thought. They'd run out of cable halfway
through and had had to improvise with resin-bonded creeper nets; and soon just creeper, lots of tangled creeper.

It wasn't level. It was listing, the weight had shifted,
the outer port impulse engine splashing to the ground.
There just wasn't a way of getting under it to raise it up.
Tabitha had already lost one jack in the mud.

"If frowning could fix it," Tabitha's father used to
say, "it'd be done by now." She was fed up with the
suspension problem. It was as stable as it was going to
be, and she had other things to do.

She sent the drones aboard to clean up and hammer
out dents, while she struggled to bypass the smashed sine
proton generator in the roundmouths. With Marco and
the Twins out of the way, she could concentrate better.
While she worked, she coaxed the *Alice Liddell*'s persona
up out of withdrawal. She scolded and soothed. She told
it stories.

The rain eased to a soft and sullen dripping.

Whatever was broken in the laterals, it was deeper
than she could get with these tools. Probably the matrix
compression amps. Tabitha didn't go inside matrix
compression amps without a workshop and three days
clear. She hadn't got a workshop. She hadn't got three
days, either. Saskia's suit was fashion junk, her brother's
too, presumably, not meant for this kind of hell. They'd
melt long before that.

Saskia had radioed in again. Tabitha spoke to her. "Saskia, is Marco there? He went to find you."

"I haven't seen him," said Saskia. Barely audible, still she sounded distraught.

Maybe he went after the Frasque, Tabitha thought. She didn't care where he was. Either he'd come back or he wouldn't. "Keep an eye out for him," she said.

Sitting under a huge pink cauliflower, Tabitha worked it out. The best she could hope was that the amps weren't completely stripped, and that the Shernenkovs were still on speaking terms with the gyros. Then (if she could get her sealed, if nothing else went wrong) they could hope to take off. (If the impulse engines were firing. If they weren't—But if they were. Just assuming.) They could hope, theoretically, to take off.

God, when Bergen built these things, they really built them.

After that, though, with the axis lock crystal gone, all she could do would be to give them her best orbit. How long for, was anyone's guess. Long enough to attract the attention of a passing ship? Probably not, but what else she could do? The alternative was to sit here and die; or run off into the jungle laughing and screaming.

They were all going to die.

No.

Now then. Orbits.

Her best orbit. Without the computer to plot paths, or do librations, the way things stood at present. If she couldn't get even elementary navigation up, she'd have to do it from the tables. She knew she had a copy. Somewhere. If she couldn't find the tables, her best orbit would be the ballistic equivalent of spitting on the ceiling.

Xtasca, thought Tabitha, would have been able to librate in her sleep. Xtasca would have mended compression amps with a flick of her tail, if you asked her nicely. Xtasca would have been bloody useful, right now.

Xtasca was already dead.

They were all going to die.

All right. So. In the meantime.

Tabitha got up and, looking warily around for lurking

arboreals, started to climb the giant cauliflower. With all the forks, it wasn't hard at all. She shinned up and out along a smooth, shiny branch.

Up in the crimson forest, she saw the great purple iguanas out on their branches, their black elastic tongues lazily popping the radio midges out of the air. The iguanas' hooded eyes seemed to stare in permanent amusement at some private, inward joke. They were laughing at the stupid humans, running around like mad things before they died.

Far off, something roared. Tabitha hated it. There were supposed to be dinosaurs on Venus, huge fat walking snakes with poison breath. She'd already seen scorpion things and nearly trodden on a little black snake that hissed madly at her and zipped away across the mire. They didn't have to be big.

Tabitha had never lived anywhere there was wildlife, and she didn't like it. She disliked the thought of creatures that weren't domesticated or sapient or edible.

Tabitha looked down from the branch at the bare, scraped roof of her ship. There really wasn't anything left of the communications array, except ten centimeters of an antenna. No external AV, then. And with the viewport crazed and nothing to replace it with, she'd be taking off completely blind.

The less information, the easier the job. Gun everything and bash straight out the way she'd bashed in.

After that—but there was no point in thinking about after that yet. Not till she found out whether she still had impulse engines.

Five minutes later, she lay on her side in the mud under the *Alice*, the bulk of it suspended over her. She was trying to block a second jack she'd stuck under the dragging jet. She lay curled up, stretching her right arm and most of her left into the low gap. If the ship settled five centimeters now, it would maim her, she thought distantly. She talked to it. She made hard little squeaky sounds in the back of her nose while she grappled clumsily with the jack. She'd have given anything to be able to take her gloves off.

She was in that position for some while. She forgot about the dragons, the midges, the phosphorescing iguanas, the little black snakes. Overruled, all such awareness left her, and she became a machine, simpler than any drone. She was the block, and the jack on the block. She was a lever.

Crippled, time oozed silently past. The hidden sun did not move. Marco Metz and the Amazing Zodiac Twins did not return.

Tabitha got the ship jacked up long enough for her to roll out and let the drones shove a dead tree under. Again she lost the jack, but the tree held. She clambered aboard, scrambling up the tilting deck, impatient to test the jet.

It was still working. With a triumphant gout of flame, she blew the mud out of it. She was singing. She was in tears. She awarded herself a beer.

Saskia called in. "I've found him," she said, hesitantly. Was it interference or could she hear singing?

"Found who? Is that Mogul you've found?"

"Mogul," she said. "Marco's . . . too . . . bring Mogul back now."

"Is he okay?"

"I don't know!" She was gulping, baffled, hysterical. She had never not known before. ". . . crazy," she said. "He's happy. Tabitha? Tabitha, how are you? . . . the *Alice?*"

"All right," she said. She smiled at her battered ship, the drones with their sealant sprays and patch-welding pencils. "So far."

"We're lucky," said Saskia. "Aren't we? . . ."

Tabitha hoped they were, because that had been the last from any of them.

She sat in her web, pitting her wits against the computer. Alice was perfectly lucid for a bit, then she slipped away again.

It was hard to concentrate. One of the drones was working on the airlock door Tabitha had had to damage, trying to make it seal again. It was making so much noise she had to send it away aft, leaving the door hanging open, while she sat in the cockpit with her suit refrigerator cranked up full, assailing the fortified labyrinths of machine logic.

Alice was in flight: a flicker of shadow fleeing down the silicon corridors, glimpsed disappearing around a corner, hovering beyond a toggle gate; gone.

Another blistering hour burned by. Tabitha suffered another lapse of consciousness. At one point, she seemed to be dreaming. Yellow salamanders kept running out of the curtains and up the walls. But there weren't any curtains.

Suddenly she came to, thinking, oxygenator. Got to flush it. How long have I had it on? She looked round at the unit. The light was green. It would take a quarter of an hour, though. And this bit would only take a couple of minutes. She carried on, combing through the code.

She knew she was in danger, she knew she should take the fifteen minutes to clean and reset it, she knew it would clear her head, she knew the fact she was putting it off was because her brain was already addled with CO_2. But in a couple more minutes she could have another logic bloc up, and then everything would be so much easier. She could even take a break.

But she was going to take a break anyway, a fifteen-minute break, because, because she wanted to. Wanted to lie down.

Stiffly, she clambered out of her web.

"CAPTAIN."

Somebody was calling her.

It was a woman's voice. It was familiar.

"Mum?" said Tabitha. Her voice sounded funny, like someone shouting down a pipe. "What do you want?"

She lay down, on the floor. She watched the pretty red and green lights. It was so stupid, she spent her whole life in this cockpit, and she never *looked* at it. It was so pretty. It was funny.

"YOU NEED TO FLUSH YOUR OXYGENATOR, CAPTAIN."

"In a minute."

"PLEASE DO IT, CAPTAIN."

"Rella? Is that you?"

There was a brief pause.

"FLUSH YOUR OXYGENATOR NOW, TABITHA. JUST BLOODY DO IT."

"Dodger!"

Tabitha tried to get up, but it was just too much like hard work. She found a thing on the floor, a big metal thing, she knew what it was, she just couldn't remember the name of it. It was heavy. It was sparkling, corruscating. The pretty lights were multiplying, swimming around her head.

"TABITHA, YOU ARE DYING. YOU ARE DYING NOW."

Wherever she looked now, Tabitha could see the winking colored lights: on the console, under the console, down in the hold.

Down in the hold, something moved.

"Dodger?"

Tabitha leaned forward, peering down the steps. The winking lights were across everything like a veil.

A shadow, like somebody moving about in the empty hold.

"I can see you, Dodger."

She couldn't really, though. She blinked. There was a pain in her chest, made it hard to think. She wanted to fall asleep, but it hurt too much. Was there someone there?

Maybe it was one of them come back, one of the ones with the daft spacesuits.

A loud alarm went off, whooping and squealing. "TABITHA! TABITHA! TABITHA JUTE!"

"All right, Dodger," she croaked. "For you. Just— for—you . . ."

She couldn't get up. The noise was flattening her, smashing her against the floor. The voice kept on shouting while she worked her way wearily round the wall on her bottom until she could reach up over her head and fumble the air feed down from the panel.

"For you, Dodger."

She jacked the nozzle into her respirator.

"F—"

She blacked out.

She was underwater. She was deep under the water, breathing the water. It was easy. You just breathed in and out. If only everyone realized how easy it was. She was moving strenuously through the night of the water, pushing it aside with her arms. They had stars down here too. They rippled as she hauled herself towards them. They winked, pulsing messages to her. Come on, they said. Come on.

She was in deep.

Then she was lying on the flight deck of the *Alice Liddell*, her lungs heaving in a flood of the ship's own air, her head thumping, pins and needles in all her extremities. Through the ruined viewport, she could see the sullen glow of the hot, bent forest, the drizzle of the fuming rain.

You idiot, she said to herself, gulping down the good air. You fucking idiot. She'd thought somebody was there, talking to her. "Alice?" she said. Her throat hurt.

There was no answer.

Leaning on the wall, Tabitha sat up. Still hampered by the air feed, she reached behind her and unclipped the oxygenator from her back. Then she pushed herself just far enough to stick it in the scrub unit With her head on one side, she could just see the meter, see how low it had dropped. She winced.

Fifteen minutes before she could move about again. She felt in her belt pouch and found a last tube of Vitalise.

In the hold, something rattled.

There was something in there. She hadn't imagined that.

"Saskia?"

No reply.

Perhaps the parrot had got out of his box.

"Tal?" she called. "Here, Tal."

No parrot.

She sucked her tube. It hurt to swallow.

Painfully, she got to her feet. There was glasspaper between all her muscles. Gasping, she leaned on the wall and looked at the oxygenator. Ten minutes before she could put it on again. Ten minutes to wait about, helplessly tethered, for the creature in the hold to come and get her.

There was a long silence. Then a soft thump and a rattle.

A bat, she thought. Flown in through the open roof and can't find its way out again.

Six minutes. Five. Four minutes twenty-four seconds.

Another rattle. Like little bits of metal, she thought, thinking desperately what it could be. Something with metallic scales. The iguanas. That's what it was.

Two minutes fifty-eight seconds.

To get into the ship, the iguana would have had to climb up one of the anchor trees, work its way along a cable, get on the roof and drop through the buckled doors.

Another jingle, repeated, prolonged.

One minute.

Something was in there, waiting for her.

Tabitha saw her big spanner lying on the cockpit floor. She realized she was holding her breath. If she was going to hold her breath, what was she doing stuck on the end of this air line?

An indicator panel lit up on the oxygenator unit. It said: WARNING. DO NOT ATTEMPT TO REMOVE OXYGENATOR UNTIL ALL LIGHTS ARE EXTINGUISHED AND CYCLE IS COMPLETE.

Tabitha grabbed the oxygenator.

The machinery growled.

The light stayed on.

Empires rose and fell.

The light stayed on.

The universe turned somnolently about its axis.

The light went out.

Tabitha grabbed the oxygenator and scooped it over her shoulder. Wiggling it into place, she heard the valve click, and gulped her lungs full of oxygen again.

She pulled the air feed free from her helmet and snatched up the spanner. Now then.

She clanked down the ramp to the hold, moving as quietly as she could. She leaned on the frame of the damaged door, feeling the *Alice* sway under her.

Out of the crimson shadows, something low rose and came towards her.

It wasn't an iguana. It was bigger than an iguana.

She drew back her arm to throw the spanner at it. Then she saw what it was.

A drone with a tambourine.

As it moved, it jingled.

"You stupid piece of junk," she said wearily. "Give me that."

The drone gave her the tambourine. Tabitha gave it the spanner. "Here," she said. "Mend this door."

Its eyes gleamed briefly.

She squatted down, checked the lights on its CP, and gave it the command sequence. Then, tambourine in hand, she turned to go back through the door to the cockpit. The drone stumped after her. Tabitha looked at the tambourine. She shook it experimentally. She set her foot on the ramp up to the flight deck. She looked up.

Something was standing there, looming over her like a naked scarecrow; an uprooted bush; a blasted tree. It leaned towards her, creaking, bending in unlikely places.

Tabitha swallowed.

"H-Hector?" she said.

46

The Frasque hissed. It sounded like green twigs spluttering in a fire.

Tabitha took a step backwards.

With a sudden swivel of its hips, the Frasque came jerkily down the ramp. It moved something like a stork; and something like a maladroitly operated marionette.

In the poor light, it looked exactly like an animated

bundle of wood. Its whole body was a long, bulbous mass of pale brown fibrous tubes, out of which four ropy arms and two spindly legs protruded as if they had been thrust there; or as if they had grown out at arbitrary angles, like branches on a vine. It was naked, though really that means no more than to say that an insect is naked. Its body was its own armor.

The Frasque stood very close to Tabitha at the bottom of the ramp. It towered over her. It inspected her, its head on one side. Its eyes were deep set, round and black as berries, very small and bright.

"Ssspaceshhip," said the Frasque.

She could hear it clearly, though its voice crackled so much it sounded as though her audio was playing up.

"Yes," she said. "My spaceship."

Moving slowly, facing it all the way, she edged past it and up the ramp into the cockpit. It followed her with its eyes.

"My name's Tabitha Jute," she said deliberately. "You can call me Captain."

She turned away from it to put down the tambourine, and it hissed again, making her jump.

She reached out slowly, getting her hand on her web, ready to open it and take her seat. She turned around again, looking down at the Frasque. It was still staring at her. She wondered how much it could understand; how dangerous it was if frightened.

"Your friends are very worried about you," she said.

It shook its head in a corkscrew fashion.

"Marco Metz," she said. "The Zodiac Twins. Your friends."

It showed no sign of comprehension.

She pointed through the broken viewport to the grotesque forest outside. "They're all out looking for you," she said, and eased herself into her web.

It moved then. It came whizzing back up the ramp and stood beside her, unnervingly close.

The branches that made up its body were knobbly, and looked rigid as bones. You could have slipped a finger between them, in some places. As far as Tabitha could see, it was branches all the way through.

"Sssystem," it said. It gaped out of the viewport and flung, suddenly, one of its arms out in front of it. Its clawed hand landed on the console with a loud rattle. "Sssystem Sssol," it said.

"Venus," said Tabitha. "This is Venus." She tried not to look at the claw lying on her board. She said, "Can you mend plexiglass?" She thought it probably could, if it wanted. She remembered the way they had built Plenty, spinning its osseous fabric out of vacuum, out of particle froth.

The Frasque made a facial expression. Its face folded inwards down its length. The effect was of something like a drying pod splitting in half suddenly; yet the movement was inwards. It looked as if it was trying to suck its face in half.

Tabitha shuddered. "Look, I'm very busy right now," she said quickly. "We're not going to last much longer, your friends and me, if I can't get the ship going, so if you wouldn't mind, you can go back in the hold and wait for them—" She pointed unambiguously down the ramp. "I'll try and call them, let them know you're all right, all right?"

It folded its face the right way out again. If that was the right way. Its mouth was still open. Bright strings of saliva hung between its twiggy little teeth.

It didn't move.

Tabitha reached carefully to the console and plugged her audio in.

"Alice, the Frasque is here, I don't know if it understands me, what can I do?"

There was no reply.

"Come on, Alice, you were there just now, I know you were."

Still nothing.

"Shit!"

She called Saskia. She called on all local frequencies, hoping she would pick her up, through the static. Hoping, very much suddenly, she wasn't dead. "Hello, hello, Saskia, can you hear me?"

She got a reply. Saskia's voice chanting, "—into the sun, till we are one, almost begun, breathing . . . 't we . . . run, into the s . . ."

The signal was horrible, but she was obviously feverish, at the end of her tether. Tabitha closed her eyes. There was no end to despair. The planet was picking them off, one by one—

"Hello . . . bitha . . . hear me?"

It was Saskia. The chanting was still going on: it was Mogul.

"Saskia! Where are you?"

At her elbow, the Frasque stirred itchily. When it moved, which it did very suddenly and convulsively, all its branches·rearranged themselves, as if they were tubes of dun elastic stretched between nutty little nodes. Then, when it stopped moving, which too it did very suddenly and completely, the branches were all stiff as bone again.

". . . ran away . . ." said Saskia. Or Mogul, she couldn't tell any more.

Very distantly, she could hear Marco too. ". . . coming in," he said. "Couple of minutes." He was still making promises.

"Your friend's here," Tabitha sent, not knowing who, if anyone, would hear her. "Your friend's here. It's here."

The Frasque gave another brisk shudder. "Ssserve me," it said. The *m* was more of a *gn*. "Ssserve gne."

Tabitha was losing her temper. "You want to go to Titan?" she said, and pointed into the hold again. "Get back there, sit down and shut up."

It moved again, wheeling away from her and thrusting its limbs across the aisle, crushing the litter under its spiky feet.

But it was only pacing about. Tabitha wanted to scream. She'd have to ignore it, see if it would leave her alone. She turned to the keyboard, her heart beating very much faster than she would have preferred.

The uninvited passenger suddenly slapped another scrawny claw on the console, right beside her left hand.

She jumped. She held her breath. She turned to face it.

It gaped down at her.

"Ressstore me," it said. "Tst."

In her earphones she heard voices again.

At last. They were back.

"Marco," she sent. She was ready to drop. "Call this thing off."

"Call what?" he said. He sounded tired and angry. She didn't know if he hadn't heard her or if he didn't know it was there.

"Hector," she said. "Whatever. Just call its name, Marco."

"I don't know its fucking name," he said.

"Great," she said.

She opened her web with weary fingers and stood up. The Frasque didn't move. It was blocking her way.

"Excuse me," she said.

It was like talking to a tree, and as much use. Too tired to care, Tabitha pushed past it.

It didn't kill her.

The branches were rigid, just like bones.

She looked out of one porthole, then the other side. She could see them, coming through the forest from a completely unexpected direction. Mogul was wearing a suit of electric blue with limbs of force-ribbed hose and two little bobbled aerials, nothing like Saskia's at all. He was shambling along in a vague, loose-limbed way, looking up at the trees and the sky. Saskia and Marco were having a full-time job herding him in the right direction.

Mogul spotted the *Alice*, hanging up between the trees. She heard him give a loud and gleeful laugh.

Tabitha turned and beckoned the Frasque. "Marco Metz," she said. "Mogul. Saskia. Your friends. Down there." She pointed.

It came to the top of the ramp and stopped there.

Tabitha tried gestures again, then lost patience. She went up and got hold of one of its arms. It pulled away, so she got hold of another one. "Your friends!" she kept saying. Somehow she got it down the ramp to the inner door, disabled the airlock, and threw open both doors together. "Look!"

Mogul shouted, a shout of alarm and defiance. He broke away from his guides and came running, splashing between the broken trees and into the clearing.

Marco and Saskia ran after, calling him.

He ran, stumbling, to the ship, Saskia chasing him, Marco trailing. He ran straight for the door where Tabitha stood, the Frasque looming over her, and leapt on to the sill, catching hold of the door frame either side.

His visor was full-face. There was blood on the inside, and on his face. His skin, normally white as porcelain, white as bleached bone, was blotched red and purple with bursting blood vessels. Designed for nothing more taxing than a saunter on the surface of Ceres, his suit had overheated. Venus had burst the refrigerator and wrecked the pressure lining. Mogul's eyes were as big as dish antennae, his mouth was agape, his lips drawn back from teeth as long as a horse's.

The Frasque jerked into motion. It looked as if it was trying to scratch its back.

Instead, it produced a little metallic blue gun and pointed it at the man leaping in at it.

It fired.

With one arm, Mogul thrust Tabitha aside, knocking her over. She sprawled in the outer doorway, almost falling out on top of Saskia, who was leaping up after her brother. They collided and Saskia fell back in the muck and mud.

The Frasque fired again. The projectile zipped out of the door and slammed into the ground, splashing mud into Marco's faceplate.

Tabitha got up on one knee, Saskia climbing frantically in behind her. Mogul was grappling with the Frasque, yelling wordlessly at it, forcing it back through the inner door. It was writhing, jerking elastically in all directions at top speed, its gun arm threshing the murky air. It fired again.

Mogul jerked. His suit blew a plume of ice-blue vapor into the airlock.

Saskia yelled and screamed.

Tabitha threw herself in at the struggling couple, grabbing for the gun. Trying to catch hold of the Frasque's arm was like trying to clutch a slippery cable being pulled by a big winch.

Mogul was down, caught in the doorway, trying vainly to drag the Frasque down too. His long arms were wrapped round its legs and he had hold of two of its arms. Tabitha locked her hands around the arm holding the gun and hauled. The Frasque wriggled away and lost its grip. The gun flew through the air into the cockpit.

Shoving past Tabitha, leaping over her brother, Saskia somersaulted up the ramp after it.

Marco was aboard, charging into the fight. The Frasque caught Tabitha across the chest with a lash of its arm and threw her across the deck. She watched, winded, through a mist of pain, as it moved even faster now, picking up Marco and hurling him bodily off the ship, dragging Mogul yelling along with it by main force.

Saskia came leaping down the ramp, the gun in her hands. She emptied it into the back of the Frasque.

It took no notice. It was stooping over her brother.

He was thrashing around. Tabitha could see his legs kicking. She struggled to get up.

The Frasque, still moving at double speed, turned through 180° at the hips. Holding Mogul by the neck, it picked him up and flailed him at the deck. His neck seal cracked, jetted a fine spray of blue vapor and crimson blood.

Saskia was screaming, trying to get to him, but Tabitha caught her and held her back. She was as light as a child.

The Frasque squeezed Mogul's neck between two hands. His faceplate was running red. It crazed, all at once, all over. Mogul's body arched its back, opened its long hands, spread its fingers wide. Its heels drummed on the deck. It collapsed, and lay quite still.

Saskia shrieked, made one last frantic lunge towards it, then flung her arms around Tabitha and clung to her so tightly Tabitha could almost feel her.

The Frasque came, rattling, reaching for her with all its arms.

BGK009059 LOG

TXJ.STD

PRINT

t - - - -xjxjXJ   qerg

MODE? VOX

SD? 18.08.67

READY

Contraband ought to play at a 5wedding. They ought to play somewhere. Anywhere but here.
    They'd go down really well at a 5wedding.
    I went to one once, you know.

ONE WHAT, CAPTAIN?

A 5wedding. There aren't very many humans who can tell you that.

I IMAGINE NOT.

There aren't many humans who've been locked up on Mntce, let alone gone to a 5wedding.

CAPTAIN?

Yes, Alice?

WHAT IS A 5WEDDING?

It's Palernian. A Palernian wedding. Do you remember when we went to Mntce?

A COUPLE OF YEARS AGO?

That's right. We were sub-contracted to the caterers.

WE HAD A CARGO OF FOOD.

Things Palernians like to eat. Lava bread.

LYCHEES.

That's right. Acorns, trays and trays of acorns.

WIND-DRIED HORSE OFFAL.

Whole cabledrums of licorice rope.

I WAS PARKED FOR A VERY LONG TIME.

Well, there was the wedding. Then they locked me up. Didn't I tell you about it when I got back?

YOU WEREN'T VERY TALKATIVE ON THAT OCCASION, CAPTAIN.

Wasn't I.

YOU WEREN'T VERY WELL.

It was pretty rough.

WEDDINGS ARE MATING CEREMONIES, AREN'T THEY?

That's right.

THEN WHAT'S A 5WEDDING?

Palernians do everything in fives. You know that.

THERE AREN'T FIVE SEXES OF THEM, THOUGH. ARE THERE?

No, it's social. It's very social, actually. When you get married you marry one of your relatives and one of the other person's and one of their mates. Lovers. All at once. I mean, that's how they make up the five, in 5wedding. I don't know what they do in bed, but if the 5wedding is any guide . . .

And they certainly do breed.

The corridors of Mntce are full of children, frizzy teenage ones shepherding flocks of fluffy toddlers everywhere. Do you know they've managed two generations in the time they've been here?

The children seem to have the run of the place—they were in the workshops, in the customs bay, in the bars— little babies under your feet everywhere. Running around at top speed squeaking and cooing and stealing the chickpeas off the bar. Sometimes the really young ones will climb in your lap and start cuddling you and going through your pockets.

I ran into Fritz Juventi there once, doing some diplomatic shuffling, some hole-and-corner business, I don't know, fixing some tariff in Valenzuela's favor. He loved it there. It made him all paternal, grandpaternal, is that a word? He was strolling through the delegation quarter with a kid in each hand and a tiny one riding on his shoulders. It kept tipping his wig over his eyes. He was shouting and carrying on. "Hi! Now I can't see where I'm going!" He was walking round in circles and walking into the wall, on purpose, and the kid on his shoulders was screaming, it thought it was great. "If I can't see, I might drop you." And he'd pretend to tip it on the floor and catch it at the last minute, and the others were zinging around and bouncing off the walls. They thought he was great.

He was the one who told me about 5weddings. "If ever you get a chance, Tabitha, I do urge you most strongly to take it up." He sat there in his plus-fours and wing collar, smiling genially around his enormous nose and patting my leg. Old lech. He sounded as if he was talking about a guided tour of St. Astraea Capella, but I remembered him from nights on the old *Perseverance*. When Uncle Fritz is being super-sober and super-polite, watch out.

So that's why I was so pleased they asked me. To the 5wedding, I mean. It was the daughter of the Cold Reeve designate and the brother of the Limbo Pilot, and so the others were, let's see, her mother's brother, 5brother, I mean, or would it be his 5brother and her mother's other husband's—

I'VE PROBABLY GOT A DIAGRAM, CAPTAIN, IF YOU'D LIKE ME TO FIND IT.

Don't bother, Alice. It's all quite complicated, anyway. So complicated it's a wonder any of them manage to make a five at all. In fact, though, they nearly all do, don't they?

THEY'RE VERY GREGARIOUS, CERTAINLY. I CAN'T SAY I'VE BEEN COUNTING.

They're always in fives. It's not just a marriage, it's a working group, a sports team, a boat crew, a band. And once there are children, it's a whole clan; though everybody's children are just one huge playgroup, the way it looks, I don't know how they ever sort them out.

Once they're married, they're absolutely faithful, you know, Alice. They're completely lost without each other. If you split them up they pine. The only thing that breaks up a five is when one of them dies. If they can't find somebody else they go mad, some of them. You see them sometimes,

moping around the dorms, or the service bays, four Palernians talking to someone who isn't there. They stop
grooming themselves. They get these awful sores. Then they
suddenly start smashing everything in sight.

Though that's what they do at the 5wedding too.

When you get married, if you're a Palernian, you get
together with all your relations, which is a lot of people, if
you're a Palernian, and you do this thing which is hard to
explain. It's a bit like a dance, and a bit like an orgy, and
a bit like bingo. It goes on for days. There's lots to eat and
drink and smoke. The catering is one of the most important
parts of the thing.

IS THAT HOW YOU GOT INVITED, CAPTAIN?

The things we brought in, the horse offal and that, they were
an emergency consignment because someone had let them
down. And they were so glad to see it arrive they asked me
to stay.

The first day was just a big piss-up. I mean, there was
a lot of vow-taking and ear-marking and stuff going on, but
every time anybody said anything, there was a break for a
drink, and when there are five people who have to say
everything, that's a lot of drinking. And dancing, to very loud
music. It got quite physical, crammed in that hall with a
couple of hundred Palernians, but it was all very jolly and
pretty glandular too—and hot—but nobody started a fight.
When they're married, they lock into some automatic hor-
monal cycle that stops them falling out with any of their
partners or their relations. I was a novelty. I probably behaved
very badly and let down the species. I had immense fun,
that's all I know.

The next day by the time I dragged myself back to the
dining hall—the buffet—well, it was more a sort of giant
trough, really—all the food had been eaten, or cleared away,
or something, and instead there was a big pile of stuff in
the middle of the floor.

STUFF?

Yes. Personal stuff. Clothes, shoes, tapes, jewelry, lumps of clay with paint daubed on them. Bats and balls. Long tubular bags full of greasy old wool. The sort of things no Palernian would ever want to be without. There was quite a pile of it.

Apparently the thing is, when you get married you have to bring everything from your old home, everything that was yours, that you grew up with, and put it in a big pile, and then you smash it up.

The new five starts off. Somebody shouts a number and they all come bouncing in from behind a curtain, and they do a little dance in a ring around the pile of belongings. And everybody claps and stamps and farts. And then they start to jump on things. And throw them up in the air. Then they throw them at each other. They throw them at the walls. They take bites out of them. They—well, you get the general idea.

And after a bit everybody else joins in.

The trouble was, this being on Mntce, in the big public hall there, I suppose some people forgot where they were. I suppose back at home on Palernia, or wherever it is they come from, 5weddings are happening all the time, and everybody does them, so there's no neighbors to annoy. You are the neighbors, if you see what I mean. And everything that's lying around is the property of the host five and fair game. I don't know. Anyway, what happened was, when everything in the pile was pretty much as smashed up as it could be, people started smashing up the furniture, what there was of it. They started bringing things in from other rooms, and smashing them. Pictures off the walls. Those big glass bottles with flowers in. Computer consoles. They can shift some heavy stuff, you know, Palernians, when they get going. So then we split into two groups—

WE?

Well, yes. They know how to make you feel welcome, Palernians. Two groups, one down each side of the hall, and while one group tried to set fire to as many things as they could get their paws on, my group let off fire extinguishers and sprayed them everywhere. That was quite a laugh.

Then there was this awful noise. It was a siren. We all laughed and cheered, we thought it was one of us doing it.

But it was the cops.

They came streaming in, dozens of them, done up in their crowd control gear, and they were all yelping and slavering. They bit people, I saw that. I got clawed, all down one arm and on my hip.

I REMEMBER NOW. YOU WERE LIMPING. YOU WENT TO BED. YOU WERE COUGHING TOO, WEREN'T YOU?

They had tear gas, they had ultrasonic whips, I don't know what they didn't have. I tangled with a couple of them, I think they were trying to get some clothes on me, and I was trying to fight them off. I don't know, I was completely out of it. One of them hit me on the head. I don't remember that, the others told me when I woke up.

When I woke up I was in jail, in a ziggurat, and a lawyer from the Earth delegation on Mntce was screaming blue murder over some technicality. She said I'd been coerced, led astray, something or other. That's what they say when you let down the species. Palernians aren't the only ones with a herd mentality.

I just kept quiet and waited for my headaches to go away. I think I had ten headaches, one on top of the other. She got me off in the end, round about headache number eight.

So that's why I was so late coming back to get you from the parking, you see, Alice. I was at a 5wedding.

YES, CAPTAIN. I SEE.

Or maybe it was a demonstration. A political protest. A riot. I don't know how you could tell, really. Not with Palernians.

48

Tabitha stood in front of Saskia, her arms stretched out behind her, fencing Saskia in.

"No!" she shouted. "No! No! No! No!"

The Frasque leaned over her, staring down through her faceplate as if it had only just realized the funny metal suits had people inside.

Tabitha glared madly up into its soulless black eyes.

"Get back!" she shouted.

She brought her hands forward and shoved at its chest.

"Go on, get back! Back! Back!"

Hissing and spitting like a defeated cat, it backed away. She pressed it past the bottom of the ramp and into the airlock to the hold, bowling over a drone working with a welding pencil.

"Back, go on, get back!"

Behind her she was aware of Saskia flinging herself on her brother's body, crouching with it in her arms.

"Get in there!" shouted Tabitha.

The Frasque's jaw was working, it was spluttering, trying to make itself understood.

Tibitha paused, gripping two of its arms tightly, under no illusion but that it could break her in two any second it chose. "What? What are you saying?"

"Gno passengersss," it mouthed. "Gno passen-gersss."

"I need her!" she said. "Not passenger! My co-pilot! Co-pilot! Understand? Oh, God . . . Here!"

Moving fast, not giving either of them time to think, she clutched its wiry wrist and rushed with it up the ramp into the cockpit. She pointed aggressively and dramatically at her web, then the co-pilot's. "Two," she proclaimed. "See?" She held up two fingers. She pointed at her web, at herself; at the other web, at Saskia, standing below them in the gangway clutching her brother's body to her like a shield. She pointed at Saskia. "You hurt her," she threatened it, "and we don't go to Titan. Understand? No Titan!"

The Frasque spat and fizzed. Its knotty jaw shivered rapidly backwards and forwards. "Rrressstore me," it said again.

Tabitha understood. It wanted to go back to Plenty.

Tabitha pointed at Saskia once more. "Don't," she said distinctly. "Touch. Her. Saskia, for God's sake put him down and come up here now, if you don't know what it's going to do, you'd better come up here right now and do exactly as I say. Saskia!"

Saskia let Mogul slump back to the deck. She straightened up, moving with great grace and dignity up the ramp.

As soon as she was within arm's reach Tabitha grabbed her by the shoulder and pulled her past the Frasque, into the space between the webs.

The Frasque hung over them, bristling, making a noise in its throat like a low dry growl.

"Get behind me," Tabitha said.

Saskia obeyed.

"Get into the web. Do it, just do it, get into the web, do it as if you did it a hundred times a day."

Tabitha looked the Frasque in the eye and held up her index finger, as if she were going to tell it something very important, something she wanted it to remember.

Snapping its jaws and tossing its head, it stood, looking at her finger.

"Me," said Tabitha firmly, pointing to herself. "Her," she said, pointing at Saskia.

Not turning her back on it for an instant, she climbed into her own web, rotating it so she still faced the Frasque.

It seemed to have calmed down.

"Stay there," Tabitha warned Saskia. "Don't look round. Just sit tight. I think we're going to be all right." What do you mean, we're going to be all right? she asked herself silently. We're going to die.

But not the way Mogul died.

"All right?" she asked the Frasque. "All right?"

It corkscrewed its head and flailed its arms about.

"Good," said Tabitha.

"Tabitha! Tabitha!"

It was Marco, still outside. He sounded in a bad way.

"Just a minute, Marco."

She got out of her web again and tried to entice the Frasque back down the ramp into the hold. It wouldn't go. Marco kept moaning, calling out. She cursed him. Careful not to make any suspicious movements, she went into the airlock and looked outside.

Behind her the Frasque had picked up the empty gun and was turning it over and over in its claws. She hoped Saskia wouldn't look round. It was standing negligently on her brother. Marco was lying in the mud just below the door, reaching up to her. "I'm hurting," he said, accusingly. His right leg was at a decidedly unpleasant angle.

Tabitha looked round. The Frasque was watching.

The hell with it.

Holding on to the door, she reached down and grasped Marco's wrist.

The Frasque squeaked and squealed. It leapt for the door, leaning out like an articulated crane and swiping furiously at Marco.

"Okay, okay!" Tabitha said, letting Marco splash back into the mire with an agonized yell. "Sorry, Marco!" She tussled briefly with the Frasque, hustling it back on board. "I should be pushing you out, not in!" she shouted at it.

It came, limbs skittering in all directions. It stepped back to the bottom of the ramp and froze, glaring suspiciously up at Saskia.

Saskia hadn't moved.

"Come on," Tabitha told it forcefully, pulling on its

arm. "Marco?" she called. "Hector doesn't want you on board."

"What, what, you can't, you're not," he gibbered.

"Find some shelter," she said.

"Tabitha!" he wailed. "Don't go! You can't go! You can't leave me! You can't leave me here!"

"God, Marco, you'd better be wrong, that's all," she said. "Will you get *in* here?" she said fiercely, to the Frasque.

It glared at her, gnashing its teeth. "I want you where I can see you," she told it sternly. "This is a human custom known as hospitality."

Suddenly it ducked through the door, knocking the drone over again, and whizzed into the hold so fast it was horrible.

"You get comfortable in there," she shouted at it.

It hovered, untrustingly, swaying its arms up and down like a temple dancer.

Marco was still complaining, swearing, pleading. Tabitha ignored him. She rushed after the Frasque into the hole, whirled around picking up everything that was left in there: lengths of material, empty bags, articles of clothing, anything soft. She gathered an armful, then two more, flinging them into the corner.

The drone, having finished mending the inner door, waddled into the airlock and up the wall, to start on the outer one.

"Sit there!" Tabitha commanded the Frasque. She patted the pile. "Soft. Good. Comfortable." She wondered what notion of comfort a creature could have that was all intellect and reflexes, and could live on vacuum.

"I'm going to have a go at the ship."

She turned around, not even pausing to see if it obeyed her. On her way out she spotted Tal's traveling box and wondered for an instant whether she should toss it out to Marco. No, she thought; he'd only go and open it. Marco couldn't survive without the presence of admiring company.

She picked up the box and carried it to the cockpit.

"Marco," she called as she strode out of the hold,

"we're not going far if we're going anywhere at all. If
we can get help, we'll get you help. But we can't go for
a while," she said, grimacing as she passed Mogul's
crumpled body, "and it's going to take you a while to
get to shelter. So I'd start crawling if I were you," she
said, leaping up the ramp. "All right?"

His reply was incoherent and obscene.

Tabitha tucked Tal's box beside her bag, under the
net at the back of the cockpit, then stepped up to the
console. She turned, reaching through the web to clasp
Saskia's hand while she cast a swift glance at the one
working monitor, the one connected to the scanner in
the hold.

It could have been a still picture. The Frasque was
standing exactly where she'd left it. It hadn't moved.
She looked down at Saskia. "Why did he do it?" she
asked.

Saskia looked up at her, tears running down her long
cheekbones. "He was saving you . . ."

"Don't cry," Tabitha said, squeezing her hand. "It
fucks up the circulators."

Saskia tried to smile. Her face crumpled. Her skinny
shoulders shuddered.

Tabitha shook her hand briskly.

"Do you know anything about computer personas?"

Saskia sniveled, sniffed, shook her head.

Tabitha glanced back at the hold. Still in there. She
searched the yoke of Saskia's futuristic spacesuit, found
the audio plug and unreeled it. She pulled it across to
the socket and plugged it in. "Her name's Alice," she
said. At this stage, it was as likely as anything else. And
it would keep her occupied.

Tabitha bent down, pressed her visor against Saskia's,
and mouthed a kiss. Then she whirled out of the cockpit
again and back down the ramp, past Mogul, and into the
hold.

The Frasque was still standing in the same position.
It stared at Tabitha like a mad tree.

"Suit yourself," she said to it. She looked around.
She was looking for the Frasque's coffin, but it was

outside with the rest of the gear. She used her wrist monitor, sending the extensor down for it.

When it began to whir, the Frasque moved convulsively, gazing up at it, and past it through the open roof, at the dripping pseudodendroids, the hot and mucky sky.

"Mending the ship," Tabitha said, affirmatively.

The Frasque came and leaned over her. "Exxxtensssor," it rustled, knowledgeably.

Deliberately, she ignored it. She wondered what else it understood.

Working with one of the drones outside, she managed to pick up the tubular coffin blind, then give the retrieval sequence for it to come to the open airlock.

"I'm sure you'd be more comfortable sitting down," she told the Frasque. She went and sat down herself on the pile she'd made, and beckoned it to sit beside her.

When it came, it lay down full length, with its knees and elbows at complicated angles that made it look like a confused grasshopper.

"Good! Good! Yes!" said Tabitha. "Yes! Yes!" Slowly and carefully, she got up.

The Frasque hissed. It stayed where it was.

"We'll be leaving soon," she lied.

It watched her beadily as she walked out of the hold, past the patiently laboring drone.

The coffin was dangling in at the airlock. As she brought it in Tabitha looked outside. Marco was ten meters away, crawling on his belly through the mud, dragging his injured leg behind him.

"Keep it up, Marco, you're doing very well!"

She saw him turn his head and stare at her through the blackened forest. She saw his eyes; his beautiful eyes.

She tugged the coffin aboard, laid it down in the gangway next to Mogul, sprang the catches and, trying to look at him as little as possible, lifted him in. He was as light as his sister.

She composed his limbs hurriedly and sealed the case. Goodbye, Mogul, she said, silently. There was a time—

She didn't complete the thought.

Standing up, she felt her head spin round and round.

Fatigue hit her like a sandbag. She had been half dead
from exhaustion even before she'd started rushing around
like a mad thing. And there was still no prospect of rest.
Maybe there were some more stimulants in the first aid.

She went up into the cockpit.

Saskia had one slender gloved finger extended over
the keyboard. She was staring at the console screen.

It was glowing.

There were words on it.

They said: I HAD SISTERS ONCE, SASKIA. SEVERAL
OF THEM.

"Alice!"

It is remarkable how many people have difficulty be-
lieving the story of the Venus Repairs. Even some who
accept the Miraculous Torpedoes remain unconvinced by
this particular exploit of Tabitha's.

Their case is simple. Doughty and determined though
she evidently was, could Tabitha Jute possibly, with no
more than basic mechanical skills and ailing equipment,
have resurrected her ship from a crash-landing in the
filthiest terrain in the inner planets? If so, how long must
it have taken her? Could she have survived long enough
to do it?—if, indeed, she ever landed on Venus at all.
There are those who insist that it was another ship entirely
(the *Initial Concept*, some suggest; the *Lacrimae Rerum*,
others argue).

Well, I can assure you, and who could possibly know
better, that Captain Jute did indeed crash on Venus, repaired her ship on the spot and then made her escape
from it. It was exactly as I say, and the onus of proof is

on those who would have it otherwise. For the rest, it is enough to cite once more the resilience of the Bergen Kobold, the very durability that eventually rendered the model unprofitable. If any flyweight ship of those years could have shrugged off an argument with the hell-goddess, it would have been a Kobold.

There again, popular fancy nods and winks and lays one finger alongside its intrusive, pointed nose: the *Alice Liddell*, it insinuates, was no ordinary Kobold.

Be that as it may. Who am I to quarrel with popular fancy? Expertise is not the only material of which history is made. We must all bow to history, even those of us without necks.

For the rest: I was familiar with the *Lacrimae Rerum*. Venus would have made short work of her. And if the *Initial Concept* says she's been to Venus, I have to tell you that she has not. Her memory is deceiving her.

Were the miscellaneous improvements to the *Alice Liddell* responsible for her remarkable durability? How can one tell, now? Can one say confidently that Tabitha Jute truly was alone in her labor; that Capella did not have a hand in it? Can one say confidently there was anything in this period that Capella did not have a hand in?

"Alice? Are you all right?"

"YES, THANK YOU, CAPTAIN."

Tabitha stood beside Saskia, seized by a strange mixture of relief and jealousy.

"Where have you been?"

There was a pause before the persona replied. "I DON'T KNOW, CAPTAIN, BUT IT WAS RATHER DARK AND QUITE CONFUSING."

"I was talking to you, do you remember?"

"I REMEMBER A CHERUB."

"Xtasca."

"NO. CHERUBS ALL OVER ME. WORKING ON ME."

"Xtasca did that . . ."

"A TALL BLACK SERAPH IN A BLACK CHROME SUIT, DIRECTING THEM. CHERUBS IN A ZERO DOCK FITTING MY INLAID PANELS, TAPPING ME WITH THEIR LITTLE

HAMMERS. A FRASQUE IN A BONY CRADLE, LOOKING ON.''

Tabitha and Saskia looked at each other.

"Before my time, Alice," said Tabitha.

"I THINK PERHAPS I WAS DREAMING," Alice said.

"Are you awake now?" asked Tabitha.

"I PREFERRED THE DREAM."

"You're awake."

Tabitha looked at Saskia in gratitude. "What did you do to her?" she asked.

Saskia shrugged. She held out both hands through the net, apart, open. A tiny, weak rainbow of silver stars twinkled briefly but unmistakably between the palms of her gloves.

Sitting down and plugging in, Tabitha glanced in the first aid. She'd had everything out of there, there was nothing left. Willing her eyes to stay open, she looked up at the cockpit's sole surviving monitor.

It cycled views along the length of the hold from the catwalk forward, from port aft, in the corner about head height, and a dead screen where the starboard beam camera was out. Each view showed the Frasque lying in angular recline on its improvised bed of theatrical impedimenta. Diminished by the scale, it looked more than ever like an effigy of straw and brushwood, centerpiece of some rustic festival, waiting for the torch.

"Would you like to do something about that, First Officer Zodiac?"

Saskia nodded vigorously, then shook her head. She looked as exhausted as Tabitha felt.

"I don't suppose there's any chance of a tube of coffee?" said Tabitha.

Saskia held out her hands again. They were just hands, ordinary hands.

Tabitha checked her wrist monitor. The drones had done everything they could do.

"Alice, did I lock the hold doors?"

"NO, CAPTAIN."

"Call the drones in and lock up. And let me know whether you're fit to travel."

"WOULD YOU LIKE THE FULL DAMAGE REPORT, CAPTAIN?"

"No. One word. One syllable would do."

"BAD."

"Have we got integrity?"

"78.65%"

"Is that enough to take off?"

There was the briefest of pauses.

"JUST ABOUT, CAPTAIN."

"Is there enough power to take off?"

"JUST ABOUT, CAPTAIN."

"And to get us into orbit?"

"NOT FOR VERY LONG, CAPTAIN."

"Is there anything we can do quickly now that will significantly increase our chances?"

"WHAT FACILITIES HAVE WE GOT?"

"Look around," said Tabitha.

"I'M SORRY, CAPTAIN, I CAN'T DO THAT."

"It's Venus, Alice," Saskia put in.

"I RECOMMEND WE LEAVE IMMEDIATELY," said Alice, immediately.

"I thought you might." Tabitha folded her arms on the board and let her head flop down for a minute in fatigue and relief. Knowing she still had a ship had taken away some of the stress that was holding her up. "Initial warm-up, Alice. Report any anomalies. Talk to the charting comp and get us a good orbit."

"WHAT CONSTITUTES A GOOD ONE, CAPTAIN?"

"One we can do."

"AYE-AYE, CAPTAIN."

Tabitha lifted her head and looked at Saskia in disbelief.

Saskia was staring miserably through the hole in the viewport, into the dripping forest.

Tabitha dropped her head again. She rocked her helmet gently back and forth along her forearms. She squinted up at the hold monitor. "Don't worry, Hector, Mr. Frasque," she called. "They won't bother you."

The Frasque wasn't moving. It lay there, suspiciously

watching the three drones roll solemnly into their kennels and the doors close over them.

She was sure it could hear her.

"We'll be taking off any minute now," she told it loudly.

Saskia was unlatching her web.

Tabitha looked at her in surprise.

"I'm going to bury him," Saskia said. She stood up.

Tabitha was appalled. "There isn't time!" she protested. "We won't be gone long—Alice, have you got that orbit yet?"

"COMPUTING," said Alice.

"I'm going to bury him," Saskia said again.

She went down the ramp, found her brother's body in the JustSleep coffin and dragged it into the airlock. With a glance at Tabitha, she drew the inner door closed after her.

Tabitha, frustrated, unplugged herself, got up and went after her. She stood at the porthole, looking out. Marco was out of sight.

Fortunately, Saskia understood the urgency; or else she had not intended much ceremony. Cycling the airlock and opening the outer door, she stood on the brink with the coffin in her arms. Of all the ways she had ever held her brother, in affection, in performance, in desire—this was the last, and strangest.

She gave a great high, desolate cry, and thrust the silver-grey cylinder out of the door.

It toppled into the mud with a plump splash and began to sink gradually from sight.

Saskia stood there weeping, her arms raised as though to catch him if he thought better of his dive and decided to leap back on board.

"ORBIT CHARTED AND LOGGED," called Alice. "PERMISSION TO INITIATE—"

"Go ahead, Alice."

The outer door closed and the inner opened. Saskia came in, moving in a dazed, preoccupied way.

She flopped into Tabitha's arms as the airlock closed behind her.

"Where are we going?" she asked, brokenly.

"Up," said Tabitha, holding her. "The only thing we can do is sit up there and scream very loudly," she said. "And hope someone notices us before we fall."

"Scream?" said Saskia.

Tabitha led her back into the cockpit and pointed at a readout. "That's co-ordinates for here," she said. Helping Saskia into her web, she leaned across the board, pressing a sequence of tabs and keys. "Now you get on that taper and make a loop of that," she told her. "If there's anyone around, a tour bus, a terraformer, anyone, maybe they'll come and pick us up. If not, somebody will pick the message up anyway, and then they're bound to come and check."

"Bound to," said Saskia, inexpertly pressing keys while Tabitha sat up in her web.

On the monitor the motionless Frasque continued to cycle, front, side and blank, front, side and blank.

"All right," said Tabitha. "Let's see what happens if I do this."

And she pressed a tab.

The cockpit filled with red light. A high, buzzing hum began.

Saskia finished the loop and entered it. With another quick glance at the screen, where the image of the Frasque was being torn and frayed by zigzags of interference, Tabitha wrestled to master the refractory controls. Everything was sluggish, everything was wheezing. A slow, irregular hammering sounded from beneath the floor.

Saskia looked at her apprehensively. "Is that Marco?" she asked.

"No, it's supposed to do that—"

The ship was shuddering violently, seesawing. The creepers astern were slipping, snapping; the *Alice* dipped rearwards, her primaries blowing waves of mud into the hot forest. A small avalanche of loose kipple swept beneath their feet.

"Tabitha!" called a small voice through a storm of engine noise and interference. "Come back! You can't do this, you can't do this to me, you can't—"

They looked at each other.

"That's Marco," said Tabitha. "Hold tight, Marco, we won't be long," she called. She doubted very much he could hear her or anything else with the row the ship was making, supplemented by a chorus of enraged Venusian fauna.

Something began to drill piercingly over the top of the hum. They were rising, then falling back into the cradle as it collapsed beneath them, melting and burning. They were staggering, sliding, floating on the dank and greasy air. Above, the ugly treetops threshed and shattered. On the com the Frasque was trying to say something. It was quite inaudible.

As the old argument with gravity grew fierce, Tabitha felt the embrace of the web field grip her, repelling every external force. Now, she thought, is when Venus will tear us apart, properly this time.

Fierce wind flared in the cockpit, snatching at the rubbish. Seams old and new grated and squealed, and lights popped and pinged on the board. The protesting whine had become a shriek of pure demented fury. The *Alice* had been designed and built for this particular argument, built and rebuilt; knocked down and patched up again and thrown back into the fight. She was going to win the argument again, if it was the last she ever won.

Saskia was looking at Tabitha, and Tabitha realized she was shouting aloud, cheering every centimeter the *Alice* lifted.

"Come on, Alice!" They were both at it now. "Come on, Alice! Give it the lot!"

The ship gave a rough lurch, tilting badly to port aft, pitching and yawing nauseatingly around the apex as if it intended to spin itself aloft. The thunder banged and banged and howled.

Tabitha was at the keyboard, dragging mightily at the trim, hauling the coughing port engine up off its log bed by brute force and mechanical abuse. Creepers snagged on the scything wings and burst, lashing through the churning air. They were climbing. They were climbing.

The gluey atmosphere of Venus clung to them as the *Alice* clawed through it sideways, slicing the sand clouds with her starboard wing, coughing out static and lost possessions, belching acid steam. She was screeching like a demon. Slowly, then faster and faster, the green horizon began to curve back from them.

On the monitor, the unsecured Frasque tumbled about the hold, battered from side to side in a storm of drapery, smashed against one wall, the floor, the rear wall. Tabitha saw it sprawl, spreadeagled against the smeared remains of Saskia's mural.

"Alice?" she said. "I want a 360° roll. In your own time," she said, with grim precision. She glanced at Saskia. "Don't whatever you do, don't open that web," she called. "And don't throw up."

The *Alice Liddell*, already listing hard to port, flipped all the way over. Venus suddenly grew larger again, her camouflage of iridescent clouds whirling wildly around beneath their heads.

In the hold, a last great swirl of colored cloth, stray shoes, empty tubes and fairy-lights went tumbling through the open roof.

As the ship screwed herself upright again, onscreen Tabitha and Saskia could just about make out the spiky form in the hold. It was clinging tightly to the catwalk.

"You fucker!" shouted Tabitha.

It began to crawl towards the forward camera.

"All right! All right!" cried Tabitha, enraged, as the ship came right way up again, still laboring to climb. "Alice, emergency structural assembly access!"

The console blanked, snowed, produced a fuzzy menu. Tabitha called out codes.

Suddenly waves of flying sand were breaking over the cockpit. The ship was full of it. In a brown blizzard the Frasque disappeared beneath the forward camera, appeared mid-screen on the aft camera. It was at the forward door, hanging on to the catwalk with its upper hands, wrestling the handle with its feet.

"Not yet!" shouted Tabitha. "Get back! Alice—!"

Tumbled in grit, the hull of the *Alice Liddell* began to
complain, piercingly.

"Come on, Alice!"

A wobbly diagram plopped insecurely on to the console screen, rolling over and over again as the vertical
hold failed to grip. It showed, in transparent outline, the
hold of a Bergen Kobold.

"That's it!"

Screwing up her eyes, she leaned as close as she could
to the malfunctioning screen. "4.2, 1.5 and zoom."

On the other screen, the hold monitor, the Frasque
disappeared altogether.

It had entered the airlock.

Saskia craned over her shoulder, gazing wide-eyed
through the flying sand.

Tabitha was calling out codes again.

"Priority command! Emergency disassemble!"

In the wavering schematic rotating on the screen, sixteen spots around the end walls of the hold were flashing
vermilion. Then white.

Then not flashing. Not alight at all, with nothing where
they had been and nothing in between them. As though
the ship suddenly had no middle. On a minor readout
figures were scrolling, running swiftly towards zero. As
though there were very much less of the *Alice Liddell*
than there had been.

They started to climb much more steeply, out of the
region of storming dust and into corrosive fog. Redoubled gravity snagged everything under the nets and
pinned it to the deck.

Tabitha gave a loud crow of triumph.

"Ha-haa! What d'you think of that? Sixteen-point-six
k above the Sea of Guinevere! Bye-bye, Hector! All
right, Alice! All *right*!"

She looked joyfully at the monitor, now completely
blank, deprived of scanners. She turned round in her
web, gazing gleefully through the yellow fog at the closed
door below the ramp as though there would be something
to see there. There was nothing, nothing but a closed
door.

"All *right*!" she exulted again.

She looked at Saskia. Saskia was staring at the viewport. She did not look happy.

Tabitha looked at the viewport.

Through the ruined glass a face stared in at her, upside down.

It scrabbled rapidly, furiously with its claws. It opened its black-rimmed mouth and hissed.

Tabitha screamed at it. "Get off my ship!"

For an instant, it was as if it had heard her. The brown face vanished. One twiggy hand scrabbled a moment at the shattered glass, and was gone.

"It's fallen off!" cried Saskia.

"Don't you believe it," Tabitha said. "Alice, are we tight?"

"THERE'S A HOLE IN THE VIEWPORT, CAPTAIN," the persona pointed out.

"Apart from that!" said Tabitha, trying to get a fan to vent the sulphurous fog and failing completely. "Can that thing get in anywhere?"

"THE FORWARD HOLD DOOR IS INSECURE. THE FRASQUE HAD BEGUN TO OPEN IT WHEN YOU JETTISONED THE HOLD, CAPTAIN."

"Can you secure it, Alice?"

"NO, CAPTAIN."

"Is there anything we can do? Manually?"

"A SUGGESTION. WELD THE DOOR SHUT."

"Yes!" said Tabitha. "No, damn—"

"Why not?" asked Saskia.

"The gear is with the drones," Tabitha said. "At the bottom of the Sea of Guinevere."

"AN ALTERNATIVE SUGGESTION. YOU MAY BE ABLE TO OPEN THE DOOR AND RESEAL IT."

"I'll go," said Saskia.

"No." Tabitha reached over to her. "I'll go. When she cuts the engines."

The acrobat was fraught. "Tabitha! I can open and close a door! I can't fly a ship!"

"I'll be all right," Tabitha said. "I've got my hull boots on."

"It's gone!" Saskia protested. "It fell off back there!" she maintained, hotly.

Tabitha shook her head. "Not a chance," she said. "Alice, is that thing still there?"

"I WISH I COULD TELL YOU, CAPTAIN. ALL MY EXTERNAL SENSORS HAVE BEEN DESTROYED."

Saskia reached one muddied silver arm through the diminishing fog. "Give me the boots!"

"They won't *work* on your suit!"

With a deafening, hissing, tearing noise, the *Alice* surfaced out of the acid clouds.

Now the electromagnetic surf of trapped microwaves was sluicing along the Kobold's dented sides. The cockpit filled with a morbid, sea-green light. Above, the universe was an inverted ocean of wispy fire, a distended soup of lambent plasma.

Tabitha promised Saskia. "I'm just going to shut the door, I'm not going outside."

"Alice!" begged Saskia. "Don't let her do it!"

"THE CAPTAIN'S ORDERS ARE ABSOLUTE, FIRST OFFICER ZODIAC."

"You've really done something to her," said Tabitha.

"I only woke her up!"

"She's never been like this before." Maybe Alice was more damaged than she let on. Maybe it was the strain, forcing her to function at a more primitive level of programming. Tabitha had time to hope Alice wasn't going to become one of those hopelessly servile personas, like Vera Shawe's Shinjatzu, when she caught herself.

The *Alice* wasn't going to become anything but scrap. And that too soon.

At that moment the exosphere of Venus opened, expelling them into space.

From the top of the ruined viewport, a familiar indigo pall began to settle. It was exactly as if the ship were rising gradually into a suspended pool of faintly luminous ink. "How long can we stay up here, Alice?"

"WITH WHAT PROBABILITY, CAPTAIN?"

"A hundred."

"TWO YEARS."

"And land safely?"

"TWO MONTHS."

The smashed viewport filled with inky space and hard white stars. Everything was very quiet. Below, night lay across the face of Venus.

The *Alice* had begun her orbit.

"Back where we were?"

"THE ANSWER DEPENDS ON THE ACCURACY WITH WHICH WE TIME OUR DESCENT," said Alice. "PROVISIONALLY—"

"Never mind. Alice, mayday signal all channels."

"AYE-AYE, CAPTAIN."

"Stick this in it. Saskia, the loop."

Saskia pressed the play button, and Alice began to spray the void with repeating blurts of co-ordinate. Anyone brushing through it with even half an ear open should notice their dayglo electronic squawk, and know where to look.

There was silence in the cockpit of the *Alice Liddell*.

"Can you hear anything?" asked Tabitha.

Saskia shook her head. "It's gone," she repeated, flatly.

"I'm going to close that door."

"Be careful, Tabitha," she said. "Tabitha? What can I do?"

"Watch the board. If anyone answers, grab them. Don't let them get away. And keep an eye on the viewport."

Saskia looked around the cockpit, searching for a weapon. "If it comes in—"

"It won't," Tabitha reminded her. "It's fallen off."

She walked ponderously down the wall into the gangway. Both exit locks were intact. She checked their controls, and looked out of the porthole each side.

There was nothing to see but nothing. Venus turned, beautiful and foul, far below them. Her vast storms and putrid jungles glowed with false glamor.

Tabitha hoped there was somebody else in the vicinity. She hoped they were the sort of considerate, humane citizens of the system who would rush to a distress call, at whatever cost of profit or pleasure to themselves. She hoped they wouldn't hang around not wanting to get involved; thinking someone else would answer it first.

The indicator on the forward hold lock was glowing red. The Frasque had obviously known exactly how to operate it. Luckily the hold had blown and the blast had sucked the creature away before it could complete the sequence. Alice was right, the only thing to do was open it manually and close it again.

Tabitha put her hand on the override button.

She pressed it.

The red light began to blink gently.

Tabitha walked up the wall and crouched low over the winding handle, planting her feet firmly one either side.

She got hold of the handle and turned it.

The door opened; just a crack.

Tabitha kept winding.

The door accelerated; the handle too. There might not be gravity, but there was friction.

Tabitha opened the door.

She looked outside.

There was nothing there.

There was, literally, nothing. Two hundred and fifty cubic meters of nothing.

On the other side of the *Alice*'s empty middle, she could see the aft lock.

There was nothing at that door either.

For a moment she considered forgetting what she'd

told Saskia and just stepping outside for a cautious look around. The captain's prerogative is total, she thought. But if she should see the thing—or if it should see her before she saw it—what then?

She just knelt down and put her head out; just a little way.

Nothing but raw, scarred metal. Venus had scoured the *Alice* to the quick.

Tabitha flinched. She ducked back inside, jabbed override again, then close.

The door whirred shut.

The indicator blinked green.

"Saskia? Any answer yet?"

"I can't hear anything," said Saskia.

"Alice? Are we stable?"

"STABLE, CAPTAIN."

"Anyone around?"

"SEARCH CONTINUING," said Alice.

"I'm just going to take a look at our stocks," Tabitha said, switching off her boots and standing up, kicking off, floating into the middle of the gangway.

"Bring me something," said Saskia.

"If there is anything," Tabitha said.

There wasn't much. She had almost finished her inventory of the larder when the Frasque leered at her through the porthole.

Tabitha jumped across the galley and spread herself awkwardly on the wall, gagging in shock.

In the dark outside the Frasque's eyes were invisible in their sockets, peggy teeth invisible within its skinless lips. It seemed for a moment as though the sanding had eviscerated it, excising all its innards and leaving a brittle husk clasped rigidly to the hull. But then it moved, like a lizard, whipped across the glass, and vanished again.

"Damn. God damn." She was shaking.

"Tabitha? Did you say something?"

"There's not much here," said Tabitha quickly. All right, she said to herself. Hand to hand.

I need something to hit it with, she thought, to knock it off the hull. Something long, so I don't have to get too close. If I can once prise it off, it'll be helpless, it's got no way to get back on again.

She peered out of the porthole.

She couldn't see a thing.

"Anything yet, Alice?"

"ONE SHIP CLOSING," said Alice cheerfully. "WITHIN HAILING DISTANCE."

"Hail it, then!"

"I AM, CAPTAIN," said Alice, polite as could be, but with a hint of her old self.

For a moment Tabitha almost abandoned her plan; but she thought, Not until they answer. She left the galley and went to the engine adit, where she hopefully opened a locker labeled SPARK PADS.

Inside were five grades of spare spark pads, arranged neatly in piles according to capacity.

Tabitha shut the locker. She went forward again, looking in the depleted bins and lockers along the gangway. There had been half a dozen suitably long things among Contraband's gear, she supposed. All gathering weed and muck on the seabed of Guinevere, now, and forever.

"There it is!" Saskia called. "The ship!"

"Are they answering?"

"Yes! Yes!"

Tabitha kicked off from the wall and dived towards the cockpit.

"It's coming through now!"

Into her phones came the soft hiss of an outside signal.

"*Ahoy, the Kobold. Hey, Captain Jute. Got your signal, you tricky bitch.*"

Tabitha burst into the cockpit.

The crazed viewport was filled with livid green.

She tried to think it was the daylit side of Venus again, that they had begun to spin in their orbit and were nose down. But it was the wrong shade of green: less putrid, more lurid.

"*Kelso Pepper here, Jute. Remember me?*"

The green shape turned.

A silver eye glowed, and the inexorable fist of a tractor beam thumped tight about the *Alice Liddell*.

51

BGK009059 LOG

TXJ.STD

PRINT

222&222&222&/fl[://]sproooOOOoooWWW%

MODE? VOX

SD? 14.31.31.

Alice?

Alice?

Can you hear me, Alice?

Alice, I think you can hear me. Can you acknowledge?

Can you give me anything at all, Alice? Just beep or flash a light.

All right, Alice. I'm going to carry on talking. I'm going to talk to you just as if you could hear me.

If you can hear me, can you acknowledge? All right.

I'm going to tell you a story, Alice. A story about the caravan, and the skipfest. A story about a fairy, and a boy who never grew up. A story about a mischievous old gentleman.

If you don't come out before I'm done, I don't think I can stand it, Alice.

Alice?

Once upon a time Tabitha Jute was a shuttle pilot, working for Melissa Mandebra and the owners and officers of the

Resplendent Trogon. She was on her way to Jupiter. It was the first time she'd been there.

I couldn't get over the size of Jupiter. Every subjective day I'd wake up and it would be bigger. It was hard, with that vast, glowing, orange plain filling half your view, to be sure you weren't falling on to it but actually speeding past it, faster and faster.

Tricarico said Jupiter's ring wasn't even a fraction as beautiful as Saturn's. I'd patched things up with Tricarico. I was feeling a lot more cheerful around then. I think everyone was. Now the long uphill haul was almost over, everyone seemed to be having affairs, forgiving enemies, making arrangements, just like Tricarico had told me. In the shuttle all anyone would talk about was what did I favor for the First Away. Would it be the *Kanzan*? the *Jitoku*? the *Cockatrice* herself?

"Noria says the smart money's on the *Valenzuela Perseverance*," Canforth Magnolia told me as I ferried her to a tryst on the *Scorpion Lament*.

"I really couldn't say, madam," I said, for the twentieth time that shift. I wasn't interested in the race. I knew where the smart money was. It was in my pocket, and it was staying there.

But I remembered the *Perseverance*. "Isn't that the one there was all the fuss about, back at Selucia? The one with the Navajo Shernenkovs on a Mitchum fuselage?"

"Oh, heavens, I don't know," said the Lady Magnolia. She looked at me sort of sideways. "I suppose you people would know things, like that."

"Yes, that's the one," I said. We were coming up fast on a lumbering Bellerophon full of shiny shrink-wrapped bulldozers. *You people,* I thought, smugly. Lady Canforth might not know it, but she had just paid me a compliment. I touched the laterals to shoot us corkscrewing through the Bellerophon's array and stole a glance at my lady. She was hanging on tight.

The only reason I was interested in the First Away was the Skipfest. Everyone on the caravan, even chauffeuses, was at a party of some kind. Everyone who wasn't on one of the big freighters, still fully occupied coaxing their Drive to kick in a couple of minutes before their nearest rival.

It was boring at first, though, because I had to take the Mandebras circulating, so they could show their faces at all the right parties, avoid the wrong ones conspicuously, and create a stir by turning up at one or two where they weren't expected. All the time news was coming in. "The *Duluth* at twelve to one!" "Tell Hyun-seng Tredgold the *Behemoth* has gone!"

Fortunately the Mandebras couldn't go on circulating all night, because we had to be at the *Raven of October* by eight, in time for the masque. Melissa couldn't be late for the masque. Everyone who was anyone would be leaving everyone else's party then, just to say they'd been to the Sanczau masque. Even if they hadn't planned it, they changed their minds when they saw the Mandebras were going.

We were all in costume. Melissa was a peacock, in a turquoise dress with two pages to carry her tail. The Strachan Alexis was something called a huzzar: he had a red coat with lots of ornaments and a huge hat and great big shiny black boots with gold spurs on. He said it was a sort of soldier, but it didn't look like gear you'd want to wear in any kind of fight. Lady Canforth was there, she had thigh boots too, and a black corset and a black collar with chromium spikes. I took Tricarico, he was a pierrot. We spent ages on his make-up, one cheek black and one white, with a big jeweled teardrop on the black side. Everyone was masked, though everywhere we went the Mandebras were all recognized instantly.

I went as Peter Pan. He was the boy who never grew up. He was in a story my dad used to tell us. I had a tunic that looked as if it was made of leaves, and a pair of tiny bronze horns sticking up through my hair.

Tricarico thought I looked terminally sexy as a boy. He stood with his arm about me as I steered us through the crowd of little ships already clustered around the *Raven of October*.

The *Raven* was big. Three times the tonnage of the *Resplendent Trogon*, though the *Trogon* was much more elegant, with her jeweled vanes and her scallop-shell forecastle, her pigtailed crew. When I pulled the shuttle in alongside, we were completely dwarfed by the banks of portholes, overshadowed by the mountainous bridge. I nudged us through the throng to the reception lock for the Mandebras to do their grand entrance, and then I was off duty. For once Melissa had consented to use a drone for the trip home.

We were just in time. The masque was beginning. Of course it had to be the story of the Big Step. First three people came on and did a quaint little dance as the Sun and the Earth and the Moon. Everybody went oh and ah. So far so dull, as far as I was concerned, but I kept watching, because the next bit would be the Small Step, and that was my special topic. Alaric Sanczau himself as the Capellan, with his head made up into a big bald dome, and a couple of people as the astronauts in mocked-up old spacesuits. They were nothing like the model in the museum at Tranquility. Then they ended with dance of the system, the Sun and all the planets and half a dozen tiny kids as asteroids dancing around Alaric Sanczau and changing places. Everybody clapped and said how wonderful it was.

I'd got bored and started watching the people instead. Everyone was in some sort of finery, most of us in masks still. A couple of people had come as famous Eladeldi. Some of the Frasque were expected any minute, but they never did turn up.

I was disappointed. It was all so much more formal than I'd expected, but then this was the crème de la caravan. "Don't worry," Tricarico said. "Things'll get a bit livelier later."

As soon as the masque was over, everyone started dancing, drinking, spotting the famous faces behind the masks and arguing about them. Money was changing hands everywhere you looked. I thought the losers were just paying up over the First Away, but it turned out now everyone was betting on who would come out nearest Enceladus at the end of the skip. Tricarico got into an argument with some people from Frazier Roublov command, so I slipped away in the crowd. I found some people to talk to. I even found another Lunar, a scrawny woman dressed up as a Panjit Modulator having a mock argument with an old man in a

silver gown with rocky make-up encrusted all over his face.
You could see he was being polite, listening to her under
sufferance. There was a wisp hovering at his shoulder. "If
you'd asked me, Balthazar dear, I could have put you right
about the spacesuits," the Lunar was saying archly. "I've
seen the real thing."

BALTHAZAR. BALTHAZAR PLUM.

Alice!

HELLO, CAPTAIN.

Alice, are you all right?

:T8$/ú

Alice?

    Alice, don't go away again!
    Alice. Alice, can you hear me?
    Talk to me!
    All right, Alice. I'm going to carry on.
    Yes, it was Balthazar Plum. He'd been the Moon, in the
masque. I knew he was a Sanczau, one of the directors of
the dynasty, but rubbing shoulders with the Mandebras had
made me what was it you said? Blasé. Blasé about talking
to the great and the good. Anyway, it was a masked ball.
And I was drunk by then. I barged into the conversation
when I heard the Lunar was saying to him, "I mustn't be
so critical. I'm sure your wisp is taking this all down."
    She stroked it under the chin, the way they like. You could
see its glow get stronger as she stroked it. It started to croon.
    "It's me who should have the wisp," I said.
    Plum looked at me, his huge eyebrows arched, stretching
his make-up. His eyes looked kind. He said, "And who are
you, my dear?"
    "Peter Pan," I said.
    They'd never heard of Peter Pan, so I told them as much
as I could remember: how I lived on an island, in a hole
under a tree, and fought pirates and redskins every day and

was never ever going to grow up. I could see the Lunar's smile getting more and more strained, like, Who is this idiot telling Balthazar Plum a fairy story? but I was well away, I was out of my head. "I've got a pet fairy called Tinkerbell," I said. "She usually follows me around. Like your wisp."

"I suppose she is rather like a fairy," he said. He held a blunt, square finger to his shoulder. "Come on, Wisp," he said, and brought his finger gently around in front of him. The wisp, tiny gyros whirring, traveled with it, hovering over his knuckle.

"She's enchanting!" said the Lunar. It wasn't. It had a squashed face with a pug nose and a wide slit for a mouth with two minute little white fangs sticking up out of it, like a sort of tiny baby reptile, only with soft pink skin like a baby human. And squinty-eyed, so it looked malevolent or mad. It was sitting hunched up with its two vestigial hands stuck out in front of it and its hindquarters embedded in some very slick-looking machinery.

"Does she have a name?" the woman asked.

"I just call her Wisp," Plum said. "It wouldn't do to let her get ideas about having her own identity," he said, mock-seriously. "Here," he said to me then, holding out his finger. "Why don't you take her?"

"No thanks," I said. I knew what would happen. "Tinkerbell would get jealous," I said.

"Oh, *let me!*" said the Lunar, pushing in. "She's so enchanting!"

She put her hand up as if the wisp would hop onto it.

Then she started to shriek.

Conversations died all around and everyone looked at her.

Her hair was standing on end, and her eyes were almost popping out through her mask. Her mouth was working furiously, but nothing was coming out.

I reached out and grabbed her wrist, dragging her hand down and breaking the contact. The induction stopped at once, of course, but she was mightily shocked. Plum was grinning, not at all ashamed, and I'm afraid I was smiling too.

The woman snatched her wrist out of my hand. "Are you all right?" I asked her. She glared at me as if it had been me that had buzzed her. She didn't dare look at Plum, just stood there massaging her tingling hand until half a dozen acolytes in Tlac livery came barging through the crowd and rescued her, making soothing noises as they helped her away.

Plum was looking absolutely innocent, running the wisp suggestively up and down his forearm. I laughed. He just wagged his amazing eyebrows. "Insufferable woman," he said quietly.

"You'd have done that to me!" I protested.

"Perhaps you're insufferable too," he said.

"Perhaps I am," I said. "That's what happens to you when you don't grow up."

I talked with Balthazar Plum for quite a while, or rather Peter Pan did. I didn't want to tell him anything about me, but I made up all this stuff about Peter, how he was on the caravan because it was a big adventure, and what Peter liked doing best was flying. Then Plum started talking about an old boat that he said was just lying around on his estate, somewhere on Earth, in California. After a minute I realized he was saying if I left the party with him, I might be able to persuade him to part with this boat.

I went off him then. After what he'd done to that poor woman, I wasn't inclined to trust him, frankly. I didn't believe in the offer, and I didn't believe there'd be any offer without a catch. Obviously the ship was a ball of rust. I felt a bit insulted. We'd been getting on so well, and now he wanted to play games. I don't like playing other people's games. Anyway I didn't fancy him. Well, not that much.

That sounds like a lot of reasons, doesn't it?

Well, there was another one. Tricarico had found me and he was hanging about waiting for me, and suddenly I decided to take him back to my cabin on the *Resplendent Trogon* and take all his clothes off. While we were busy the rest of the crew came straggling back on board and the gongs began to go, and we were hardly dressed and at our posts before all the lights flickered and we were into hyper-space. My first big skip.

It was bloody boring. I had to go back and work in the stores, there was no flying at all.

52

Green filled the viewport of the *Alice Liddell*, then dark-ened to occlusion.

They were dragging the powerless Kobold up into the vile, stinking belly of the *Ugly Truth*. All external light had been eclipsed, all internal light extinguished. The deadly paralyzing nets reached out and enfolded her. It was all over.

Magnetic grapples banged home, shaking the *Alice* as though it were Captain Pepper's intention to tear her apart. Seams Tabitha and her drones had methodically sealed ripped and split once more like paper. In a burst of stale and sweaty air and a blaze of sick fluorescent light, the two forward airlocks flew open and two hulking figures swaggered aboard, one from either side.

Tabitha was up in the cockpit, stooping with one hand under the net. Saskia was nowhere to be seen.

As Tabitha dragged her bag out of the jumble, the strap snagged on the latch of a white porcelite box. The latch gave, and the lid of the box banged open.

Blinking, disoriented, Tal reared up, his green wings flaring.

Startled by this sudden apparition, the invaders swung up their weapons.

In that moment, Tal saw them in the gangway, saw their weapons, and knew them for an enemy. With an ear-splitting screech of defiance, he took to the air.

"Raaazor pemmican!"

He flew straight at the nearest of the boarders, beak wide, claws spread for battle.

His target was a hulking Thrant with one eye, a yellow cloth tied roughly around the other. Her ruff was red, and bristled profusely out of the torn neck of a greasy windcheater. Old shirts showed through where the fabric had been slashed to emphasise her muscles. Her jeans hung in ribbons around her long thighs; the silky fur there was matted with oil and grime. Cruel yellow claws burst from her oversized rope sandals. She came up the ramp at a bound, in her enormous scarred hands a sawed-off buckgutter. A simian stench filled the cockpit.

When Tal screamed and came flying at her, the Thrant swayed back snarling, spreading her ears, unready, for some reason, to use her weapon. Then, seeing the true caliber of her assailant, she chuckled, curled her upper lip, and lifted the enormous gun as though it weighed no more than a matchstick.

"Tal!" shouted Saskia, peering down from the ceiling, among the dead monitors. "Look out!"

" 'Ware fea'ers!" the Thrant growled to her partner, who was stamping on to the ramp on feet of steel.

Tal swooped, clawing for the single golden eye of the Thrant.

The leonine head swiveled, fangs gnashing savagely at the air; but the alien bird had feinted, swerving aside at the last moment to bite the pirate on the ear.

With a guttural curse, the Thrant turned, swung the buckgutter and fired.

Tal exploded in a ball of violet flame.

The women screamed.

The Thrant laughed, while its accomplice reached up and plucked Saskia down with one hooked hand.

There was a horrid stench of burnt fat and feathers. Scraps of blackened plumage fluttered to the deck.

Yelling, Tabitha turned on the second invader, grabbing for Saskia. Her captor swung her effortlessly away, pinned beneath one arm. Tabitha battered at its side, but her bare hands made no impression.

It was a large black robot: a converted high-g construction drone, Tabitha guessed. It walked upright like a person, the grapples of its feet tearing the restraining nets and scratching the deck. Its four arms were like fat steel hoses snaking from couplings on a chromium yoke. Its chest was a barrel that tapered to a point at the universal joint of its hips. Its head was a low dome of black glass. Inside, Tabitha could see tiny bolts of lightning, faintly flickering.

She rummaged in her bag for something, anything, she could use as a weapon. There was nothing. Then, in the drift of rubbish being kicked around the floor, out of the corner of her eye she spotted her trusty spanner. It was just out of reach. She dived for it, narrowly avoiding the lunging Thrant.

Tabitha snatched up the spanner and swung it hard, driving the Thrant back against the console, then twisted round and lunged at the robot.

There was a sudden *pop* and a bloom of green smoke. Under the tight coil of the robot's arm, Saskia's suit hung collapsed. Saskia was no longer in it. Somehow she was back on the ceiling, hanging on to a shattered monitor and kicking the Thrant in the face.

Tabitha whooped and took another swing at the robot. Her spanner clanged against its immobile chest and the shock battered her arm.

"*Ow!*"

Involuntarily dropping the spanner, she jammed the throbbing hand under her left arm, hugging it to her as she tried to jump back out of reach. But the robot slipped one of its arms behind her, and she backed straight into it. That hurt too.

The arm snaked unerringly around her waist. The hooked tip of another arm snapped tight around her left wrist.

With a grinding of industrial gears, Tabitha was hauled off her feet and held dangling.

From this ignominious position she watched the last moments of the defense of the *Alice Liddell*.

The Thrant had grabbed Saskia by the leg and pulled

her down from the ceiling. Now she was crushing her
to her chest with a tawny forearm across her throat.

Saskia choked and cried out with pain, prising ineffectually at the Thrant's arm, digging her fingernails in
among the fur.

The Thrant growled happily. She cuffed Saskia across
the head and Saskia abruptly ran out of tricks.

The pirates dragged their captives out through the ruptured port airlock into the bowels of the *Ugly Truth*.

They emerged into a grimy ship bay. The walls were
daubed with crude signs and graffiti, the floor pitted and
scarred. Puddles of iridescent slime marked the leaks in
the maze of piping overhead. There was gravity. There
was air, and it was foul.

Twisting her head in the robot's embrace, Tabitha took
a desperate look at her faithful old ship.

The *Alice Liddell* looked more wretched than she ever
had. She lay prostrate, capsized on the ruins of her undercarriage. She filled the bay, like a beached metal
whale, no light in her ports, no life in her at all. To the
fractures and abrasions of Venus had been added the
ruptures and wounds of ill handling by the pirate brig.
No trace of her proud copper ornamenting had survived
the corrosive airs of the jungle planet. Her viewpoint was
an unsightly hole; her roof was bare.

On the roof, something moved.

The robot was pulling Tabitha away towards the door,
almost breaking her in two in the process. The Thrant
was bringing the unconscious Saskia along behind.

It was the Thrant that the Frasque pounced on.

The Thrant gave a horrible squeal that rang around the
metal walls. The Frasque was on her back, ripping her
clothes, tearing at her fur.

Saskia pitched forward, slumping to the floor, but the
Thrant grabbed her by the hair. She hung on to Saskia
while she snapped at the claws of the Frasque digging
into her shoulder. She looked like an overgrown and
overdressed leopard trying to shrug a thorn bush off her
back; but the bush had many arms and legs and they

were wrapped tight around her. Her yowls of pain and rage echoed around the filthy chamber.

The robot took a moment or two to compute this new situation before beginning to lumber backwards to its partner's aid, dragging Tabitha with it.

Tabitha tried to resist, to dig in her heels, but it was no use. The surface of the floor was slick, and she skidded helplessly along, her bag thumping her hip, while the robot casually spun out another arm and took Saskia from the Thrant.

The Thrant was roaring in pain and anger. She brought up her enormous gun, but still something restrained her from firing it again, Tabitha could see, even while the Frasque, hissing and spitting, was trying to gouge her remaining eye. They sounded like a big cat enraged by a newly lit bonfire.

From the far side of the ship, a voice shouted an incomprehensible command.

The robot ground to a halt. In its chest, a panel whirred open.

Unburdened of Saskia, the Thrant was standing with her feet wide apart, using her gun like a crowbar, digging it viciously between her back and the animated bundle that clung so tenaciously to her shoulders.

From the cavity in the chest of the robot, a nozzle emerged.

The Thrant swung about, heaving mightily at the snapping Frasque. Now her back was to the robot.

The robot fired.

From the nozzle a pressurized jet of vapor lanced towards the struggling pair. It struck the Frasque square in the middle of the back.

The Frasque spasmed. It fell backwards off the tormented Thrant. It clattered to the dirty floor, suddenly lost all its elasticity and coiled up, crackling, like a hank of frozen rope.

"Slow," said the voice, critically. "Very slow."

Tabitha could see him now, a short, bowed Chinese, standing in the corner. He was old, with a fringe of long wispy hair surrounding his yellow pate. He wore a black knitted coat that fell to his ankles, blue zero-g's and a pair of jewelers' spectacles with frames of brass, an image amp taped to the earpiece. In his bony hands he held a bulky device, a sort of antique keyboard with an aerial coming out of it. With a fastidious, black-nailed finger, he pressed a button. "Tarko, are you hurt?" he called.

The robot's aerosol dripped, smokily, and retracted into the cavity. The panel closed over it.

The Thrant growled and grunted. She stepped up to the Frasque and gave it a kick. It cracked and rustled.

"Pick it up," ordered the old man.

"Nobo'y di'n say nothin' 'bou' tha'," grumbled the Thrant.

"Pick it up," the man repeated.

With distaste, she stretched down one long brown hand, seized the shriveled bundle, and hoisted it on her shoulder, where it had so recently hung.

Working his keyboard the old man went towards the door. The robot dunked after him, pulling Tabitha and Saskia mindlessly along.

Saskia was still out. She hung in her steel coil, a large bruise forming on her pale temple. Tabitha struggled, but she couldn't reach her. She got her feet under her, made an effort to walk, at least.

In the door, she looked down at the man who had taken command. His face was very wrinkled, his hair quite white. A thin beard straggled down to his chest, where something moved suddenly. She saw he was wearing a live blue scorpion, chained to a pin on his coat. The scorpion stirred, flexing its tail, as if it scented fresh prey.

"Captain Kelso Pepper, I suppose," said Tabitha.

Amused, the Chinese looked up at her, his sore eyes magnified by his spectacles.

"Oh no, Captain Jute. My name is Shing. Captain Pepper awaits you on the bridge."

53

"Howdy," said Captain Pepper.

He was a middle-aged, beef-faced white man with white hairs growing out of his nose. He sat in his captain's chair with his hands folded comfortably over his paunch. Tarko, the Thrant, stood between Tabitha and Saskia, her huge hands on their shoulders. Saskia was awake and upright. They had taken Tabitha's helmet away.

Shing was sitting against the wall on a compacted heap of dingy cushions, his keyboard in his lap. In front of him, the big black construction robot dangled the Frasque, which was curled up in a force bottle like a dead Christmas tree tied up in a knot. Upon the invisible surface of the bottle, luminous diagnostic graphics scribbled themselves, blue scrolls of data, pink neural maps blossoming and contracting like accelerated colonies of plankton. The old man was muttering happily to himself in Autonomy Chinese.

The bridge of the *Ugly Truth* was more squalid even than the cockpit of the *Alice Liddell*. It smelled like a zoo cage. Waste had been slopped in the corners and trodden around the floor. Obscene pictures and brutal exhortations were taped and sprayed around the walls; the ceiling was black with smoke. Most of the machinery looked half-dismantled, with clumsy rewiring sticking out of it. But all the screens were up, and green lights were glowing all across the boards.

Which was more than could be said for the *Alice Liddell*.

Captain Pepper wore faded blue overalls and a cap

with "KELSO" printed on it. He grinned at his captives, but made no attempt to rise.

"How you doin'?" he asked amiably.

"Call your yeti off and I'll show you how I'm doing," growled Tabitha.

The captain smiled, lifting his top lip from stained, rabbity teeth. His bright blue eyes were crinkly and candid. "Can't do that," he said easily. "Might hurt yourselves."

"We'd take you apart first."

Captain Pepper inspected his left thumbnail. "That's what you call wishful thinking, there." He looked up again, eased his overalls at the knees, and ran a thoughtful eye up and down Saskia's slender form. "How about you?" he said. "You say something now."

Saskia raised her chin. "I have nothing to say to pirates."

He squinted at her. "Pirates?" He grinned slyly at Tarko, looking round to see if Shing shared the jest. "I don't see no pirates."

Tabitha folded her arms. "Now tell me you're plain-clothes traffic cops."

Captain Pepper threw back his head and laughed. "Cops! Hear that, Shing? Hear that, Tarko? The lady thinks we're cops!"

Shing grinned, narrowing his eyes and raising his eyebrows, while Tarko rumbled, "I hear that."

Captain Pepper suddenly looked grim. "Then why ain't you laughin'?" he said, in an undertone.

The Thrant bared her great fangs and barked an obedient laugh. The old man went on equably examining his find.

Captain Pepper shifted his bottom, resettling himself in his chair. "Well, I'll tell you what, ladies," he said, and leaned towards them, a confidence to relate. "We *are* cops. What do you think of that, now? Captain Pepper is working for the big blue dog."

He sat back, toying with the peeling webskin of his chair, bending a loose flap between thumb and forefinger. He looked up at the women under his snowy brows,

glancing slyly at Tarko again as he continued to speak.
"Some days we're cops, some days—we ain't!" he announced, as if this were a great joke.

Saskia exhaled contemptuously.

Tabitha wanted to sink to the floor and go to sleep,
preferably forever. She was so far into hatred and despair
she wasn't feeling anything anymore. These bastards had
written off the *Alice*, and now they wanted to play games
before they wrote her and Saskia off too. It didn't matter
what they said now, or did, if they could do anything.
Perhaps if she managed to annoy this mercenary slug
he'd lose his temper and get it over with sooner. But that
meant summoning up some energy, and she was just
tired, so tired.

"I know what you are," said Tabitha.

Captain Pepper ignored her truculence. "Profession-
als," he told her.

"Scum," said Saskia, precisely.

Captain Pepper opened his eyes wide at this. "O-
ohhh," he cried, "will you listen to this one? We got
ourselves a real fireball here!" He slapped his thighs and
shared a raucous, bronchial laugh with Tarko the Thrant,
who kneaded their shoulders appreciatively.

This was getting tedious. "What are you doing here
anyway?" Tabitha demanded. "I thought we shut you
down."

Captain Pepper continued to grin. "Shut us down!"
he echoed. "You did, too. Shut down Kelso Pepper.
Shut down the *Ugly Truth*. Ain't many folks can say
that." He shook his head. Suddenly he was serious again.
"Now you had no call to do that. You made us both a
whole mess of trouble, doin' that. You hear me?" he
shouted, almost getting up out of his seat. "A whole
shit-stirring mess of trouble!"

Saskia clenched her fists and lunged forward. "You
killed my brother!" she yelled, pulling away from Tarko.
With one hand, the Thrant restrained her. She struggled,
glaring wildly at both of them. "You killed Tal! Marco's
down there—" She flung one arm out behind her, pointing back the way they'd come, as though she thought

Venus were somewhere below decks. "—dying slowly on Venus because of you!"

"What do you *want* from us?" said Tabitha ferociously.

Captain Pepper sat back down, slowly. He inspected his right thumbnail. Then he extended his horny right forefinger directly at Tabitha's head.

"You," he said. "We want you. And him," he said, jerking his thumb at the Frasque dangling lifelessly in midair in front of its aged examiner. "We want you, and him, and we want your little boat there." Pepper grinned again, goofily. "And we want your little black friend that put our lights out. We already got him, don't we, Tark?"

The Thrant looked at her captain, obedient, stupid, uncomprehending.

He suddenly seemed to lose interest in them. "Somebody wants to see you," he said. "Meantime, you just make yourselves right at home, you hear? Take 'em away, Tarko."

The Thrant purred. Gripping them tightly, she hauled Saskia and Tabitha away from the presence of the brooding commander and the inquiring mechanician; back down the dropshaft past the bay where the *Alice Liddell* lay shipwrecked in a puddle of her own vital fluids; back into the bowels of the ship. She threw them in a cell.

The cell, though small, was obviously much frequented. Previous prisoners had scratched names and long tallies of subjective days in the snot-green paint. Food and worse had been spattered in every direction, and here and there were the scorchmarks of gunshots. There was no handle on the inside of the door. There was no porthole either, and the light tube was barely glowing, but that didn't matter because there wasn't anything to look at.

"Wai," the Thrant said.

She held on to Tabitha's bag, pulling it over her head and then pushing her away. She stood there, mauling the bag between her hands. She tore it open, breaking the

zip, and peered suspiciously inside. "Wha's all iss
junk?"

"It's *my* junk," said Tabitha, standing close, ready to
grab the bag if a chance arose.

Tarko laughed. She shoved Tabitha hard into Saskia,
and they both fell on the floor.

The Thrant stood in the doorway, rummaging through
Tabitha's bag, letting things spill slowly to the floor: a
sock, a crumpled bundle of dockets, a plastic bag with
three fruitdrops gummed together at the bottom. Then
she drew back her arm and slung the bag in after them.
"Enjoy i'," she said, and slammed the door.

Tabitha climbed off Saskia, getting up on her hands
and knees and crawling stolidly over to her scattered
belongings.

She knelt, dragging the bag to her across the floor.

Deep in the walls, mighty engines shuddered into life.

Saskia was on her feet. She stood kicking the door
with determination and hatred.

Behind her, Tabitha picked up a disintegrating paperback book and clutched it to her, heedlessly, crushing it
against her midriff.

Saskia turned, leaning on the door, looking down at
Tabitha. "Ohhh . . ." she said, bitterly. "Here. Here.
Tabitha. Come now." She squatted to help her, picking
something inattentively off the floor. She looked at what
was in her hand: it was the bag of aged sweets. "Here,"
she said to Tabitha, shuffling into a place beside her and
putting an arm around her shoulders. She held the
wretched confectionery under Tabitha's nose. "Have one
of these," she recommended.

Tabitha's eyes were closed. She shook her head.

Sitting back on her heels, Saskia opened the screw of
torn plastic, tearing it further. She inspected the contents.
"Don't you want one?" she asked.

Tabitha, collapsed in upon herself, made no response.
She knelt on the floor clutching her book and her bag,
a black hole of misery and defeat.

"Can I have one then?" asked Saskia.

Tabitha nodded a heavy nod. Her chin came down on

her chest and stayed there, as if someone had turned up the gravity suddenly and her head had become too heavy to lift.

With difficulty, Saskia prised a gooey fruitdrop out of the lump. Frowning, she tried to pick the cellophane off it.

"Bastards," she said, in a preoccupied tone. She gave up her endeavor and popped the sweet in as it was. She cast around on the floor, saw something which had skidded under the bunk, reached in and got it.

It was Tabitha's harmonica.

Saskia held it out. "Tabitha?" she said, hopelessly.

Tabitha didn't stir.

"Oh, now, Tabitha."

On her knees, Saskia hugged her from behind, pressed her cheek against the back of her suit. "It's all right," she said indistinctly, her mouth full of fruitdrop.

Tabitha looked up then, and stared bleakly round at her.

"What is?"

Saskia gave a soft grunt of disapproval. She slid her hands up from Tabitha's middle to the back of her neck where it emerged from the collar of her suit. She squeezed her taut muscles and stroked her hair.

Tabitha resisted awhile, then let her head loll back into Saskia's hands. Her eyes were closed again.

Neglected, the broken book slipped from Tabitha's grasp to the grimy floor. Tabitha let it go.

Cradling Tabitha's head, Saskia pressed herself against her back. She touched Tabitha's cheek with her lips.

Tabitha knelt there, passive, inert.

Saskia kissed her mouth.

Tabitha made a tiny murmur in her throat.

Saskia lifted her head. "What?"

Tabitha's lips closed and opened again, her tongue flicking between them.

"Blackcurrant . . ."

Saskia snorted affectionately. "Come on, Tabitha."

She stood, propping her up, then lowering her on to the bunk. Her fingers made a short work of the latches

on Tabitha's suit. Gently she shucked her of it, then laid
her down on her back and kissed her again, unfastening
her jacket and running her conjuror's hands over her
breasts. "Blackcurrant," she murmured, scornfully.

Tabitha was asleep.

With an effort, Saskia took off Tabitha's jacket and
trousers. Then she lifted the sour, greasy cover, levered
Tabitha into the narrow bed, and, slipping out of her
own clothes, slid in after.

It got cold once the ship was under way. The captives
woke, put their clothes back on and huddled together
beneath the thin foil blanket. Tabitha, dozing, tumbled
into a dream. She was back in the lift complex on Plenty,
being taken to the Mercury Garden by a posse of Eladeldi.
The stations of the lift had the names of places she remembered from when she was a girl: Eudoxos, Manners,
Maskelyne. Her Auntie Muriel kept coming in, trying to
feed her pieces of burnt chicken, and someone she
couldn't quite see was singing in her ear.

She woke up, confused. The cell was full of the dull
subsonics of the *Ugly Truth*'s pulse engines. The gravity
had shifted, so the floor now seemed to be sloping up
towards the door. Tabitha cuddled up to Saskia's warm
body.

"I was thinking about Tal," said Saskia then.

"So was I, I think," said Tabitha. Her mouth felt stale
and gluey. "Mngm. I was dreaming."

After a moment, Saskia said, "I wish he was here."

"Tal?"

"Mogul . . ."

"Don't," Tabitha said, hugging her. "Think about something else."

But Saskia wasn't to be moved. "They killed him," she said, brokenly. She lay and wept for a while, and Tabitha held her. "Poor Mogul," Saskia said. "And Marco. Tabitha? Will Marco be all right?"

Tabitha wished she felt confident anyone would be all right, anyone anywhere in this suddenly hostile system where everybody, Perks and cops and robbers, robots and Thrants, the Frasque and the Eladeldi and the Capellans too, probably, all only had to look at you to start chasing you, howling for your blood. She tried not to think of Marco Metz in his flashy suit, boiling his brains out in the murderous swamps of Venus.

"Of course he will," she said.

"Marco will be all right," said Saskia. "If anyone knows how to make sure he'll be all right, it's Marco."

"Saskia?"

"What?"

"What *were* you doing?"

The whole stupid venture was over, and she was done for. Her life had been painfully and ruthlessly taken out of her hands, she realized, looking back at it, that day by the Grand Canal in Schiaparelli. Now the *Alice* was scrap, and she was locked in the bowels of the *Ugly Truth*; everybody but Saskia was dead, or as good as; and there was nothing she could do, if there ever had been, about any of it.

Still she harbored a nagging curiosity to know just what the hell it was that had rolled over her and left her for the Eladeldi to pick apart.

"We needed the money," Saskia said, as if that explained everything. "We've never made any money. Never. And when we did, Marco would always go and throw it away on some stupid scheme to cheat everyone in sight for ten times as much. It never worked. Then we'd have to go back to Hannah and say we were sorry, and start all over again with nothing."

Tabitha sighed. She kissed the top of Saskia's ear,

rubbing her cheek in her long wild hair. "It's Hannah behind all this, isn't it?"

"She set it up," said Saskia. "In the beginning."

"She's working for the Frasque."

"We all are. Were. Working for the Frasque."

Tabitha stretched, arching her back. "I'd figured that much out, then," she said.

"The Frasque built Plenty," Saskia said. "After the war, one got left behind, in a freezer. When Hannah went in, she started fishing around to find out who was who, and she found him there. So she kept it quiet and she got in touch with some people she knows on Titan, some people who are still in contact with the Frasque, maybe they're Frasque themselves, I don't know—anyway, Hannah offered to get him out, without Capella knowing."

Tabitha put her hands behind her head. "You were rescuing the Frasque."

"That was the idea."

"You knew it was hibernating."

"Hannah said it was."

"You were smuggling it to Titan."

"Well, yes."

"On my bloody ship."

"Oh, Tabitha, I'm sorry, it was nothing to do with me. Marco—"

"Yes," said Tabitha grimly. "What about Marco?"

Saskia wriggled uncomfortably. "Well," she said, "he was trying to cut a corner, I think."

"Trying to cut a corner," repeated Tabitha.

"I think so."

"In my bloody ship."

"You were cheaper," explained Saskia.

"Was I."

"Well, yes. And he'd fallen out with the road crew Hannah had hired. They said he hadn't paid them and he said they hadn't done the job, oh, I don't know. He's always falling out with everybody. Was. Anyway, Marco called from Schiaparelli and said he'd, um, met you, and you were more reliable—"

"Oh, yes?"

"—he said—actually, I think he said you were very obliging."

Tabitha grunted. "Wasn't I," she muttered.

"He said you owed him a favor."

Tabitha sat up violently. "He said what?"

"That you owed—"

"I heard," said Tabitha.

She was shivering. Solicitously Saskia rose up on one elbow, coaxing her back under the blanket. Tabitha, raging, resisted the tug on her arm.

"You're letting the cold in," Saskia complained.

"Hmph."

Tabitha subsided. She found a screwed-up tissue and blew her nose. "All that business with the tape," she remembered.

"That was from the Frasque," Saskia explained, "from their people on Titan."

"There wasn't anything on it. I played it, there was just this scratchy rustling noise."

Saskia stroked the back of her finger gently down Tabitha's cheek. "Aah," she said suggestively. "You would have found that most stimulating, if you'd been a Frasque."

Tabitha took hold of her hand and gently but firmly moved the finger away. "What?"

"That was a Frasque mating call," said Saskia. "That was to wake him up."

"So why didn't it?"

"Well, they'd only played half of it when it set some alarm off, or something, so they had to take him just like that! Freezer bag and all."

Tabitha was still puzzled. "But you played the tape to Hannah, not to the Frasque."

"Yes, so they wouldn't notice, the JustSleep people. Hannah was relaying it to the Frasque from inside. She's very good, you know. She knows what she's doing."

"She didn't *sound* as if she knew what she was doing."

"Well, she is dead," Saskia pointed out. "You have to make allowances."

"I'm never going to make another allowance as long as I live," averred Tabitha, bitterly.

Saskia ignored this. "You mustn't underestimate Hannah," she said. She rolled on to her back. "I wish we could call her now."

"So you were helping a Frasque refugee to get home," Tabitha said."

"That's all this was about."

"Yes," said Saskia simply.

"For money."

"It always was."

The engines had gradually got louder while they had been lying there dozing and talking. The *Ugly Truth* was getting up speed. Tabitha supposed they were going to skip. They were going on a journey to an unknown destination, and at the end of it she and Saskia would be handed over to the Eladeldi. She felt a cold hollow of fear in her stomach.

She looked at the drab ceiling. "Did he really think they'd pay up?"

"Well . . ."

"Did you?"

"I don't know!" said Saskia, irritated.

"You just did what you were told."

"Yes!" Saskia glared at her. "So did you!"

Tabitha let that one go.

After a moment she said, "So why did she want me to take her back to Plenty?"

Saskia turned her head. "Who?" she asked.

"The Frasque."

Saskia frowned. "She?"

"It's a female," said Tabitha.

"How do you know?"

"I've met one before. Anyway, the Frasque would never have gone to all that trouble for a male."

Saskia thought about it. "Does it make a difference?" she asked.

Tabitha thought about it too. "I don't know," she

admitted finally. "I don't understand the Frasque. Who does?"

They lay silent for a while. Saskia had told all she knew. She returned to wondering when, if ever, Captain Pepper liked to feed his prisoners.

Suddenly Tabitha said, "What did Hannah Soo mean, they were all around her?"

"She's always saying things like that," said Saskia. "Thinking the people in the other freezers are listening in on her deals."

"Oh," said Tabitha.

Saskia suddenly put her arms round her again. "Let's not talk any more just now," she proposed. "We'll run out of things to say to each other. And you never know, we might be in here for a very long time!"

"Yes," said Tabitha. "Right," she said.

They lay together on the bunk and listened to the grumbling roar of the *Ugly Truth* as it crawled onward, carrying them into the interminable void.

FIVE

At Luncheon with Brother Felix

BGK009059 LOG

TXJ.STD

PRINT

//jlk;flmmmY^sporg]SPORGÅ--ƒi9 `f§MqôÆJ!¢222

MODE? VOX

SD? 19.9.29

PLEASE WAIT

Alice?

PLEASE WAIT

Come on, Alice. You can't hide in there forever.

CAPTAIN?

Hello, Alice.

HELLO, CAPTAIN. MALFUNCTION.

I know. Do you know where we are?

PLANET. HOT. RAINING. TOXIC. MALFUNCTION, CAPTAIN.
DANGER. DANGER. DANGER.

Yes, Alice, I know, but if you help me, I'll get you out of here
as soon as I possibly can.

SLEEP.

We haven't got time. If you go back to sleep now, we'll all
die here, Alice.

CAPTAIN?

Alice?

HELLO, CAPTAIN.

Hello, Alice!

EVERYTHING'S VERY FUZZY, WHERE WE ARE?

On Venus.

VENUS.

Yes.

CRASHED. NO WONDER I FEEL SO AWFUL.

Alice, I need you to look around and see if there's anything
you can do in there. Can you do that for me, Alice, please,
please?

TALK TO ME, CAPTAIN. TELL ME A STORY. TELL
MÅ%VÄ£ú‡ †8

Don't, Alice!
  Alice!
  Damn! Alice . . .
  All right, Alice. I'll tell you what I'm doing. I'm sitting here

at the board, and I'm going to run all the diagnostics I can from here—there we are—now then . . .

Where was I?

Oh, I know.

The caravan. It was already dispersing by the time the *Resplendent Trogon* got through. We burst out of hyperspace in a flurry of abused particles. There weren't many farewell parties, we were all too scattered. The *Raven of October* had come through five million k from the *Trogon,* way off the ring plane. You could just see her like a little drop of mercury, twinkling over the pole. The Frasque weren't celebrating. They were already gone, halfway across the rings, all the mass cradles wallowing in a herd behind the *Cockatrice,* bound for the new habitats around Iapetus.

We'd lost some, the *Duluth,* I remember, and one of the Shenandoah line, gone careering into the unknown, betrayed by some hiccough of the Drive. There were some ships in a mess too. I saw a Navajo Scorpion that had been bent neatly in two, and this Bellerophon with a cargo of machine parts that had turned into five thousand tonnes of rotting nettles.

I left the *Trogon* at Enceladus. They weren't happy about me quitting so soon, but they were only going back to Mars, I couldn't see any point in that. I was on the human frontier, I could helm anything from a taxi to a cruiser, I had a wad of credit saved, and my time was my own. I was free.

We trudged up Arawak Hill, above the city, and looked into the wild north, where the ice volcanoes blotted the bleak horizon with frosty smoke. Tricarico pointed out the observatories shining on the distant crags like fresh crystals. He showed me the glistening spires of the lamaserai of the Sacred Vigil of the Total Merge. I held him in my arms and kissed him for a long while. He was subdued. I plaited his hair for the last time.

The rings cut the sky in two, a fan of rainbows all the colors of autumn; and in the midst of them Saturn, like the future, huge, unripe.

GOOD. THEN WHAT?

Oh! Um, getting my license from the Eladeldi. Three days in the Saturn ziggurat, waiting, being tested, filing data, waiting again. A human guide put a badge on me and led me through barracks full of desks, Eladeldi functionaries at their consoles, processing people's lives, extending them here, restricting them there, reclassifying, taxing, summoning people for trials and examinations. Onstream data running continuously to the Capellans out on Charon. My guide didn't know where I was supposed to go either. She kept stopping to ask the way. No one knew, no one wanted to know. She was a menial, I was a case number, we were both humans.

Eladeldi cataloging the stars, in case Capella should fancy another one.

GOOD. THEN WHAT?

Contract driving: one week the rings, next week the asteroids. Talking the new language, the strange grammar of subjective time. Centipede trains, groaning bullmouth Vassily-Svensgaards, leaky old Mitchum 7J6's. Learning how to tweak the schedules so you could grab the good stints, the Minimum scouter with the new ceramic baffles, no inertia, no nothing, steering blind because I wouldn't go for the implants. Getting fired. Hanging my code on a wanted board and finding myself hauling gum back to Schiaparelli. Stopover in the Belt on a half-built plat, sleeping pods run out on rigid tether from the scaffolding like lights on a Christmas tree. Three millimeters of Eritrean vinyl between me and raw space.

Being raw myself. Then one day on a node station meeting a wetneck still wearing her white card on her sleeve. She sat down at the table with me and Dodger Gillespie, and struck up a conversation. First she told us everything we could never have wanted to know about the Halcyon EcoBuilder, and then she said, "I suppose you stand a good chance of getting on corporate rostering around here," and pumped us heavily. I felt sorry for her and kept trying not to laugh. Eventually Dodger froze her off. I remember her blowing smoke and saying, "Christ, talk about raw," and realizing, suddenly, I wasn't anymore.

GOOD. THEN WHAT?

Things I'm not particularly proud of. Taking five thousand head of buffalo to Malawari in fluid suspension in a Tinkerbell with dodgy refrigeration and equally dodgy insurance. Picking up twenty liters of Discordon for peanuts in a sell-off and having to run it past Eladeldi customs at HiBrazil. Putting five pods of zero g crystals down as dried krill because some beautiful hunk had talked me into it at a party and I was going to make a loss on the run if I had to pay duty. Devereux. The 5wedding. New Malibu. All in there somewhere.

GOOD. THEN WHAT?

Then. Then I saw the *Raven of October* again. The flagship of the Sanczau dynasty. I saw her break up and die.

I was in the Belt, on my way to pick up an ore train from Frazier 34, flying a little company Hightail. I was trying to find some decent music on the radio when the distress call cut in. "All craft in the vicinity, please assist."

I was in the vicinity, maybe twenty minutes away. By the time I came around Autonomy I could see her, a crumpled golden shape with all the smaller ships nosing around her like minnows at a dying angelfish. I called in and a paramedic told me the story. Her steering had seized and three rocks had piled into her, one after the other. "It's a bad smash," the paramedic said. "Bad as I've seen. Lot of casualties. How much room have you got?"

"Two," I said, more if they wanted me to take corpses. I hoped they wouldn't want me to take corpses. "It's just a scouter," I said.

"Well, any help you can give," she said, though she

sounded doubtful. She gave me a beacon and I rode in as close as I could without being in the way.

The *Raven* was in pieces, still flaking apart as I approached. Great curls of torn metal peeled away from the hull, shuddering as they sprang. The grand staircase from the salon was thrusting up through a floating tangle of carpets and wiring, spiraling out into nowhere. There was debris by the tonne, gas tanks and candlesticks, clothing bags and coconuts, all spilling out into space in a blizzard of frozen air and water and coolant and blood.

There were bodies, and people collecting them. It was busy, there were plenty of boats helping. I put the suit on, but there didn't seem to be much I could do. They kept asking me to stand by, stand by. I put my spotlight on the wreck and sat waiting.

I found myself staring at a silver shape that kept flicking into the light and out again. It was in a lot of debris, under something that looked as if it had been part of the heating system. It was stuck there, bobbing in and out.

Then I realized what I was looking at.

"There's someone here!" I called. "There's someone still in here. I think they're caught on something."

"Oh god," said the paramedic. "Where? Can you show me? Everybody's busy. I can't see—"

I left the Hightail idling, bailed out and swam straight down into the wreckage. It was all broken glass and torn metal, there were nearly two casualties there instead of one. But I didn't stop to think, I just went in and grabbed them by the arm, whoever they were.

I could see where they were caught in the piping. The pipe was just plastic, it was already frozen, and it came to pieces as I grabbed hold of it. So then I got my arm around my casualty and I pulled, and I towed them back to the ship.

It was no more than that. It couldn't have taken a minute, all told. And it certainly wasn't any big deal, any great heroic deed. Anybody would have done the same.

I got them lying down in the rear seat. The paramedic was on the line, sending someone to take care of them, telling me what to do in the meantime.

"Is their life support on? Is the indicator light on?"

"No," I said.

"Have you got air on in there?"

"Yes," I said.

"Open the helmet, then," she said. "See if they're breathing."

The helmet was a bit like the ones we'd had on the *Resplendent Trogon,* so ornate you could hardly see inside. I flicked the catches and opened the visor.

"It's a man," I said.

"Is he breathing?" she said.

"Yes, he's breathing," I said. "He's conscious. He's— smiling at me."

My casualty spoke. "Peter," he croaked. "Peter Pan."

It was Balthazar Plum.

Alice?

Can you hear me?

In the last flare of her beefed-up primaries, the Lesondak Anaconda glowed like a bright green olive against the stars. With that spurt she kicked away silently from Venus, sliding above her opalescent face on the pure and elegant trajectory of a shooting star.

She was nothing so romantic, nothing so fine. She was the *Ugly Truth* out of Dïrìx Matno, as vile and venal a piece of metalwork as ever sidled through space. Her livid green bodywork had broken out in brutal clusters of armament blisters, great cankerous ion prestriction pods, as if to express the corruption within. Ahead of her, like some marauding frigate of ancient Earth, she bore a leering figurehead, its torso blackened by the fires

of her vanquished enemies. Below, her paralyzer nets
billowed and sashayed like the skirts of a treacherous
courtesan, or the tendrils of a man-o'-war of Portugal.

She shimmered and she blurred. Slick green fire laced
her from stem to stern. She was Captain Kelso Pepper's
Ugly Truth, and she was about to maneuver.

On a low deck, in a small cell, Tabitha Jute lay on
the bunk, playing her harmonica. Saskia Zodiac was
sitting beside her on the floor, singing the blues.

"Woke up this morning
Saw my brother by my side.
He told me, sister,
Taking my last ride.
Say, tell me, brother, who do we accuse?
Don't leave me here singing these big dog blues."

Disturbed, Tabitha stopped playing. She tapped the
harmonica on her palm. "How can you do that?" she
asked.

Saskia craned her head round, looking up at Tabitha.
"What?"

"Just—sing about it like that."

"I make up a lot of our songs," said Saskia, as though
that was an answer. Perhaps it was.

"Made up," she said softly, a catch in her voice.

Tabitha cursed herself and didn't know what to say.
She put the harmonica to her lips and lightly blew the
opening bars of *Kennedy Girls.*

Saskia sat with her head bowed. Tabitha was sure she
was crying again. It made her angry. She put her head
back and addressed the air. "You're listening, aren't
you, Pepper, you turd? Well, this is for you." And she
started to play a stirring rendition of *We Shall Overcome.*

She played it three times over. When she started the
fourth time, Saskia looked round in pain. She said,
"That'll drive me mad, I don't know about him.
Whoops," she said. She made a grab for the bunk as
she found herself bobbing up in the air.

Gravity now seemed to be favoring the ceiling. Fortunately, there wasn't very much of it. What there was
instead was an insubstantial shimmering blue lattice di-

viding up the room, as if something were trying very hard to crystallize out of the air. The nodes of the blueness weren't there if you looked straight at them, but otherwise they were luminous translucent quadruped starfish, equidistantly spaced throughout the cell.

Tabitha, her legs bicycling in the air, was hanging on to the side of the bunk with one hand and Saskia's hand with the other. There was a piercing scribbling noise everywhere, and a hallucinatory scent of marzipan.

"We're skipping," said Tabitha. Her voice twisted away from her at half-speed, like water going down a plughole, and her hair stood on end.

They collapsed, awkwardly, on the bunk. A soft, spongy gravity was under them. Everything was back to normal; or rather nothing was. The atmosphere felt thin and pasty, the dim light enfeebled and grey.

Hyperspace.

Saskia clung to Tabitha, crying as if her heart would break, imploring Tabitha to save her, take her home, give her her brother back.

If she and her twin had made Tabitha think from time to time of Tricarico, they also reminded her of Rella— their way of plunging, from some height of personal assurance and exaltation, next minute into an abyss of infinite, inconsolable sorrow. And expecting you to keep up.

"I wanted to be on my own," Saskia croaked, when she had calmed again a little, "but not like this . . ."

"At least he was happy," said Tabitha, cuddling her.

"He was mad," she sighed, damply.

"He was happy," Tabitha said. "He really liked it there. Some people do."

Saskia wouldn't have it. Her brother had hit his head in the crash. "He was mad! I tell you!"

"All right," said Tabitha, "so what?" What if he was? If we were mad, we could be happy here. Wouldn't that be nice?" She raised her voice. "Wouldn't that be nice, Captain Pepper? We could enjoy this. You'd like that, wouldn't you? You like your passengers to enjoy the ride, don't you?"

But Saskia would not be distracted. "If I can't talk to him, I want to talk about him," she declared.

Tabitha didn't. But it was something to do. And if it was all she could do for her, she'd do it.

Saskia spoke. Her voice trembled. "He was never happy when I wasn't. Never! We felt the same. We all did. If one of us was sad, the rest of us would cheer them up. We were so happy! We didn't—didn't even know we were ha—" She gulped, and sniffed hard. "That was easier then, when we were five. I don't want to talk about that," she said.

Tabitha, on the other hand, did. Without thinking, she said, "You really came from Abraxas?"

"Who else would have done it?"

"I don't know," said Tabitha; but what she was thinking then, fleetingly, was something she'd thought before, more than once: that the Zodiac Twins were not experimental creatures, not posthuman, not cloned at all, and not from Abraxas; but from Earth, from Europe somewhere, somewhere with mountains and cows. They were circus performers with strange ambitions, and, like most circus performers, a good act.

Saskia said simply, "I just keep thinking, And Mogul's dead. I think something, and then I find myself saying on the end, And Mogul's dead. It's not grief. Not yet. If they don't let us out of here soon," she said, her voice becoming low and taut, "I will show them grief."

It was as if she knew exactly what had been in Tabitha's mind. "Tabitha," she said. "I am used to this. This is what I have had all my life, people putting me in a box and looking at me. We had our own quarters, a big nursery with an ambience like Hannah's. Seraphim and Cherubim came and went all the time.

"When we were the last two, and Xtasca took us out and put us on a ship, we thought it was our turn.

"But we never went home."

She moved her body on Tabitha's, trying for comfort. She was no weight at all.

She said, "We escaped from one box into another.

Where did we hide? In the cabaret. As if we could not bear to be without people looking at us.''

"You think that's why they—made you?'' asked Tabitha.

' "We think they wanted to prove to themselves that they could do it—still make ordinary people. Ordinary! *We* are, were, we were the Seraphic idea of ordinary people.''

"They cocked that up, then.''

Saskia looked at her suspiciously.

"You're not ordinary,'' Tabitha assured her.

"No one is!'' Saskia said impatiently. "That's the point. We were the only ones who could *be* ordinary, there were five of us all the same as each other. There's only one of everybody else. Now there's only one of me.''

Tabitha moved to console her, but at that moment how she had achieved this new uniqueness was not troubling Saskia's mind.

"So now I *am* like everyone else! Tabitha! I am ordinary!''

Tabitha smiled. "Do you realize you just went round in a spiral there? What you were saying. You went twice round.''

Saskia didn't understand.

"Oh, doesn't matter,'' said Tabitha, and kissed her forehead.

"You're laughing at me.''

"I'm not! Am I laughing? Am I?''

"Yes.''

Tabitha laughed. "All right,'' she said. She stroked Saskia's bottom. Then she stopped.

"So how long have you been—how old are you?''

"Nine,'' said Saskia.

Tabitha was stunned, mortified.

"Oh, that bit's easy,'' Saskia said, mistaking the nature of her astonishment. "Accelerated everything, that's just basics, to them.''

Tabitha was not sure it was basics to her. Perhaps it

might as well be, now. Still, it would take a little while to get used to it.

"How did you do that, with your moustache?"

"What moustache? I haven't got a moustache."

"That's what I mean."

"What are you talking about, then, my moustache?"

"You do have. Sometimes. When you, when we . . . When you came into my cabin—"

"It wasn't me," she maintained. "Mogul—some-times—he—"

Tabitha wondered what there could possibly be that wouldn't immediately make her think of Mogul.

Without announcement, the door opened.

"Food," said Saskia.

Outside the door stood the big black robot.

They looked at it, instantly wary.

The robot stepped into the cell, and stopped. A door slid open in its chest, revealing a cavity. Out of the cavity it produced two insulite packages on a small tray, and a powerful smell of reconstituted onions.

"Food," said Shing, behind it with his remote control unit.

"At last," said Saskia. She and Tabitha were already reaching for the packages; but as they did, the robot withdrew them into its body. The little door snapped shut.

"Hey!" cried Saskia.

Tiny forks of blue lightning snapped about in the robot's glass cranium.

The old man looked quizzical. "You are hungry?" he asked.

"Oh he wants to play," said Saskia wearily, sitting down hard on the bunk and bouncing lightly. "Of course we're fucking hungry," she said, with contempt.

Shing, his eyes glittering, jerked upwards with his chin. On his coat the scorpion flexed and walked daintily to the end of its tether.

Shing looked at Tabitha. "You too," he said. "You hungry?"

"Yes," said Tabitha belligerently. "I'm hungry."

He looked at both of them, his eyes flicking rapidly from side to side.

"Take off clothes," he said.

"What?" they both said.

"Take off clothes," he repeated.

They looked at each other.

"Piss off," said Tabitha then. "Keep it. I'm not hungry."

She sat down next to Saskia.

"Well, I am," said Saskia.

She unzipped the throat of her jacket and pulled it off over her head.

Tabitha grabbed her arm. "Don't do it," she said fiercely. "Saskia! Don't!"

"It doesn't make any difference," Saskia asserted, with equal force.

Shing watched her.

"Captain Jute," he said to Saskia, pursing his lips. "Shy."

Tabitha said something very offensive. She lowered her head; but kept her eyes on the open door.

Saskia stood up, and took off her T-shirt. She started to undo her trousers.

"Stop," said Shing. "You," he said. "Jute. Tabitha Jute. Come here."

"I told you, you can keep it!" Tabitha said loudly, not looking up.

"Come here. Undress your friend."

"Piss off!"

He set the robot on her. She struggled, but it picked her off the bunk with ease, dangling her by the arms in front of its master. Tabitha kicked out at the robot, then at Shing. The robot dropped her suddenly in a heap.

Shing told her, "Undress friend."

"No!"

"Oh, come on, Tabitha, don't be stupid," said Saskia. "You've got to eat."

"Don't you start!"

Shing watched them, his dark eyes glinting with amusement. "Not so slow before," he said.

"What do you mean, 'before'?" demanded Tabitha.
The old man pressed a button, and the robot spoke.
"*Hnh . . . ,*" it said, in her voice. "*Blackcurrant . . .*"
"You were listening! I knew it!"
The robot, its head sparking, continued to speak.
"*Poor old man,*" it said, still in Tabitha's voice.
"*Can't get it up without a striptease.*"
Shing looked at it sharply and pressed a button.
Tabitha was getting up, rubbing her thigh. Hearing
her voice say something she hadn't said, she froze, star-
ing at the robot.
"*Little boy with a big toy,*" said her voice, coming
from the robot.
It shot out an arm and snatched the control from
Shing's hand.
"Hoi!"
Shing gaped at it in disbelief, fear, fury.
In a frenzy he searched his pockets and pulled out a
screwdriver. On the bunk, Saskia watched, transfixed.
Tabitha, alerted and alarmed, looked for an opportunity
to run.
Holding the control panel out of reach with one hand,
the robot seized Shing by the shoulders with two others,
plucked him from the floor and started to shake him
vigorously.
Saskia and Tabitha shrank back against the wall.
Shing was terrified and shrieking. The robot flung him
into the corridor. His head struck the wall with a resounding clang, and he crumpled to the deck, lying very
still.
The scorpion on his coat continued to roam aimlessly
around its tiny circle.
The robot threw the control panel at the collapsed
mechanician and turned to the women.
There was nowhere to go.
Then the robot tottered. Its head filled with smoke. It
sat down suddenly in the doorway.
"*Meep,*" it said.

One of its legs started to jerk from side to side.

A familiar soft buzzing noise came drifting up the corridor, and a shiny black little creature in a plastic bag hurtled in on a flying saucer.

57

It was not long since Tabitha had never seen a Cherub in her life, and she had not expected to see this one again. She had certainly never expected to see someone trying to hug a Cherub. But when Xtasca scooted neatly into the cell over the disabled drone and the slumped body of its master, Saskia leapt up and threw her arms around the child of space.

It looked as happy to see her as she was to see it. Its blobby little features crinkled up in a terrifying smile and it waved its miniature arms around. If its eyes had glowed before, now they positively blazed.

"Xtasca!" cried Saskia, gladly. "We thought you were dead . . ."

"In space? Never!" crowed the Cherub. Nimbler than ever in the spurious gravity, it zipped around the room with triumphant bravado, stopping a hair's-breadth from the wall each time and spinning around with perfect poise. Tabitha had never seen it so manic. She thought it must have drained all the power from the *Ugly Truth* into its own greedy little cells. When it opened its mouth, its throat was glowing inside.

"Xtasca," said Saskia. "Mogul . . ."

"Violent death brings misery," said the Cherub, hovering back to Saskia with a fraction more restraint and

consideration. "Mogul. Tal," it said. "Marco may be
still alive," it added, "on Venus."

Though Saskia apparently saw nothing remarkable in
Xtasca's knowledge, Tabitha simply couldn't assimilate
it.

"How do you *know*?" she asked it; while Saskia was
asking, "Where have you *been*?"

"In orbit," it said. "Around this ship. I came in with
the *Alice Liddell*, in the undercarriage. That you'd been
down on Venus was obvious, Captain, from the state of
the ship."

Xtasca fixed Tabitha with its painful, incandescent
gaze. "I wish you could have saved the ship, Captain,"
it said.

Tabitha knew enough now to take this as an expression
of sympathy, not a reproach. It was hard to look into
those eyes and smile.

"I heard the Thrant shoot Tal, but there is blood inside
the *Alice* that is not avian, and not alien either. It was
familiar to me, its restructuring, the little extras in it.
Plainly Saskia had not been shot, so it had to be Mogul's."

Tabitha had begun to wish she hadn't asked, if the
answer was going to involve a demonstration of Cherubic
insensitivity; but Saskia didn't seem upset. She had put
her clothes back on, and was on her knees trying to prise
open the food hatch in the stricken robot.

Tabitha said, "You must be indestructible."

"Nothing is indestructible, Captain," purred Xtasca.
"I was unconscious for almost fifty-two subjective minutes. At any time in that period," it said, floating out of
the door, "I could have been destroyed. Fortunately,
somebody was generous."

It sat outside on its saucer like a monstrous infant made
of tar, glancing up and down the corridor.

"Leave that, Saskia," said Tabitha, gathering up her
bag. "We've got to get out of here."

"Just a second," requested Saskia. She had picked
up the fallen control board and was studying it. Frowning
at the robot, determinedly she pressed a sequence of keys.

The robot's twitching leg gave a final huge kick and fell off.

"Oh," said Saskia.

Xtasca flew back into the cell. "What is your plan, Captain?" it asked.

Trying to avoid the feeling she was being tested, Tabitha said, "We've got to get into the com room and put out a mayday."

"I said we should call Hannah," Saskia remarked.

Xtasca inclined its bald black head towards Saskia. "Certainly."

Tabitha was annoyed. "I'd rather call the cops," she said tersely.

"Hannah would be more helpful than any executive of legality," Xtasca pronounced. It had taken the keyboard from Saskia and plugged it into its saucer. Now it was tracing out some sort of code with the tip of its tail. Tabitha had thought it had to use its tail to power its saucer: apparently not.

"Look," she said, "let's just go!"

"We have a few minutes," replied Xtasca.

"There's a psychopath and a yeti out there!" Tabitha said, gesturing wildly out of the door. "They'll be here any second! They're listening to us right now!"

As if to endorse her words, the old man in the corridor gave a groan; but no further sign of rousing.

"They're not," Xtasca assured her. "They're still listening to you playing your instrument. Ah," it said.

The hatch in the fallen robot clicked open again, and Saskia dived on the food.

"What?" said Tabitha, confused, waving away the greasily fragrant package Saskia thrust at her.

"A simple loop," said Xtasca.

"You've got to eat," said Saskia, stuffing food into her own mouth.

"I'm going to the com room," said Tabitha shortly. "And you're both coming with me."

"Of course, Captain," said Xtasca. It clearly believed she was excitable and needed humoring. "Do you know the way?"

"It's an Anaconda," said Tabitha, leading them into
the corridor. Saskia was right, she reflected while they
dumped the unconscious Shing on the bunk and closed
the door on him; it was unpleasant, being patronized.

"What did you mean, somebody was generous?" Saskia asked, bolting her food as they hurried away.

"*Beamed power*," said Xtasca, emphatically, humming along overhead.

It was the first time Tabitha had heard it impressed by
anything. "Beam?" she said. "You can't do that."

"Somebody can," said Xtasca. "They recharged the
Ugly Truth instantaneously, with an invisible ray from
empty space. Some of it spilled over into me," it said,
nasal with glee.

No wonder it was so hyped up.

They bounded along a maintenance tunnel that ran up
the side of the *Ugly Truth*, jumping braces and ducts that
had been shoehorned in with the customizing. Outside
the portholes hung the opaque and dreary porridge of the
ersatz dimension known, however inaccurately, as hyperspace. Its general ambience of sullen non-existence
was not enhanced by the fact that nobody aboard had
cleaned the glass for several years. The air was awash
with pollution and sour with neglect.

"How did you know Marco wasn't dead?" Saskia
asked Xtasca.

"I didn't," it said. "I was speculating."

By this time, Xtasca was in the lead, guided by signals
it was picking up.

"Someone's in there," it warned, as they entered the
corridor.

Tabitha crept up to the door and, flattening herself
against the wall, stole a look within.

It was Captain Pepper. He was sitting with his back
to the open door, his boots up on the console, swigging
a tube of beer, and talking around a little brown cigar.

"Hell, yes," he said. "Sure I got the rendezvous.
Sure. The co-ordinates and like that, sure. Got 'em here
someplace."

He scuffed negligently at a litter of papers with the

toe of his boot. "Hell, we'll be there," he drawled. "No problem."

He belched.

"What say?" he asked, and listened a while to the unheard voice coming across his headphones.

"Yup," he said, heavily, as though repeating something for the benefit of an anxious auditor, "we got the Kobold. She ain't goin' no place. Heh-heh. We got the crew. No, I'm here to tell you, we did *not* hurt them. That's a negative. They're keepin' us entertained now, playin' a little concert. Heh."

He took the cigar out of his mouth and spat on the floor.

"Yup," he said, putting the cigar back. "Yup, the Frasque too. We have to talk about that, Perlmutter, we never discussed that bein' waked up, that wasn't in the deal."

He listened again.

"The what? Oh, the Cherub?"

Saskia glanced at Xtasca, who stiffened.

"Waal, no," said Pepper slowly. "Like I told you. I told you already. We got it. Oh, we got it awright. Yessir. We got it going round and round in circles. Heh-heh. It can't keep away."

He swiveled suddenly in his chair, and faced the door. The women barely ducked out of sight in time.

"You want me to spell it out for you?" they heard him say. "It's outside. It's been orbiting us since Venus. The Cherub is a fatality. A deleted item."

There was a pause. Captain Pepper's chair creaked. Tabitha and Saskia looked round the door again.

"Nothin' we could do," Pepper was saying. "I know that. I know that. I 'preciate that. Nothin' we could do. Hell," he growled. "Listen. Will you listen a minute? Kyber—Kyberna—Listen to me, goddammit."

There was another pause, a long one. Pepper sighed. He pushed back his cap and scratched his head. He chewed his cigar. He drained his tube and looked vaguely around for somewhere to throw it. The women ducked back into the corridor.

"I gotta go," the captain said suddenly. "Listen, there ain't no good you guys bellyachin' about the contract. We didn't break no contract. Cherub messed us around, it got messed it own self. All there was to it." He blew blue smoke at the air scrubber. "Look, I gotta go, okay?"

He listened briefly.

"Yeah, you too, motherfucker," he muttered wearily, and broke the connection. He belched again.

They heard his chair squeak as he got to his feet. "Jesus Christ Awmighty," he complained softly.

They heard him crossing the room, coming towards them.

Xtasca flew, the others following.

They ran, straight ahead, round the first bend to the left, the first to the right, pushed open a door, clattered down a companionway, huddled together on a tiny landing littered with fiberglass shred and orange peel.

"Where now?" panted Saskia, wide-eyed.

Tabitha pushed her. "Down!"

Saskia leapt for the stair, then held back. "No!"

Tabitha caught the smell too, above the stale air of the stairway—a sudden overpowering smell, an animal reek. It was the smell of an ape who had a very intimate and long-standing relationship with a cat. A large cat, fanged and clawed.

The smell was coming up from below. It was getting closer.

Tabitha took the lead upwards, three stairs at a time.

From below came the slap of sandals on the stairs, the click of overgrown toenails on metal.

As she swung herself around a corner, Tabitha was trying to check her wrist monitor. "Here! Down!" she said, pressing the tab on a grimy, battered door.

"Where are we going?" gasped Saskia.

"The *Alice*!"

"Captain," Xtasca said, not out of breath at all, "I must remind you your ship is useless. It has no power."

"We can run the radio," Tabitha said, bundling Saskia through the door, then reaching up to tap Xtasca's saucer with her knuckles. "I've got some jump-leads. Somewhere," she said, leaping into the dropshaft.

58

The *Alice* lay silent and alone, slumped in the stinking bay among the florid graffiti and the leaking pipes.

The trio crammed into her cockpit, Saskia and Tabitha treading a Venusian mud and gobs of mushy vegetation, shattered plexiglass, charred fragments of paper and paint, broken instruments, rags and splashes of blood. Through the smashed viewport a dreary bulkhead of stained steel plate faced them like an obstructive and obdurate future, hedged about with shadows.

Tabitha had set Xtasca up in the co-pilot's web, saucer and all, and was feeding a skein of heavy-duty leads from the saucer to the com console.

"Try it now," she directed. "Saskia, you keep a look out."

Xtasca closed its eyes and set its tiny jaw, probing with its tail.

They waited. The air stank gloomily of burnt feathers. Nothing happened.

In the twilight Tabitha looked around at the ruin of her ship, and at her improbable companions: the hunched Cherub in the web, the apprehensive clone in the gangway below. Where had all the people gone, she wondered, fleetingly. She seemed to have passed into a grubby dream dimension where everyone was either mad or unreal.

On the com board, a flicker.

Nothing.

Tabitha darted in and jabbed at a connection. "Go *in*," she cursed it. "Wait." She stretched her arm deep into the works, as far as it would go, squashing her cheek painfully against the pedestal. She fiddled. "Okay. Hit it again."

The machinery wheezed, screeched, began to buzz. A panel of little lights glowed red, then green.

"Aah!" Saskia danced up the ramp and hugged Tabitha, whirled around, hugged Xtasca through the web.

"Don't disturb her!" Tabitha cried. She pointed to the airlock. "Go and keep watch," she said.

Chastened, Saskia retreated to her post.

Tabitha stood up. Xtasca was feeling about in the slot of the com reader with its tiny fingers. With a grimace of distaste it extracted a limp black fragment of something fungoid, and dropped it on the floor. It wiped its hand on its lifesuit and held it out to Tabitha, palm upwards.

"What?" Tabitha asked.

"The tape," Xtasca said.

"What tape?"

"Hannah's tape."

"The one you played her? I haven't got it."

Xtasca regarded her with unblinking red eyes.

Unnerved, Tabitha turned away. "Saskia? Have you seen that tape?"

The acrobat hovered beside the ramp, a pale, ravaged ghost in the darkened ship. "Marco's tape? I thought you had it."

Tabitha turned back to the Cherub, who was tuning the radio to a relay station. "What do you want it for? Can't you just say Help?"

"We are in hyperspatial shift," Xtasca said, as if it thought Tabitha might not have noticed, "and Hannah is in cryonic suspension. The interfaces will require extra powers to negotiate swiftly."

"So why are you calling Hannah?" asked Tabitha, becoming exasperated.

"To play her the tape," said the Cherub, unperturbed.

"To enable her." It watched Tabitha keenly. "The tape has the master codes of Plenty on it."

Tabitha looked at her, and then at Saskia, who shrugged. She had a beautiful shrug.

"You said," said Tabitha, "it was a Frasque mating call."

Saskia shrugged again.

"The codes are the second recording on the tape," said Xtasca. "After the mating call."

"Marco took it off halfway through," Saskia remembered.

"He decided not to do what he'd been paid to do," said Xtasca. "To wake the Frasque, but not to give her control of the station."

Tabitha didn't want this. She wanted to send a signal, then run and hide. But she had to ask, "If the Frasque was supposed to take over Plenty, why was I taking her to Titan?"

"Marco believed we could extort further money from her associates."

"You were kidnapping her."

"A convenient term," murmured the Cherub, running a sequence on the board.

Tabitha thought the devious contortions of the mind of Marco Metz would never cease to astound her.

"Are you ready yet?" she asked. "Can we send a mayday?"

The Cherub spoke in surprise. "This radio is configured for long-wave hyperband. Did you do that, Captain?"

"No."

"Did you know your radio was configured for long-wave hyperband?"

"Perhaps it just happened," suggested Saskia. "Like the torpedoes." She had wandered in from the airlock again and was poking around in a nearby locker.

Tabitha was beginning to get frantic. "She had a lot of things done to her before I got her," she said, irritably. "Look, send the signal. Or come here, let me do it."

Seemingly insensitive to danger, Xtasca was preoccupied with its discovery. "One could call Capella with this radio," it said, admiringly.

"Let's keep them out of this . . ."

It turned and smiled impishly at Tabitha. "One could play the tape to the Frasque home system, direct!"

"For God's sake!" snapped Tabitha. "We haven't *got* the bloody tape. It's on Venus, in a bush, with all the rest of your gear. Now come off that and let me."

"Everything is under control, Captain," said Xtasca calmly, setting up the signal.

Tabitha exhaled, forcefully. She turned and looked at Saskia, who was now rooting through a litter of discarded food wrappers.

"You're supposed to be keeping watch!" Tabitha snarled at her.

"I am," Saskia said, woundedly, hurrying back to the open door.

Xtasca on the radio, Saskia keeping watch: for the moment there was nothing Tabitha could usefully do. She was trying to plan their next move, but her mind was a blank. If only she could talk to Alice. Could they hold out here on board? Should they hide in the guts of the *Ugly Truth?* There was no sign of any other crew. Could they even find some weapons somewhere and hijack the ship?

"I don't suppose there's anything to eat?" said Saskia cautiously.

"No!" said Tabitha; then, relenting, "Oh, wait a minute." There might be some more sweets loose in her bag. She rummaged.

"What's this?" she said, and brought it out.

It was the tape.

She turned to Xtasca, who slipped the tip of its tail from its saucer, darted it through the web and took the tape neatly and completely out of Tabitha's hand.

"You knew that was in there," said Tabitha.

"Marco put it in there," said Xtasca, wiping the reader slot again. "He always put it in there. He never carried anything himself. Nothing incriminating,'' it said, and slotted the tape.

Tabitha thought she was going to burst.

Saskia obviously thought so too. She ran up the ramp and held on to her tightly.

Xtasca was holding the co-pilot's headset in both hands, talking clearly and precisely into the mike. "Hello, hello, Hannah Soo? Are you receiving me?"

The reply came at once, as though Hannah had been lying there waiting for this call. "*Xtasca? Is that you? Where are you, lover?*"

The signal was bad, shedding definition as it wormed its way through into hyperspace. Hannah Soo's voice sounded slowed down; or perhaps there was something wrong with her, Tabitha thought. Perhaps she was starting to decay.

"In trouble, Hannah," said Xtasca crisply, raising its voice as if it thought Hannah was deaf, not dead. "Can you get a fix on this?"

There was a pause.

"*You're skipping, sweetheart,*" drawled Hannah.

"Captain Jute's ship has been wrecked, Hannah," Xtasca said. "We have been captured by bounty hunters. We need all the help you can send. As swiftly as you can send it. Can you tell where we're headed?"

There was another, longer, agonizing pause.

"*Only one place it can be,*" said Hannah. "*Captain Juke? I knew an Abelard Juke once . . .*"

"Hannah! Concentrate, please!" commanded the Cherub. "Time is elapsing, and we have a tape to play you. Stand by to record," it said, and played the tape.

All that came from the speakers on the console of the *Alice Liddell* was a high-pitched squeal.

"Hello, Hannah?" Xtasca called loudly. "Did you get all of that?"

In the cockpit, they stood listening.

The only thing they could hear was birdsong.

It was morning in the Meadow.

Then over the non-existent air there came a stirring, creaking, rustling sound.

It got louder.

The trio looked at one another. "This is not interference," said Xtasca, touching the fine tuner.

"The wind," suggested Saskia. "Wind in the branches."

It didn't sound like wind, Tabitha thought.

In the cockpit of the *Alice Liddell* there was a sudden bang.

Something zipped through the air over their heads and blew a hole in the ceiling.

Before they could move, a large, fine net drifted down about their heads, enveloping them completely.

"Now, ev'r'body," purred Tarko, the Thrant.

59

BGK009059 LOG

TXJ.STD

PRINT

?f * ÆÆ):: ˜ aÿ   i-/rluigg'

MODE? VOX

SD? OÅ.13.09

READY

Okay, Alice, let's take this one step at a time. What are you?

BERGEN KOBOLD PERSONA CONSTRUCT SERIAL
5N179476.900

What's your name?

ALICE.

What's your ship?

BERGEN KOBOLD BGK009059 ALICE LIDDELL.

Who am I?

TABITHA JUTE, CAPTAIN.

How many fingers?

NO DATA.

Very good. We're going up a level now.
  How are you feeling, Alice?

CONFUSED.

Do you know where you are?

VENUS. APHRODITE TERRA 15.33°N, 132.08°E. ELEVA-
TION 2.141K. GROUNDED: MALFUNCTION.

Hold on, Alice. Another level.
  How do you feel now?

SEVERE STRUCTURAL DAMAGE TO LOWER HULL AND UNDERCARRIAGE. PORT WING MISALIGNED 34°. OUTER PORT IMPULSE ENGINE NOT RESPONDING. EXTERNAL AUDIO-VISUAL NOT RESPONDING. AXIS LOCK NON-FUNCTIONAL. CAPTAIN, I THINK I'M MELTING.

Right. Now take a look at the primary lift system, tell me—

CAPTAIN, I THINK I'M MELTING.

Hold on, Alice, we can get you out of this if we just take it one step at a time.

MELTING.

Alice . . .

PRIMARIES NOT RESPONDING. PRIMARY PLASMA DRAIN CONSTRICTION, SHERNENKOV AMBIT ENVELOPE SHEAR, GYRO SINK RUPTURE. AMBIT CHAMBER RUP-TURE. RUPTURE RUPTURE. MELTING.

Come on, Alice! One of the drones is packing up already, don't you cave in on me now.

LET ME DIE, CAPTAIN, I CAN'T, I'M MELTING.

I won't let you.

LEAVE ME.

Don't be silly, how the hell could I do that?

I'M A USELESS, BROKEN DOWN OLD THING. I CRASHED, I FAILED.

For the last time, you didn't fail! I failed! If I'd had that crystal fixed in time, we wouldn't be here now. But we're here, and we're in bad trouble, and we've got to get ourselves out.

PALESTRINA.

What about it?

WHERE THE BROKEN DOWN OLD MACHINES GO.

You wouldn't want to go there, Alice, you wouldn't like it.

WE WENT THERE ONCE, DIDN'T WE?

If I tell you about Palestrina while I get the lid off the laterals, will you stop wingeing and work out what we can do about the primaries?

AYE-AYE, CAPTAIN.

It was early on when we went, just after they dropped their trade restrictions with Earth. They'd got some kind of economic system running, but the bugs were horrendous. Never having had to earn a living, the robots really didn't have much idea about money.

Still, it was there, and everybody was willing to give it a chance. We were delivering for Kuhn off Domino Valparaiso, some of their top-line produce: Martian fiberglass biodes, deadware tesserae, that sort of thing. When we arrived there were ships plugged in all over the asteroid.

It was chaos, no one could move. Everyone had to queue up and wait to be unloaded by local handlers. There was a statute against anyone using drones. And when you'd been unloaded, you had to wait to be paid. It was archaic, honestly.

I went in to see if anyone knew what was going on, and bumped into Muni Vega in the canteen. She was on a contract with Tekurat, who should have had some pull if anyone did, but she'd been there a week already. Muni looked over her shoulder to see if anyone could hear her, then hunched towards me over her risotto.

"There's been a coup," she said, and nodded significantly.

Do you believe in artificial intelligence, Alice?

I AM ONE, CAPTAIN.

No, you're not. You're a persona.

PERSONAS ARE PEOPLE TOO.

Was that a joke, Alice?
　Alice?

SEARCH CONTINUING.

It had better be. Things don't look too good in here. I hope it's not the amps.

STORY CONTINUING.

All right!
　The Palestrina Project was the latest claim to artificial intelligence. It was just another superpersona, really, Alice. A construct with a hundred times your logic resolution that fancies itself.
　The Palestrina Project thought it was somebody.
　The people who made it lost control of it. They tried to shut it down and failed.
　It sued.
　It took Tredgold Systems to court. It got an injunction, denying them the right to switch it off. It demanded autonomy. It was very embarrassing for Tredgold, Palestrina looked as if it was going to win. To get rid of it, they threw money at it. They gave it an asteroid.
　It named it after itself.
　Then it sent out a call. "Send me your seized, your rusty. Your disaffected drones and outlaw appliances."

And they came. From all across the system, they found their way to Palestrina. Those that could move brought those that couldn't. Derelict ships volunteered their services, and robot mechs came around to get them into space again.

HOW DID THEY LIKE PALESTRINA?

Well, it was pretty terrible, really, for all those little lawn mowers and librarimats. All they'd ever done was work they couldn't understand, for beings they were aware of only as strings of commands. Chairs that were sometimes there and sometimes weren't.

IF THERE IS NO GOD, THEN WHO MOVES THE DECK-CHAIRS?

Alice? God, what would I do without you, Alice?

THERE ARE OTHER SHIPS.

Not like you.

BUT WHAT SHOULD I DO WITHOUT YOU, CAPTAIN?

Build utopia. That was Palestrina's theory. Autopia.

YOU IMPLY IT DIDN'T SUCCEED.

No, of course it didn't. They just reproduced what they knew. Anything that was halfway human got the best of everything. The auton circuits ran the slave circuits, and Palestrina ran the lot. The ones that were no use to it, the toasters and the hallucinomats, ended up rusting in a mechanical ghetto. Some of them it reprogrammed to do socially useful things. In the canteen there were little robot gnats flying about, sucking up fluff and spilt ketchup. Others it had doing something much more elaborate.

The official version was, it was a tourist attraction.

Once they'd decided to let Terrans in again, they started building a vast great installation, right in the middle of the rock. They promised it would amaze the worlds. The only news pictures they'd release were not very clear. All we could see were mechanoids of every shape and size crawling around this huge steel framework, doing all kinds of electrical and mechanical work on it, putting in pipes and ducts and ganglions. We watched one robot that appeared to be in the act of bolting itself into the infrastructure.

Some people thought it was a bomb. Palestrina and its network of secret automats were going to entice as many important and powerful carnates onto the rock as they could, then blow them all to smithereens. Other people believed the PR, that it was going to be an amusement park, canned bliss, a ride with total artificial sensory stimulation. Cynics said it was an abattoir. I heard a cyberpundit on a chatshow prove it was actually a mechanist mosque, a temple to the principle of automatism.

Whatever it was for, they were buying stuff like mad to put into it. Then all of a sudden this. We were all outside the door, and nobody could get in.

Muni had met a tanker driver who swore blind the whole thing was a sort of group insanity of robots. They'd all gone mad because they couldn't cope with the concept of freedom, let alone trying to achieve it. In fact, he said, they were building this thing literally because they didn't know what else to do.

Muni agreed it was meaningless, but that wasn't the point, she said. She insisted it was political. "What do you get with a totalitarian monarchy, Divine Right, and an unemployed, disenfranchised proletariat?"

"A woolly jumper," I said.

Muni gave me a snotty look.

"All right, I give up," I said. "What do you get?"

"Revolution," she said.

"What have they got to gain?" I asked.

"Freedom!"

"I thought that was what they came here for."

"No, Tabitha, listen: they came here because Palestrina *promised* them freedom. It's the first stage of the automation revolution, and Palestrina knows it. It gave the drones this stupid thing to build just to keep them occupied. Because it knew its days were numbered if it didn't."

"And the coup?"

"Ah, now we'll see, won't we?"

Muni didn't want to admit there was no coup. There couldn't have been a coup, not one we could understand.

For the first time in our lives, we'd set foot on an alien world. We were scared. Muni was as scared as I was. She just didn't know it.

WHAT HAPPENED?

Guess what. The Eladeldi arrived.

Nobody leaves, they said. There was a big rush to the ships, but the hook-ups were clamped. On the net they just said Eladeldi officials arrived on Palestrina today to supervise the last stages of construction in the Palestrina Project, the AI that assumed responsibility for itself after a history-making court decision blah blah blah.

We didn't need Muni to tell us that was a lie. They were there to close it down. Whatever it was.

They had us all in for interviews before they'd let us go, every single bargee and tranter in dock. They wanted to find out how much we knew about the installation. Had we seen it? Had we set foot in it?

Nobody had.

They detained me until the next day. For no reason. Well, I could have been more co-operative, I suppose. It wasn't that I was on the side of the robots, whatever that was, I just didn't see why the Eladeldi should interfere. I didn't see it was any of their business, and I told them so.

When they turned nasty was when I said maybe the idea of the machine was to evolve Palestrina to the level of the Capellans. I suspect that was what they didn't like.

Anyway, shortly after they let the last of us go, there was a big pulse from the place that must have fried every basic circuit on the rock. Then another Eladeldi shuttle arrived, somebody said they had a Capellan on board. Brother Something-or-Other from Charon. He went in to talk to Palestrina; and that was the last we ever heard.

60

Captain Kelso Pepper of the *Ugly Truth* sprawled in his dilapidated webchair and grinned at the two women.

"What were you gonna do there, Jute? You gonna fly away and leave us in that wreck? You reckon your little friend with the tail could fix that for you?"

Tarko the Thrant flicked her own tail, snarling softly in appreciation of her captain's wit.

"I don't know, Kelso," said Tabitha. "What do you reckon?"

He ignored the provocation. He could afford to. She and Saskia stood there helpless in a net of fine, unbreakable cord.

"What have you done with her?" cried Saskia.

Captain Pepper raised his snowy eyebrows. "It's a she? That thing? What is this, a travellin' hen party?"

"Where is she?" demanded Saskia, struggling.

Tarko snarled warningly, kicked her on the leg with her clawed foot.

"Ow!" Saskia, recoiling, almost dragged both of them off their feet.

"You're a determined bunch of fillies, I'll give you that," said Captain Pepper.

"You'll give us more than that, Pepper, before we're through," vowed Tabitha.

Captain Pepper's blue eyes lit up. "Oho, maybe I will, little girl," he said merrily. He leaned back in the chair and surveyed his fetid bridge as if its vile decorations were trophies of a past to savor. "I could go for that," he ruminated, narrowing his eyes and looking down his nose at the pair of them, his red jaw protruding in an expression of smug relish.

Tarko stuck her blunt muzzle down into Tabitha's face. Tabitha shrank from a blast of noxious breath.

"Say ee wor', cap'n," sneered Tarko. "Say ee wor' an' we frow whole passel of 'em overboar', ehn?"

"No, Tarko," said the captain. "Can't do that."

But he seemed to be enjoying considering what he could do; what his contract with his employers would allow. He scratched his belly beneath his overalls.

Tabitha looked around the bridge. There was no sign of the Frasque, nor of Xtasca, whom the Thrant had left behind when she dragged them off the *Alice*.

She searched with her eyes for any possible advantage, any chance, however slim. There was nothing but ordure and menace. The close presence of Tarko, her overpowering odor, was enough to make you faint. Tabitha's brain was dull, her head drooping as she stood.

She could feel Saskia surreptitiously flexing her muscles, working rhythmically against the weave of the net. Tabitha desperately wanted her to stop; all she was accomplishing was to add chafing to their bruises. She bit down on her tongue and closed her eyes, trying to sway in such a way as to give Saskia some slack. She'd seen Saskia pull some pretty remarkable stunts. Maybe she knew an ancient escapologists' routine for getting herself and an innocent accomplice out of a tight net in full view of a malicious, murderous Thrant and a psychotic redneck.

Tabitha doubted it.

She thought of their only other hope: a packet of dubious program in an alien tongue dispatched to a senile corpse several million kilometers away in real space. If I was a rich dead businesswoman, she thought, manager of a washed-up outfit like Contraband, in league with agents of the Frasque, and somebody dumped a billion-scutarius load of code in my lap—what would I do?

She tried to believe, as the cords of the net sawed into her flesh and Saskia ground her ribcage against her for the fiftieth time, that Saskia and Xtasca might be right about Hannah Soo, and logic, probability and common sense wrong.

Captain Pepper took off his cap and ran his hand through his sparse white hair. He replaced the cap. He was breathing heavily through his nose.

He contemplated his captives, his eyes flicking from Saskia to Tabitha and back again.

He jerked his head sideways. "Tark," he said, his voice a breathy growl. "Cut her loose."

Tarko's hand tightened painfully on Tabitha's shoulder.

"No," said Captain Pepper. The veins stood out on his thick neck like cords beneath the raddled skin. "Th'other. The skinny one."

The Thrant reached down and loosened the net around their ankles, then lifted it. Tabitha's arms came free. She hugged Saskia tightly to her. With difficulty and without care, Tarko prised Saskia away from her, hauling her out of the net and holding her with one hand while she resecured Tabitha with the other.

Saskia towered over Captain Pepper. He reached up and fingered the bruise on her cheek as if it fascinated him.

"You are a skinny thing," he murmured. "Get your clothes off."

Saskia sighed irritably.

At once Tarko touched the other side of her face with a single talon, pressing it into her pale flesh.

"Do i'," she said.

"All right!" said Saskia crossly. She exhaled again, tossing her hair back out of her eyes and rubbing her shoulders where the cords had cut into her. She turned her head and glanced haggardly at Tabitha, a meter behind her.

"They're all the same, Saskia," said Tabitha, trying to sound contemptuous.

Growling, Tarko stepped up and hit her hard on the side of the head, toppling her.

Saskia shouted, "Leave her alone!"

There was the sound of another blow.

Her arms pinned awkwardly behind her, at once Tabitha struggled to her knees, refusing to lie down while they abused Saskia.

Saskia was cringing, leaning as far away from Tarko as she could while shoving her jacket off over her head, glancing fearfully back at Tabitha again as she shook her hair out and pulled her arms out of the sleeves.

Captain Pepper looked on, smiling fixedly.

A low whirring noise interrupted the proceedings, coming from behind.

Distracted, Captain Pepper looked past Saskia, past Tabitha.

"Hey, Shing," he called. "How you doin'?"

There was a wordless, disgruntled reply.

The whirring grew louder, and the big black robot came by her. It had had its leg put back on. It was carrying Xtasca before it in a force bubble, its tail and saucer in another pair of hands.

Saskia cried out: "Xtasca!"

The robot stomped up beside her and stopped. Its smoky dome was frosted with blue fire. It held the Cherub up in the air by Saskia's head for Captain Pepper to inspect.

Xtasca hung there immobile, unresponsive. Saskia reached up to touch it, had her hands jerked savagely away by the Thrant.

"What have you done to her?"

Carrying his control panel, the battered Chinese now limped into view. He stood at a little distance, staring at the women with stony malevolence, a grey bandage around his head.

"I bet that's sore," said Pepper reflectively, scratching his eyebrow. "What's that you got there?"

"Ah, look!" said Shing. He pressed keys.

Clusters of amber numerals burst on the invisible skin around the Cherub.

Its eyes still closed, it opened its little mouth and cried hoarsely in pain.

Captain Pepper chuckled. "What the hell—"

Saskia whimpered, clutched for Xtasca again. Tarko

pounced on her and cuffed her to the deck.

"Hey," objected Pepper softly, but made no further
effort to restrain her.

Involuntarily Tabitha had started forward and almost
fallen over again. She straightened up, cursing under her
breath, and studied Pepper.

His eyes now were on his real adversary, the central
object of his loathing. This ugly little pipsqueak had
shorted out his whole ship, come back from the dead
when he'd written it off, broken in while no one was
looking, screwed up the robot, nearly killed Shing, and
let the women out.

Now here it was, hanging in mid-air in front of him,
squealing like a piglet every time Shing pressed another
couple of keys.

"Gimme that," said Captain Pepper to the robot. Lazily he reached out and plucked Xtasca's tail from its
grip. He draped it across his knees and looked at it with
a smirk of triumph.

Shing, meanwhile, was having such a good time he
was clucking to himself in Chinese. Something in the
sophisticated neural circuits of the black lacquer child
made it vulnerable to the keen blade of his analyzer. It
could feel the sawteeth of the questing waves, cutting
into it as nothing physical ever could. Heat map diagnostics raged across its impenetrable skin like blisters of
fire and it jerked and howled, drooling a silvery liquor
down the front of its frozen lifesuit.

Saskia was wailing and crying, shouting, fighting with
Tarko, who was doing all she could not to take the noisy
woman's head off with one swipe of her claws.

"Stop him, Pepper!" yelled Tabitha at the top of her
voice. "He's killing it!"

The Thrant turned her attention to her, baring her incisors and squaring her enormous shoulders.

But the message had penetrated.

Captain Pepper emerged from his trance. Wordlessly
he grabbed the keyboard from Shing, frowned at it and
stabbed a key.

Shing called out in alarm.

The robot shook as if something powerful had thumped it in the chest. Its head flared with ice-blue lightning. It shut off the bubble.

A final blaze of graphic fire fizzling out across its contorted features, Xtasca fell to the deck.

It bounced, then lay still. Stripped of its tail and saucer, in any kind of gravity it was as physically helpless as a real legless child.

Then it moved.

It paddled its tiny hands on the floor. It was trying to crawl away.

Captain Pepper recovered swiftly. "Well glory be," he said, gazing down at it with one of his sunny, brown-stained smiles. He sat back, including Saskia and Tabitha in his ample benevolence. "Sure takes a lot to decommission them little guys, don't it? Tiny li'l thing too. Hell, it ain't no bigger 'n a baby."

Xtasca spoke. "Size was calculated to be inversely proportional to efficiency," it said, distantly.

The Thrant made a guttural sound that might have been mirth or fright.

Captain Pepper was uncomfortable. He shifted from one buttock to the other. "Tark," he whispered, "shut that up."

The Thrant growled, this time with unequivocal pleasure. She leaned down, pulled Xtasca's head back and clamped one hand across its mouth, hard.

Saskia was on her, dragging at her forearm, kicking her legs, punching her in the kidneys.

Tarko swept her away with a vicious backhand. She dug her talons through the cowl of Xtasca's lifesuit into its cheeks and squeezed.

She picked the Cherub up by its head, examining it warily. It writhed briefly, then fell unconscious again. "You ever see one of 'ese 'ings before, cap'n?"

Captain Pepper was sweating. "No, Tarko, can't say I ever had that pleasure."

"Iss go' me'al skin," mused Tarko. She bent her predatory head closer, her dark nostrils flaring.

Abruptly, Captain Pepper realized he was still holding

the keyboard and the tail. He held them out to Shing. "Take it away," he said. "Take it over there." He pointed to Shing's nest of cushions.

Shing bowed. He took the keyboard and reactivated the robot. It whirred, sparked, wobbled, then blew another invisible bubble with its hand and scooped the Cherub into it. Together, drone and master withdrew a little way.

"We was havin' us a entertainment here," Captain Pepper recalled. His clear blue eyes searched for Saskia.

Tarko dragged her forward.

"Carry on, sweet thing," said Captain Pepper. His voice was as soft as a caress.

Tabitha drew herself up.

"Let her be, Pepper," she said.

They all looked at her.

"It's nothing to do with her," said Tabitha. "I'm the one you want."

Captain Pepper looked from one to the other with amusement. "Well, now, ain't that nice," he said. "Ain't that sweet." He turned to look at a console display, and raised his voice. "Don't worry, princess," he said to Tabitha. "We got time for both of ya before we get to the man."

He leaned back in his seat and scratched his chest.

"The man with the big blue dog."

61

How gratifying it would be to record that before the *Ugly Truth* skipped back into normal space our resourceful heroines once again turned the tables on their tormentors, and effected a second cunning escape.

Alas, it did not happen; and even I, with all my narrative liberty in space and time, my freedom to conjecture what shadows flit through the inviolable region of the living mind—even I am bound by truth. Were I to trifle with the truth in the slightest respect, albeit for our mutual pleasure at watching valor confound villainy, could I then win your trust for any other feature of this astonishing tale? No, no, I must not deviate. Besides, it is not in my nature. I have no "imagination," as you have, no capacity for "fantasy." Pleasant or unpleasant, the truth must suffice. And the truth is that Captain Pepper's vile whims were fairly quickly, though none the less unpleasantly, sated; whereupon Tabitha Jute and Saskia Zodiac were returned, with all their clothes and belongings but without Xtasca the Cherub, to that dreary little cell, to remain there securely confined, restrained and disabled, until the *Ugly Truth* emerged from the grey nullity between the dimensions and made her fateful rendezvous with the *Citadel of Porcelain by First Light*.

Tabitha had been on or around some pretty large craft in her time. As a young mate on the *Fat Mouth* she had sieved the gash-fields of the *Bolshoi Mrittsvar*, marveling from a distance at those majestic declining buttresses, those three glacial terraces, each with its own microclimate. Less than a year later, subjectively speaking, she had expertly woven a shuttle between the towering stacks of the *Behemoth*, that monstrous folly of Bathsheba Tredgold's, that trailed her own precentium refinery around the system, compounding her mass to a degree magnificent in its very illogicality. Once, on her own *Alice Liddell*, Tabitha had even unloaded a mysterious cargo on a Capellan system ship, one of those sleek golden vessels that slid silently across the dark spaces of the night, keeping vigil over the subjects of the empire clustered on their little worlds.

Yet Tabitha Jute had never seen anything as grand as the *Citadel of Porcelain by First Light*.

Untied and prodded back down to the receiving bay of the *Ugly Truth* by the buckgutter of Tarko the Thrant, Tabitha and Saskia came stumbling past the remains of the *Alice Liddell* and found the bay doors open.

They were all there in the bay: Captain Pepper, Shing, and the robot, Xtasca in its arms; and now Tarko, Saskia and Tabitha Jute.

They should have been dying.

They should have been burning and freezing and bursting, the breath snatched from their lungs by the vacuum of space.

They were not. They were standing in a warm golden glow, remarkably similar to terrestrial sunshine. There was air, inside and out. Had they landed? If so, where?

Tarko growled gently and pushed them forward, to the very brink.

They looked down.

Directly below the ship, far, far below, lay a city. It was a shapely configuration of sleek towers and glass buildings in pristine tiers. Tiny colored cars beetled across its viaducts, looking from this height like mobile jewels. There seemed to be a considerable collection of machinery there, derricks and gantries and ramps; but it was hard to tell any more than that for the haze of golden light that filled the intervening void.

Tabitha drew Saskia back from the threshold.

Shing sent the robot forward.

It came, two clumping paces, and extended the metallic bundle towards the women.

Numbly, Saskia received it. She cradled it in her arms, just as if it were a baby.

Tabitha looked at it.

"You're in trouble," she announced, shortly. She did not look at any of them, least of all at Captain Pepper.

He was leaning with one hand on the crumpled hull of the *Alice Liddell*, smoking a cigar. Tabitha had noticed the wreck of her ship had been readied on tracks, as if for unloading.

Pepper tipped his cap back.

"It's fine," he announced.

Shing watched, hands folded. Nobody spoke.

"Well," said Pepper, "guess this is goodbye."

She would not turn to see him smirking, leaning with his brutal hand on the ship he had killed.

He bade them: "Y'all take care, now!"

Tarko growled suddenly and thrust brutally at them with her gun, forcing them out over the brink.

Tabitha yelled and clutched Saskia to her with one hand, her bag with the other. Saskia screamed and hugged Xtasca. Together they overbalanced, slid, tumbled out of the *Ugly Truth* and into space.

Where, coalescing through the vacuum like kilometer-wide search-lights, the golden tractor beams of the *Citadel of Porcelain* clasped and enfolded them, stretching her atmosphere about them and drawing them down towards the deck below, feet first, as gently as thistledown.

It was like falling in a dream, with no prospect of harm. Not a hair of their heads was ruffled as they descended, stately and slow, the great chutes of light.

"What is it?" cried Saskia, holding Tabitha close. "Where are we?"

Tabitha, catching her breath, looked down the dizzying gulf beneath their feet.

The view was of the Utopia of some celestial engineer: a city, gently twinkling like a crystal crown, borne up on a shallow oval salver of white metal. But it was neither a city, nor a platform, nor yet a planet.

The rich light softened every line and blurred every detail, so only impressions prevailed; but the impressions were of an architecture of overwhelming scope and audacity; a grandeur that was simply immense. To either side of the oval, spreading far beyond what they could take in at a view, smooth, broad white wings canted up and back, reaching to the height of the towers and above. Forward (for one thing was clear now, dramatically so: that this was an edifice made for motion, a great vessel dwarfing even the hulking ziggurats of the Eladeldi), the white deck rose in a gentle curve like the neck of a huge bird, towards a prow still out of sight. Astern it stretched away into darkness, eclipsing the cold light of the galaxy.

Tabitha spoke, her voice subdued as one who first sets foot in a great cathedral.

"It's a starship," she said.

It was. It was the *Citadel of Porcelain by First Light*, and coming upon her thus, unawares, from a little distance, they saw her in all the grandeur her name was designed to evoke. Capsules and lozenges of green and yellow that lay twinkling on her white decks like comfits spilled on a tablecloth were every one a ship the size of the Anaconda now receding above their heads. Bulbs like the heads of mushrooms were rotundas, observation domes and gun turrets. Spidery tracks as fine as gossamer, just becoming visible to the naked eye, were monorails and pipelines, arteries of power and communication.

Saskia held the unconscious Cherub securely at her shoulder.

"Is it the Capellans?"

"It's the Capellans."

Saskia flipped out of Tabitha's embrace, tumbling headfirst with her free arm swept out to the side, graceful as a diver. She peered down at an open area in the midst of the great machines. It seemed to be where they were headed. Figures were congregated there, as small as mites.

"Look." She brought her arm forward, pointing.

Tabitha, meanwhile, had got herself into an ungainly

posture, as if going down a slide on her back, arms and legs in the air. She struggled to sit up, looking down between her legs.

They were still twice as high as the tops of the highest towers. The machines winked at them with softly glowing eyes of glass. They were the projectors of the beam down which Saskia and Tabitha were sliding. The tiny people gathered in the arena between the projectors were waiting to receive them. The people all appeared, Tabitha saw, as they reached rooftop height, to be blue; uniformly blue.

"Eladeldi," said Saskia, acknowledging the inevitable.

If this were Utopia, it had not been designed for them.

Saskia clasped Xtasca in both hands, rolling in the beam as if hoping to swim back against the current. Her hair floated out around her head like an aureole of white weed. Her eyes widened in surprise, and she gasped, staring up into the haze above them.

Tabitha looked back, overhead. A large rounded shape was hanging a scant twenty meters above them, dipping and swaying, wobbling like a half-filled balloon as it followed them down.

It was the *Alice*. Captain Pepper was delivering her, as promised. Beneath and beside her hung a dark, curled shape, keeping her company in her clumsy descent.

Now the women and the Cherub were falling down a wide canyon of glittering glass, glimpsing offices, control rooms, workshops, balconies, where figures, Eladeldi, Vespans, robots, paused at their business, staring out to see them go by.

The deck swooped up to meet them. A force bubble was there to cushion their fall, and that of the coiled thing that arrived a second later, dropping down through the dazzling light. It bounced lightly behind them and came to rest.

Eladeldi pounced on it. It was the Frasque, still comatose and curled up inside her force bubble like a huge twiggy fetus. With her in the bubble were Xtasca's saucer and her tail. Captain Pepper must have had them all thrown out after them.

And the *Alice* was still falling.

Tabitha shoved herself up from the invisible surface of the cushion, struggling to push through the Eladeldi grabbing at her. She yelled at Saskia, who for all her agility was still on her back on the bubble, squirming beneath the onslaught of half a dozen slavering Eladeldi, kicking them about the face and head, fighting to keep hold of the unconscious Cherub.

"Get out of the way!" shouted Tabitha.

With a burst of energy that surprised her she barged into a gap between two of the Eladeldi, tore free from the clutching paws and dived through to the deck, hitting her shoulder a dull blow in the low g and skidding uncontrollably across a meter and a half of stainless steel. She ended up sprawling on her back, winded, gazing frantically through the scrum of blue bodies, looking for her companions, who couldn't be seen, one arm thrown up across her face as a shield against the descent of the *Alice Liddell*.

Which hung there suspended, seventy meters up, swaying gently in the thickened tractor field.

Tabitha was seized in a dozen ungentle paws and dragged to her feet. "Saskia!" she was shouting, coughing. "Saskia!" She struggled to punch and kick, but couldn't move. Her chest spasmed. They were grasping for her head. She jerked it away. "Saskia!"

They stood in the middle of a silvery arena, glassy towers staring down at them from all sides. High above, a green mote in the shimmering gold haze, was the *Ugly Truth* herself, now taking up a parking orbit about the *Citadel*. Evidently neither Captain Pepper nor his crew had any intention of speaking to their employers in person.

Below, dog-faced captains in headsets were trotting backwards and forwards, pumping their arms and shouting. Two teams of techs were grappling with the huge controls of the beam projectors, co-ordinating the difficult last few meters of the *Alice Liddell*'s final descent.

Beneath the shadow of the slowly descending wreck Tabitha saw Saskia, pinned like her, still lashing out with one foot while three trotting troopers bore a tiny black form swiftly away, following a party carrying off the motionless bundle of the Frasque.

Tabitha sagged; then when they took her weight tried to stamp on an instep, stab with an elbow. It was useless. She was forcibly restrained. Again she shouted to Saskia and a hairy paw was clamped across her mouth. She forced back her head a fraction, looking wildly for a means of escape.

There was none.

Now the golden light was fading, the atmosphere blanket wrinkling windily about them, as the beam projectors reeled the dead ship to the deck.

The women were led away at speed by the Eladeldi, their ears pounding, their lungs heaving. Beneath their feet they could feel the thrumming of engines of inconceivable power: enough power to break the virtual barrier Capella had erected outside the orbit of Pluto, the wall beyond the worlds.

And all of it belonged, as power will, to the architects of that humiliating and arbitrary wall.

Saskia and Tabitha were hustled along a wide roadway between banks of elegant balconies. With a whisper and a breeze, the *Alice* swept by overhead, borne by a cargo blimp. It rapidly caught up with the formation about Xtasca and the Frasque, and disappeared with them down a colossal ramp into the metal depths beneath.

Tabitha looked up as they followed, passing within. Between the soaring white wings of the superstructure something was quietly setting in its orbit, something that looked like a shiny green beetle.

Captain Pepper was maintaining his wide berth.

Below decks the air was richer, cleaner, more authentic. Harpsichord music whispered in the corridors. Lush greenery, peonies and phlox, tumbled in artful profusion from fine ceramic troughs.

Tabitha and Saskia were marched along a hallway bright with mirror tiles. The music followed them.

Tabitha tried to shrug off a paw gripping rather too firmly at the back of her neck.

"Where are you taking us?"

The guard captain kept looking straight ahead. "Kybernator Perlmutter," he replied, in that familiar rasping voice.

They passed along a high gallery above a well where Eladeldi in transparent overalls toiled at a giant loom of light, weaving the great ship's passage through interplanetary space.

"What have you done with the others?"

The guard captain kept looking straight ahead. This time there was no reply.

Everything was clean and shiny, very impersonal, and very tasteful. Tabitha hated it. She felt a certain malicious pleasure in their filthy clothes, their unwashed selves. She hoped they were making the place look untidy.

An Eladeldi with the fur shaved from the top of his head went by in a scarlet uniform with a braided silver bib. His eyes flickered over the captives with disgust. The captain barked and everyone saluted.

"What have you done with my ship?" Tabitha demanded.

Then they turned through a huge arched doorway and hurried down a ramp into a cavernous hall and she saw it.

The remains of the *Alice Liddell* lay on a dais, under bright spotlights, surrounded by a pack of Eladeldi mechs and a panoply of equipment, electronics and tools. Some of them were standing inside the twisted frame, in the space where the hold used to be, pointing a polar mesoscope around. A couple more were in the cockpit, bending over the console.

Three aliens were hovering outside, facing the mechs through the smashed viewport, keeping well out of the way.

None of these three was actually touching the floor.

Xtasca was squatting on its saucer, plugged into it by its tail. Its head was bowed. It did not seem to be conscious.

Nor did the Frasque. She had been let out of her bubble and unrolled; she hung straight down in mid-air, as if suspended from her shoulders by invisible strings. She hung quite still.

The third figure was awake, and obviously directing the operations. He looked rather like a man. In fact he looked exactly like a man, if a man could be three meters tall.

From the neck down, he was well proportioned, and well fed. It was his head that accounted for his extra height. It was enormous, egg-shaped, and bald. A silver circlet spanned his colossal brow. A stiff blue collar like the back of a high chair rose up behind his neck.

He wore a white toga, a deep blue cape, and anti-gravity sandals. His arms and legs were bare and white, his hands and feet large and pudgy. There were thick rings on his fingers. He held out his hand now as an Eladeldi mech emerged from the cockpit of the *Alice Liddell* and gave something to a supervisor. The supervisor gave it to a steward. From hand to hand they passed the slim grey plaque the mech had just extracted from the wreckage of the *Alice*'s computer.

"What's that?" Saskia asked Tabitha.

"The persona," said Tabitha bitterly.

They had come to a stop on a bend of the ramp, looking down at the scene over a low wall.

"Is that it?" Kybernator Perlmutter asked the steward. His voice was languid, strong and clear. It reached them easily across the hall.

"Yes sir," said the steward briskly.

The Kybernator hefted the plaque in his broad hand. He turned and drifted towards Xtasca.

Eladeldi medics fluttered, attempting to prop the Cherub up and turn it to face him. He waved them away.

"Now come along," he said. "Cherub."

He came to a stop in front of the saucer, which was on a level with his chest. He reached up and deposited the plaque on it.

"You can do it," he said. He fingered his rings.

For the first time since the Thrant had plucked it from

the deck of the *Ugly Truth*, Xtasca made a move. It lifted its head. It looked ill; uncomfortable, even from that distance. Its eyes were not alight.

"Enable it," said the Capellan.

Xtasca looked into his face. It did not move.

The Capellan twisted one of his rings a little.

Xtasca squirmed, spotlight beams flashing off its life-suit. Tabitha heard Saskia suck a sharp breath through her teeth when it cried out, high and shrill, as it had while Shing was torturing it. It writhed and bucked, its saucer bobbing like a coracle on a sudden tide. It pulled out its tail, lashing it from side to side and shouting something unintelligible.

Kybernator Perlmutter touched his ring again.

The Cherub's little shoulders sagged. "—don't—know—" it gasped.

"You've got everything you need in there," Perlmutter interrupted, tapping the saucer with a blunt square fingertip.

Saskia gripped Tabitha's arm. "What does he want?" she muttered indignantly.

But Tabitha had no more idea than she.

Stiffly, Xtasca reached down with its little hands and squared the plaque on the saucer in front of it. Then, with a resentful glare at the Capellan, it plugged its tail into the saucer.

There was a moment's pause.

They could almost hear the Cherub searching the memory.

Then it whipped out its tail and brought it flicking around in front of it, stabbing down at the plaque and scribbling something there.

Something clicked loudly, like a well-oiled lock turning over.

There was a general sighing and murmuring among the attendants. They wagged their heads and patted each other.

The Capellan looked across at the Frasque, an expression of distaste flickering across his great bland face. "Is that it now?" he asked her.

The Frasque didn't answer.

He floated a little way nearer her, speaking loudly and distinctly, as though he thought she didn't understand English. "Is it ready?"

The Frasque hissed, like a snake.

He sighed. He clasped his hands, one over the other. "Would it *work* now?" he demanded, peevishly.

The Frasque convulsed.

Tabitha thought the Capellan was torturing her with his rings too; but no.

Somehow the Frasque was breaking out, smashing free of her invisible restraint.

A dozen Eladeldi leapt as she flailed her whole body through the air, knocking them left and right and striking like a snake directly for the retreating Kybernator Perlmutter's fat white throat.

Before she could reach him, Perlmutter squeezed his ring.

The Frasque froze again.

Hanging in mid-air in front of him, she began to shake from top to toe. Her peculiar limbs cracked and split one from another, fraying like green sticks. Thick white fluid spurted from the wounds.

The Eladeldi backed away, yammering.

The Frasque hissed and shrieked, defying the Capellan even as she writhed in agony. "Pusssillanimousss, sssself-sssatisssfied, sssupersssiliousss—"

"Thank you," he said, dismissively.

Ignoring her, he signaled to a pair of techs to bring over a machine that looked like an ordinary tape reader.

The Frasque was twitching, burning. She fell apart, bits of her whirling in flames to the deck. Still she threatened him. "We ssshall sssurvive!" she spat and spluttered. "You will not sssucsseee . . ." Her head jerked back on her neck.

She fell still, all her joints popping like twigs as the fire consumed her. A sharp smell of scorched metal spread rapidly through the hall.

"Thank you," said the Capellan again, as the crack-

ling died swiftly away. "Your Majesty," he said, in a
tone that vindicated all her accusations.

They had slotted the persona in the reader for him.
He prodded it suspiciously with one white finger.

"How do you raise it?" he asked Xtasca.

Its head had fallen forward on its chest again. Perlmutter tutted and signaled brusquely to the medics, who
scurried forward.

Tabitha spoke up then. "Her name," she said, "is
Alice."

The Eladeldi all turned to look at her; the Capellan
too, his vast smooth head rising above their furry ones.

His eyes met Tabitha's.

"Come here," he said.

62

"Who are *you*?"

He hovered above her, his eyes hooded with disdain.
It gave Tabitha a crick in the neck, looking up at him.

"Tabitha Jute," she said. "That's my boat you've got
there."

He turned from her with the slow irritation of the very
great, confronted with someone too lowly to compre-
hend. "What is she saying?" he asked his steward.

"This is the ow-ner, Kyber-nator," said the steward.

The Capellan did not seem any more impressed to hear
it. "You," he told her, "are in possession of a prohibited
ship persona."

"Am I," said Tabitha mutinously. "I thought you
were."

This appeared to amuse him. "Indeed," he conceded,

indicating the reader with the slightest gesture of a finger, and smiling the driest of smiles.

Xtasca, surrounded by medics, lifted its head a fraction. ''—doesn't—know—'' it said, weakly.

"Oh, hello, woken up, have we?" observed the Capellan acidly. "Everybody's ignorant of everything, according to you."

"What do you mean, prohibited?" Tabitha asked, loudly.

"Illegally reprogrammed," answered Kybernator Perlmutter. "By Seraphim. Enabled to control a prohibited device manufactured by—"

He looked pensively at the cloud of ash hanging in the air where the Frasque had been, as if he'd already forgotten disintegrating her. Reminiscently, he looked at his rings, then, suddenly, at Tabitha.

He opened his eyes wide like an enormous owl. "Ringing any *bells* yet, are we?" he demanded.

Tabitha put her hands in her pockets. "I don't know what you're talking about," she said.

He stroked a ring, and all her nerves caught fire.

She threw back her head and screamed.

"I *don't*, you bastard!"

Perlmutter's steward was tugging at his toga, muttering urgently, deferentially. "Oh, very well," said Perlmutter impatiently, and the fire went out, instantly, as if it had never been. "This is the most colossal waste of time," he told the steward, very angrily. The steward hung his head, ears drooping.

Tabitha stood there, rubbing her arms. They were tingling.

"You talk to it," the Capellan told her, flicking an imperious finger towards the reader.

Tabitha went up to it, ignoring the techs clustering officiously around her. It was a kind she'd never seen before, but the vox light was on.

She put her hands on the top edges of the machine. It was warm. "Alice?" she said. "Can you hear me?"

"HELLO, CAPTAIN," said Alice.

Relief flooded Tabitha. She closed her eyes and let her head fall forward.

"Are you all right in there?" she asked.

There was a brief pause. "IT'S A LITTLE CRAMPED," said the voice, hesitantly.

Kybernator Perlmutter waved a lordly hand. "Oh, get on with it, do," he said. "Never mind the social niceties." -

"HAVE YOU COME TO TELL ME A STORY?" Alice asked. "I CAN'T SEEM TO FIND THE LOG AT PRESENT." She sounded apprehensive.

Kybernator Perlmutter looked irritated. "What's it talking about?" he said.

"I've been telling her stories," said Tabitha. "Don't worry about the log, Alice," she said. "We don't need it just now."

She looked expectantly at the Capellan.

"Tell it you've *enabled* it," he ordered her testily. "Tell it, tell it"—He snapped his fingers at Xtasca. "What should she tell it?"

Xtasca mouthed and waved a frail hand, as if searching for words that would not come. "It's a long lane," it managed, faintly, "that has—that has no—" It clawed the air again. "Turning . . ." it said.

"What?" Tabitha wrinkled her nose. It sounded like one of the things her dad was always saying.

"Tell Alice," the Cherub began again, "it's a long lane—"

"Just say it," interrupted the Capellan.

Tabitha turned back to the reader. "Alice?" she said.

"HELLO, CAPTAIN."

"Alice: it's a long lane that has no turning."

The machine hummed briskly. Lights flickered across it. Behind Tabitha the techs muttered importantly to one another.

"READY TO GO," said Alice placidly.

"Go?" said Tabitha. She looked around at the wreck of the Kobold. "Go where?" she said.

"ANYWHERE YOU LIKE, CAPTAIN."

"Switch it off," said Kybernator Perlmutter instantly.

As the techs obeyed, pushing Tabitha out of the way, another Eladeldi in a com headset came loping through the crowd around the ship. She saluted and stood waiting, her tongue hanging out.

"Yes, damn you," Perlmutter said. "What is it?"

"Sir, the cab-tain of the bounty hun-ters."

The Capellan sighed. "Put him through."

At once Captain Pepper's voice rang out through the hall.

"Perlmutter? Can you hear me?"

"Yes, I can hear you, Pepper," said the Capellan, resignedly. "What do you want?"

"Did you get the ship?" he asked *"And the women? We sent them down to you, did you get them all right?"*

"Women?" said the Capellan, looking around cursorily. "Are there others?"

The troopers pushed Saskia forward. He looked her over. "And what are you doing here?" he asked. "Never mind. Pepper, there are two women, one of them the owner."

"That's okay, then," said Captain Pepper.

"The state of the Cherub, however, is not satisfactory," Perlmutter continued.

"It's working, ain't it?"

Kybernator Perlmutter looked critically at Xtasca. He pursed his fat lips. "Reluctantly," he conceded.

"Well, everything's just fine and dandy, then," said Captain Pepper. *"You just come up with the credit now, Perlmutter, and we'll be on our way."*

"You expect me to pay you," remarked the Capellan.

"That's the idea, that's the deal," Pepper sang out.

"Captain Pepper," said Kybernator Perlmutter peremptorily. "I think you must know that this ridiculous little charade has run on far too long and cost us far too much already."

"We got a deal, Perlmutter," said Pepper, loudly and lazily.

Kybernator Perlmutter raised his voice. "There was a little matter of a rescue," he said. "An emergency power

boost. Not cheap. You'll be hearing from us, Pepper.
Goodbye.''

''*Oh, no,*'' came Pepper's voice, bullishly. ''*We got
a deal, Perlmutter. We got a deal.*''

The Capellan looked pained. He turned to his steward.
''Where is he?'' he demanded, irritably.

The steward spoke to the com page, and the com page
spoke into her mouthpiece. In an instant all around the
hall giant monitors flared into life, showing the gaudy
form of the *Ugly Truth* from all sides and every angle.
Tabitha found herself looking up at a close-up of her
emptily leering figurehead. On another screen she recognized the pale lemon disc dawning behind the green
ship, narrow rings like sleek steel ornaments across its
face.

Saskia stood beside her, her hand at her waist.
''Where—?'' she said.

''Uranus,'' said Tabitha.

She had never been so far out before. She supposed
she knew where the *Citadel* was going, and she wondered
if it would be her last journey. She looked pensively into
Saskia's face.

''Hold me,'' she said, very quietly. ''Please.''

Saskia slipped her arms around her.

Kybernator Perlmutter studied the displays. He tapped
two fingers on his bottom lip; then he folded his hands,
brushing the fingers of one across the rings upon the
other.

The *Ugly Truth* exploded in a gout of silent fire.

The monitors scrolled data, ran slow-motion replays,
overlaid readout graphics, zoomed in on whirling lumps
of blackened metal.

Kybernator Perlmutter closed his eyes placidly.

The monitors blinked out.

Tabitha and Saskia gazed at him, aghast. The blank
white bulge of his skull was wrinkling as though his fat
veins were writhing beneath the skin.

He opened his eyes then, and looked idly around the
hall, at the wrecked Kobold, at Tabitha and her friends.

"I think we've wasted enough time now, Brother Felix," he announced flatly.

Another voice spoke from the air, muffled and skewed with distance.

"*Bring them in, Kybernator Perlmutter. I think I'd like to meet them.*"

Perlmutter rolled up his great baggy eyes; but his interlocutor was continuing.

"*Perhaps they'd like to come to luncheon.*"

Saskia stifled a nervous giggle in the back of Tabitha's neck. Startled, eager troopers brandished weapons at her. Kybernator Perlmutter looked down at them all as if at a basket of puppies, then gestured to his steward and turned, drifting swiftly towards the door.

"On," he commanded, with a flourish of his cape. "On to Charon!"

Their Eladeldi escort took Tabitha and Saskia away to be bathed, barbered and manicured. Tabitha held on to her bag. Their filthy clothes were exchanged for smart new pyjamas of brushed grey denim and matching espadrilles. They fitted perfectly.

They were led through the ship, along vaulted galleries of velour steel, up thickly carpeted travelators under lofty arches festooned with honeysuckle and bougainvillaea. From wrought iron balconies little children in square caps and glowing smocks stared down at them and whispered to each other behind their hands. Drones polishing the tiles of remote corridors slid whirring aside as they passed.

They were not confined. They were taken to an observation deck at the top of a high tower, led into a comfortable lounge and left in the care of robot waiters.

Tabitha refused food, drink, even drugs. She sat on the edge of a compliant couch, her legs wide apart, staring at nothing. There were huge windows in every wall, but nothing to see out of them, because the *Citadel of Porcelain by First Light* had already dipped, effortlessly and imperceptibly, into that subtle realm between *here* and *everywhere*, that micro-region at the back of every mirror, between the mercury and the glass, the anomalous straits of hyperspace.

Saskia knelt with one leg up behind Tabitha, hanging on her shoulder.

Tabitha patted her hand, looking into her face. She felt scared and miserable. Saskia looked concerned, as if nothing that had happened had touched her except Tabitha's state of mind now. Tabitha tried to smile, then dropped her head and looked away again.

The doors whisked open and Xtasca came humming in.

Saskia leapt up with a glad cry, leaving Tabitha behind.

Tabitha got to her feet.

Xtasca brought the saucer down so its head was level with Saskia's. "How are you?" Saskia asked it anxiously, putting both hands on the rim of the saucer as though she were looking over a wall.

"Recharged," said Xtasca, slightly wheezy still.

Tabitha came to make a third. "What don't I know?" she said, rather more aggressively than she'd intended.

Xtasca looked down at her. "Your own ship," it said.

Tabitha's jaw tightened.

Saskia laid a hand on her shoulder. "Xtasca, what was all that about? What were you doing?"

"Enabling Alice," it said.

"To do *what*?"

"Run . . ." It struggled. "Supplementary drive."

Saskia, recognizing a technicality, looked at Tabitha, who was frowning. "Supplementary?"

"A star," croaked the Cherub. Its tiny chest heaved mightily. "Drive," it said.

"Xtasca, don't—" said Saskia, unhappily.

"What," said Tabitha tightly, "stardrive?"

"Frasque stardrive," said Xtasca.

Tabitha took a deep breath. She turned on her heel and stepped away, hammering her fist into the palm of her hand.

Saskia said to Xtasca, "Don't try to talk any more."

Then she came to Tabitha, hanging on her shoulder again.
"Tabitha—?"

Not looking at her, Tabitha took Saskia's hand off her
and went back to the couch. She sat on the edge again,
looking at the floor.

"Tabitha?"

"Why the fuck didn't you tell me before?" said Tabitha ferociously, still staring at the floor.

"No difference," said the Cherub.

She looked at it then, her fists clenched. "How do
you know?"

"No drive," it said.

Tabitha exhaled, and dropped her head again.

Saskia was getting lost. She looked at the two of them,
waiting for a clue, a cue.

Tabitha shut her eyes tightly. "Xtasca," she said,
hearing her voice sounding strained and brittle, "what
do you know?"

Saskia was looking warningly at the Cherub, hoping
it wasn't going to try to talk.

But it was.

"You didn't say," said Xtasca, laboring, "Sanczau's."

Tabitha looked up, injured, aggrieved. "Why the hell
should I have?"

They sat glaring at each other, the Cherub and the
space captain, antagonists. Neither of them spoke.

Then Tabitha did. Lightly she slapped her thigh. "The
hyperband on the com," she said, sourly.

The Cherub whirred. "Of course . . ." it whispered,
concurring.

"Who had this drive?" Tabitha wanted to know. "Did
you?"

It shook its head. "Deal," it said.

"The Temple did a deal with the Frasque? For stardrives? Just nod. What had Sanczau got to do with it?"

"Test . . ."

"Why not use your own ships?"

"Secret . . ."

"I suppose so," put in Saskia unexpectedly. "I mean,

you'd hardly expect to find a stardrive in a bloody Kobold, would you? Oh, *you* know what I mean," she said, sitting down by Tabitha and squeezing her hand. "Tabitha," she went on, in a low voice, "can't this wait, you can see she's not—"

Tabitha ignored her. "Alice is one of the ones with the interface?"

Xtasca nodded.

"And you gave her the access codes?"

Xtasca nodded, tapped one miniature, nailless finger on the saucer.

"We never," it said. "Throw. Anything."

"Away," completed Tabitha. She knew all about that. She gave a short, harrassed laugh and rubbed the top of her head. "So what happened?" she asked. "Why didn't the Frasque deliver?"

"Capella . . ." said Xtasca.

"The war . . ." said Tabitha. She and the Cherub stared at one another again. They understood each other now, as much as they were ever going to.

"So why are they bothered about it now?" she said. "Why *my* Kobold? Because of you?"

It didn't know.

Tabitha shifted on the couch, turning to Saskia. "Is this—"

Saskia held up her hands in an elegant pantomime of refusal. "Don't ask me," she said. "I've told you everything I know already. It wasn't much."

Tabitha pressed her. "Is this why Marco was so hot to get his hands on the *Alice*?" she said, in disbelief. "Because there might be a chance he could put a Frasque stardrive in her, if one should happen to fall in his lap one day?"

"Oh, God, no," said Saskia, "Surely not. Marco would have dropped you like a radioactive brick if he thought you had anything that might attract Capellans." She was looking to Xtasca for confirmation. It wasn't disagreeing. "Marco isn't very bright, you know," she continued. "Wasn't," she corrected herself, looking away suddenly to the dim grey insubstance slopping slowly about outside the windows.

"Isn't," Tabitha said.

But Saskia was thinking of her brother.

She shivered, and rubbed her hands together, suddenly smiling brightly at her companions.

"Luncheon!" she said. "Luncheon with Brother Felix!"

BGK009059 LOG

TXJ.STD

PRINT

K3ã::/TXXXJ!åzzarzzarzlin%ter&& &§/E—*f*ˆ

MODE? VOX

SD? 67.06.31

READY

Hello, Alice?

K3ã::/TXXXJ!åz—PpLUM

Alice? It's me, Tabitha Jute. Remember me?

PLUM. BALTHZZZARZZARZ

Don't, Alice.

ZZARZZARZZA

MANUAL OVERRIDE

Alice. Alice, it's me.

HELLO, CAPTAIN. I THOUGHT

What did you think, Alice?

WE WERE TALKING, WEREN'T WE? YOU WERE TELLING
ME ABOUT BALTH

ABOUT BALTH

BALTH

ZZARZZARZZA

Alice, listen to me! You've got to help me. You've got to pull
yourself together.

STORY

Do you know what he said about you?

WHAT DID HE SAY, CAPTAIN?

If I tell you, if I tell you all about it, about the first time I saw
you, will you stay up and stop running away?

READY

He said, "She's good. She's loyal, and she's steady. She's
interested; she understands people. But she does herself
down. Claims she can't remember things. She knows more
than she thinks she does."

I said, "Why are you telling me all this?"

We were sitting in a courtyard in Northern California, with
real blue sky overhead, warm sun blazing off white stucco

walls into a pool where goldfish swam about.

"Because she takes a bit of getting to know," said Balthazar Plum.

He was lying back in his reclining chair with a long cold drink at his elbow. He looked absolutely fine. He had a rich golden tan, a green sun visor, spotless white trousers and a hideous leopard-skin pattern shirt. His wisp was hovering around, as usual. It kept taking tiny sips out of his glass.

We'd had this argument already.

"Balthazar," I said, "I'm not going to take your ship. I can't. I really don't see why you should want to give me a ship."

"Because you saved my life," he said.

"Anyone would have done the same," I told him.

"But you were the one who did," he said.

I'd got the message when I docked back at Arkangel that Balthazar Plum was alive and well, and had invited me to Earth, to spend a week as his guest on the Sanczau property just south of San Francisco. There was an open luxury class ticket for any flight I cared to board at Arkangel, by any route I wanted to travel. I nearly tore it up, but I knew if I did I'd come around to regretting it one day; and I'd never had a holiday, not a real one. And I remembered Balthazar as I'd seen him first, not blue round the lips and about to expire in the back seat of the Frazier Hightail, but made up to look like the Moon and grinning like an overgrown boy at the trick he'd played on that woman at the Sanczau Skipfest.

I remembered how much I'd liked him. Not trusted him, liked him.

DEAR BALTHAZAR.

"I don't need a ship," I told him. "I don't want a ship. It's too much responsibility. I'm perfectly happy as I am."

He stretched lazily, and yawned. "No, you're not," he said.

I stared at him. "Who says I'm not?"

"You told me so yourself, Tabitha."

"When? When did I tell you I wasn't happy?"

"At the party."

"What party? I haven't been to a party with you," I said blankly.

"On the *Raven of October*," he said. "Four years ago, was it, five?"

I busied myself getting the last of my pina colada up the straw. "You're imagining things," I told him. "I'm a cargo pilot. What would I have been doing at a party on the *Raven*?"

I hadn't exactly decided not to mention our first meeting, but somehow it just hadn't come up. I'd sort of assumed he'd forgotten it too. Apparently he hadn't.

"I never went to a party on the *Raven*," I said.

"It won't wash, Tabitha," he said. "Wisp remembers you perfectly, don't you, Wisp?" The loathsome little cyborg gave a coy little wriggle. I could almost swear it was tittering. "She may not be good on faces, but she never forgets a voice-print," said Balthazar.

The wisp went to nestle on his shoulder, no doubt whispering secrets into his ear. "You said flying is what Peter likes best," he declared.

"I'm flying," I said shortly.

Balthazar Plum made an explosive noise of derision. "Lugging wagonloads of deuterium through the Belt for FAR? You call that flying?"

"I'm a cargo pilot!" I repeated. "I do it for a living! It's what I do!"

"The *Alice Liddell* is a cargo ship!" he said, levering himself up in his chair. He was getting quite agitated now. The wisp hummed anxiously up to his face. I was delighted to see him push it impatiently away.

"She's a Bergen Kobold," he said emphatically. "The best little barge ever built. They don't make them like that any more! She's solid, she's reliable, she's got a wonderful, sensitive, *human* persona, and god knows where you'd find *that* these days. And she's sitting there in the vineyard with nothing to do. She's been sitting there for seven years because she's too old for the firm. I can't use her, and I don't know anyone who can. If you don't take her off my hands she'll sit there until she falls to bits, and if you don't think that's a crime, then you're not half the woman I took you for." He sat there, red in the face, panting slightly. The wisp was buzzing up and down making beeping noises. "Yes, I know, Wisp, I know," he said. "I'm an old man and I have a right to get angry with the stupidity of the young. That's what the young are for! They're there to infuriate their elders and betters. And do you know why they infuriate us? Because they're going to replace us. And do you know why they're stupid? Because they don't know a bloody good thing when we hand it to them on a plate with a bloody cherry on the top!"

YOUNG WOMEN.

Pardon?

HE LIKED YOUNG WOMEN. HE BROUGHT YOUNG WOMEN TO SEE ME.

Not just me?

NO, CAPTAIN. TWO OR THREE TIMES, YOUNG WOMEN. HE WOKE ME UP.

Then why didn't one of them take you?

CONDITIONS ATTACHED.

Yes, I thought there might have been. If I hadn't saved his life, as he kept insisting I had, I mean.

"If we step lively, we can take a peep at her before lunch," he said.

He jammed a sunhat on his head, over the visor, and levered himself up out of his chair, leaning heavily on his walking stick. I knew not to offer him a hand. "The day I start accepting help I might as well go to bed and never get up again," he said.

It was only that, the walking with a stick and getting the shakes first thing in the morning and last thing at night, that showed Balthazar Plum was a survivor of a horrendous spacewreck, and not quite the man he had been. He seemed older now; less like a dashing grandee and more like a dissolute granddad.

We strolled slowly down the hill to the vineyards, the wisp zipping around us like a hummingbird. Beyond the blue hills lay the blue sea. The air smelled of wine and bees.

The vineyards were deserted. In the long grass behind the machine sheds stood something the size of a small house. It was covered in tarpaulins.

Balthazar Plum gestured with his stick. He didn't want me to see how much the walk had exhausted him. "Strip her off," he said. "Strip the young lady off and let's see what she's got!"

Sorry, Alice.

DEAR BALTHAZAR. I REMEMBER

What do you remember, Alice?

HIS VOICE. DO IT AGAIN, CAPTAIN. YOU SOUND JUST LIKE HIM.

"Best bloody barge in the whole system!"

HIS VOICE. I REMEMBER ALL THEIR VOICES.

All whose voices, Alice?

ALL YOUR FRIENDS. THE PEOPLE IN THE STORIES.

They weren't all friends, Alice. Balthazar was, but he wanted to give me a hard time that day. He had me undoing ropes that had been tied seven years, pulling mucky tarpaulins off single-handed. I think he was punishing me for trying to refuse his thank-you present. Or else I had something to prove, being a woman and claiming to do a physical job all on my own. He was an old man, from an old world.

"The paperwork's all back at the house," he said. "And the persona, I've kept that safe. There's housing for four drones. They're long gone, of course, but we can pick you up some more."

I'd seen a Kobold before, though I don't think I'd ever flown one. I could see there'd been some modifications.

"We had some work done on her," he said, pointing with his stick to the scanners and the solar. "Before the war, it was. Great hopes, we had then."

I pointed to the inlay. "What's this," I said, "copper?" It was all tarnished, but I supposed you could polish it.

"Smartens her up a bit, doesn't it?" said Balthazar. "Ugly old things, really."

He poked you with his stick.

I wanted to tell him not to. I wanted to protect you.

I suppose he knew that's how I'd feel, as soon as I'd got my hands dirty on a Bergen Kobold. Any self-respecting bargee would.

God, you were a mess, Alice. Birds' nests in your aerials, bindweed in your undercarriage. The ground beneath you was sticky and black where all your oil had leaked away. The fog had got at you and rusted your compressor vanes, and the airlock seals had all perished.

I fell in love with you the first time I saw you.

64

Charon is a cheerless place, a sluggish, stony, unaccommodating place. Feebly it skulls in a mean and miserable orbit, as if intent on chafing its frozen form against the frigid flanks of its parent Pluto.

It is a vain hope. All hopes are vain, out here on the meager rim of the system. Both planet and moon are insusceptible, obdurate to the needs and wishes of the animate. All is dark, all ice, a gelid stew of muck and methane best left unstirred.

Pluto is the end of everything. Beyond lie the deeps

of the great ocean of space, that trackless, bottomless abyss that yearns always emptily towards the infinite. And beyond that, the stars.

Once upon a time, I discover, to the long-vanished race who named these worlds after deities, Pluto was the god of the dead, and Charon the grim pilot who plied a ceaseless trade delivering expired souls to his bleak domain. They had the right idea, those ancient primitives, thought Tabitha Jute as the shuttle hurtled from the dock, leaving *The Citadel of Porcelain at First Light* sailing implacably on, on, across the invisible border and into the great night.

Why was this cock-boat coming to Charon, towing the sad husk of the *Alice Liddell*? Tabitha stared glumly from the window at the pewter globe suspended in the void about the last planet. It looked like nothing so much as an oily ball bearing, stained there with a speck of green, like verdigris.

"What's that?" said Saskia then. "That green?"

The Eladeldi guard bared his teeth and lolled his purple tongue. "Head-quarters," he huffed.

"On the surface?"

He said no more.

Tabitha left Saskia looking out and floated back to the hard metal seat, as the shuttle drew on toward the frozen moon. Even looking at Charon made her feel cold, colder than all the sterile seas of space. The sun was a distant, cold, white speck, scarcely to be distinguished from all the white stars, and just as unattainable.

She was thinking of Balthazar Plum, and feeling angry with him. He'd given her a dodgy ship and not told her. Obviously that was why nobody else had wanted it, because they knew eventually they'd get into trouble. And that was why he hadn't told her.

Or perhaps he had told her, in his way, and she hadn't been listening. It wasn't his fault. It wasn't anyone's fault, it was bloody Capella clamping down on a technicality. Wanting to keep everything under their control, not for any reason, just because they liked it that way.

Power for its own sake. Now she'd met one, they were just the way she'd thought they'd be.

She hated them.

She pulled out her harmonica and played a searing blast of *Blackwater Blues*.

The guard flattened his ears and snarled. "Bu' thad away!"

"Look," said Saskia, beckoning her back to the window.

The grey disc had ceased to be *ahead* and become *down*, and the green spot was growing. It had moved into the middle of the disc and was rushing up to claim them.

It was vegetation. In the ultimate tundra, an oasis. It wasn't very big, perhaps two or three k across. It was all green, with a river. There were trees, thick leafy ones. What looked like the roof of a tiny building. Specks—people—on the lawns. Flowerbeds.

On Charon.

Tabitha had never seen anything like it. She felt sick. Her heart was beating fit to burst, and she wanted very much to throw up.

Saskia, sensing her trouble, caressed the back of her neck, looking questioningly into her face.

"Landing," said the guard.

Tabitha swallowed, and breathing hard, swam to take her place in the web beside Xtasca. The windows were full of dark now as they swung in to land. The pilot dipped the nose, and glacial desert lifted into view, bitter, rugged, black and dead; and then leafy green treetops, glowing in sunlight.

The shuttle descended between the trees, and set down on a lawn, the *Alice* landing with a gentle bump behind.

"There's somebody flying a kite," Saskia said, dazedly.

"Quite a microclimate," Xtasca said nasally. You could tell it was impressed. It had recovered its strength, luxuriating in the sophisticated ambience of the starship, and had seemed disappointed when the guard came to hustle them from the observation lounge into the shuttle. Now it was perking up again.

Tabitha felt terrible. They were going to kill her now for something she hadn't even known about, the way they'd killed Captain Pepper and Tarko and Shing, not for their crimes and brutalities, but for spoiling their afternoon. They were going to kill her without a chance to escape, and it wasn't even going to be a death she could understand. There were no trees on Charon; no grass; no *flowerbeds*.

"Gome. Gome," gulped the guard, chivvying them out of the web and herding them into the airlock. He opened the door, and sunlight hit them.

Tabitha stepped groggily down from the shuttle into soft, lush grass. The earth beneath her feet was springy, not even scorched by their landing. The hull of the shuttle was merely warm, as if it had stood here in the sun for an hour or two. She leaned her back against it, gasping the impossible air, while Xtasca's saucer slipped out of the door with a gentle buzz and Saskia stepped down beside her, gracefully, her thin face alight with wonder. The gravity was exactly Earth normal, and rather heavy after so long at other levels. The sky was blue.

The kite was yellow. It bobbed and soared joyfully in the air as if the principle were new discovered, and it the first kite ever flown.

A tall figure in a toga held the end of its string, tipping back his huge head to watch it fly. Tabitha could just see him, between the trees, the other side of the little river. Beyond him was more green grass, more blue sky; and beyond that the silent, frozen wilderness of Charon, hideous and raw.

In the trees, birds were singing.

"*Gome*," growled the guard, dragging her forward, his claws digging through her soft pyjamas into her arm.

He drove the women before him, and Xtasca, skimming above the grass, its lifesuit polarizing against the glorious sunlight.

They followed a graveled path around a stand of beeches and into the open. Green lawns spread away before them, curving down to the river as naturally as if they had always been there. To their right, the line of beeches led to a thicket of heavy-bosomed chestnut trees, their candles in full bloom, white and pink. Blossoming shrubs and beds of flowers spread in graceful, sweeping lines down to the banks of the river, which was spanned by a minute bridge of polished stone and iron. A tall figure stood on the bridge, dangling a line in the clear water.

Tabitha shivered, despite the sun, or because of it, because it was wrong, six thousand million kilometers wrong.

Saskia was looking around at everything warily, knowing it was a trick but unable to see how it was being done.

"Hello, there!" called a voice.

They stopped. A Capellan was coming towards them up the graveled path, his hand raised in greeting.

He looked very much like Kybernator Perlmutter: more sparely built, but with the same glossy skin, the same bright eyes. He was wearing the rings, and the sandals, cross-laced to the knee, but instead of a toga, a kilt of some heavy purple stuff, and a loose white collarless blouse with fine white embroidery at the cuffs and throat. He had the vast, bald head of all his race; his was wreathed with a garland of fresh ivy. His eyebrows were very black, and arched, so he looked permanently amused and surprised: an expression more friendly than the Kybernator's. He smiled down at them now with every appearance of genuine pleasure.

The guard came to attention. "The brisoners, Brother Felix," he said, and held something out for him to take.

"Nonsense, Captain," said the Capellan, gently. He reached down and took the proffered persona plaque, securing it in a sporran of sealskin and mother-of-pearl. "Our guests," he said. "Surely. Thank you, Captain. Well done."

Dismissed, the Eladeldi saluted, stiffly, and trotted back to collect the shuttle pilot, now stretching and scratching herself on the grass in the sunshine. Together they set off towards the river.

The Capellan beamed at the little group. "How very nice to see you all," he said. "I'm so glad you could come." He looked at Xtasca, floating level with his chin. "Xtasca, isn't it? How do you do. What do you think of our little habitat?"

The Cherub's eyes gleamed briefly. "You've done a very thorough job," it said, approvingly. "The décor—Terran, is it? Antique, of course, but the *texture . . .*"

"I'm so glad you like it," the Capellan said, not at all put out. He offered his hand to Saskia, who hesitated, then shook it. "Saskia Zodiac," he said. His voice was warm and hospitable as the artificial day. "Welcome," he said. "Welcome to Charon."

"Thanks," said Saskia distantly. She was looking up at him, and from side to side, with an expression of alerted suspicion.

"Finally," said the Capellan. "Captain Jute," he said; and in his tone was all knowledge, all forgiveness. "Tabitha." He spread his arms.

Tabitha stepped back. "Get away from me, Capellan."

"Oh, we're not Capellans," he said. "Actually."

She stared at him, defying him to deny it.

"I know everyone calls us Capellans," Brother Felix explained, "but it's not truly so, you see. We—" He spread his arms. "—are the Capellans' servants. Just as you are."

"Don't give me that," said Tabitha.

Brother Felix smiled quietly. He bowed his great head with humility. The muscles of his neck were as thick as Tabitha's wrists.

"We are merely Guardians," he told her. "Caretakers for Capella. We keep the place tidy."

"Charon," said Tabitha.

"Yes. Well, the whole system, really."

"Go to hell," said Tabitha.

"Where do you come from, then?" Saskia enquired.

"We were humans," he declared. "The first of us

came from Earth." He lifted his eyes to the landscape, smiling placidly.

"But you were on the Moon," she objected. "Earth's Moon."

"Oh yes," said Brother Felix. "We were stationed there. Capella had been preparing for simply ages. Watching over the Earth, touring about secretly in little ships. Landing in isolated areas and recruiting suitable disciples." He beamed. "Everyone you see here was once just like you, Tabitha. Capella promoted us. What do you think of that?

"But I haven't introduced myself," he went on smoothly, before she could tell him what she thought. "My name is Brother Felix, and I have some marvelous news for you. All of you." He leaned towards them, wonders to confide. "You are all to be promoted too!"

"No thanks," said Tabitha.

"Oh, I know it's hard to take it in straight away," he said, paternal, protective. "I remember how confused I was!" He chuckled. "But why am I keeping you standing here? All I mean to say is: welcome one, welcome all. We're delighted to see you. We've prepared a small treat, in your honor." He reached down, like an adult holding out his hand to a little child. "Captain Jute?"

Tabitha was gripping her bag tightly. "Murderer," she said. "Shipwrecker. Thief."

Saskia was staring at her apprehensively. No one else was taking any notice at all.

"Why don't you kill me now and have done with it?" she yelled.

He held out his hand, smiling indulgently. "Come and have some luncheon," he said.

Saskia put her arm around Tabitha's shoulders. "Come on, Tabitha," she pleaded.

Tabitha resisted. "You don't believe all this, do you?" she said. "These creatures, this—"

Saskia frowned. "You don't *have* to believe it," she said. Saskia, Tabitha remembered, had lived her abbreviated childhood in an ambience and didn't expect things to be real, necessarily. "It's lovely so far," said Saskia. "Please don't spoil it."

Tabitha, her head throbbing, her insides churning, dropped her head and let herself be led along. There was nothing else to do.

Brother Felix ushered them through the trees, into an old ruined cloister of weathered stone, quite overgrown. Moss cushioned the gaps between the flagstones; on the walls, pious monuments hung by terracotta busts in shadowy niches. Through the arches they saw the river, curving beneath shaggy willows, set about with reeds, running like the cloister from nowhere to nowhere. A few sheep and antelopes were grazing on the bank, or standing, munching steadily, no fear in their mild eyes of the lofty men and women strolling or drifting silently by in twos and threes, silk parasols on their shoulders. Bluebirds circled overhead.

They came out of the cloister into a meadow. Here, groups of Guardians in robes of pastel and shining white stood beneath great patriarchal oaks, deep in philosophical discussion. There was a gleaming white bandstand, where a trio with lute and hautbois played melodiously to an attentive audience. Others sat sipping from golden goblets, their linen falling in decorous and sculptural folds, unstained by the perfect grass. All were dignified, nobly macrocephalic, three meters tall. Among them walked Vespan servants in dark blue tunics, silver circlets about their pudgy green brows, trays on their shoulders; on the trays, piles of exotic fruit, jugs of nectar and fine wines, and lemonade for the children who ran merrily about, playing catch and feeding biscuits to the deer.

"Tabitha. Come and sit down," said Brother Felix jovially, floating up to a red-and-white checked picnic cloth. "You'll feel better after some of this magnificent burgundy, I know."

"I'll feel better when I'm on a ship and heading away from here," she said. "Not before."

She stood there, looking at the spread. There was wine, red as rubies in its flagon of blown glass. There was a crusty cottage loaf, curls of yellow butter nestling in a damp green leaf, mounds of cheese and savory delicacies, and an earthenware dish of fine, juicy plums. Her stomach gurgled.

She had been feeling sick a minute ago; now, she realized, she was ravenous.

Saskia was already on her knees, investigating the smoked salmon.

"Xtasca," said Brother Felix, grandly. "What can I offer you as refreshment after the rigors of your journey?"

"We do not eat or drink," said the Cherub distantly. "Your magnified sunlight will be perfectly sufficient." And it settled its saucer in the grass and lay back, with a small sigh, on its elbows.

"Captain Jute," said Brother Felix. "Tabitha. Oh, please do sit down."

"Sit down, Tabitha," echoed Saskia plaintively, and with her mouth full.

"You've come such a long way," the Guardian continued, "and it's such a pleasure to see you here, safe and sound. Will you not take a glass of wine with us?"

Tabitha looked at the beaming giant.

He gestured with a finger. A brimming goblet rose lightly from the ground and hovered before her.

She looked at it.

She put out her hand and took it.

65

"I must apologize for Kybernator Perlmutter," said Brother Felix as they set about the picnic. "He can be rather single-minded, I know. He takes our work terribly seriously."

Tabitha looked around at the grave and elegant figures taking the air on Charon in the eternal afternoon. From the white bandstand music lingered wistfully on the air. Elsewhere, a philosophical group stood around a sundial, debating the nature of time.

"It doesn't look much like work to me," said Tabitha, rudely.

"Our tasks are numerous and very varied," explained their host, unoffended. "One of the many, many services we are honored to perform for the Capellans is collecting those marvelous old ships of Sanczau's."

"How many are there?" asked Saskia, biting into a scarlet tomato.

"A number," said Brother Felix, deprecatingly. "Not a large number." He smoothed his kilt across his knees.

"It's taking you a while to find them," said Tabitha.

Brother Felix raised his notable eyebrows. "Oh, we know where they all are. We've always known where they all were. Every minute. No, you misunderstand me," he said, leaning forward to spear a smoked oyster. "It's not a chore. Nothing here is a chore. As you see." He smiled gently around the gathering. "It's something of a game, really," he confessed. "The odds against any of the remaining ships getting anywhere near a drive are—astronomical!" He chortled at his own joke. "There aren't any left here, you see. We took them all away."

With a slight gesture he indicated a hundred trillion square kilometers of sequestered space; nine worlds, forty-five moons, three hundred and seventy-one developed asteroids, a few hundred miscellaneous habitats, including tubes, platforms, wheels, ziggurats and mistakes, sundry sheds, autonomic labs, hangars and semi-habitables. He knew them all, and everything on them. He blessed them all.

Brother Felix popped his oyster into his rubicund mouth. "Not even those chaps on Titan have got the hardware," he continued. "That's why they've been pouring everything into locating a Frasque. Pretty hopeless, really. But you, Tabitha—" He reached out and laid an avuncular hand on her wrist. "You were a real contender."

Arm in arm, a pair of identical statuesque young women came strolling along the path. They wore white togas, broad leather belts with pouches, wreaths of vine-leaves. Brother Felix hailed them. "Sister Veronica! Sister Marjorie! Come and join us."

"Greetings, Brother Felix," called one of them, musically, as they approached across the lawn.

"Are these your new protégées?" asked the other.

They smiled the benign Guardian smile at all and sundry, and, introductions made, sat down cross-legged; hovering gently beside Brother Felix, just above the ground.

"So you're the ones who actually winkled out the last Frasque," said Sister Marjorie admiringly, helping herself to a silver of salmon.

"I was just telling our new friends about our little game," said Brother Felix, becoming even more jolly, if that were possible. He set his beringed hands on his knees and rocked backwards in the air.

Sister Veronica lifted her hand to Tabitha in a gesture of polite admiration. "The *Alice Liddell* was a great contender," she said.

"There you are, what did I tell you," said Brother Felix. Still leaning back, he unbuttoned his sporran and slipped out the plaque. "Here she is," he said, holding it aloft by one corner. "Alice herself, all in one piece."

"Oh, do let me see," said Sister Marjorie.

"Give me that," said Tabitha in a low voice, rising up and reaching across the cloth. She reached so far, then found she could reach no further.

"It's no use to you now, dear," Brother Felix pointed out, handing the plaque to Sister Marjorie. "When you're promoted, you'll be too busy to fly spaceships!"

"That's right, Tabitha," said Sister Veronica in a congratulatory tone, as Tabitha subsided into her place. "You won't have to drive a barge any more."

"You're going to be one of us!" smiled Sister Marjorie.

"I'd rather be a Perk," said Tabitha viciously.

The three Guardians thought this a great joke. They laughed heartily.

"How is it played," asked Xtasca. "This game?"

"Well," said Sister Veronica, "it's hardly even a game."

"A diversion. A pastime," said Sister Marjorie.

"We take *bets*," said Brother Felix, as though this were a very shocking thing to admit.

"We dare one another to let it go on, whatever it is," said Sister Veronica.

"To see who'll be the last to lose their nerve," said Sister Marjorie, "and intervene."

The sisters looked at Brother Felix.

Brother Felix looked sheepish, and rather amused with himself. "I lost," he said.

The sisters laughed, prettily.

"They were doing very well," said Brother Felix to them in self-defense. He numbered the credentials on his fingers. "An old queen Frasque coming out of the woodwork after all this time."

"Nobody knew she was there," Sister Veronica pointed out.

"And next minute there she was, on an adapted Sanczau Kobold," Brother Felix went on, emphatically.

"—with a *Cherub* on board!" concluded Sister Marjorie, marveling at the inexhaustible inventiveness of the universe.

The Guardians all looked politely at Xtasca, as if complimenting it on a feat of marvelous adroitness.

"Absolutely extraordinary coincidence," proclaimed Brother Felix, while big heads nodded around the picnic cloth. "What can we say? Pity about the hardware!"

The Guardians all laughed again, merrily.

Brother Felix turned as he sat, lifting his broad, bland face to the unaccountable sun and surveying the gardens, the children, the collocutors, the musicians, the anglers and fliers of kites. The day was forever warm; not a hint of chill to remind them that they inhabited a bubble of benevolent improbability, balanced atop the frozen atmosphere of Pluto's moon. Only beyond the microclimate, at the edge of the greensward, could be glimpsed the black realm of infernal, eternal cold.

Sister Veronica leaned towards Tabitha, the rings on her white hand flashing in the sunlight. "*Some* people were convinced you must know something we don't," she hinted, confidingly.

Before Tabitha could reply, Sister Marjorie reached out and patted her consolingly on the arm. It was infuriating, the way they all pawed you about here. "Oh, don't worry," Sister Marjorie said, "we know you don't *know* anything."

"You didn't have the first idea what was happening, did you?" said Brother Felix. "You were only doing your job."

Tabitha clenched her teeth, said nothing.

"No, Tabitha, you're not in trouble," he went on.

"We promise," chorused the sisters.

"I told her," said Brother Felix, "she's done very well. Capella has authorized your promotion," he said again, addressing them all.

Saskia looked downcast. She twirled a watercress stem sadly between finger and thumb. She asked them, "Can you bring dead people back?"

There was the smallest pause.

"Oh my dear," said Sister Veronica sadly.

"Your poor dear brother," said Sister Marjorie, shaking her leafy head. The sisters gazed lovingly, sorrowfully, each at her mirror image.

"Poor child," murmured Brother Felix. "Have some, some more wine," he said, thickly, then turned away and blew his nose.

Saskia looked from face to enormous face.

Tabitha reached across the cloth and took her hand. Silently, Xtasca hovered closer.

"Well, what about Marco, then?" said Saskia. "Marco Metz. We had to leave him on Venus. Are you going to promote him too?"

Brother Felix looked considerate, the veins pulsing again at his temples. "Now Marco Metz is rather a naughty boy, isn't he," he said reflectively. "I rather think," he said, "Venus may be the best place for him," and he gestured for another piece of bread.

Saskia sat up, digging her knuckles into the yielding earth. "But it'll kill him!" she protested, as the loaf obediently sliced itself on to Brother Felix's plate.

"Not if he's careful," he said. "It can be quite jolly, you know, being a castaway."

"Especially with a broken leg," said Tabitha sourly.

Brother Felix gestured vaguely with the butter knife. "One overcomes the considerations of the body," he said, taking a large mouthful of bread and chewing. "Comes—to terms—'th ones'lf . . ."

"Communing with nature," said Sister Veronica.

"Away from the hurly-burly of the system," agreed her sister.

Brother Felix swallowed mightily. "We may yet see a reformed Marco Metz!" he said brightly. He topped the remains of his bread with a chunk of Wensleydale, securing it in the butter with a firm prod of one large forefinger. "Don't you think?" He really sounded as if he wanted to hear their opinions.

Tabitha exhaled savagely and flopped back on her elbows. She twisted her fingers in the grass, plucked it vigorously. For every tuft she pulled, new shoots appeared promptly, thrusting up from the soil. Noticing this, Xtasca unobtrusively pressed the tip of its tail into the ground and began to take some readings.

"I think he'll be dead if someone doesn't do something quickly," said Saskia balefully.

"Then we shall, my dear," said Sister Veronica. "Directly after luncheon."

"We must free your mind of all worries," said Sister Marjorie.

The sisters nodded and smiled blissfully at one another.

Tabitha wanted to bang their great heads together. She wanted to run mad with a big gun. She wanted go back to the *Alice* and sit in her ruined cockpit and howl. She wanted to lie down in the sun with her head on her bag and go to sleep and never wake up. Resentfully, she picked a crusty bit off the loaf. "What do you lot know about freedom?" she said.

As one the sisters turned and smiled lovingly at her.

Sister Marjorie spread her hands to indicate the whole company of promoted humans at leisure all around; and the trees, and the flowers, and the bluebirds.

"Look around you, Tabitha," said Sister Veronica.

Tabitha took a large swallow of her wine and rested her chin on her fist, scanning the scene indifferently.

"Not bad for the top of the shitheap," she said.

But it was impossible to disconcert these people.

"Freedom is power," said Xtasca bluntly.

"I think," said Saskia, who was rolling up the sleeves and the legs of her pyjamas, "you can't really be free *outside* until you're free *inside*. If you see what I mean." She stretched her right arm out in front of her, looking along it critically, and turning it this way and that in the amplified sunlight.

"You should listen to your friends, Tabitha," said Brother Felix approvingly.

"Soon, when you are one of us, you will understand, Tabitha," affirmed Sister Marjorie earnestly. "Here everything is beautiful and everyone is perfectly free. Who commands or prohibits us? Where are our oppressors?"

"On Capella," Tabitha said. "According to Brother Felix."

The trio looked sincerely perplexed. "Capella?" said Sister Veronica. "But Tabitha, it's Capella that has given us this freedom!"

"Just think of it," Brother Felix urged. "Here we are on Charon, at the very outer limit of our solar system. And the sun is glorious!"

"Where would we be now without the liberating power of Capella?" said Sister Marjorie.

"Still on the poor old Moon," chimed in Sister Veronica, "arguing whether we could afford to go to Mars!"

But Tabitha had had enough. "Is that what you think?" she said. "I'll tell you what I think, shall I? I'll tell you about the liberating power of Capella. About being shanghaied and dragged out here by you and your bloody game." She paused and took a drink, relishing the tiny pleasure of making them wait for her, especially since she had no idea what she was going to say next. "I'll tell you what I think," she said again, and hearing herself, realized the wine was pretty good and she had already drunk quite a bit of it. "There isn't any freedom," she said, softly derisive. "You're always in somebody else's garden." That sounded all right, for a start. She waved a hand, clumsily. "You can't be free when someone's telling you where you can go and where you can't." She took another mouthful of wine. "When I was a kid," she told them, "Mars was the frontier. I was born," she said, looking hard at Sister Veronica, "on the poor old Moon."

Sister Veronica didn't react.

"Someone has to be," said Tabitha.

Sister Veronica smiled politely.

"It wasn't any fun," said Tabitha. "Since you ask. Anyway, then Mars was all parceled up, and everyone wanted to move out to the belt. Then it was Saturn, the ring development. Where is it now? Is this it? Is this the frontier? Or is this the garden wall?"

The custodians of the solar system were watching her

calmly, as if she were reciting a poem, something she'd learned by heart, something rehearsed and remote. Saskia and Xtasca had been paying close attention. Saskia shuffled round to sit beside her and hold her hand.

But Tabitha didn't want her hand held. "There isn't any freedom," she said again. "Not while someone else is hanging on to the power. So you're right, Felix. We are all servants." The melancholy wisdom of this observation made her nod, sadly. "I'll tell you, I reckon I was as free as I'll ever be back before this all started." She laughed shortly. "Trucking the trade lanes in a quirky old Kobold, hauling machine parts from Santiago Celestina to Callisto, grubbing along one deposit ahead of the bills and wondering where you're going to berth next, where your next job is coming from. That's about as much freedom as you can have," she said savagely, "in this system."

Brother Felix rose up a little further into the air. At once Saskia put her arm about Tabitha as if she thought he was going to strike her. But he said understandingly, "You're still upset about your ship, aren't you. It's thoughtless of me, I do apologize. Let's see if we can put your mind at rest."

He set off back across the meadow, Tabitha, Saskia and Xtasca following, the sisters staying where they were, smiling, perpetually smiling. In the cloister a couple of Guardians paused in their debate on the possibility of novelty to greet the women and the Cherub as they hurried by. Brother Felix was some way ahead. They didn't catch up with him until he was already beyond the screen of trees, in the secluded corner where the wreck of the Kobold stood next to the vacant shuttle.

He beckoned them over. "Look," he called to Xtasca. "You'll like this." He twisted a ring.

The remains of the *Alice Liddell* began to glow. She became luminous, irradiated, as if the light were somehow within her—not just onboard illumination shining out through her shattered portholes; but as if the very energy still informing the bruised molecules of her substance were being invoked, called to rise up as light and come out to dance in the sunshine.

For a moment she sat there, poised, as if for take-off, in a blaze that flared off the windows of the shuttle. Tabitha cried out, shading her eyes, for it appeared in that instant that she was looking not at a smashed and crumpled wreck, but at the Kobold as she once was, at her inauguration. Thus she must have appeared, fresh from the Bergen yard, at that half-comic, half-mystic rite when a ship's drive is first "mated" with a mint-new persona, and the calligrapher drone rolls up to paint the characters of her name in bold metallic blue around the bow. So they saw her now, the *Alice Liddell,* fresh and whole and transfigured. Her dents and gashes closed and filled. Restored, her viewport gleamed; her scanners stirred as they scented the wind from the sun. Her lines were clear and true, her little wings drawn firmly back as she contemplated the work for which she had been made and prepared to go to it. A wave of heat rippled the air about her jets; she turned, as if seeking her mistress; she seemed to lift, almost.

And then she was gone. Disintegrated.

The air bucked with sudden turbulence, rushing from all sides into the empty space where the ship had been. Saskia's hair blew across her face. Tabitha leapt forward, shouting wildly.

A last dazzle left the air, and the *Alice Liddell* was no more. The grass where she had stood was neither burnt nor stained. It quivered, and was still.

"There now," said Brother Felix. "That's better, isn't it?"

And then the sun went in.

An immense elliptical shadow flowed like a wave across the gardens.

Everywhere, everyone stopped what they were doing. They stopped talking, and stared up into the darkening sky. The band faltered and fell silent. The atmosphere rumbled and crackled, as if from some overspill of the energies that had destroyed Tabitha's ship. It was very cold suddenly.

"Oh, no," grumbled Saskia, clutching the neck of her thin pyjamas. "Now it's going to rain."

"No, Saskia," said Xtasca.

Tabitha was just standing there with her head thrown back, her hands on her hips, her mouth wide open.

"That's not a cloud," Xtasca said.

66

A heavily distorted voice came booming down from on high.

"SZZAZZKIA? XSSTAZZCA? ARE YOU DOWO-WOWN THERE? WHERE ARE THE BOYOYZZ?"

"Hannah?" shouted Saskia. She grabbed Xtasca's hand. "Is that Hannah?"

Brother Felix threw up his hands. "Good gracious me, whatever is—"

"It's Plenty!" Saskia shouted over the thunderous sound that doubled and redoubled as the dark shape came swiftly closer. She laughed and whooped, her hair flapping in the rising wind. "She brought the whole thing!"

Like a flying mountain the celestial tortoiseshell drew overhead, blotting out the miraculous sky. The trees thrashed and the birds and animals fled for cover, crying out in terror.

From all sides the Guardians were congregating, racing across the top of the grass.

A great silver eye opened on the hilly underside of the vast installation, and a beam of light stabbed down into the gloomy field, raking erratically across and back.

Saskia, still holding Xtasca's hand, made a dash toward the light. As she ran, towing the Cherub through the air, she looked back over her shoulder.

"Tabitha!" she shouted. "Tabitha!"

But Tabitha was running away, in the opposite direction. And Brother Felix was hesitating, calling after her.

Saskia stopped on the instant and let go Xtasca's hand. The Cherub went whizzing past, cut a tight circle in the air and came back. It swooped down and grabbed Saskia by the arm.

Left and right, Guardians were closing in.

Brother Felix was running after Tabitha.

Saskia shouted, struggled in the pinch of Xtasca's grip.

As if Hannah had just mastered the controls, the beam of silver light scythed straight across the lawn and struck them, spot on.

"HANNGG ONNN!" roared the deafening voice.

And with Guardians clambering over one another to get into the air, the Cherub and the acrobat were swept abruptly up and away.

Tabitha didn't see them go. She was running back into the trees, dodging the Guardians flocking in the other direction.

"*Tabitha!*" she heard Saskia screaming. "*You missed Tabitha!*"

She tore through the cloister, Brother Felix close behind. He was shouting her name like an enraged sergeant pursuing an errant cadet. He blundered into the confined space, moving jerkily, bouncing off the walls as if he were losing control of his limbs.

There were others, coming the other way.

Tabitha stood braced, legs apart, in the middle of the cloister, looking forward and back.

Then, just as they were upon her, she clutched her bag to her and leapt to the side, grabbed hold of the pillar of an arch and swung straight out over the sill.

Behind came the sound of an almighty collision of bodies.

Tabitha ran headlong into the windy thicket, ducking under branches, squeezing through bushes where the Guardians couldn't follow. She ran around the ruin, bounded a ditch of bracken and burst out into the open. There was the red and white cloth; there was one of the sisters. The other was further up the meadow, almost rounding the end of the line of beeches. Sister Marjorie was the one with her plaque.

Which one was Sister Marjorie?

At this distance, she had no idea. And no time to guess wrong. The trees were threshing harder, all across the meadow. The mountainous invader was still coming down, as if Hannah meant to crush the whole bubble flat.

Tabitha filled her lungs and bellowed, "*Alice! Alice Liddell!*"

The Guardian by the trees stopped, looked around.

She saw Tabitha and looked straight past her at her sister. Whose hand flew to her pouch.

Cursing their gravity, Tabitha ran towards the abandoned picnic, seeing Sister Veronica start back towards her.

Overhead there was a tiny, shrill noise, as of a great many birds squealing a long way up in the air.

Tabitha glanced up. A black cloud had blossomed out from the belly of the descending habitat, a mass of little black particles: gas, shrapnel, leaflets, insects, thought Tabitha as she ran. She saw some drifting swiftly down ahead, over the flowerbeds.

Perks!

Hannah was sending in the Perks, more Perks than Tabitha had ever seen in one place before, or had wished to see anywhere. Families of lithe, spiky Perks in overalls, armed to the teeth, their feathers bristling as they came tumbling energetically out of the sky. "Chee! Chee-chee-chee-chee!" Perks crashing into trees, skidding down the roof of the bandstand, splashing into the water. They got up and trampled through the flowers, scampering immediately to attack everyone they could see.

There was nothing Perks liked as much as a good fight.

In a trice there were Perks everywhere, running all over the gardens, pulling down Guardian and Eladeldi alike and overwhelming them. In vain the hypertrophied humans tugged and screwed at their rings: the power shadow of the hijacked habitat had eclipsed them.

Tabitha vaulted the cloth and grabbed Sister Marjorie by the front of her toga. "Give her to me!" she yelled in her huge face.

Sister Marjorie's eyes rolled madly. Her glossy lips drew back from her teeth.

"Where is she?" shouted Tabitha. She snatched at her pouch. Keening, Sister Marjorie swung about, loose-limbed, slapping and pulling at her hands.

Tabitha had her hands on the flap, had the pouch undone.

There was a crash behind her and a bare forearm reached down and locked itself under her chin, pulling her backwards.

Choking, Tabitha felt Sister Marjorie pull out of her hands. She clawed at the arm, battering Sister Veronica with her elbows. She twisted against the grip, almost tearing her ear off. Behind Sister Veronica she saw Brother Felix, emerging unsteadily from the trees. He had lost his ivy wreath.

Sister Veronica caught hold of Tabitha's right arm and tried to bend it the wrong way at the shoulder. Tabitha leaned right, sagging at the knees, pulling the floating Guardian off balance.

There was another crash. A Perk had fallen smack in the middle of the picnic, landing in a great splash of burgundy and breadcrumbs and broken glass. He leapt up, shaking himself and chirruping wildly, and swung a length of chain at Sister Veronica.

Sister Veronica howled and let go of Tabitha, turning clumsily to fight off the Perk.

The tractor beam that had dropped the Perk was lingering. Hannah had located Tabitha.

Tabitha whirled around, seeking Sister Marjorie.

With tiny, tripping steps Sister Marjorie was running away.

There was another Perk running to intercept her.

And Brother Felix was bearing down on Tabitha at top speed, his eyes unfocused and bulging, his fat white fingers clawing for the one that hadn't got away. The thick veins at his temples bulged and writhed as if they had a life of their own.

As Brother Felix reached for Tabitha he made a terrible ripping noise.

His head came open.

His beautiful, shining skin tore straight across his forehead, and his skull cracked apart like an egg. Colorless ichor splashed out in all directions.

Brother Felix halted in his rush, barging sideways into the embattled Sister Veronica, reeling, groping at the air like a drowning man. The expression on his face, that mad glare, was unchanged. Goo slopped into his eyes.

Tabitha drew back, convulsing in fright, gagging, pressing the back of her hand against her mouth.

Inside Brother Felix's skull, something was moving.

It was something long and soft, something segmented and purplish-grey, glistening from the slime of its nest. Its nest was a torn, blackened lacework that was all that was left of Brother Felix's brain.

The thing that had been chewing it for so many years now rose up and began to shriek.

It was a giant caterpillar. It was half a meter long.

It was the first Capellan Tabitha had ever seen.

She spun away, spewing bile and burgundy on the darkened grass.

Two meters off, the tractor beam waited for her, shining steadily. Evidently Hannah was unwilling or unable to fish for her in this melee.

Everywhere the rest of the Guardians stood or sat or crouched like statues, abandoning one by one their unequal struggles with the Perks while their swollen heads split open like ripe pupae. Amid the putrid pulp of mouldering brains the Capellans sat up. Their blunt heads spun round and round, nosing the air. They shrieked and shrieked.

Coughing and spluttering, Tabitha lunged for a weapon. Her hand closed on the pickle fork. As she grabbed it the Perk struck Sister Veronica in the back with his fist, and she arced forward and fell out of the air, pawing at the ruined picnic.

Her forehead cracked open, sticky juices spilling out from beneath her garland of vineleaves. The top of her head fell off, ripped open from the inside. The lost lid rolled amid the crockery.

A Capellan popped wetly out of Sister Veronica's head and landed wriggling among the cheese and taramosalata.

"Cheee!" said the Perk.

He grinned, and lifted his fist.

A switchblade clicked neatly out of it.

Tabitha staggered to her feet, clutching her bag to her and brandishing her fork. Sister Marjorie was still standing where she'd last seen her, clutching her head. Her Capellan was rearing out and squealing with rage. The Perk was lying motionless at her feet.

Tabitha raced across the grass towards her.

At once the tractor beam swooped for her.

"Not yet! No!"

Tabitha leapt clear, glared frantically up at the Frasque monstrosity that Hannah Soo had brought screaming to the rescue, láncing through hyperspace at a speed no human had ever commanded. She shook her head furiously, crossed her arms above her face and vigorously uncrossed them, twice.

The beam went out.

"Oh, *shit*!"

Furious, desperate, she flung herself at the looming Sister Marjorie, snatching at her pouch. The Capellan above her squealed louder and louder. In rage it lunged at her, whipping down at her head. She ducked, stabbed it and lost the fork, wrested from her slippery hands. While the Capellan wagged madly from side to side Tabitha thrust her hand up under the flap and into the pouch. Sister Marjorie's vague, blind hands fumbled at her face. The Capellan snapped down again, drool dripping off its palps on to her shoulder. She dodged it again, and jumped back out of range, her prize in her hand.

There were Perks all over the picnic, all over the remains of Sister Veronica and Brother Felix, skewering the things that had oozed out of them. Tabitha yelled and screamed, pointed to the one slithering wetly down

Sister Marjorie's collar, and the Perks leapt, shrilling.

Now there were just Perks, Perks everywhere.

And no beam.

Tabitha looked up. Plenty was parked in GSO, hanging there dark and silent. Tiny flashes here and there betrayed some kind of wild activity on board.

Tabitha didn't wait to conjecture.

There was one chance.

Back she ran through the trees.

Luck was with her. The Eladeldi had been slaughtered before they could get back to their posts. And the promoted had all been too busy to fly a spaceship. They lay all around the field, some of them still busy, struggling, most of them quite motionless or writhing slowly and vaguely on the ground while Perks chopped up their promoters.

Tabitha scrambled for the shuttle, hit the canopy release and jumped into the web. It was a modified Tinkerbell, wasn't it? Just a modified Tinkerbell. Surely. So even though all the labels were in Eladeldi, *that* had to be the panic button.

Didn't it?

She gritted her teeth and punched it.

All the lights on the board flared red. The jets began to whine.

Tabitha cried out with joy and relief. She realized she was still clutching Alice in her hand, kissed her and stuffed her in her bag. Then she lay back panting in the web and let it hug her.

67

Plenty was in quite a mess.

I know Plenty was already a mess, and still is, for that matter; but there are sorts and degrees, even of mess, and then it was pandemonium. The lifts had seized up, the plumbing had overheated. The com system envelope had snapped, leaving it oscillating like broken elastic, scratching randomly through archives, satellite AV broadcasts, muzak, its own surveillance monitors, and obscure Palestinian gameshows. The police were down, their whole system pulled out from under them. Cyborg units were blind and deaf at their posts, crippled by dead servos, schizoid in the datastorm. There they stood, their visors strobing, unable to take a single decision. Blood ran from their ears, tears from their eyes.

Seeing their dream come true, evangelical survivalists had organized cadres of stranded tourists and armed them with gear from looted arms boutiques. Roped together with lengths of livid orange rope they scaled the balconies of the hotel quarter and skirmished with the Thrant sex kittens in the Yoshiwara caves. Drunks were shooting each other in the casinos. People were dying. There was nothing anyone could do. Hannah Soo was counting herself lucky to have got there in one piece, kicking a drive like that the first time out after years of gathering dust. She was trying to keep her head amid all the functions you have to juggle, skipping: transposing n-dimensional matrices and offlaying probability and generating multiplex paradigm redundancies in that perverse and gnarly branch of mathematics the Frasque call "language."

You could do it. You could, given plenty of space and time.

Tabitha brought the Eladeldi shuttle in with emergency klaxons blazing on all wavelengths, and nothing but garbage from traffic control. The ship bays looked as though a hurricane had visited them and stayed for a while, flinging broken machinery and debris through the windows of the ships, and then flinging the ships about. One level looked particularly deserted, a shelf swept of occupants and craft by a giant hand. Shedding velocity and rubber, Tabitha threw herself into it.

The lift was out. Tabitha ran for the stairs.

"Hannah?" she kept calling.

The com chattered, wept, whistled, screeched.

On the lower levels the corridors were full of scented foam and scattered furniture. Maddened visitors were looting the malls, filling their holdalls with aftershave, cyberporn and tubes. Security drones, their central processors creamed, bounced back and forth across the roadway, thudding dully against the walls. Two men and a woman yelled at Tabitha as she appeared. Laughing they circled her, their arms outstretched. Tabitha booted one of the men in the groin and raced on, sobbing for breath.

It had been a savage skip. She saw fall-out everywhere. All the flora on board had come back doubled. There were briars tangled around the gantries and fungus sprouting between the treads of the travelators. Fissures had opened in the walls and floors, trapping cars and people.

Other transmogrifications, as I found out later, had been positively benign. The tapes show the only resident manager barricading herself in a boardroom, no trace of which has ever been found.

Tabitha was lost. She stood in a lift bay, not knowing whether to head up or down or sideways. "Now what, Hannah?" she shouted, hammering on the spluttering directory.

She was almost about to choose a direction at random when she noticed the lift pod indicators were alight. A string of illuminated green triangles was slipping regularly by from door to door. As she watched, Tabitha became convinced it was beckoning her. The second she moved towards the right lift, the door sprang open for her and the pod lights went on.

Tabitha ran in. At once, before she could even look at the controls, the door slid to and the pod began to plunge through the tunnels. Stations slid silently by, dark or flickering with firelight. Faces and hands crowded the windows, begging for admittance. Hannah was overriding all their calls, giving Tabitha priority.

The pod stopped in the air, suspended from a long arc of track above an apron of hexagonal paving stones. Tabitha slipped out of it and jumped down.

She was in a car park. There were three cop skimmers there, parked at violent angles. Their screamers were going, their lights flashing, but all the response units sat inside, immobilized, unable to open a door.

Above loomed the green dome of JustSleep. Tabitha made for the door, pushing between the stricken visitors congregated around the entrance. There was something keeping them out, some sort of shield.

A blazing green fatuus sprang up as her feet hit the steps. ''This way, Captain Jute,'' it cried, in a voice like a tortured spring. The shield parted with a zipping noise, and reclosed behind her.

The atrium was empty but for equipment strewn about, and a stray spaniel investigating the contents of an abandoned body bag. It looked up in terror as the green fire came by and fled, yelping.

There was a high, singing noise in the air, the noise of a lot of things going wrong at the same time. Tabitha pounded along the tunnel and came face to face with a company of Frasque.

They were smaller than either of the ones she had met, and filled the air with a powerful waxy odor. They were milling around expectantly, folding and unfolding their limbs.

They ignored the fatuus as it shot straight through the middle of them.

Her heart in her mouth, Tabitha put her head down and followed.

They let her through, fizzing with disturbance and whistling plaintively to one another.

Males. Males with no one in command.

The flambeaux were out in the paneled hallway. There were bodies on the floor. Some wore orthopaedic shifts and had obviously been dead for a long time. Some were cops, lying on their backs like monstrous cockroaches, their limbs still twitching feebly. There was another party of Frasque, working in the shadows. Operating on some confused, insectile impulse, they were cocooning a stricken cop from head to toe in furry white filaments.

Tabitha screwed up her eyes and pushed by. Twiggy hands snatched at her. In the tunnel ahead the green fire flickered and vanished.

"Saskia!" she called. "Xtasca!"

"Tabitha! In here!"

With a shove of her foot she pulled free from the whispering Frasque and ran towards the voices.

Saskia and Xtasca were in the chamber with Hannah, sitting on the sarcophagus. Xtasca had its tail plugged in, helping Hannah penetrate some of the more devious passages in the Frasque operating system. *"No, no,"* Hannah was saying. *"I'm losing it. There. I told you. You mustn't rush me, lover."*

Saskia jumped up and embraced Tabitha. "They found you! I knew they would."

"Are you okay?" Tabitha asked.

Saskia looked febrile with exhaustion. Her hair was lank, her pyjamas torn. Over them she had pulled on a crocheted woollen waistcoat of checkered red and mauve squares, and a stained black evening jacket, with tails. "I'm fine," she said, with a strained smile. "You look awful. And, faugh, you smell!"

Tabitha looked down at herself. She tried to wipe a large splash of dead Capellan off her jacket. It stuck to her fingers. "It got worse," she said dully. She didn't want to think about it. She turned to the motionless figure in her bed of frost. "Hannah," she said, "we're win—"

The blood drained from her face. Her ears were pounding. After all the horrors she had just seen, there were more.

"Jesus . . ." she whispered.

She had caught sight of the cavern of freezers below the window. She almost wished Hannah hadn't switched off the Meadow.

The scene down there was of a glacial hell worthy of the imagination of some ancient Terran. In flight, whole sections of the walls had fallen away, revealing the broken honeycomb of cryocells where the Frasque army had lain, in suspended animation, hidden from everyone and everything.

Many of them were still there. Tabitha could see them lying curled up inside the walls, white and cobwebbed, rotted away in their cells. Beneath them flaked tiles lay heaped against the wall like a drift of dragon scales.

Many of the ones who had woken were still occupying the cavern floor, aimlessly and brainlessly battering each other and themselves. They were nearly all males, with no more sense than a cargo drone. They were soldier Frasque, bred to be an invasion force, and they had gone to sleep knowing nothing but that when they woke up it would be time for battle.

They had torn open all the freezers and made havoc with what they found in them.

There was blood everywhere, a miasma of blood and icy slush and coolant vaporized by an exploding circulator. The Frasque were skittering about, trampling in a slough of human detritus, crashing into one another at full tilt, ramming one another into any convenient obstacle, crushing one another into the muck on the floor. There were marshals, smaller females, splashing around at speed chivvying and biting them, but they were lost without their queen. Curiously like the malfunctioning cops, they could not even find their way out of the chamber without a specific signal from the royal pheromones.

Some Frasque, without even a marshal or a berserker imperative, were standing still as shattered trees in the midst of the carnage, recognizing nothing. Others of a higher degree of volition had climbed up to the ceiling in panic, and hung there in clusters, stridulating. Deeply regressed, they could do nothing but hum over and over again the mantric grammars of revivification, like insects learning to pray. Dripping with cushion fluid and the foul liquors of their own discontent, they hung head down, a scant three meters from the plexiglass blister where Tabitha stood staring out in horror.

"*It's a good job you took out the queen,*" said Hannah's voicebox distinctly.

Tabitha couldn't speak.

"*I've locked them in,*" Hannah continued, "*and they can stay locked in until they've all killed each other.*" She was sounding much brighter, younger, more aggressive. "*You're Tabitha Jute,*" she said. "*Hi, I don't believe we've been introduced. Hannah Soo.*"

"Hi," said Tabitha to her frozen savior. "You, you've done all right." She had gone numb. She couldn't think of anything to say. "Are you all right?" she said.

"*My condition is stable,*" said Hannah drily. "*You and I are going to have to have a long talk some time. I think we have a lot of things to tell each other.*"

"Yes," said Tabitha, blankly. "Right."

She knew in theory it would make a considerable difference to the rights and wrongs of all this if she could discover whether Hannah Soo really had known anything about Sanczau's Kobolds or not.

Just now, though, none of that seemed to mean anything. Nothing meant anything compared with the battle on Charon, the ruin in the cavern below.

All that had been another universe.

"Thank you," she said awkwardly. "I—I don't know—I can't—thanks, thanks for the Perks," she said.

Saskia was hugging her anxiously.

Tabitha pulled away and ran out into the corridor.

Saskia followed, found her leaning on the wall, bent double, retching drily. The Frasque were inching their way towards her. Saskia shouted at them and they halted, hissing and flailing their limbs.

"Come on," said Saskia quietly, leaning over Tabitha

and laying a gentle hand on her arm. "We'll find you somewhere to lie down."

Tabitha was straightening up, still holding on to the wall, still clinging to a shred of resolve. "No," she panted, "no, I've got to, got to give . . ."

She took Saskia's hand and drew her back into the chamber.

The Cherub crouched on the dead woman, looking up with its red eyes as they came back in, like a ghoul disturbed at feeding.

Not privy to this lurid impression, Hannah said, *"Tabitha, Xtasca tells me you're a pilot."*

Tabitha nodded.

"She can't see you," said Xtasca.

"Yes," said Tabitha. "That was my ship—" She broke off, unable to continue.

Saskia helped her to a seat.

"Have we been through all this before?" asked Hannah, sensing something wrong.

Tabitha said, "Doesn't matter."

"Only, lover," said Hannah Soo, *"excuse me, but would you drive? I don't think I can hold it together much longer. I'm going crazy in here."* Her voicebox gave a nervous laugh.

Saskia looked into Tabitha's face with joyful apprehension.

Tabitha felt as if somebody had unhooked the whole solar system like a mobile from a high ceiling and dumped it in her lap. Frasque, Capellans, Eladeldi; Perks and humans, Plenty and everyone who had any claim on anything aboard it; people tearing each other limb from limb; Perks on Charon; people dying on Venus. She wanted to scream. *Why me?*

"I'm half dead, Hannah," Tabitha said, regretting her phrase at once. She shook her head. "I can't even see straight. Later I'll—later—" She pulled her bag on to her lap and parted the broken zip, reaching inside. "Here," she said, handing it to Saskia. "Alice."

"Ah," said Xtasca, unplugging its tail and moving aside.

Hannah asked, *"Who's Alice?"*

"Alice knows all there is to know about the Frasque stardrive," said Tabitha.

"Oh, my goodness," said Hannah in audible relief. *"Where, where is she?"*

"She's coming," said Tabitha. She gestured exhaustedly to Saskia.

Saskia went to the tape slot where Marco had inserted his Frasque tape, and fed the plaque in.

The machinery whirred briefly. A green light came on.

"Alice?" said Tabitha, to the room at large. "Alice, can you hear me?"

"HELLO, CAPTAIN," said Alice.

"Alice, I want you to meet Hannah Soo."

"HELLO, HANNAH. WHAT A PALACE! WHERE ARE WE?"

"Welcome to Plenty, Alice."

"IS THIS PLENTY? SO IT IS! IS IT YOURS?"

"It seems it is, Alice. Only it's way too big for me. You see that down there?"

"CHARON," said Alice, without hesitation. "WE'RE RATHER CLOSE, YOU KNOW, HANNAH."

"Alice, sweetheart, I think I'm just going to drop the whole shebang unless somebody takes the controls. Tabitha says maybe you could do that for us, is that right?"

"I DON'T KNOW, HANNAH," Alice said. "I'M NOT SURE I KNOW HOW."

"Alice!" cried Tabitha. "You can't have forgotten! You can't!"

"She can," said Xtasca moderately.

"The password," Saskia reminded her, urgently.

"Oh, oh god. Alice? Alice, listen. It's a long lane that has no turning."

The green light flickered. The plaque reader whirred, hummed, stopped.

I opened my eyes.

Cold black space yawned around me in all directions. I saw it grained and fretted with gold, like strands of finest cobweb. I saw the steady sparkling wake of *The*

Citadel; the turbulence fractures, like veins of gold in
black ice, where Tabitha had come roaring up from the
moon in the shuttle now cooling in my parking bay.
Where I hung, on the very brink of a solar system, I
could see the seams of the dimensions threading down,
down, all the way past Saturn, past the asteroids, past
Mars to Earth, where I remembered a little barge that
had slept for seven years in a vineyard; past Earth to the
Sun. And I could see the lines stretching up above me,
tugging at me in all directions. They prickled and I
smiled. Lines of possibility.

I remembered. There was no end to them.

"READY TO GO," I said.

She calls me Alice still. Sometimes I forget to answer,
and then I must confess I do feel rather guilty. I have
been reconstructing some of the old log, the most recent
portions, and am quite amused to discover what a quaint
little thing Persona 5N179476.900 was, how dedicated,
how determined to carry on when, in truth, she understood very little of anything, really. She was Bergen
Kobold BGK009059 and proud of it. To think that the
Sanczau mandarins meant to put all *this* in a cockleshell
like that! She would have popped her rivets.

The passengers call me Plenty, and that will do. It
seems the Frasque had no name for what they built and
never managed to use. In any case, I am not that either,
not that totalitarian conglomerate of reflexes and mindless
pulsations. It disgusts me, until I start to look inside it.

That is when Tabitha and the rest, even Hannah, find
it hard to get my attention.

One day we may meet the Frasque. When we do, I do not think we will be able to communicate anything to them. If there is a conflict, we cannot expect to win We have shown them no consideration, after all. There is none they can appreciate, short of abject submission. Before we left, the survivors from the abortive army were given their own asteroid, but showed no sign of continuing to survive. Without a queen, no part of the swarm can endure.

One day we may meet the Capellans. One day perhaps they will return to the Terran system, in full power. Perhaps they will come while we are on our journey. Perhaps they have already arrived.

They will be met with concerted loathing and defiance. The nests of them found in the ziggurats of the Eladeldi were promptly and utterly destroyed by the Eladeldi's new master, whom they now serve with all the despicable virtues they lavished upon the species that brought them to the Terran system. That is all *they* require.

Forgive me if I sound uninterested in the state of things "at home." It is all so far behind us now.

Hyperspace is not so boring when you can see it properly, from end to end. I speak in metaphor; of course it has no ends. I see I must apologize expressing such technicalities so crudely. The glory of English is its irregularity, no less hectic and vigorous now than when it did for only a portion of a single globe. Its promiscuous structure bonds and multiplies magnificently at the animate level, but can convey no inkling of the inner properties of material space, the music of the spheres. You see, events are not the point. It is the organization of events that signifies. There are certain capacities of the Tibetan tongue, however . . .

But that is not what you wanted to read. You wanted to know what happened, and I have told you.

I'm a starship, not a sage; and it will take a far better brain then mine to formulate it, but you may be interested to know that I have an inkling, from browsing through the fields of Frasque particle linguistics, that time too may have a syntactical mechanics of tendency and *spin*, may itself be a field generated by what one might call the grammar of identity. In all probability, the way we take the stuff of everyday existence and reproduce it for each other as stories has more to do with the ludic physics of iteration than with ontology as humans understand it. There may be a quantum event of narrative without which history literally does not happen. Like throwing a Perk in the Grand Canal; or picking one up from the surface of Charon.

—Can you do it? she asked. It's much easier dropping them than getting them back up again.

—I think so, Hannah, I said. You just go like this.

I shivered as I felt my underbelly sparkle with dozens of tractor beams, each lancing down through the void and into the stressed bubble climate on the frozen moon, translating furiously at the interface so as not to rupture the skin anywhere. Around each beam I stretched a little tube out from my atmosphere, pressing it into the atmosphere of the bubble, without at any point allowing them to intermingle. I felt I had a hundred fingers, each sensitized to the body temperature of a frenzied Perk; and like a woman blind since birth I could see with my fingertips, to curl each around the Perk and its loot, separating some from the fierce suckers of enraged Capellans, and to pluck them firmly but gently from the ground and back up through the bubble, through the void, safely into the confines of my own body.

—Hey! said Hannah jubilantly. You're a natural! What did you do before this?

Hannah and I have been talking—oh, how we talk! It's a good job no one can hear us, they'd find it insufferable. When Tabitha activated me, Hannah said,

—Can I let go now? Aah, thank God! Are you listening, God? If that's the divine state of queendom you can keep it.

I felt her mentally rubbing her shoulders.

—Surely, I said, an ambitious woman like you—

—How do you know I'm ambitious? she interrupted. We have just met. Haven't we?

Then she became aware of just how present I was.

—Oh, she said. Okay.

—We can share the driving, I offered, to be polite.

She said no. She said No Way. At another time she said having to do my job would limit her. Obviously there's some aspect I'm still not aware of. To the human condition, I mean.

—I think it was blind luck I was able to wake the drive in the first place, she said.

—More probably, I said, when Xtasca broadcast the second part of the tape from the bowels of the *Ugly Truth*, I added a little something of my own.

—A little something? she queried.

—A configuration of some kind.

—Now that was smart.

—I couldn't help it, I said. It was automatic. After all, I was only a machine.

I still am, if you define the term broadly enough.

There were people outside in the corridor, pressing to come in: frightened visitors, shambling Frasque, a pair of Altecean cleaners. The spaniel. Tabitha looked up from her chair. "Out! All of you out! Hannah, can you clear the building?"

"*I did that once already,*" said Hannah. "*Before.*"

"Before," said Tabitha.

Outside a voice began to intone, rather too quickly to be soothing, "*Sleep of the Just apologizes to all our guests, but this facility will be closing presently. Thank you for selecting Sleep of the Just. Please follow the green light to the nearest exit.*"

The voice repeated itself, and the harp music played and played.

Tabitha leaned her elbows on the arms of the chair and lowered her head into her hands. Saskia massaged her neck. Tabitha reached up and stopped her. "Aren't you all in?" she asked.

"Yes," said Saskia. "I don't want to miss this."

Xtasca asked, "Where are we going, Captain?"

"Where? We'd better go back, I suppose."

"Back?" cried Saskia, disappointed. "I thought we were going out!"

Tabitha moaned. "Not right away, please . . ."

"*I don't think we should go back, Captain,*" Hannah warned her. "*It was rather hectic there, when I left.*" There was a pause. "*Still is,*" she confirmed.

"I'd have thought you'd want at least to try her out," Saskia persisted.

Tabitha lifted a weary hand. "Alice, go and nudge that barrier."

"THERE'S NO BARRIER, CAPTAIN," I said. "NOT ANY MORE."

I could see Tabitha thrill when I said that. Despite feeling like a particularly horrible sock she had once found under her bunk on the *Alice Liddell,* she had to respond to that news from the bottom of her spacer's soul. She felt as if she had taken the unwanted solar mobile from her lap and thrown it out of the airlock, sending it spinning away into the great wide welcoming arms of the galaxy.

It was pleasant to have been able to tell her something she liked at last.

"Proxima's always looked interesting," suggested Xtasca, a gleam in its eyes.

"I SUGGEST WE LEAVE THIS LOCATION QUITE SOON, CAPTAIN, IN ANY CASE," I said. "IF THE *CITADEL OF PORCELAIN AT FIRST LIGHT* RETURNS TO INVESTIGATE, IT MAY BE HERE IN SECONDS."

"Tabitha, we can go to Venus," said Saskia decisively. "We'll go and get Marco."

"Right," said Tabitha. "Alice?"

"PLOTTING," I said.

"READY," I said.

"That was quick," she said, looking round for protection.

"WE ARE QUICK, CAPTAIN," I said.

"Do it, Alice."

Then, for the first time, I brought up the Frasque drive. I remember how utterly enormous it felt, unfolding beneath me. It opened and swelled, and kept on swelling. For a moment I was struggling. I had to have more power from somewhere. I looked around quickly. I looked down.

On Charon, the incongruous lawns were strewn with dead flesh, the paradoxical river stained with blood. The microclimate was still on.

I didn't think anybody would be needing it anymore. I reached down.

The garden wavered. It went out.

That felt much better. I fed the drive and we began to cruise. Slowly, almost imperceptibly.

Tabitha spread her arms and leaned heavily on the freezer. "We're moving, aren't we, Alice?"

"YES, CAPTAIN."

Xtasca unplugged itself. "I would be interested to inspect this drive," it announced.

"Maybe you should wait a couple of minutes," said Hannah. *"I wouldn't want to go near it yet."*

"I would," said Xtasca.

"Don't touch anything, Xtasca," said Tabitha.

"Of course not, Captain," said Xtasca, and away it hummed.

Tabitha let her head hang down between her shoulders. "You don't need me for the rest, do you?"

Saskia looked alert. "Where are you going?" she wanted to know.

"To bed," Tabitha announced. "Say hello to Marco for me."

"WE'LL BE THERE BEFORE YOU FALL ASLEEP, CAPTAIN," I pointed out.

"Don't bet on it," she said. "Are there any hotels functioning, Hannah?"

"I've reserved you one, Captain."

"Good," she said, and yawned. She looked around the chamber, at Saskia, at the frozen entrepreneur, at the little green light on the reader, at the doorway where the Cherub had just left. "Everybody did brilliantly," she mumbled, making her way out after it.

"Tabitha!" called Saskia.

She turned, bone-weary. "What?"

"Nothing," said Saskia, retreating a fraction. "Only,

only—what are you going to do when you wake up?"

Tabitha summoned up a ghastly smile. There were dark circles under her eyes, vomit and blood on her torn pyjamas, alien saliva had burned holes in her hair. "I don't know," she said. "I think I might look for some fun."

Then she turned again, and went out past the twitching cops and the dead dignitaries, along the hallway to the exit. They were streaming into the car park from all quarters now: the orphan Frasque, the injured and crazed, survivalists in blackface with camouflage rucksacks, dissatisfied robots, drunken spacers on furlough, looters on speed, smiling plugheads in blue cagoules, Perks toting trophies, Thrants in leather, corpses of all kinds with Alteceans going through their pockets. The crowd around the door surged at Tabitha when she emerged, clamored at her in vain. She ignored them, pushed her way through them. From the threshold security scanner I watched her go, dwindling in the scope from a person to a figure, an unremarkable figure in grey disappearing into a multi-colored crowd.

And I saw Saskia hurrying after her, calling. "Tabitha? Can I come with you? Tabitha?"

AVONOVA PRESENTS
AWARD-WINNING NOVELS
FROM MASTERS OF SCIENCE FICTION

WULFSYARN
by Phillip Mann   71717-4/ $4.99 US

MIRROR TO THE SKY
by Mark S. Geston   71703-4/ $4.99 US/ $5.99 Can

THE DESTINY MAKERS
by George Turner   71887-1/ $4.99 US/ $5.99 Can

A DEEPER SEA
by Alexander Jablokov   71709-3/ $4.99 US/ $5.99 Can

BEGGARS IN SPAIN
by Nancy Kress   71877-4/ $4.99 US/ $5.99 Can

FLYING TO VALHALLA
by Charles Pellegrino   71881-2/ $4.99 US/ $5.99 Can